MURDER AT THE SEVEN DIALS

A BOW STREET DUCHESS MYSTERY
BOOK ONE

CARA DEVLIN

First Cup Press

Any references to historical events, real people, or real places are used fictitiously. Names and characters are products of the author's imagination.

ISBN paperback: 979-8987612507
ISBN hardcover: 979-8987612514

CHAPTER ONE

London
April 1819

The boy navigated the dark and narrow alley with a breed of confidence only street urchins possessed. Stealthy and fearless, he dodged shoulders and carts, moldering crates of rubbish, and took an agile leap over the splayed legs of a vagrant. A person could adjust to a certain level of comfort with this sordid side of London, where Covent Garden and Long Acre met with the Strand and Temple. The gilded people of Mayfair and Knightsbridge seemed worlds away instead of just a few miles due west.

Hugh Marsden considered himself one those adjusted sort.

He trailed the scrappy lad, known to him only as Sir, through a sooty warren of streets and alleyways, trusting the boy's nose for trouble—and reward—without question.

Sir had arrived at number 19 Bedford Street at half past eleven on a Tuesday evening. He'd pounded incessantly upon the front door of Hugh's modest and narrow, three-story terraced house until the wood had swung away from his fist, to be replaced by an unimpressed valet glaring down at him.

From his chair in the upstairs study, Hugh had already folded the most recent copy of the Hue and Cry gazette. Sir's particular knock was unmistakable. The late hour, concerning.

"You want to see this one, Mister Hugh," Sir said, gasping for breath when Hugh met him in the foyer.

As a principal officer at Bow Street, Hugh no longer walked the night streets as a foot patrol, as he once had. In fact, he'd been just about to turn in for the evening, and Basil, his ever reliable valet-turned-mother-hen, reminded him of it.

Hugh ignored him and kept his curious gaze on Sir. "Is it serious?"

Sir's answer—a dramatic expression of revulsion—was bait enough. Hooked, Hugh told Basil to fetch his coat.

"I'll signal for a cab—" the valet began, but Hugh interrupted, "No time. We're on foot, Sir," and then bounded away, barely one sleeve into his greatcoat.

He chased the lad, ignoring the stitch in his side. The wiry eleven-year-old, however, contained the boundless energy of a foxhound.

"The bloody nob's still there!" Sir shouted over his bony shoulder.

And with that little nugget of gold, Hugh ran faster. Wherever *there* was and whatever crime he'd committed, if it led to a conviction at the magistrate's court, a fine ten pounds would land in Hugh Marsden's pocket—so long as he was the one to bring the man in. Though not part of his pound-a-week salary, Magistrate Poston liked to keep things competitive among the officers and patrolmen. And Sir would be in for a crown, too.

At last, the lad stopped running and let Hugh catch up. He pointed toward a dingy row of terraced housing, where a crowd clustered at the bottom of the entrance steps. Hugh ripped off his hat and raked his fingers through his hair, the roots damp with perspiration.

"How do you know it's a nob?" Hugh asked. Sir held out his palm, the creases blackened with coal soot and street grime.

"Oh, he be a gent, Mister Hugh. I know me a gent when I see one."

He ignored the boy's outstretched palm and pushed through the bedraggled crowd, into the mouth of the building. "Where?"

Sir remained attached to his heels. "Third floor, second room, left. Now where's me coin?"

Hugh edged through the crowd at the base of the common stairwell. The blockade was made up of prostitutes past their prime and long overdue for a bath.

"Bow Street's 'ere, girls," one of them crooned as Hugh took the steps two at a time.

He wore nothing that would mark him as an officer with the Bow Street force, like the navy coats and red vests the mounted officers wore, but he supposed these ladies knew how to read a fellow by his clothes. Straight away, they would have noted the cut of his suit, clean and pressed. That alone marked him as unlike the men of their usual acquaintance. They would have caught his scent as he passed, which lacked the stale brume of alcohol and cigars. They likely noticed the flintlock pistol at one hip and the iron wrist cuffs dangling from the opposite.

"Didn't know Bow Street 'ad such a fine bum!" The particularly uninventive comment followed him up and around the bend in the stairwell.

Granted, they were not paid for their creativity.

Sir barreled up the stairwell, his palm still out and thrust up in front of Hugh's chest. The persistent, stunted wretch.

"What's the man done?" he asked as they climbed the narrow steps to the third floor.

"He's done murder, that's what he's done. Now where's me

coin? I got a sick baby brother and me mum's got the wheezes real bad, and then me Da, he—"

"Save the sorry tale of your plight for the nuns, Sir. You'll get your coin when I get my man."

Which, by the looks of the crush of people up ahead, might not happen after all. If another foot patrol had arrived, he'd have jurisdiction, and Hugh might as well go home.

He forced his way through the spectators.

But wasn't prepared for what met him.

Blood, he had seen before. However, in his near eight-year service to the magistrate, he'd not seen blood like this.

It painted the walls in frenzied streaks, spattered lines, and bursts of mist. The gore had rained upward upon the ceiling and had soaked what had once been a snowy white counterpane on an elegant, mahogany tester bed.

He noticed her legs first; the vulgar, suggestive splay of them, as if she'd been mid-coitus when killed. The victim wore black stockings, and though ripped, they were still clasped to lace garters around her thighs. Hugh stepped inside the room and met the glare of the night watchman.

The old man's weathered face told a story of salt and wind and open sea. When he walked toward Hugh, a limp in his step layered in a past injury that likely prevented the man from finding work. Every parish in London had a revolving circuit of night watchmen, most of them impoverished old men without any other way of earning wages.

"You a Runner?" the night watchman asked.

"Officer Marsden." He refused to call himself a Runner. The term made him out to be little more than a messenger running orders for the chief magistrate. He was an officer now, ranking above regular foot patrol and conductors, and despite the building commotion outside, it appeared he was the first to arrive.

"Well, I can't get 'im up," the watchman said. He gestured toward the floor, to the space behind two grey velvet chairs sitting arm to arm. Hugh took his hands out of his pockets at the sight of the second man, this one the 'nob' Sir must have been referring to.

He sat upon the floor, his legs drawn up and his head tucked down, arms wrapped around his knees. Blood soaked his shirt and trousers. His hands, too. A gold band encircled the left ring finger, though the gleam was smothered by gore.

Hugh averted his eyes from the man and took stock of the rest of the furnishings: more heavy mahogany tables, fine Turkish rugs, the pair of plush velvet chairs, a japanned six-fold screen set beside the bed, and several deep green, striped silk bolster pillows scattered about the floor, covered in sprays of blood. Fine paintings hung on the walls, but there were no trinkets, and the cupboards near the cook stove were currently in use as bookshelves.

"See Mister Hugh? I says he's done murder. Cor, look at that mess!"

Hugh spun toward the open doorway. Sir's eyes were full-moon wide as they gazed upon the dead woman's body. Hugh crossed into Sir's line of sight and reached into his waistcoat's breast pocket. He withdrew the promised five shillings. Hearing the coins sing, Sir tore his eyes from the gruesome display and whisked the coins away the moment they clattered into his palm.

"Run off, now," Hugh said. "Before you give yourself nightmares."

Sir made a spitting sound with his lips. "Seen plenty of cold meat, I 'ave."

Hugh had no doubt. Most people would be casting up their dinner, but Sir hadn't so much as blinked. He took another shilling from his pocket and held it up. "Fetch a hackney and have the jarvey wait outside."

Sir swiped the shilling and took off. Hugh then turned back to the night watchman and the blood-soaked man, huddled on the floor. He was indeed wealthy. The furnishings gave it away, as did the tailored cut of his clothes. Even spattered with blood, Hugh could tell they were expensive. Likely bespoke on Savile Row.

Though furnished well, this was not the man's permanent residence. More likely the place where he met his mistress. The man rocked forward and back, clutching his knees. He wasn't about to run, but Hugh wasn't ready to approach the man just yet, either. He stepped toward the tester bed, bracing himself for the necessary inspection. He'd already observed the splay of her legs, so his eyes went to her face.

Damn.

Like Sir, Hugh had seen plenty of dead bodies in the five years he'd been with Bow Street. He'd yet to become immune to the initial cramping a dead body brought to his gut, or the hollowing sensation that came when he looked into a pair of wide, unseeing eyes. But there was something especially miserable when he came across the body of a child, or as in this case, a young woman.

He cocked his head for a better look. She'd had her throat cut. It hadn't been done cleanly. The flayed skin appeared ripped and jagged, as if her killer had started and stopped a handful of times, cutting clumsily into the same section of throat more than once.

The woman had been butchered. Hugh lifted her left hand. The nails hung back loosely, torn and bloodied. She'd fought for her life, and she'd bled heavily for it.

Likely no more than five and twenty, her cheeks were smooth and unlined, the delicate skin around her eyes still firm. Her eyebrows were groomed to thin arches, darkened with kohl, and the pallor of death made the rouge on her cheeks more prominent. A cluster of onyx gems dangled from one ear lobe, while the other was bare. She was not the man's wife, that much Hugh knew. Though she wore stays and a chemise, she lacked a pair of drawers, which left her lower half exposed.

The chatter in the hallway stroked Hugh's attention; five people crammed themselves in the doorway, all of them craning their heads for a gander.

"Shut that door," Hugh growled to the watchman. The old man startled but did as told, limping over to slam it.

"Did you find her as she is now?" Hugh asked. The night watchman didn't answer. "Have you touched the body, or moved anything?"

Hugh would not give anyone, even an old man with a bum leg, the benefit of the doubt. He knew too much about base human compulsion to not automatically wonder if this man, or any of the vultures outside, had moved her, or what little she wore, for a look at her. Hugh also knew when he was being fed a lie, and so he watched the old man as he returned to the bed.

"Haven't touched a goddamn 'fing," the man said. "Check me hands for blood if ye like."

He didn't need to. The old man grimaced, looking as if he'd rather take a swim in a latrine than touch a dead body.

She'd kept herself shorn, Hugh noted, feeling a bit of a violator himself. However, the simple fact spoke volumes. She was likely a prostitute, and a costly one who wished to keep herself clean for the man currently muttering to himself on the floor. He probably let these rooms just to meet with her. These were not furnishings a female would surround herself with. No, this was a man's room. She had come to him.

"When did you arrive?" Hugh asked the watchman next.

"Half hour since. Forty minutes, most."

With a sigh, Hugh touched the gore coating her neck. His fingers drew back with blood, tacky and just starting to congeal. He then turned his hand and touched the woman's bare arm. Her flesh wasn't warm, but it hadn't gone stone cold either. She'd been dead for perhaps an hour.

"And you've sent for the parish constable?" Hugh asked.

Bow Street wouldn't be dealing with the woman's body. That responsibility fell to the constable, who would fetch a cart and deliver the body to the coroner, who would then hold an inquest to determine how the woman had died. It would be a brief inquest. Hugh glanced at the man on the floor. *This* was the person Bow Street would be dealing with—and Hugh would be the one to deliver the bastard.

Hugh left the tester bed and approached the man, whose head was still tucked down with his forehead pressed against his knees.

Had he killed the woman in a fit of rage and then collapsed in hysterics? Most killers would have fled before someone could stumble upon the scene and make the hue and cry out over the streets to draw the night watchman. Finding a corpse and the killer in the same room was not common.

In fact, it felt just a little bit wrong.

"The nob wouldn't budge," the watchman said.

Hugh circled the man. Something glinted in the oil lamplight on the floor by his right hip. Using the toe of his boot, Hugh nudged it aside. The knife looked like a utility blade, shaped long and thin. A fillet or boning knife. Blood colored the steel and the simple wooden handle. He sent the blade skimming across the floor, just far enough aside so that the man wouldn't be able to reach for it should he get the urge.

Hugh lowered himself into a crouch. "What's the woman's name?" There was no point in pleasantries.

"Audrey." The man's drawn-up legs muffled his voice.

"And her surname?"

"Audrey."

Hugh sighed. "Why don't you tell me your name?"

"Audrey."

Audrey, Audrey, Audrey. The bounder had either lost his senses or was playing at it.

Hugh, tired of staring at the crown of dark blond hair streaked with blood, asked the man to lift his head. He got the same response: *Audrey*.

So, he grabbed a fistful of the man's hair and tugged his head back, exposing his face. Tears and blood left bisecting rivers down the man's cheeks. His lids fluttered, as if he were fighting to stay awake.

"Oh, hell," Hugh muttered. He released the man's hair, and his head flopped down again. Hugh got to his feet, his knees cracking as they straightened.

"What?" the watchman asked.

Sir had said it was a nob, a wealthy gentleman from the other half of London, and he'd been dead on. However, this was no run-of-the-mill gentleman. No wealthy merchant or businessman, or even a member of the landed gentry.

"He's a peer," Hugh answered. He knew him too, from a time when Hugh possessed more ties to *le bon ton* than he did to lower society, as he did now.

The man sitting at Hugh's feet, soaked in his dead mistress's blood, was Philip Sinclair, the Duke of Fournier. A goddamned *duke*.

"This tap-hackled bloke's a peer?" the watchman crowed. Hugh took a whiff of the duke. He certainly looked and acted intoxicated, but he didn't smell it.

Hugh hooked Fournier's arm and wrenched him to his feet. Though taller than Hugh, he was probably a stone lighter. Still, it proved difficult to hold him. The duke's legs were like two poles of gelatinous aspic.

"Ye lettin' 'im loose then?" the watchman asked.

As a peer of the realm, the duke would be granted some protection from the law. As if being born into wealth and titles were not enough, these men and women were also exempt from the basic rules that governed the masses below them.

It was something Hugh despised.

The lack of justice, the favoritism, the elitist mindset that decreed that certain people with certain blood were fundamentally better than others, had been a thorn in his side for a very long time.

There were many constables and foot patrolmen who would have chosen to handle the duke swaying at Hugh's side with kid gloves. They would have rather trundled him back to his fine home located on whatever stately square it sat upon rather than face the public blow back that would come with arresting him.

Hugh Marsden was not one of them.

"He'll come with me to Bow Street," he replied, and then jerked his chin toward the dead woman behind them. "And for her sake, I'm going to do everything I can to see he gets a rope at Tower Hill."

CHAPTER TWO

Lamps threw guttering flickers of light over the stone steps to number 4 Bow Street. Audrey Sinclair peered out the carriage window, restless. Carrigan had drawn along the curb more than ten minutes ago, and though she'd wanted to immediately leap from the conveyance and storm inside the magistrate's offices, sheer willpower and respect for her brother-in-law's sensibilities had kept her planted to the bench seat.

Michael would arrive any moment, she was certain of it, and then the pair of them would descend upon Bow Street together. She shivered beneath her cloak.

This was not happening.

This could not *be* happening.

A clattering of wheels and tack announced another carriage's arrival, and her driver leaped down from the box, shaking the chassis. The fringe of beaded tassels clinked against the window's glass as Carrigan pulled open the door and extended his gloved hand. Audrey's heart squeezed, almost painfully, and her knees went a bit soft as she came down onto the pavements. Michael descended from his carriage and immediately saw her.

"You should not be here," he said, his deep voice as gruff as usual. Tonight, however, it held an additional snap. "This is no place for you, Audrey."

His comment was not unexpected. She'd spent the entire ride from Curzon Street preparing for it.

"He is my husband," she said. "I refuse to sit at home and wait."

Patience and grace were virtues that duchesses of the realm were supposed to exude. However, when one's husband had just been arrested for murder, one didn't cling to such stiff-necked rules.

Her brother-in-law knew her well enough to forgo arguing, and simply made a growl of discontent before ascending the front steps, his great coat flapping behind him like the dark wings of an avenging angel.

The second son of a duke, Michael was a titled noble, and Audrey prayed the magistrate would kneel to his power. If anyone could exonerate her husband and secure his release from this wretched place, it was him. He was a persuasive man, and Audrey had every faith he would sway the fools who had arrested Philip in the first place.

Then again, Michael had not been successful in persuading Audrey to remain at Violet House.

Well past midnight, she'd been awoken by the sounds of a commotion just outside her bedchamber. She'd opened the door, revealing their butler, Barton, and her sleepy maid, Greer, both wearing dressing robes and expressions of alarm. A message had arrived. "*From Bow Street*," Barton added in a whisper.

As Audrey took the sealed note, she could only think of Philip, and how he had not been at home when she had turned in for the evening. The moments after reading the brief message were now mere pulses of memory, overwhelmed quickly by her orders for Barton to ready a carriage, to send a footman to Lord Herrick's on Grosvenor Square, and for Greer to help her dress.

This had to be a terrible misunderstanding. Surely, she would leave Bow Street with Philip at her side.

Michael, or Lord Herrick to those not welcome to address him so informally, signaled the first man he and Audrey spotted within the narrow house's foyer. Though first a residence, number 4 was now a place of efficient business. Audrey spied a sitting room and a large desk directly before the front windows, its top piled with stacks of papers, bound texts, and news sheets. Guttering lamps lined the walls along with street maps of London, each a spidery network of ink veining out from a tight center cluster.

Despite being quarter to two in the morning, there was a hum of activity in the room. Audrey avoided looking directly at any of the men and women who were milling about the place, some sitting forlornly upon a bench, one rubbing a bloodied eye and crying, and another arguing loudly with a foot patrolman. The air smelled of burning oil, tallow, sweat, and unwashed clothes. Michael's stern voice brought her attention back to an officer approaching them. He had the clean, starched look of a man of some import, and the stern eyes of a man who was greatly vexed.

"Your business, my lord?" the man requested.

"We demand to see His Grace, the Duke of Fournier. I am Lord Herrick, His Grace's brother, and this is Her Grace, the Duchess of Fournier. Take us to him at once." Michael's tone brooked no argument.

But argue the official did. He pursed his lips and flared his nostrils. "His *Grace* is awaiting legal counsel in gaol."

The sarcastic emphasis placed on *Grace* landed like a slap to the cheek. How dare this man disrespect Philip? Audrey narrowed her eyes.

"Our solicitor, Mr. Potridge, is en route," she said, forcing the man to take notice of her. "Lord Herrick is His Grace's counsel at this time."

She'd tasked Barton with sending a second footman to the

family's longtime solicitor before she'd set out from Violet House, where she and Philip had lived since their wedding nearly three years ago. The neoclassical monstrosity had been built by the fourth Duke of Fournier, Philip's grandfather, and it was their London residence, whether Audrey liked it or not. And she roundly did *not*.

She'd simply never found an appreciation for the cold and austere lines of Violet House. The name, so soft and dainty, suited it as well as a dowager wearing pink. The home had been christened 'Violet' after the fourth Duchess of Fournier, though Audrey had always thought the then duke should have considered the duchess's middle name, Griselda, and named it accordingly.

"This way then," the Bow Street official said, his bitter dislike apparent.

Michael waited until Audrey had stepped forward to follow, and then fell into step behind her. She barely kept pace with the disgruntled official, her Indian silk cape heavy around her shoulders, and her legs still clumsy and wooden from shock.

Murder. Bow Street had placed her husband under arrest for *murder*. She still hadn't a clue who they believed Philip had killed. It was absurd. He would never kill anyone. *Never*.

When the officer opened the front door to number 4 and took the steps into the street, she faltered. Surely the man was being facetious, tricking his unwanted visitors into leaving. Curious and skeptical, she followed, but when he reached the doors of a tavern across the street, she balked.

"Exactly where are you taking us, sir?"

Lamps had been extinguished inside, leaving the windows dark. The officer flipped through a brass ring of keys.

"We hold prisoners in the cellar of the Brown Bear, Your Grace." He grumbled his reply, the keys on the brass ring clanging together. As his pale white fingers touched each one in search, Audrey shivered.

She could only imagine what those keys would whisper to her should she have the chance to hold them. She made a fist underneath the rippled silk of her cloak, her kid gloves creaking in the damp and chilly April night air. She would touch nothing. It was awful enough having to be here in the first place—she certainly didn't want to subject herself to any visions of past arrests, or whatever unpleasantries those keys, and her curious ability, would surely show her.

Michael drew to a stop beside her as the officer unlocked the tavern door. It swung wide, and the stale odor of cigar smoke, ale, and grease made its way up her nose. Audrey started forward, only to be barred entrance by the officer's outstretched arm.

"The holding cells aren't no place for a lady," the officer said. Audrey bristled.

"I shall decide that for myself." She moved around his outstretched arm and entered the tavern.

It was shadowy and quiet, with only one lantern in the back for light. The officer closed and locked the door behind Michael, and then led them forward again, to another door near the single lantern. He led them through it and down a twisting set of bare board steps, into a raw, dank cellar.

"I've got Lord Herrick and the Duchess of Fournier here to see the duke," he told the guard standing at the bottom of the stairs.

"No women, Ruthers, you know that. Take her back to the offices."

Audrey was still trapped on the step behind the officer when she heard that deep-throated reply. She swept past Ruthers and the other Bow Street man and entered the cellar before either could dare reach for her arm. "I will not be taken anywhere."

She saw Philip and drew to a sudden stop. He was seated on the edge of a cot on the opposite side of the cellar. He had his head in his hands, his eyes pinned to the floor. The clothing he wore did not belong to him—worn trousers hung like canvas sails and a white shirt was stained with yellow patches beneath the arms. Philip wasn't a dandy in the least, but he appreciated fine clothing and spared no expense for quality. Sitting there, hunched over, elbows upon his knees, he looked as gritty as a sailor just come to port. It was his mop of fair hair she recognized, and his long-fingered hands gripping the sides of his head. Only they, too, were grimy.

"Philip—" She moved forward, and a shadow peeled off the cellar wall. A man, tall and wiry, entered her path.

"Your Grace, I insist you return to the offices."

It was the man who'd spoken to Officer Ruthers a moment ago. He wore a waistcoat but no jacket. Audrey's eyes skipped to his forearms, exposed by shirtsleeves rolled sloppily to his elbows. His hair appeared dark and unkempt in the dreary light of a few lanterns.

"Step aside. I would see my husband," she replied, teeth clenched.

"As I am in the middle of questioning him, that will not be possible," he replied, sounding as though his own teeth were clenched.

Michael entered her light of sight. "You will cease your questions until our solicitor is present—which should have come about hours ago. Why was Potridge not sent for?"

The man barely acknowledged Michael. Instead, he rolled down each of his sleeves with measured ease.

"Philip?" Audrey called, watching him for some reaction. But her husband only rocked forward and back, his head still cradled in his palms.

The man finally finished covering his forearms and said, "His Grace has not been the most cooperative of men."

"And for that you refused to send for his solicitor?" Audrey replied, her temper simmering anew. He'd been thrown into this dank, dark cell. Accused of murder. Why on earth *should* he cooperate?

"I assure you, had he supplied his solicitor's name, I would have sent for him straightaway. However," said the man, whom she could only assume was another Bow Street officer, "His Grace has not uttered one coherent word since I found him in Seven Dials, drenched in blood."

Audrey looked again at her husband's borrowed clothing. He'd been given these rags because his clothes had been covered in blood? And disposed of? She dearly hoped not. If she could touch his things, close her eyes, and concentrate, allowing the energy they held to enter her, she might be able to see the truth.

Any item—large or small, metal or glass, stone or fabric—retained a bit of energy, and for some reason, one Audrey had long ago stopped questioning, she could not only feel this energy, she could *see* it. The energy appeared as images, gasps of memories. If she could hold her husband's clothing, she might be able to see what occurred before this austere officer had thrown him into the tavern's cellar.

"The Seven Dials?" Michael scoffed. "Absurd. The duke has no business in that part of London."

He was right. The Dials was a seedy neighborhood, rife with thieves and vagrants. Her husband wouldn't venture there. Unless, of course, he'd taken up his old habit. Audrey frowned. *No.* He'd promised he was finished with that business.

"Whose blood?" she asked.

The Bow Street officer hesitated, as if considering withholding the answer. Audrey was ready to demand a response when he finally replied, "Miss Belladora Lovejoy. An opera singer at Drury Lane."

The mention of the Theatre Royal at Drury Lane gave her pause, but with the officer's eyes hinged on her, she knew to keep her expression unaffected. Philip had a box at both Drury Lane and Covent Garden and enjoyed attending—much more than she did. Had he known this woman?

"And you believe my husband killed her?"

"Yes."

"What proof do you have?"

"That is for me to present to the magistrate when he arrives in the morning."

The man's refusal to answer kicked like an insult—something Audrey, as Duchess of Fournier for the past few years, was not accustomed to.

"As acting counsel for His Grace at present, you *will* disclose to me what led you to arrest him," Michael said.

It took the officer another few seconds to release Audrey from his intent glare. When he finally did, she drew in a silent gulp of air. Who the devil was this man?

"He was found in rooms leased under a fictitious name, with Miss Lovejoy's mutilated body in close proximity. He was the only one present at the time of discovery, drenched, as I stated, in blood. The apparent murder weapon, a boning knife, was at his side."

The words were nonsensical. Audrey could not comprehend any of it. Her instinct to shout *No!* to everything the man said reared its head, but she kept it in check. She would not make a scene and be ordered out of this cellar.

"My husband does not keep an apartment in the Dials," she stated levelly. "Have you searched for the man whose name is attached to the lease?"

"He doesn't exist. As I told you, it is a fictitious name," the officer replied.

"How can you be so sure?" she pressed.

He paced the width of the cellar taking short, agitated strides. "The landlord confirmed His Grace was the tenant. He knew him by the name supplied on the lease, a Mr. Maxwell Penny. He has been leasing these rooms for months. Your Grace—" he stopped and clenched his hands into fists. "I understand this is no way for a wife to learn of her husband's liaisons—"

"*Stop.*" Audrey's voice cracked off the walls. The man did as she commanded and stared at her once again. "You are wrong, officer—what is your name, sir?"

By his pressed-thin lips, he appeared to be fighting the urge to groan. "Principal Officer Hugh Marsden. And my apologies, but it is quite certain. Due to Miss Lovejoy's...appearance when she was discovered, it's clear that she was in the duke's rooms as his mistress."

"Enough," Michael barked before Audrey could argue once again. "There is no need to be vulgar."

"On the contrary, Lord Herrick. Considering where we are all standing, there is no escaping it," Mr. Marsden replied, his dark eyes still centered on Audrey. Almost as if he suspected her of some crime as well.

She kept her mouth shut as Michael went to Philip's side.

"Say something, brother." He leaned over to peer into Philip's face, which was aimed at the dirty floor. "My God, you must speak for yourself. Explain what has happened."

"He won't," Mr. Marsden put in. "I suspect he is in a fair amount of stupor."

Michael straightened his back and turned to glare at Mr. Marsden. Audrey kept her eyes upon her husband. He wouldn't stop kneading the tops of his thighs with his fingers. They were unclean, with dirt around the nails. Or perhaps, she thought with a shock of horror, it was not dirt at all.

"And why wouldn't he be? Thrown into a hole such as this," Michael said, still sneering.

Mr. Marsden ignored the comment. "I'm bringing him before the magistrate in a few hours—"

"Not before Potridge arrives," Michael cut in.

"Then you best hope he arrives soon." The officer reached for a coat upon a stool and tugged it on.

Audrey went to Philip's side, her skirts brushing against the dirty cellar floor. She didn't care about the filth. She crouched before him, taking his stained fingers into her hands. Had she removed her gloves, the touch might have shown her something. Nothing definite, though. Objects were easiest to read, while skin-to-skin contact was more fickle.

"Philip," she implored softly. "Look at me."

His eyes darted back and forth, as if watching some frantic action playing out on the cellar's packed-dirt floor.

"I don't know what has happened, but whatever you say, I will believe it." She needed him to look at her. Needed those eyes to latch onto hers. Until then, he would be lost, a prisoner to whatever hell he was currently trapped in. "Darling, it is I, Audrey. Please, Philip—"

"You are wasting your breath, Your Grace."

Audrey shot to her feet and swiveled to glare at him. "And you are an interminable brute, Mr. Marsden."

He smirked. "Nothing like what you're used to in Mayfair, is it?"

"And you would know, wouldn't you?" Michael murmured. Audrey looked at her brother-in-law, but he had his scathing glare hinged on the Bow Street officer. Mr. Marsden flicked him an apathetic glance. "That's right, Marsden. I know who you are."

Audrey frowned. How did Michael know this man?

"Call me a brute or anything else you please," Mr. Marsden continued, unmoved by Michael's comment. "I'm merely doing my job."

"My husband is not a murderer. I don't know what you've done to him in here—"

Mr. Marsden cocked his head and took an angry step toward her. "Do you imply that I've attempted to beat a confession out of him?"

"I said nothing of the sort!" Her nerves flared to life as a measure of control slipped. Never had she been made to deal with a man as crude and raffish as this.

A spark of smugness lit his eyes. He'd affected her, and he appeared pleased with himself for it.

Michael slid in between them, his broad shoulders obscuring the officer's figure. Almost immediately, Audrey's boiling blood dropped to a simmer.

"Have Carrigan take you home," he said to her.

She shook her head. "Philip should not be alone."

"He won't be." Michael took her shoulders in his hands; hands that boxed at the Sturgis Club every Thursday evening. Philip had confided Michael's penchant once, along with Michael's concern that his brother should box as well. *As a way to improve my health,* Philip had muttered with a vault of one fair brow. *Seems to believe it will improve my virility.* The memory of her husband's wry grin hit her hard.

"I will remain here and make sure Potridge arrives," Michael added.

The truth shed over her then: Within a few hours, her husband would be standing before the magistrate on charges of murder. An opera singer of questionable reputation had been slain in his leased rooms. Rooms Audrey had not known about. Her throat cinched tight. He'd promised that he was finished with keeping secrets. He'd promised things would go back to the way they used to be when he and Audrey had been able to confide in each other. Confessions Audrey could have never shared with anyone else. Philip accepted her, and she accepted him. Secrets and all.

Or at least, that was what Audrey had believed.

"Go back to Violet House." Michael's hands squeezed her shoulders. "Do not accept any callers today, Audrey."

Did he take her for a fool? Of course, she would not accept any callers. The whole of London society would wake up to the scandalbroth of her husband's arrest. The most tenacious gossipmongers among them would descend upon Violet House under the pretense of support and solidarity, while all they would truly be after were details, of which they could flaunt at the next luncheon or tea or ball. Audrey suspected Lady Dutton, a Dowager Viscountess, would be the first one to call, followed swiftly by her archrival, Lady Shoreham, a young, widowed countess currently shocking the *ton* with a barely concealed affair with Lady Dutton's son-in-law.

There were only three people Audrey trusted explicitly. Two of them were currently in the prison cell with her, and the third was Michael's wife, Geneva.

Michael released Audrey's shoulders. His promise to stay with Philip gave her a thread of relief. He wouldn't allow any brutish Bow Street officer to so much as touch him. She took one last look in her husband's direction. He was still rubbing his fingers over his thighs, his eyes cast to the floor. What was he seeing inside his mind? What wasn't he sharing with them?

"I will show you out, Your Grace," Mr. Marsden grumbled as he picked up a covered box, four hands long and equally deep.

"It is hardly a challenge to show myself out, thank you," she replied, stepping past him, and starting up the stairs, into the empty tavern.

"All the same, I can't have you wandering the Brown Bear unaccompanied," he said, practically treading upon her heels as they left the cellar.

She bristled at that word: *wandering*. As if she were a heedless puppy or young child.

At the entrance, he reached past Audrey's arm and opened the door before she could do so herself. He stood aside, balancing the box in his other hand, and with a mocking dip of his head, murmured, "Your Grace."

His disdain for her—no, not for her personally, but for her station in society—was written all over his person, from his expression to his tone to the piercing bite of his glittering brown-eyed glare.

"You do realize, Mr. Marsden, how foolish you will look when my husband is proven to have nothing to do with this crime?"

However, a tremor of unease slipped up her spine at all the things the officer had said. Philip's secret rooms, the dead singer, the blood, and the weapon...her husband's clear shock and uncooperative manner...none of it made him appear innocent. But he simply could not have killed the woman. He simply could *not* have been having an affair with her. Of this, more than anything else, Audrey was absolutely certain, because her husband and dearest friend, the Duke of Fournier, was not, and had never been, in the least bit attracted to women.

Mr. Marsden huffed a laugh as he crossed Bow Street and made his way toward the magistrate's offices. "I am in little danger of looking the fool."

"Prove it," she said as a hasty idea formed in her mind.

He stopped in the middle of the street and peered at her. "Excuse me?"

"Prove what you know, sir. Show me the murder weapon."

He had to have it somewhere. If Audrey could only touch it, even just for a few seconds, she would be able to glean images of knowledge.

The officer shuffled the box in his arms, his patience clearly beginning to wane. "The murder weapon has its place as evidence, but it will hardly prove everything I know."

She eyed the box in his arms again and guessed at the contents.

"Yes, but *I* will know whether or not the knife belongs to my husband, you see."

Her point was about as dull as a spoon and Mr. Marsden rolled his eyes before continuing toward the front steps. She followed, ignoring her driver, Carrigan, as he started to open the carriage door.

"I find that doubtful, Your Grace," he said, entering the offices. "You didn't even know he kept rooms."

His rooms. Yes, of course!

Mr. Marsden had let the door shut behind him, but she pushed it open and followed. He kept his back to her, turning down a long corridor.

"I wish to speak to the establishment's owner, if you would be so kind as to give me the address," she said.

At this, Mr. Marsden flashed her a smile, followed by a burst of laughter. "Establishment is too kind a word for that scum hole."

He scuffled with a small ring of keys taken from his pocket and unlocked a door. It was a closet of some sort, its shelves cluttered with other boxes. He slid his box into an empty spot and slammed the door, locking it again. There was no chance she'd be able to get into that closet without being seen. But maybe she could find something else to touch in Philip's secret rooms.

"The address, *sir*," she persisted.

A certain misgiving creeped into the crook of his smile. "I'll give it to His Grace's solicitor, once the fellow arrives."

His impertinent, high-handed dismissal set her blood back to boiling.

"*I* am asking you for it *now*."

"I would advise you not to travel to the Dials alone." Not a shred of humor remained on his tone, and Audrey was happy to hear it. There was nothing amusing about this situation, and the man's smile had unsettled her.

She remained quiet, simply waiting for him to speak. She would not leave until she had the address and well he knew it. Finally, he shifted his square jaw and relented.

"Mercer Street. A collection of rooms called Jewell House."

Shock that he had granted her the address nearly tied her tongue. She'd expected more of an argument, in fact. A belated moment later, she was able to speak. "Goodbye, Mr. Marsden."

With a tight nod, she turned and made her way from Bow Street headquarters.

CHAPTER
THREE

The hackney drew to a stop along Mercer Street. Audrey, seated on the edge of the tattered bench inside the hired carriage, felt ill. What she was doing was absurdly dangerous.

As she'd waited all day at Violet House for Michael to call on her or send some word about what had happened, she'd held out hope that a visit to Seven Dials would not be necessary. Surely, the magistrate would allow Philip to return home. Surely, Mr. Potridge would have figured some way to free her husband from suspicion. He was a gentleman. A *duke*.

In all the years Audrey had known him, never once had Philip shown any propensity toward violence. Why, even when they had been children on their neighboring estates in Hertfordshire, Philip would groan when Michael and Tobias, their youngest brother, would whittle sticks and play at fencing. He'd always been much more interested digging for beetles and ants in the grass with Audrey and little Cassandra, Philip's baby sister.

Whatever Mr. Marsden had found in those leased rooms at Jewell House, whatever he believed he'd pieced together, was just plain wrong. And for the several hours she spent pacing first the morning room, then the study, and then the library, Audrey had clung to the hope that the powers that be would agree with her.

But they had not, and so here she was.

No duchess should travel by hired hackney in the dead of night to the Seven Dials, and if she did, she should not be going alone—just as the awful Mr. Marsden had advised. However, had she suggested the trip, Michael would never agree to accompany her. Her place for the time being, Audrey had been told, was inside Violet House. *Until all this blows over,* Michael had said after downing the first of what would be three drams of single malt.

The magistrate had commanded that Philip was to be kept in a private room at the Brown Bear until he chose to cooperate. Mr. Potridge's arrival, a quarter hour after Audrey had departed, had not roused her husband from his delirium. With no verbal acceptance or refusal of charges, with nothing to say for himself, and his behavior as it so oddly was, he was deemed unfit for release.

"Any other man in his state would have been thrown into Newgate, or an asylum," Michael had declared on his third dram. Philip's title was the only thing keeping him from such a fate. And at least he'd be out of that cold, rank cellar.

The driver of the hired hackney took his time unfolding the steps and opening the door for Audrey, though she could hardly chastise him for it. The old man was the furthest thing from her own robust driver, Carrigan. But Carrigan would not have taken her here, at least not first without informing Barton and the housekeeper, Mrs. Moore, to make sure he didn't lose his position.

She descended onto Mercer Street. The cloak she'd worn as she'd slipped out the back door of Violet House was pulled high over her head, obscuring her face. The chances of being seen and recognized were slim, but Audrey saw no reason to risk it.

"Will you remain?" she asked the driver as her serviceable boots touched down onto the paving stones. The night was damp and chilled, the rain that had fallen glistening in puddles along the street. Her nostrils traced horse dung and coal smoke, refuse, old fish, and sweat.

"Aye, miss," he answered. She slipped him partial payment of a shilling and hoped his word was honorable.

Audrey peered up at the building before her.

"This is Jewell House?"

The driver nodded and scrubbed his nose with the back of his hand. The carriage lantern threw shadows into the creases of his face. "Aye, miss. If ye don't mind the cheek, miss, 'tisn't a place for a lady such as ye'self."

Her plain dress, cloak, and footwear, as well as hailing a hack three blocks from Curzon Street, had apparently done little to mask her blue blood.

The dark exterior of the building showed few rooms lit with lantern and candlelight, and most windows were obscured with drapery. She didn't know which rooms Philip had been renting and had no way of finding out without alerting someone, such as the building's landlord, that she was there.

"Thank you for waiting," she said to the driver, ignoring his warning that she didn't belong. He was correct, of course, but she had come too far in her plan to be cowardly now. Philip needed her help.

The front door to Jewell House, being a common door used by many people throughout the day and night, was unlocked. Audrey clasped the cool metal knob and pushed the door open, stepping into the darkened entrance hall. Not one lamp or candle had been left burning for the building's residents or visitors. But when Audrey shuttered her eyes and let out a long breath, the knob still clutched in her ungloved hand, an image gasped in Audrey's mind: A pair of boys darted forward and bounded up the stairs, each one holding a small glass lantern. Their shoes slapped on the steps and their voices echoed as slight vibrations against her ear drums; voices only she could hear.

She knew it for what it was—the most recent energy the doorknob retained, passed on to her in a vision. But it was too recent. Philip had been here the previous night.

Audrey pushed back further, closing her fingers tighter around the cool metal. The light shifted and sunlight filled the hallway, more people churning into view as the daylight changed from burnished afternoon to dewy morning then faded once more to blue dawn. The images came to her in strokes, each one more jagged and grainy than the one before. They would soon disappear altogether; objects could never maintain deep wells of clear energy.

Audrey bit the inside of her cheek, giving another push with her mind. It was like turning pages in a book, flipping through them with eager impatience. The next gasp was dense, practically impenetrable. A man shuttled down the steps toward her, but it was so far in the past she could barely make out anything more than a head of dark curls, thick arched brows, and a small mole on his cheek as he floated past, thinner than smoke.

She'd pushed too far. The doorknob fell dormant, leeched of its energy. Frustrated, Audrey released it and searched for something else to touch. Her eyes landed on the newel post at the base of the stairs, and when she settled her hand atop the carved wooden sphere, she moved backward through the energy more slowly. Patiently. She was rewarded when swirls of bare flesh, shoulders, and mounded décolletage came into view. A crowd of murmuring women had gathered in the entrance hall by the light of many lanterns.

They parted in annoyance as a gangly boy pushed between them, followed by a man in a light brown suit. *Mr. Marsden.* The women cackled as he kept on the boy's heels. Audrey took a step forward, her vision hinged on the officer as he took the steps two at a time. At the top, he grasped the newel post and flung himself around the bend.

The image was lost, and Audrey was again in the darkened vestibule of Jewell House, alone. Her skirts hindered her ability to take the steps as quickly as Mr. Marsden had, but she rushed up them as quickly as possible. At the landing, she grabbed hold of the next newel post and dug into the energy until she found him again. The image was clearer this time; fewer people had touched this newel post during the day. She saw Mr. Marsden turn at the top of the steps and she hurried after the memory, nearly forgetting to be afraid of the darkened stairwell as she climbed.

At the top, she clutched the wooden newel and reached for the energy he'd left behind. It had taken years of taming her visions before she'd learned how to control them. To manage them and make them abide her. Before, when Audrey first realized she could see the memories of inanimate objects, confusion had lead her toward panic, and then eventually, overconfidence led to carelessness. A carelessness that had cost her greatly.

But now, she knew how to work through the barrage of images. How to slow them and make them behave. Most importantly, she knew to be discreet about what she could do.

On the third floor of Jewell House, Audrey watched Mr. Marsden's lingering energy as he approached a door down the corridor. There, a crowd of people had gathered. Audrey released the image and found herself, once again, alone in the dark. The door was locked. She'd expected such an obstacle. Reaching into her upswept hair, she removed two of her pins. It had been years since she'd picked a lock. Five, at least, since she'd learned to free herself from her room at the Shadewell Sanatorium. Her midnight forays onto the roof to breathe freely, chart the stars, and dream of an escape had been the only things to carry her through those two years of torment.

She'd become quite good at it back then, but of course, had found little need to lockpick anything since. It took a minute for her to maneuver the pins just so but felt the lock give way as voices and shuffling feet sounded down the hallway. Audrey swept inside the room, closing the door behind her, her hands shaking. The voices traveled by the door in a jumble of slurred speech and cockney.

She exhaled and turned to face the room she'd just broken into. It was only slightly brighter in here with moonlight coming through a trio of windows along one wall. She reached into her cloak's pocket for the stub of a candle and a palm-sized tinderbox. Her chambermaid, Mary, kept the tinderbox at the hearth. Anticipating the need to light a candle, Audrey had taken a wax candle and the small steel box of flint, steel, and char cloth.

The paltry moonlight guided her hand as she struck the chip of steel against the flint, which was settled within the packed bit of jute. The jute caught aflame, and she touched the candle's wick to it. The glow cut through the gloom.

The room was modest, with few furnishings and decoration, though what was there—the plush chairs placed before the fire, the woodwork on the mantle clock, the numerous candlesticks, a table lamp—was of quality. None of these items were familiar, though they were all distinctly masculine. And completely out of place. The kinds of people who lived at Jewell House and the surrounding buildings would not live half so fine.

With sinking spirits, Audrey moved deeper into the room. The wax candle's light didn't reach far, so she was standing almost within arm's reach of a tester bed by the time it materialized out of the darkness. The bed's frame was all that was left, the mattress having been removed. A strange black spatter painted the wall behind it.

Her stomach turned, and with a jolt, she skittered backward. This was where the woman had been killed. Mr. Marsden had said she'd been found in a precarious position, and Audrey realized now that he'd meant upon the bed. The black spatters. They were her blood.

The heel of Audrey's boot came down onto something, and whatever it was ground into the floor. It felt like a small rock, but when she lifted her foot, saw it was a drop pearl and black crystal earbob, strung on wire with a slim hook. Audrey crouched. It belonged, she presumed, to the opera singer.

Gathering a breath, she picked up the piece of jewelry, pinching it between her thumb and forefinger. With barely a nudge from her mind, the earbob's energy leaped into view. A chaotic blur of the room spun around her. Pale white arms flailed before Audrey's eyes...a woman's arms. Her fingernails clawed into the floor as someone dragged her. Her eardrums vibrated with gargled screams and panicked breaths.

Horrified, she dropped the earbob. It fell to the floor, and the memory vanished. The candle's flame warmed her cheek as she stayed there, crouched next to the piece of jewelry. *Belladora Lovejoy*. The name of the opera singer. The woman whose arms Audrey had just seen thrashing. She'd been knocked to the floor. Attacked. How many more moments had passed before she'd been murdered?

The earbob had more to show her, and Audrey had no choice but to watch if she wanted to prove her husband innocent. Perhaps the true murderer would be revealed in the bundle of retained energy clinging to the piece of jewelry. It would be nothing she could show Mr. Marsden or the magistrate, or even Mr. Potridge or Michael. Philip, of course, would believe her, but that was only because he knew what she could do. He had been well aware of it before he'd proposed marriage, and he'd promised to keep her secret so long as she, in turn, kept his. At Bow Street, she had not been able to explain that *if* Philip had chosen to stray, he would have done so with another man.

However, Philip had promised Audrey that he would never take a lover without first telling her of his intentions. She had agreed to do the same, though that had not yet come to pass, and she couldn't imagine it would. Theirs was a marriage of friendship and respect, and she trusted Philip. Whatever had happened to Miss Lovejoy in this cursed room the evening before, it was not at all what Mr. Marsden believed it to be. She had to find out how her husband had become involved in this madness.

Audrey prepared herself for another plunge into the last

memories the earbob offered and picked it up again. She opened her mind to the shaky, fragmented vision of being rolled over. Miss Lovejoy's battering arms again came up into view, beating back some dark outline. Audrey made out the profile of an ear, the side of a closely shorn head, dark hair the color of ink—

"What are you doing in here?"

Not a voice from the vision.

Audrey shot up from her crouch. She spun around, lashing out with the candle into the space directly behind her. A firm hand caught her forearm. In the second before hot wax lurched onto the burning wick and doused the small flame, Audrey saw the shadowy face of the man who'd sneaked up behind her.

She cursed under her breath. "*You.*"

CHAPTER FOUR

"Of all the stupid things I've witnessed over the years, this one truly shines," Hugh said, his fingers still wrapped around the duchess's slim arm.

"Unhand me," she demanded, yanking free of his grasp, and stepping aside.

Hugh had entered the duke's rooms soundlessly moments ago to find the lady crouching near the four-poster. Sir's tip-off that the duchess had indeed gone to Jewell House as expected had sent Hugh's temper roof-ward.

"This is a crime scene, Your Grace. It is also the middle of the night. You should not be here lurking about, *alone.*"

The naïve, utterly careless chit. Did she have no idea what went on beyond the sculpted lawns of her manor house? Last night at Bow Street, when she'd marched right into the cellar of the Brown Bear, dismissing his order to leave, he'd known she would be a condescending snob. Though, he hadn't quite believed she would be so senseless as to visit Jewell House alone.

He had given her an address, but she had known which room belonged to the duke, and so how ignorant could she truly be?

"I certainly could not have come here during the day," she answered.

"You should not have come at all."

The duchess moved again, this time toward the windows. "How did you know to find me here?"

He snorted a laugh. She'd lacked any finesse in extricating the address for Jewell House from him. Almost immediately, Hugh had sent one of the lackeys at Bow Street to find Sir. The boy had been instructed to report back should she make her way to the Dials, and just past midnight, Sir's rapid knocking on his front door had roused him. He'd flagged a hack and left for Jewell House within minutes.

"The question, Your Grace, is *why* have I found you here?"

He took a step toward her, wanting to shepherd her into the thin moonlight falling in bands across the room. He wanted to see her expression. Lying women tended to hike their chins or flare their nostrils; they often fidgeted with their fingers or hair or earlobes.

"It is simple," she said, her face still lost in the darkness. "I'm here to conduct my own investigation."

He felt no humor in this, only a stab of reproach. "Need I remind you that *I* am the Bow Street officer, and *you* are a duchess?"

"I require no reminder. However, I wonder if perhaps you do? I have told you time and again that my husband is innocent and yet you refuse the possibility."

"Forgive me for favoring *evidence* over the delusional opinion of a suspect's wife," Hugh replied, his jaw tight. The woman infuriated him with the way she so comfortably sat upon her privilege and rejected the sound facts of the case.

"I am not delusional." Her voice grew soft. Defensive. Hugh stopped to consider; his senses were well honed to play off another person's weakness.

"No, perhaps not. Perhaps you've come here not to investigate, but to tidy up."

The air between them went rigid. "What do you mean by that?" she hissed.

"Odd how you so easily found your way to your husband's rooms, when last night you claimed to know nothing of them."

She stayed quiet, though Hugh imagined her pulse had just taken a running leap.

"The slighted wife of a powerful duke, shoved aside for some tart of an opera singer," he went on, aiming to lead her out. He did not for one moment believe the grasping woman standing in the darkened room before him was a murderess, but the sooner she felt offended, the sooner she would trot right back to her fine home and leave his case alone.

"Absurd," she replied. "You cannot frighten me with your ridiculous theories. If I had been the one to kill Miss Lovejoy, do you truly believe I would be here, proclaiming my husband's innocence? Wouldn't I instead allow my philandering husband to take the blame?"

Hugh wished the candle she'd been holding hadn't gone out. He didn't enjoy arguing in the dark. Something about it balanced the scales and allowing this duchess any amount of power was a mistake.

Her husband was a murderer, and yet she had endangered her own life coming here to investigate, as she'd called it. Investigate what? An empty room? Hugh had scoured it thoroughly after delivering the duke to Bow Street but had found nothing to point to a scenario different than the one presented to the magistrate. The only difference tonight was the missing mattress. It made the four-poster look skeletal in the moonlight. Hugh imagined it had been hauled outside and burned. The people of St. Giles re-used much around here, but there could be no second life for something with so much gore soaked into the fibers.

"Whatever your intent here, it was misguided and foolish.

Come with me. I will see you home." Hugh was finished with this room and with the tedious Duchess of Fournier.

She was not unlike other young ladies of her circle with a newly minted title. Hugh didn't keep a close eye on the gossip of the *ton*, but he thought he'd heard of the lady's marriage to the Duke of Fournier a few years back. A bit of scandal had been attached to it, but Hugh hadn't cared enough then to dig into it. He still didn't, though it might shed some light on the goings on from last night.

"No need." She swept past him. Hugh traced a warm, honeyed scent. "I have a carriage waiting outside."

He'd seen the worn coach and its hunched jarvey when he and Sir had arrived. The usual footpads and whores had been milling about, along with a few lads likely on their way back to Bertrick's flash house with their pickings. The Canary wasn't too far down Little White Lyon, and it was only one of the dens of thieves and criminals in this scum hole. The duchess was lucky she'd made this far without being accosted.

Hugh followed her from the room—which had been locked up by the landlord on Hugh's orders the night before, to keep the vagrants out. He eyed the duchess's trim figure as she exited Jewell House and wondered if she'd found a key among her husband's possessions at home.

"Don't be naïve. By now, a thief could be sitting in that hack you've got waiting outside. I will see you home safely."

"I am not going home," she announced. "Nor do I wish for you to deliver me anywhere at all."

It had been a long time since Hugh had been forced to converse with society's upper crust. He had not missed the acute feeling of being several shades less worthwhile than those around him. It was how he'd felt his entire childhood.

There had been some benefit to growing up in the servant quarters of Neatham House, the ancestral seat of the Viscount Neatham. Hugh's mother had been nanny to Lord and Lady

Neatham's children, and she'd been allowed to keep Hugh with her. He'd been given a proper education—something a servant's child was never afforded.

For a time, Hugh believed his mother was an exception because of her position. As nanny, she was needed by the viscount's children at all hours of the day and night. However, as Hugh grew older, and his resemblance to the viscount became more and more distinct, he began to understand the whispers, stares, and upturned noses he received. His mother's position as nanny wasn't the reason Lord Neatham allowed for Hugh's presence. Guilt was the reason, and because the viscount had been a fairly decent man, he'd taken responsibility for the boy and for Hugh's mother.

"If you are not going home, I can only presume that you intend to carry on with your personal investigation," he said as he and the duchess stepped into the thick brume outside.

The dense smog was a sour-looking greenish yellow by the light of the carriage lanterns and gas-lit streetlamps. The hackney's jarvey climbed down from his driver's bench and opened the coach door for his approaching customer. Hugh stepped in front of the duchess and glanced into the hack, to make sure the inside was empty.

"You've concluded your investigation, haven't you? Leave me to mine, sir," she replied.

The duchess glared at him until he stepped away from the hackney door, and then she ascended into the cab. While she may have wished for a quick exit, her jarvey stood waiting for her instruction. Hugh remained where he was, hands deep in his trouser pockets, and waited as well. From inside the coach, she grumbled, "Oh, for heaven's sake, the Theatre Royal, Drury Lane, if you will."

The jarvey tipped his hat and closed the door. "Aye, miss."

Hugh went to his own hired hack, where Sir still lounged inside. Any other child, and Hugh would have been sending him home to bed, but from what he'd gleaned about his young cohort, the boy might very well be safer riding around London in the middle of the night with a Bow Street officer.

"I've earned me coin, haven't I?" Sir asked as Hugh instructed the driver to follow the hackney cab.

"Stop whining. We've one more stop to make."

Within minutes, they were pulling up behind the duchess's hackney cab outside the theatre. Though it was well on to one in the morning, the night's performance had ended not long before. Actors and actresses would still be hanging about, he figured, and he had the sinking sensation that the duchess intended to speak to them. What in hell kind of duchess would lower herself to speak to the performers?

A desperate one, he mused.

He and the duchess descended onto the curb at the same time. Her plain cloak and serviceable boots could not detract from her regal poise or air of entitlement. When she speared Hugh with a vexed look, he took no small amount of pleasure in it.

"Must you follow me?" she asked.

He left the hack once again, with Sir groaning and grumbling inside.

"I'm curious what you think you will discover here," he replied.

The duchess walked past the grand columns and through the front doors to the theatre, as if she had done so a hundred times. She likely had. Hugh had been to the opera on two occasions, and neither time had he used the front door. He hadn't sat in the house, either, but had gone about with some inquiry business backstage, in the warren of halls and dressing rooms. Once to arrest a stagehand, and the second time to question an actress accused of thievery.

"I would like to know more about Miss Lovejoy," she answered him as they entered the foyer. It was empty except for a few men sweeping the floors and polishing the handrails of the split stairwell, which branched off to the left and right to ascend to the upper level. The men paused in their work but quickly carried on, averting their eyes, and minding their own business, as they had likely been trained to do.

The duchess came to a halt, appearing suddenly hesitant.

"What is the matter?" Hugh asked.

She bristled, her chin hitching. "Nothing at all." *A lie.* The hitched chin gave it away. She strode toward the workers, probably just to turn her back on him. But he could sense discomfort and uncertainty beneath her hesitation.

The duchess was clearly not familiar or at ease with taking control of a situation, and though she put on a good front, he knew why. Pampered and coddled, the woman had likely never had to make a weighty decision in her life. He'd known duchesses and countesses and ladies of every peerage rank, and he'd never met one who wouldn't lower her head in deference, or simper when she knew it was the requisite response.

Then again, flickers of a rebellious nature kept sparking up in the Duchess of Fournier's eyes, which were, he'd noted, the color of new ferns springing from a forest floor. Either that or viperous green.

"Pardon," the duchess was saying to the workers when he caught up to her. "I'd like to speak with the theater manager. Where might I find him?"

"Backstage, madam," one man replied, standing his broom up. "Would you like an escort?"

Hugh moved past them. "That isn't necessary."

"An escort would be lovely, thank you," she replied, louder than necessary. Hugh sighed and paused to let the worker pass. The duchess met Hugh's eyes as she bustled by as well, one thin brow arched high.

He took up the rear, her cloaked figure soon swallowed by the darkness of a slim corridor leading backstage. Patrons of the theatre didn't tread here; the carpet felt like old moss beneath Hugh's boots instead of thick pile, and the walls were papered with broadsides and newspaper clippings rather than embroidered silk. Only a single tallow candle was lit in a crimped tin sconce. When they entered the light, the duchess spoke to the worker.

"Sir, are you familiar with Miss Lovejoy?"

The worker slowed, his back straightening with tension. Hugh felt the same surprise. He'd thought she had only accepted the offer for an escort for arguments sake, but perhaps she'd had a keener reason.

"I am, madam. Or I was, at least," he answered after a prolonged moment. They moved out of the light and back into the shadows.

"Was she currently performing in a production?" she asked next.

"Yes, madam."

Hugh was accustomed to brief answers; sometimes even no acknowledgement that he'd asked a question at all. As was the case earlier today when questioning the duke. Whenever that happened, Hugh knew to curb his questions and try a difference tactic. The lady walking the corridor ahead of him, however, nosed on like an eager hound, oblivious to the worker's resistance.

"Did Miss Lovejoy have any admirers that you're aware of—"

"Here you are, madam." The man opened a door, flooding the corridor with bronzed light. He held out an arm, tucked his chin, and allowed the duchess to pass. As soon as Hugh fell into step behind her, the door closed, and the worker was gone.

She let out a long breath.

"You step heavily, Your Grace." She glared at him, and Hugh raised his hands in submission. "I'm simply saying if you want answers, it will serve you well to be a fox instead of an elephant."

Her full lips pinched. "I do not require your help nor your advice. Why have you bothered to follow me, Mr. Marsden?"

Hugh stifled the answer that leaped to his tongue: *Because you're blinded by desperation and conceit and are wading into dangerous waters.* She would only tell him to go, and though it tempted him greatly, Hugh could not leave the lady alone backstage at a theatre.

He sauntered past her, into the cluttered and narrow passageways snaking off stage. He dodged racks of costumes, furniture, and all manner of props as he followed the buzzing hum of voices. The odor of sweat, smoke, and perfume met his nostrils, and then Hugh turned a corner and found himself in a room full of light, mirrors, and frothy, bright colors.

Men and women in half dress mingled together, casting off costumes and stage makeup. Every eye lifted and landed upon the two intruders. Conversation ceased. One man, tall and lanky and wearing nothing but a waistcoat and trousers, his chest and arms bare underneath, continued to whistle a tune as he wiped one side of his face with a cloth. The garish paint streaked off, revealing badly pitted, dark brown skin. He kept on with his whistling as he ran his eyes over Hugh and the duchess, who had gone still with shock. Likely, he thought, from the display of so much flesh and bosom. He suppressed a smirk.

"The theatre manager," Hugh said. "Where can we find him?"

A moment ticked by as the actors and actresses eyed one another, silently deliberating. The man with the pockmarked skin quit whistling and licked his lips.

"That way," he answered, pointing down the corridor. He offered nothing more, and Hugh backed up. He caught a fold on the duchess's cloak and gave it a brief tug.

She gasped in offense, and as soon as they were moving along the corridor again, lashed at him. "There is no need for you to manhandle me, Mr. Marsden."

"I wouldn't have put it past you to stay and stomp around the room asking your questions."

"If I chose to do so, it would be none of your concern."

Abruptly, Hugh's indulgence ran dry. He stopped and turned, causing the duchess to come just short of crashing into him.

"You seem woefully ignorant of your own actions tonight,

Your Grace. You might be accustomed to your world parting like the Red Sea before you, but I advise a better look at your surroundings. No one here gives a damn who you are."

She glared, first in shock and then, as her eyes narrowed to slits, in fury. "It is not your responsibility to act as my guide, Officer Marsden. I neither asked for it nor do I want it."

"On the contrary," he said, his patience unraveling. "You are the wife of a murder suspect I've just sent before the magistrate. I would be remiss in my duties if I turned a blind eye to whatever you are currently doing to thwart my investigation."

Twin, depthless pupils flared with new fury. Any well-heeled lady of the peerage would have turned up her nose and ignored him. Once again, the duchess deviated from her set role.

She took a step closer. In the stuffy, tapered corridor, Hugh scented the barest trace of rose water. He held himself perfectly still as she set the delicately squared edge of her jaw.

"Are you so afraid that I will succeed in thwarting your case?"

"Hardly."

"Then I wonder why you've chosen to tag along with me tonight."

"Perhaps it is because I am a gentleman," he said through gritted teeth.

Her lips bowed into a sudden grin. "A gentleman. Why, Mr. Marsden, you should join the actors and take to the stage with a line so well delivered."

She nudged past him, her shoulder brushing his arm. Hugh didn't know whether to laugh or groan with frustration. The woman had gall, that much was evident. And she had the right of it: Hugh was no gentleman, not in title nor in practice.

Still, her dismissal pricked and drew up memories like beads of blood. A face surfaced in his mind. Lady Eloisa Neatham, so young and demure and fragile. So easily broken. The Duchess of Fournier might be young, but she was neither demure nor fragile. At least not in any visible way. He scowled as he stayed on her heels toward a second room, aglow with lamplight. This was the reason he avoided the elite whenever possible. They reminded him far too much of his life before Bow Street.

The headstrong duchess whisked right through the open door, into the lit room. It housed a cluttered desk, lamps, a number of cabinets, a few racks of clothing, and a slim bed, the bedding of which was unmade, along with a chamber pot pulled out from underneath the bedframe. It looked as if the manager lived here.

"Excuse me, sir," she said to a rumpled-looking man in shirtsleeves behind the desk, his attention on a ledger before him. He lowered his pipe and blinked owlishly.

"My lady?" Astutely and swiftly, he'd recognized her position. He stood up and immediately reached for the jacket over the back of his chair.

"I'm sorry to bother you at this hour," she began. Hugh noted it was the first apology she'd made that night. "However, I'm looking for some information on an actress you've employed."

The manager visibly stalled as he shrugged into his jacket and extinguished his pipe. He put on a showman's smile, filled with gracious hospitality. Hugh kept his own expression blank when the manager's eyes skipped toward him, then away.

"Of course, my lady, but first, may I introduce myself? Ignacio Bernadetto, at your service." He bowed deeply after coming around the desk to stand before the duchess. As he straightened, Bernadetto reached for his top hat, on the chair in front of the desk, and popped it into place.

"Mr. Bernadetto, it's a pleasure to make your acquaintance. I'm Audrey Sinclair, Duchess of Fournier."

At her name, the manager's welcoming grin sunk faster than a rock tossed in the Thames. His complexion turned ruddy, and his throat bobbed as he swallowed hard.

"Your Grace." He ran a palm down the front of his jacket. "You are here to inquire about Miss Lovejoy."

Hugh stepped into the cramped office. "You are aware then,

that the Duke of Fournier was arrested in connection with her death?"

Bernadetto observed Hugh, his nostrils flaring as he took stock of him. Quickly, he must have deduced he was not of the same station as the lady, for he sniffed at him. "And you are, sir?"

The duchess spoke before Hugh could. "A private inquiry agent assisting me with the gathering of facts."

She peered at him, those spring green eyes flashing with a dare to refute the statement. He bit back the urge, wanting only to keep Bernadetto talking. If he knew Hugh hailed from Bow Street, he might clam up entirely. It seemed the duchess had the forethought to know that, too. The sooner she got her answers, the sooner he could shuffle her back into a carriage and to the fashionable square her grand home was perched upon.

"I see," the manager said, his eyes still lingering on Hugh's face another moment. He then cut his attention back to the duchess. "Yes, I am aware the duke has been arrested, though I am not sure I can help you with anything else."

The lack of condolences told Hugh that Bernadetto was not in the least sorry to hear of the duke's predicament.

"Did His Grace frequent Miss Lovejoy's performances?" Hugh asked as the question came to him.

"He has a box, yes, and he attended a number of our productions."

The duchess took the opening. "Whether Miss Lovejoy was performing or not?"

"Belladora was in nearly every production, Your Grace," he replied, his cold disdain beginning to leak through his earlier pretense of cordiality. "I cannot know if His Grace attended for the sake of the arts or for the sake of...something else."

"Did she have many admirers?" Hugh asked before the duchess could protest Bernadetto's statement.

The manager let the tension out of his shoulders as he circled back behind his desk. It was a tired, loping motion, and Hugh presumed he and the rest of the theatre troupe had struggled through the night's performance.

"Her fair share, I suppose. She received bouquets and notes after every performance for being so lovely and expressive and... attentive to her audience."

"But not just any audience members," Hugh said.

He knew how the theatre worked. Roles were not handed out based on merit alone. To operate, the theatre required wealthy patrons, and those patrons held sway over who received lead roles. Had Miss Lovejoy had a patron of her own, and he wished to see her in the lead role time and again, it could be easily purchased.

The duchess's suspicious glance hinted that she had caught on to his meaning.

"You are inquiring as to whether or not Belladora had a benefactor," the manager stated.

"Did she?" Hugh asked.

Bernadetto settled into his chair once again and crossed his legs. "Her personal affairs are not for me to discuss. I will not tarnish her memory with such loose gossip."

"We do not intend to tarnish her memory." In her fervor, the duchess stepped closer to the manager's desk. "We intend to find the man who harmed her."

A new voice entered the room from behind them. "You mean the man who slit her open like a pig."

Hugh swiveled on his heel, his hand reaching under his jacket to the smooth handle of his pistol. The whistling man from the dressing room stood just outside the office entrance. Hugh berated himself for not having heard the footsteps coming along the corridor. It wasn't like him not to keep an ear open. It was the duchess's presence, he suspected. He'd been busy sparing her attention when he should have been directing it to better use—like not allowing their exit to be cut off.

"Away with you, Porter," Bernadetto hissed.

The man, Porter, ignored the order. "Who do they want to

help, I wonder...the bastard sitting in the Stone Jug, or our sweet Belladora?"

Like chins hitching or fingers fidgeting, Hugh had learned to pay close attention to words. Porter's use of 'our sweet' chimed like a warning bell.

"The man who has been arrested is not the man who killed Miss Lovejoy," the duchess said.

Bernadetto shot up from his seat. "What?"

"That hasn't been proven," Hugh bit off, keeping his eye on Porter. The actor blocked the only exit.

"However, we *will* prove it," she went on. Hugh sent her what he hoped was a clear and persuasive glare to cease speaking.

Porter took a step inside the office. "You see, Ignacio, they just want to spring the blue blood. They don't give a damn about what happened to Belladora."

"I didn't say that—" the duchess began.

"Porter. *Out*," Berdadetto barked. Once again, the command went ignored.

"The nob was there, covered in her blood."

There had been dozens of people peeking inside the apartment before Hugh arrived. The tales of what they had seen had likely gone out far and wide within hours, but Hugh wondered if perhaps Porter had been there, as one of the onlookers.

"I don't deny that, but he wasn't her benefactor. Who was?" the duchess pushed on. Hugh wanted to throttle her. And by the look of Porter's bulging eyes, so did he.

"She weren't no ladybird," he growled.

Not a kept mistress? Hugh didn't believe it for a moment. It was simply the way of their world. Porter was either lying, ignorant, or he was protecting someone.

"Your Grace. Sir," Bernadetto said, addressing them. "I think you should take your leave. We have told you what we know."

Hugh wanted out of this backstage warren, but he couldn't walk away from a lie. "Her roles. Who purchased them?"

If he could get the benefactor's name—*the duke's* name preferably—he could serve up his case like a roast on a platter to the chief magistrate, Gabriel Poston.

Bernadetto rubbed his temple and bared his teeth. "Miss Lovejoy needed *no* endorsements, sir. If she had an arrangement with a gentleman, I was not aware of it, nor was it my business to pry. Now I would like you to leave, at once." He made a half-hearted bow toward the duchess. "Your Grace, forgive me my terseness, but it has been, as you can imagine, a trying day."

The duchess wouldn't turn her back on Porter, who still stood within the doorway. It was perhaps the most intelligent thing the woman had done all day.

"For us all," she said, and with a tight nod to the manager, moved toward Hugh and the door. Porter remained where he was. Though taller than Hugh, the actor was lanky and had an underfed look to him. He would fight well, Hugh determined, fueled as he was by anger.

"Step aside," Hugh warned, his voice low, his hand flexing on his pistol's handle.

"Porter," the manager said, this time his voice like the lash of a whip.

The actor heeded the order and cleared the doorway. Hugh saw the duchess through first, and then followed, turning back to make sure the man didn't lunge after them. Porter slipped into Bernadetto's office and the lamplight inside blotted out as the door shut.

"Here." Hugh cut ahead of her and opened the door to the corridor that the broom sweep had shown them through.

"I know where I'm going," she replied as she shuttled past him.

"Do you? What a relief." He slammed the door shut, closing them in darkness.

He heard her skirts swishing on ahead. Hugh took long strides over the old carpet to catch her just before she entered the light of the single candle sconce. He knew it was a mistake as he reached for her elbow, and yet he still did it, jerking her to a stop. Alarm and...something else...widened her eyes as she stared up at him. Fear? That's what he thought he saw before she wrenched her elbow from his grasp.

"I can't bloody begin to count how many mistakes you made back there," he said, his tongue loose and wild, his blood pumping fast.

The duchess gathered herself up, looking as if she were ready to launch a fleet of war ships right at him. "At least I asked the questions that needed asking!"

"And what answers did you receive that will help the duke? None. You bungled it all up by giving them your name."

"My name?" she echoed, incredulous. She was a dragon, all hard scales and flaring nostrils. If she could have breathed fire, Hugh would be ducking right then.

"You tossed your title out before you, no doubt believing it would buy you respect and what? Some level of importance? However, this time, *Your Grace*, that name of yours tripped you up and sent you sprawling."

Hugh pressed forward before she could respond. "The people here, they don't give a damn about you or your husband. You are nothing to them. Belladora Lovejoy was their friend, their colleague. And you traipsed in there and told them the man arrested for her murder was innocent, dashing their hopes for justice. What did you believe they would do, thank you? Devote themselves to your cause?"

The flame of the candle reflected off the tin shield behind it, scattering low, changing light over the duchess's face. Pricks of color stained her cheeks, and her eyes looked glassy. Whether it was with ire or humiliation, Hugh couldn't be certain.

"Philip was not her benefactor," she said, twirling around a direct answer to his question like any skilled debutante. No, nothing so young and innocent. This was a married woman of status. Far from a debutante. "You heard them both deny that she possessed one."

"A woman can have a lover without him keeping her as a mistress," he scoffed. Her color darkened, and Hugh felt a pinch of remorse. "You opened this door, Your Grace, so you should be prepared for unsavory truths."

"As you should be, Mr. Marsden, like the fact that you arrested the wrong man," she replied before moving farther down the corridor, drenching herself in darkness again. "That Porter fellow seemed overly protective of Miss Lovejoy."

Once they were back in the foyer, with the candelabras snuffed out and the broom sweeps gone, he fell into stride beside her.

"She had her admirers in the audience, as well as among fellow performers. I'm sure Porter was one of them," he agreed.

Jealousy could have been why he'd so vehemently denied Miss Lovejoy was a kept mistress. It gave Hugh a moment's pause as he opened the door for the duchess and held it wide as she glided outside, drawing up her cloak's hood. Jealous men killed in mad rages. He'd seen it a number of times before. Women killed as well, though it was rare for them to use blades. Women chose poison more often than not, or a bullet direct to the back of the head. The opera singer's body had been mutilated, and it could not be denied the person who'd done it had been in a violent rage.

If Porter had followed Miss Lovejoy to the duke's rooms and seen them together, it was possible he could have lost his temper. He nearly had tonight. But then, why leave the duke without so much as a scratch? And how had the duke's clothes become so wrecked with blood?

"You look like you've swallowed old mutton. What has come to your mind?" the duchess asked as she came to a stop beside her hired hack. The jarvey and his tired nag, and even more tired carriage, still sat in front of Hugh's own.

"Nothing that I care to discuss," he replied, and then, remembering the etiquette ingrained in him as a child, bowed slightly and added, "Your Grace."

She scoffed, the scraping sound in her throat unladylike. "Don't pretend at good manners now, Mr. Marsden. You've already sworn and shouted and jostled me around plenty this evening."

He wanted to refute her claims but couldn't. It was true. His reputation was already in shambles among the peerage, and his lack of patience with the whole lot of them was why.

"Very well. No more pretending. I warn you off from this absurd investigation of yours. You're out of your element, duchess. Keep going, and you could get hurt."

"You are quite right—I am out of my element. But you see, I'm not afraid of getting hurt." She moved toward her hack, the jarvey having already opened the door for her. He handed her in, but caught the door when he went to shut it. She held it open a moment as she looked down at Hugh.

"What I am afraid of, is becoming a widow," she said, then latched the door. "Goodnight, Mr. Marsden."

She slid back, out of view, and Hugh curled his hands into fists. The woman was a stubborn ox.

"Are we done yet?" Sir called impatiently from the open hack door. Hugh hopped inside. Home beckoned, but not until he knew for certain the duchess had, at least for tonight, ceased her efforts.

"Nearly." He rapped the roof. "Follow her."

CHAPTER
FIVE

Audrey sat in bed, her back against the pillows, the satin counterpane drawn to her waist. The fire in the grate animated the blue silk walls of her bedroom in a quivering dance of black and orange flickers. She'd been sitting in place for more than a quarter hour, looking at the drop pearl and black crystal earbob lying atop the counterpane at her side. It was such a small thing, and yet it occupied the space as well as any sleeping husband. Not that Philip shared her bed. This was her room; her bed and hers alone. Her husband had never slept here, though he did come in once a week or so to maintain the façade of a traditional marriage. In the beginning, they would have great fun with it, teasing the servants by making a racket. Now, however, they'd tamed themselves and usually just had a brandy and a chat.

Belladora Lovejoy's earbob appeared a harmless thing on the bed of satin jacquard, but Audrey knew it was far from innocent. It had already given terrifying images that her memory would cling to forever, and the moment she touched the earbob again, more would come. Mr. Marsden had interrupted her earlier. The piece of jewelry still had more memories to give before it fell quiet and dark. Once it did that, it would be just an earbob. Empty. Safe.

There was no choice in the matter. She had to hold it. Had to help Philip in any way possible. Already, she knew the man attacking Miss Lovejoy had not been the duke. She'd seen a glimpse of his head, his dark, shorn hair, his ear. But there might be more to see; perhaps his whole face.

Audrey dreaded it. Dreaded feeling like she was the one being attacked, so close to Miss Lovejoy's memories she could feel the smothering weight of sheer horror.

The man at the theatre, Porter, had been dark haired, his skin a deep brown. But his skin had been pitted, and the side of the face she'd seen in the vision had been smooth and white. Bristled, but unmarked by any scarring.

She'd made mistakes with her questions at the theatre, she wouldn't pretend otherwise. Not that she'd ever admit it to that insolent Bow Street officer. Audrey touched the crook of her elbow, where his hand had grasped her earlier. Though it had not been skin-to-skin contact, she'd seen something. The image had been fast and jagged. A woman's face. There, blooming in Audrey's vision, all loose russet hair and creamy skin, and then gone again.

That had never happened before. She wore gloves whenever fashionable—and thank goodness they were—and avoided touching people. Skin contact hardly ever caused visions to erupt, blinding her to the real world, but when they did, they struck hard. Energy with that sort of power was never a current memory, but one that haunted the person. One that consumed them so completely that it was always there. Always present. Whoever the woman with the russet curls was, haunted Mr. Marsden deeply.

Audrey batted away the curiosity. Mr. Marsden was not her ally, no matter the lie she'd told Mr. Bernadetto. When she'd arrived at Violet House, the jarvey had helped her down and quietly informed her that the other carriage had followed them from the theatre. Audrey tipped the jarvey handsomely before going inside. Barton, her butler, had let out an audible sigh of relief when he met her at the door. While he hadn't questioned her directly, he'd made comments that demanded some sort of explanation of her absence—all of which she'd bypassed by telling him she felt ill and was turning in for the night.

While Greer had been stoking the fire in the grate and readying the bed, Audrey had peered outside, searching for the officer's carriage, half thinking it would be parked along the street. It hadn't been, and she'd felt silly as she let Greer undress her.

Audrey now sat with her head throbbing and her eyes dry and hot as she stared at the earbob. She needed sleep, and she couldn't do that until she'd taken every memory the earbob could give her.

Get on with it, you ninny.

Audrey closed it into her fist.

Battering arms, flailing and hitting. Blurred images, dark and vicious. Shouting, grunts, and panting breaths. Swathes of firelight and bared teeth. The images chugged further into the past, and Audrey made out the exterior of a fine brick terrace house, a brass plate—47—above the door. White columns, an endless row of them, fronted every home along the street.

Gray speckles closed in from the edges of her vision. And then, blackness.

Audrey sucked in a breath and opened her eyes. She uncurled her fingers. The earbob rested in the center of her palm; the edges of the crystal had pinched grooves into her skin. It was just an earbob now, all energy, all clues, leached. And not one face. Not one piece of information that she could follow. At least not easily.

She couldn't think through the muddle of her exhausted thoughts. Audrey set the earbob on the bedside table and sank into her pillows, closing her eyes. Behind them, she saw the russet-haired girl, Mr. Marsden's livid expression, and the jumble of images she'd just hurtled through.

It was only when she woke from a dreamless sleep a few hours later that she remembered with a cramp in her chest that Philip would not be at the breakfast table as he usually was. He was always so pleasant at breakfast, while Audrey knew she was a bit of a grouch before she could sip her chocolate.

The morning before his arrest, they'd been having breakfast together and reading the gossip columns, as usual, sharing a laugh over the description of Lady Dutton's gown the previous evening at Lady Granger's annual musicale.

"*There is, without doubt, a peacock somewhere in Kew Gardens that is missing every last feather. It is a sad affair when a creature sacrifices its beauty to help enhance another's, and the effort falls so short of success,*" Philip had read aloud, laughing as he'd reclined in his chair, crossing one leg, and sipping his tea.

"That is cruel," Audrey had commented, attempting not to smile.

"To the peacock," he replied.

A knock upon her bedroom door drew her from the memory, her weak smile fading completely.

"Come in, Greer," she called.

Greer had been serving her for the last three years, having been assigned the position of lady's maid when she and Philip had married. Nearing middle age, Greer had served the previous Duchess of Fournier, Philip's mother, until the woman's death a handful of years before Audrey took the title. She was a quiet, loyal lady's maid, who rarely smiled and yet never appeared cross. Diligent was the term Audrey would use, as well as content. Serving a duchess as lady's maid was, next to housekeeper, the highest rank among the serving class and much respected. Greer exuded confidence and pride in everything she did.

Even now, as she entered the bedroom and immediately went to the windows to draw back the drapes, she did so with bustle.

"Good morning, Your Grace," Greer said. She set a stack of folded linen on a bench and immediately entered the large, attached boudoir, where Audrey's clothes were kept.

"Will you be taking breakfast in your room, or in the dining room, Your Grace?"

Audrey wanted nothing more than to sit in bed all day, denying the real world was unfurling outside the four walls of her room. Which was exactly why she had to get up and get moving.

"In the dining room," she answered, shoving back the counterpane. Greer emerged with a dark plum day dress, so dark it was nearly ebony. The gown was plain, with minimal embroidery and not an inch of lace.

At Audrey assessing eye, Greer said, "I thought this would be appropriate."

Audrey took a deep breath; it was as close to a mourning dress as one could get. She set her jaw. "Another color, Greer. Green, I think."

With a bob of her head, she disappeared back into the boudoir.

Audrey dressed and took breakfast alone, the footmen and maids all abnormally subdued. The house was so quiet, the soft, steady ticking of the clocks sounded like heartbeats in every room and hallway. To her relief, Barton maintained his usual show of persnickety irritation as he swept into the sitting room just before noon.

"Lady Redding to see you, Your Grace," he said, adding, "*if* you are at home. And if I may, Your Grace, Lord Harrick advised yesterday that callers be kept to an extreme minimum. If you would like me to see the lady out..."

"That isn't necessary, Barton, thank you. I will see her."

He sniffed his disapproval, but Audrey only shook her head and smiled. She appreciated Barton's attempt to spare her what would no doubt be an agonizing half hour in the presence of the Viscountess Redding. Audrey, however, knew her as Millie.

Her older sister by ten years, Millie had never paid much attention to Audrey while growing up. She'd been looking to marriage by the time Audrey had been ready to leave the nursery and hadn't much time to spare a seven-year-old pest who hid in hedgerows to jump out at her older sister and whatever beau had called on her that week.

It was just the two of them, Millie and Audrey, the brother born between them having died. James had been kinder to Audrey, though he'd still been six years her senior and had been too busy to play or climb trees with her. He'd caught a fever at Eton, and he'd brought it home to Haverfield, their home in Hertfordshire.

Audrey had been shut up tight in her nursery rooms on the upper floors for her own protection, unable to see anyone for days. Her nanny would sit with her, leaving only to fetch meal trays. It had been unbearably hot and stuffy in those rooms, even with the windows open to the spring air, and Audrey had been sticky and irritable. No one would let her see James. No one would even take a letter to him. She'd written a whole page in her broad scrawl, telling him that once he was better, she would teach him a card game she'd grown rather good at.

She wasn't sure how many days she stayed tucked in that nursery. A whole week? Maybe more. All she knew for certain was that when her nanny finally took her by the hand and led her out, Audrey had emerged into a world where James and her father were dead. Papa. Audrey hadn't even known he'd fallen ill. No one had told her. She'd been so furious that she'd yanked away from her nanny's strangling embrace and run. Out of the house, through the lawns, into the woods, and the fields beyond. No one had chased her down, and it had felt like hours later when she saw the imposing roofs of Fournier House through a clump of trees.

Tired, hungry, and a little scared at how quickly dusk had fallen, she had strolled into her neighbor's circular drive, where a few footmen spotted her. The next thing Audrey knew, she was lying on a silk sofa in a cool sitting room, munching on lemon ice with the lady of the house fretting over her. The former Duchess of Fournier had shed real tears when Audrey told her about James and her papa. She'd then beckoned Philip, who'd been James's age, and he'd played jacks with her while a carriage was prepared to bring her home to Haverfield.

She'd fallen a little bit in love with Philip that day; him and the duchess and the rest of Fournier House, that was. Now, *she* was Duchess of Fournier. Philip was her husband, and he *did* love her, though just not in the way Audrey always imagined she'd be loved one day. It was quite all right by her though. She loved Philip as a friend, the very best of friend.

Her eyes were watering when Millie entered the sitting room behind Barton, and she blinked to clear them.

"Thank you, Barton," she said, standing to greet her sister.

It had been months since Millie had paid her a visit. They had seen one another at balls and dinners, but Millie didn't often call on her, and Audrey, guiltily, avoided calling on her as well.

Millie took Audrey's gloved hands, and Audrey held her breath, prepared for something like what had happened the night before with Mr. Marsden. But the moment passed without a bursting vision, and Audrey exhaled.

"Tell me the rumors are not true," Millie said before she'd even settled herself on the edge of a slipper chair.

It had been more than twenty-four hours since Philip's arrest. Plenty of time for gossip to have bled into every household in London, aristocratic or common. A duke had been arrested for a grisly murder. Now that she thought of it, Audrey couldn't believe Violet House hadn't been overrun with callers. Or perhaps Barton had only allowed notice of Millie's arrival because she was a blood relation. It wouldn't surprise her to know her butler had taken up the task of fending off nosey busybodies.

"Of course, it isn't true," Audrey replied. "Philip hasn't killed anyone."

Her sister's rounded figure seemed to expand as she held her breath. "But he has been arrested? He is in prison?"

"Yes, but—"

"This is disastrous!" Millie shot up off the sofa and toward the hearth. "He is utterly ruined. How could he have allowed himself to be caught in such a compromising situation?"

Audrey frowned. "What have you heard, exactly?"

Millie briefly met her eyes, but she looked overwhelmed and embarrassed. "Nothing a lady should have heard."

Audrey suppressed a sigh. Her sister had always been a bit of a prude. Not to mention self-centered. She wanted to scream at her for thinking first of Philip's reputation, and nothing of his innocence.

"You heard she was an opera singer," Audrey guessed.

Millie made a hissing sound and stalked back toward the sofa. "Actresses...they're all immoral light skirts."

The pain on Mr. Bernadetto's expression, and the fury on Porter's the night before came at Audrey. "She's dead, Millie. Loose morals or no, she was murdered."

Millie pressed her lips thin, looking so much like their mother, Audrey shivered. "And your dear duke stands accused."

Millie had never cared for Philip, though Audrey suspected it wasn't anything to do with him personally so much as it was the fact that he was a duke, and that he'd asked for Audrey's hand instead of Millie's.

A dozen years after seventeen-year-old Millie exchanged vows with Viscount Redding, a doughy-chinned middle-aged man, her sister had become a widow, left with four children and a substantial fortune. By then, Philip, the new Duke of Fournier, had been on the market, and Millie had wanted him, four-year age gap be damned.

Audrey clasped her hands in her lap. "You know him. You *know* he would never do such a thing."

Millie shrugged and sat again on the slipper chair. "What do we really know of our husbands? Don't be naïve, darling. They lead secret lives, and we must pretend we're ignorant of them."

"Perhaps that's how it was with Lord Redding, but things are different between me and Philip."

Millie shook her head and laughed. "Dear Audrey, I forget how newly wed you are. But come, we must prepare for what happens next." She sat taller, her figure, made full and voluptuous from children, appeared too constricted within the confines of her day dress and spencer. "Decamping to Fournier Downs is the only option for you while the courts sort everything out. Now I know mother will be mortified, but I do believe, with time, she will come from Haverfield to call on you—"

"Fournier Downs? Millie, I'm not decamping to Hertfordshire."

Her sister gaped. "You cannot possibly think to stay in London."

"Of course, I'm staying." She bit her tongue before she could say anything more. Telling Millie that she'd decided to launch her own investigation, counter to Bow Street's, would result in one of her sister's histrionic fits. She'd never be rid of her then.

"Absurd! Staying on in London while your husband stands trial for the murder of his mistress—"

"He did not murder anyone!"

"—is scandalous. Withdraw to the country. Preserve your dignity while you still maintain a shred of it."

Audrey knew then that it didn't matter to Millie whether Philip did or did not kill his mistress, just like it wouldn't matter to anyone else in the ton. The arrest alone was scandal enough to ruin him forever, and her by proxy. It turned her stomach into knots, and a cold sweat crackled over her chest. How had things gone so very wrong so quickly?

"Running away will only make me look ashamed of Philip, and I'm not. So no, I will not go to Fournier Downs."

Audrey stood, the muscles in her legs sore from how tensely she'd been sitting since Millie arrived. "Now, if you don't mind, I have some business to attend to."

Her sister's mouth dropped open. "Business? Ladies do not attend to *business*."

Always so proper, Audrey thought as she moved toward the sitting room door. *And as shallow as a rain puddle.*

"As the head of this household for the time being, I'm afraid I must."

"Surely, Lord Harrick could help you in those matters," Millie said, slowly rising and following her sister to the door.

Surely, Michael would, though honestly, the only business Audrey needed to attend to right then was seeing her older sister out of her sitting room before she screeched loud enough for all of Curzon Street to hear.

"Thank you for your advice," Audrey said, as sweetly as was manageable. "I'll take it into consideration."

Millie pressed her lips thinly; it was their mother's favored expression and it settled into the grooves of Millie's face with startling ease. Audrey glanced away, not wanting to see their mother if she didn't have to.

"I'll call again in a few days. I hope by then you are ready to be more reasonable," Millie said as she swept out of the sitting room.

Audrey dropped the prim hold of her posture. Retreat to the country. It was what everyone would expect her to do, not just Millie. And perhaps she would...if she had any doubts at all about Philip's innocence.

A soft knock landed upon the door frame, and Barton appeared.

"Thank you for not offering to bring tea," she said. He'd known she wouldn't wish Millie to stay very long.

Barton bowed, his coal black hair neatly trimmed and parted. Like most butlers, his manners were impeccable, along with his presentation. He ran a duke's household and took pride in the task.

"May I be of any more service, Your Grace?"

Audrey hesitated. Seeing Millie had dredged up the past. It had been so long since she'd thought of the day James and her papa had died, and how she'd once laid in the sitting room at Fournier Downs with a longing to never leave. It reminded her of how long Philip had been her friend.

And now, he was sitting in a guarded room at the Brown Bear tavern, alone. Perhaps enough time had passed and he would be ready to speak to her. If not...well, she would simply take his hands and try to see for herself what haunted him so deeply. She would help him, whether he wanted it or not.

She looked to Barton and gave a decisive nod. "Have my carriage readied."

HER HOPE WAS on fire by the time she arrived at number four Bow Street. It had been over a full day since his arrest, and Philip had to have broken free from his stupor. He had to eat and drink, didn't he? Michael had left Violet House the afternoon before saying he'd send the family physician to inspect Philip, and as Audrey girded herself before walking into the Brown Bear tavern, she all but convinced herself that her husband would greet her with a smile and an embrace, and most importantly, words.

The tavern was bustling, unlike the time she'd last been there. Heads turned and eyes stuck, surely wondering what she was doing in such a place as this. She'd taken a few steps into the tavern and toward the bar when a serving maid approached.

"You want a table?" the woman asked, as though in disbelief.

"There is a man being held in an upstairs room, by Bow Street," she replied, trying to keep her voice low. "I'd like to see him."

The serving maid's eyebrows rose with understanding. "Take the stairs, luv. Two floors up. The Runner will see you."

The conditions of the upstairs were only slightly more hospitable than the cellar had been, with narrow halls, dingy floorboards, and smoky air. Just as the tavern maid had said, a Bow Street constable perked up in his chair when he saw her. He eyed the space behind her, as though expecting someone else—a man, she presumed—to appear on her heels.

"Madam?" he said, brow creased in confusion.

Oddly enough, being addressed as madam instead of 'Your Grace' set her at ease.

"I would like to see the man you have in holding here, sir. The Duke of Fournier."

He changed his posture and cleared his throat as his eyes swept from Audrey's face to her feet, then back up again. It gave her the insulting sensation that she'd just been shoved back an inch. Or undressed. Perhaps both.

"I'm not sure that's allowed, madam," he said.

"I have come all this way to speak to *my husband*." As she stressed her relationship with hope it would help clear the way, she recalled how Hugh Marsden had accused her of doing so the night before, at the opera. And how she'd bungled things up because of it. She bit the inside of her cheek and took a breath. "Sir, if you must fetch your superior, I understand and will wait."

The man clenched his jaw, and only then did she realize he might not have liked the implication of needing his superior's permission. But instead of being denied entry again, the man nodded once and reached for the ring of keys at his waist. He unlocked the door and stood aside for Audrey to enter.

"Visitor," he barked into the room, and then to her, added, "Just a few minutes, Your Grace."

The room was little more than the size of a butler's pantry and empty of everything but a cot, a chamber pot, a small table, and two chairs. A small window let in only a little light. A figure laid upon the cot, which was pushed against the far wall, his back to the door. Philip.

"You have a visitor," the Bow Street constable said again when Philip didn't move. Audrey's heart sank, her burning hope that he'd be back to himself doused with ice.

"He's been like this since yesterday," the man grumbled to her. "Wouldn't even speak to his solicitor, or the other lord there, his brother."

Michael and Mr. Potridge had informed her that Philip had been silent, but she'd hoped after a night spent here, alone, with time to think and to sober...

The man moved out into the corridor again. On the floor near the open door was a tray with a plate and cup. The food and drink hadn't been touched.

"Philip?" she said as she entered the warm, stale room.

His head turned. "You should not be here."

She wanted to cry out in relief. Philip's dry cracked voice brought stinging tears to her eyes as she went to him. There was no other chair in the room to sit, so she perched on the edge of the cot. He turned onto his back and sat up, his elbows braced against his knees, hands covering his face. The picture of utter despair knifed through her.

"Don't be ridiculous," she said, trying to mask the waver of her voice. "Where else should I be?"

"Violet House. Fournier Downs. Anywhere but near me."

"Millie tried to convince me of the same thing," she replied.

He lowered his hands, which were no longer caked in dirt and blood, and she wanted to weep. His eyes, usually so bright and jovial, were flat and haunted. His mouth was set into a grim line, his brows pinched. "I don't usually agree with your blow horn of a sister, but in this instance, I do. Go, Audrey."

She smacked his arm, knocking his elbow from his kneecap and sending him lilting to the side. He caught himself and sent her an exasperated look.

"You didn't hurt her, Philip, I know you didn't," she said. "Why have you not denied it? Why are you not speaking to the officers or magistrate? You must realize it only makes you appear guilty."

It was exactly how Mr. Marsden wanted it. He wanted to close his case and prove he was right, and he couldn't care less about the damage left in his wake.

Philip pulled away from her, moving backward to lean against the wall.

"Why won't you speak to me?" she asked. "You've always told me everything. You kept rooms, Philip, and don't think I'm ignorant as to why."

She gritted her teeth, determined not to give him a lecture. Not now, at any rate, and not with the Bow Street guard listening from the corridor. She quieted. "Talk to me. Who were you really seeing?"

"I'm trying to protect you." His voice strained against some emotion. Anguish. Anger. She wasn't sure which.

Audrey opened her reticule and brought out the earbob she'd stowed away inside. Philip eyed it when she held it out to him in her palm.

"What is that?"

"It's how I know you are innocent. This belonged to Miss Lovejoy. I found it in your room at Jewell House."

Fire leaped in his eyes, and he sat forward, suddenly sober. "What in hell were you doing at the Seven Dials?"

She closed the earbob in her fist. "What were *you* doing there? I know it wasn't to meet your mistress." She practically hissed the words so the man outside the pantry wouldn't hear.

Philip sealed his lips again and leaned his head against the wall, eyes lifting toward the cracked plaster ceiling. Then, in a whisper, "What did it show you?"

He knew everything about her. He had for some time, and never once had he doubted or reviled her for it.

"Terrifying things." The frantic, blurred memories were even more obscure and distorted now. "A man who was not you."

He flicked his eyes to her, knowledge behind them. "Did you see his face?"

She shook her head. "His ear. His cheek. Dark hair."

Something in Philip's eyes went soft. Horror ripped through

her. "Good god, Philip. Please tell me...he wasn't...it wasn't who you were..."

His eyes flashed. "No! Of course not."

"Then who—"

"I can't. I...I *can't.*" He sounded so pained, so anguished, that she bit her tongue against another question about his secret lover.

She knew the stubborn set of his jaw. Philip wouldn't answer. "Fine, then. Belladora Lovejoy...who was her benefactor?"

Philip sat forward, his hand clutching at her arm. He gripped her wrist before hastily letting her go. He knew that a vision might have been passed on to her. But her mind stayed woefully unimpeded.

"Stay out of this, Audrey." He shook his head and once again, leaned against the wall and closed his eyes. "Please, go. If you're seen visiting me here—"

"Dash the gossip and scandal. You are my *husband*. I will not stay out of this."

He had to know that. It might have been why he looked at her from his heavily lidded eyes with such sadness. But he said no more.

"Michael and Mr. Potridge will visit you soon, I'm sure, and please consider a story—any story—that might get you freed from this place," she said, standing. The sour odor of the room was beginning to make her head ache and her stomach twist.

"There is no excuse for the way they found me, my love. That Runner has his case made."

"There is an excuse—there is the *truth*." She hesitated by the cot. If he would only tell her who he was leasing those rooms to meet...perhaps whoever it was had something to do with this sordid business.

He knew things that he was refusing to share with her. Information that could help him. Why would he wish to hurt himself? Unless he thought he was protecting her. Or someone else. His lover, perhaps.

"Your Grace." The constable stood within the threshold. He'd given her the allotted five minutes and wanted her to leave. Staying any longer would get her nowhere anyhow.

Philip turned his head toward the wall, refusing to meet her eyes. Audrey breathed in deeply when she left the room and watched as the constable locked the door again. It was an unnecessary precaution. Philip had no wish to leave that room. Part of her believed he wanted to rot in there for the rest of eternity. But he wouldn't. If the grand jury sent his case to the House of Lords, and they convicted him of murder, Philip could very well be shunted off to Newgate. Or to the gallows.

Audrey had to find that mysterious benefactor. Not just for her husband's sake, but for Miss Lovejoy. The man who murdered her was still walking around London somewhere and could very well commit the same brutal act again.

"Will that be all, Your Grace?" the man asked once he had hooked his keys to his belt again.

"For now," she replied, and then turned to leave.

CHAPTER
SIX

The duchess's slim gray brougham had been winding down every street for the last half hour. Traveling at a slow clip, it meandered from Long Acre to Floral, to Covent Garden to the Strand, and every court and side alley along its circuitous route.

"Where in hell is she going?" Hugh muttered as the hired hack he'd flagged outside the magistrate's offices trailed her from a safe distance. He sat up in the box with the driver, much to the man's obvious discomfort.

"Not used to passengers ridin' up with me," he'd told Hugh, who'd then slipped the man an extra shilling.

"Just follow the gray brougham."

Constable Davis had shown the duchess into her husband's holding room and had then quietly flagged another constable on the street outside from the tavern's corridor window. Hugh had suspected she would return, and so he'd asked all the patrolmen present to fetch him if she showed. If he wasn't available, he'd instructed them to follow her themselves as soon as she left. Thankfully, Hugh had been speaking to Chief Magistrate Gabriel Poston about another arrest, this one a man accused of hitting his friend in the temple with a grappling hook and nearly plucking out his eye. A bloody mess, but one the accused had confessed to doing.

It was so much simpler when they confessed.

Hugh had been waiting with the hired hack when the duchess left the Brown Bear. After brief instruction to her driver, she disappeared into the stylish brougham.

And now, he'd followed her on a protracted tour of every street and passage and corner within ten blocks of the magistrate's court. Hugh was about to give up and turn back when the brougham came to a stop on Yarrow Street. He nudged the jarvey next to him, who pulled to the curb as well. Hugh watched as the duchess's driver handed her down in front of a row of terraced homes.

She stood outside one of the homes, looking at the door, and yet not moving toward it. Her driver stayed by her side, as though awaiting her command. Hugh ground his molars, his senses sharpened to pin pricks. Finally, she walked up to the door and knocked pertly, rather than sending her driver to announce her as would normally be done. She stood close to the door. Too close. And was it just his perspective or were her hands hovering near the knob?

Hugh suddenly didn't know whether to laugh or growl—she was picking the bloody lock! What sort of duchess knew such a skill? A moment later, the door opened, and she slipped inside.

Hugh held up another shilling. "Distract her driver for a few seconds."

The jarvey took the coin and turned it over between his fingers before it disappeared into his coat. "Aye, guv."

Hugh hopped to the pavements and walked toward the terrace house, waiting for the jarvey's diversion. He heard the wheels of the hack rumbling past, drawing to a stop by the fine brougham.

"Oi there, guv!" the jarvey shouted. "Are ye familiar with these roads? Looking for Clarendon."

The duchess's driver turned away, toward the hackney, and

Hugh darted up the small stoop and inside, saying a silent thank you to the duchess for not locking the door behind her.

The jarvey's voice grew muffled as Hugh entered the foyer and closed the door. The silk wallpaper was a cool shade of blue touched with mint green. He listened carefully, but the house was still as a tomb. In the sitting room, the furniture had been draped and the curtains closed to prevent the paper and paintings from fading. The house had been closed up, though there wasn't any dust gathered on the polished hand railing as Hugh made his way to the upper floors. He followed the lady's scent of rosewater.

He peered into rooms as he passed, his footfalls absorbed by thick, blue carpet. Not a masculine Prussian blue, but pale robin's egg. Everything, from the carpet to the paper to the paintings...all of it was feminine.

He heard the creak of a floorboard on the second level, and he climbed the curve in the stairwell. What the duchess was doing breaking into this closed up home was beyond his grasp. He came around the newel post and traveled down the corridor, toward the next room with its door open wide—and heard an errant floorboard creak beneath his own weight.

A gasp sounded from the room ahead. He'd given himself away. No use skulking about now. Hugh let his muscles loosen and walked with ease to the open door, pushing it all the way aside.

"I know you are here, Your Gr—"

His side vision caught something coming at his head, and Hugh ducked, raising his arms to fend off the blow. He felt the stinging impact of a weapon and grasped it—something long and metal—and he yanked it forward, out of his assailant's grasp.

"Oh! Mr. Marsden!"

The Duchess of Fournier stood behind the door, her hands covering her mouth, her eyes sparkling with astonishment. He peered at the brass bed-warming pan he held and then, with more patience than he knew he possessed, set it down atop the draped four poster bed.

"You...you're following me again!" A blush swept into her cheeks, flooding them pink like spring roses.

"I could arrest you right now for breaking into this home."

She was clever enough not to try to deny it. She dropped her hands and clasped them behind her back.

"You wouldn't."

"I would. And I will," he replied, entering the spacious room, the furnishings within also draped. "Unless you explain to me why you are here, whose home this is, and how the devil you picked that lock."

Again, she didn't waste effort attempting to deny the accusation. So, it would appear she was capable of thinking before she spoke, after all.

"It shouldn't surprise me that you haven't yet been here," she said, smoothing the short lace veil that hung from her hat's brim. Her voice had gone from breathy with alarm to brittle with dislike. "You don't even know who lived here."

Hugh hadn't, but he certainly had a good idea now.

"Miss Belladora Lovejoy."

The duchess brushed off his answer with a roll of one shoulder. "I practically spoon-fed you the answer."

He sighed, long and hard. She had just come from a visit with her husband; he likely told her about the residence.

"Did you expect to find something among her possessions that will exonerate the duke?"

She looked sideways at him. "It occurred to me that there might be something here that would tell me who her benefactor was."

Hugh crossed the room to the windows overlooking Yarrow Street. "You needn't have picked a lock to find that out, Your Grace. If this property is owned by her benefactor, then the estate papers will show as much."

It was odd, however. Hugh had suspected Miss Lovejoy wasn't living in the rooms at Jewell House, but why would the duke have kept rooms there on top of this town home for her? There would be no need to meet his mistress anywhere but here, a safe distance from the Curzon Street residence where he lived with his wife.

Hugh had followed the duchess to the manse the night before, trying to keep his eyes off the sheer magnitude of the home, and instead focusing on her hired hackney. He didn't salivate over grand homes. He'd grown up at Neatham House on Kensington Square, one of London's finest addresses. He'd known luxury firsthand.

"Yes, well...if you don't look into those estate papers, I will," she replied as she removed her kid gloves. Hugh watched her amble across the room, toward a vanity and chair.

"How can you be sure this was her home?" he asked as the duchess touched the carved lip of the chair. She paused, staring ahead at the draped mirror. A few seconds passed. Just as Hugh wondered if she was going to answer or not, she released the chair.

"I went to the theatre again," she replied. "And I asked Mr. Bernadetto."

She wouldn't look directly at him, and Hugh knew she was lying. He couldn't believe she would be so obtuse as to return to the theatre, and he also knew the manager wouldn't have lifted a finger to help the duchess in her quest to free Belladora's suspected killer. Still, he suspected it *was* the singer's home, as a second look at the walls showed several framed playbills from the theatre.

"What are you doing?" he asked as her fingers tugged on one of the vanity drawer's handles.

"Searching, as I've already told you."

"What can you hope to find? The place is shut up," he said as her hand rummaged around inside.

"Some of her things are still here," she replied, attention riveted to the drawer. "The staff must have been in a hurry to quit the residence."

Hugh harrumphed, but then opened a door to a heavy mahogany wardrobe and saw a number of gowns and pelisses. Slippers were lined up along the bottom. He opened a few of the wardrobe's inner drawers and found silk stockings and linen chemises, garters and gloves and ribbons. Nothing had been packed away, or taken by the maids, as was common when their mistresses no longer had need of their things.

He closed the drawers with a frown, and when he turned back to the duchess, saw she was holding something in her fingers, inspecting it.

"What have you there?"

She clasped it into her palm, out of view. "I thought you weren't interested in investigating."

"I'm interested in the evidence against your husband that you're attempting to dispose of."

She sent him a withering look, and then opened her fingers. A round, milky gem about the circumference of her thumbnail lay in her palm. Hugh strode toward the vanity for a closer look. He'd seen one like it before.

"The Seven Sins," he said, plucking it from her palm.

"Excuse me?" she asked, pulling on her gloves again.

"A gaming hell in Temple. These lockets are given out as tokens." Hugh flipped the locket, exposing a flat brass backing. He slid the backing aside on a miniscule hinge. "It's for storing opium," he explained.

"Opium," she murmured, staring at the locket. Doubt swept over her expression before it hardened again. She took the locket back, and Hugh let it go. He had no need for it. "So, she was a member of this gaming hell."

"Women cannot be members," Hugh replied. "They can accompany members, however, and are permitted with these tokens. You're aware of what a gaming hell is?"

Again, she slammed him with a look of derision. "I'm not a complete simpleton, Mr. Marsden. I am aware men have their clubs."

"Gaming hells are not gentleman's clubs," he said.

She turned to show interest in a painting on the wall and slipped the locket inside her reticule. He rolled his eyes. Not as smoothly done as she believed.

"The *demimonde* is not allowed entry at White's or Brooks's, but they are at most pleasure dens," he went on, making no indication that he'd seen her little sleight of hand. "I assume your husband has a membership to White's?"

The gentleman's club ranked as the best in London, reserved for only the most illustrious of ton. The Duke of Fournier had been among that ilk. Until two days ago. Now, Hugh wondered if the duke's membership had been pulled.

"Yes, but he prefers Brooks's," the duchess said.

"I can't imagine he'd have shared with you whether he belonged to any hells like the Seven Sins."

"My husband is not the gambling sort."

Just as he was not the philandering sort, as she so staunchly believed. The woman was either ignorant to a fault or playacting as astutely as the actresses at the Theatre Royal.

"As you say." He felt the bedroom grow smaller as the duchess strolled toward the front windows overlooking Yarrow Street.

The fact that he was alone in a bedroom with a duchess was not lost on him. The scandal, should anyone stumble across them in this moment, would damage her reputation, and likely earn him an ear blistering from the magistrate. Perhaps a suspension. Then again, the house was closed up, the previous resident deceased. No one would find the pair of them here. Unless someone spotted the lady's rather recognizable brougham parked out front.

"You haven't yet answered my other question, Your Grace."

She peered at him, the derision not yet fully gone from her eyes. "What question is that?"

"Your lock picking prowess," he replied. "You don't strike me as a typical cracksman."

She'd worked smoothly and quickly; she'd done this before.

"Ladies must be accomplished in all manner of subjects, Mr. Marsden," she replied lightly.

The huff of laughter was out of him before he could stifle it. Her sheer gall kept knocking his feet out from under him. "Forgive me, I thought that meant excelling at languages and painting landscapes."

"I've never been very adept with landscapes." She moved around the end of the four-poster and toward the door. "I'll bid you good day."

Hugh reached the door before she could and held the edge, blocking the corridor. "How did you learn Miss Lovejoy lived here? Don't lie to me. After last night, Bernadetto would have nothing to do with you. Did your husband give you the address?"

The duchess pulled up short. A muscle in her jaw tensed. Her fair complexion revealed every emotion rippling just under the surface. Right now, it was a curious combination of impatience and panic.

"Do you plan to share every detail of your investigation with me?" she asked.

What investigation? he wanted to reply but thought better of it. She was already so easy to provoke, and she was right about needing to leave the premises.

"Of course not."

"Then you cannot fault me for keeping certain details of my own investigation private," she said. "Now, please step aside, sir."

He stalled a moment longer. She stood close enough for her rosewater scent to push up into his senses. The duchess might have been small in stature, coming barely to Hugh's chin, but she was no waif. The cloak she wore obscured womanly curves, and for a weak moment, he wondered what kind of fool the duke was to keep a mistress when he was so newly wed to this woman. Then again, he knew firsthand how much of a virago she was.

"Duchesses of the realm do not conduct criminal investigations," Hugh said.

They sip tea, discuss fashion, gossip about their friends, and willingly forget the other ninety percent of poor, working-class men and women in London. Granted, it had been several years since Hugh had lived within the Viscount Neatham's household, but he highly doubted it was enough time for the women and men of the *ton* to develop moral consciences that extended beyond their own set.

The duchess shrugged off any hesitation at being penned in by Hugh's imposing figure blocking the door, and stepped forward to within a single hand span of his chest.

"I think you'll learn that duchesses..." she said as she came even closer, a scant inch separating her body and his, "...can do whatever they please."

With a clenched jaw, he stepped aside. Hugh watched the duchess as she strode toward the stairwell. He let out a breath as soon as she disappeared from view, and then started after her.

"You've succeeded in one thing, Your Grace."

"What might that be?" Her voice drifted from below.

"You've drawn my attention away from your husband's involvement in Miss Lovejoy's murder."

When Hugh turned down the next bend in the stairs, he saw the lady at the base, staring up at him. Hope glittered in her eyes, alongside caution.

"I found him with the murder weapon, near the body, covered in blood. He was unresponsive, calling out your name, might I add. *Audrey*," he said, testing the name on his tongue. It was impolite not using her title, though truly nothing about this situation could be deemed polite or proper. She parted her lips but quickly sealed them again. "*Audrey, Audrey*. Where were you that night?"

He reached the bottom step and they stood, crowded on the landing. The foyer was just below, the rest of the house quiet and sleeping, like a tightly wrapped chrysalis.

"At Violet House." Her voice cracked with astonishment. She clearly hadn't expected Hugh to question *her*.

"Who saw you there?"

"My maid. My butler. Everyone. Why are you asking me these questions?"

He wouldn't relent. Hell, he should have called her bluff and stood his ground upstairs in the bedroom doorway. The moment her body touched his, she would have backed down. "A husband would want to protect his wife. Perhaps that is why he refuses to answer any of my questions."

Stunned rage flooded her eyes and a second blush rose upon her cheeks. "You suggest that *I* had something to do with her murder?"

"Jealousy is a strong motive."

He was the one bluffing now. The duchess would not have been able to stab the victim as many times, or as brutally, as the true murderer had. But if a little suspicion thrown her way were to put her off from her "investigation," the cheap accusation would be worth it.

"You are despicable." She shoved past him and took the rest of the steps at a near run.

Hugh followed. "Last year, one of my colleagues arrested a viscount for public indecency."

The duchess threw him a glance over her shoulder. "What does Lord Umbridge's arrest have to do with anything?"

It was no surprise she had heard of the drunken old man's arrest. His trousers and smalls had still been around his ankles when he'd been clapped in irons by one of the horse patrolmen out on Picadilly Circus.

"By dawn the following day, a dozen lords were frothing at the bit for Umbridge to be released. The viscount, they claimed, should not be made to suffer the punishments of common men."

The lady sighed. "Do get on with your point, Mr. Marsden. My driver is waiting."

Her driver would wait all day if she bid him to. Such was the world she lived in. Everything right there at her fingertips.

"You should know that not one member of your set, beyond Lord Herrick, has come up in arms against our holding the duke," Hugh said. "He is a leper among his peers, and when his trial is heard by the House of Lords, I would not count on much support from those you call friends."

It was a cruel statement. Hugh saw the flash of injury it caused, and the touch of guilt in his gut doubled. But then she exhaled and reached for the front door handle.

"You've made up your mind about me and about Philip." A few warbling syllables were the only indication that she was affected at all. That, and the fact that she'd addressed her husband familiarly, without his title. "But the truth is you know nothing of my life, or what I am capable of. Not what my title is capable of, but *me*, Audrey Sinclair." She turned the doorknob and the noise from Yarrow Street poured inside the muffled home. "If you wish to prove your end of the investigation, Mr. Marsden, I suggest doing more than resting on your laurels. One can so easily become lazy and fat with success that they never see their opposition until it bests them."

And with that, she stepped outside and slammed the door in Hugh's face.

He waited, his ears ringing, until the sound of her carriage pulled away. The woman had the tongue of a viper, and Hugh despised the way it left him feeling turned around and dizzy. The very moment he'd felt he had the upper hand, she'd yanked it away from him again.

As he descended the steps to the pavements, leaving Miss Lovejoy's mausoleum of a home, he realized the duchess hadn't been bluffing. She would keep up her investigation until she found what she was looking for, or until she pushed too far and got into trouble. He was willing to bet the latter would come about first.

CHAPTER SEVEN

Audrey slipped off her glove the moment she was in the brougham and let out a long exhalation. That infuriating man had followed her from Bow Street most likely, and now he suspected *her*. It was ludicrous. He couldn't possibly believe she'd done such a brutal deed. He was only attempting to crawl beneath her skin and lodge there, like a thorn.

"Well, he has succeeded," she sighed, and then reached into her reticule.

She'd made the mistake of touching the opal-faced locket with her bare hand earlier, in Miss Lovejoy's bedroom, with Mr. Marsden standing on the other side of the room. Something had rushed into her vision, nearly blinding her, before she'd been able to push it into submission.

The Bow Street officer had been speaking to her, and she'd already hesitated too long a few seconds earlier, when grasping the back of the vanity's chair. An image had rolled into view then, of a pretty woman sitting before the mirror, inspecting her reflection as she took what looked like a gemstone from a purse and dropped it into one of the narrow vanity drawers. Audrey had gone for the drawer next.

The vision conjured when she touched the locket had been disturbing—a smoky room, red lights, men kitted out in full dress, women with improper amounts of flesh on display. And with Mr. Marsden speaking to her, she'd been distracted. Unwilling to waste the energy the locket held trapped inside, she had slipped it into her reticule to await a more private moment.

So now, as Carrigan carried her back toward Curzon Street, Audrey held the opal locket in her bare palm and closed her eyes, ready. Without Mr. Marsden there to watch her in that hawk-like way, she could relax.

The vision formed like a fog again—it was of a crowd inside what Audrey now knew, thanks to Mr. Marsden, was the Seven Sins. A busy faro table covered in green baize, colorful chips and playing cards, plumes of cigar smoke cloying the air. She held her breath as a man appeared, close enough for Miss Lovejoy to nuzzle his starched collar and cravat. Recognition nearly doused the whole vision, and Audrey let out a gasp. It was Augustus St. John, the Marquess of Wimbly.

He had been to Violet House on numerous occasions and had been at nearly every society function she and Philip had attended. In his early fifties, he was still a handsome man, though a bit weathered in the jowls and chin. He was wealthy beyond measure, and by no means was his marriage to Lady Wimbly a love match. The man was a notorious philanderer and made no attempt to bury his proclivities.

She calmed her excitement at seeing the marquess, clearly Miss Lovejoy's admirer, as his face drew near, his hand reaching to cup her chin. And then closer still, until Audrey felt smothered—as if the marquess were attempting to kiss her, instead of Miss Lovejoy.

She dropped the locket and the image scattered. The pale blue interior of her carriage replaced that of the gaming hell. Her heart raced, her stomach in an uncomfortable twist. Gracious, she'd never been to a gaming hell and certainly had no desire to visit one now. That sort of place was everything she was not: loose, free, lurid. But the Marquess of Wimbly had looked entirely at home in such an establishment.

He had been Miss Lovejoy's patron.

Audrey leaned her head against the squabs, thankful the risky trip to the opera singer's home had been worth her while. It was still remarkable that she'd found it in the first place. All she'd had to go on was the vision of a street of terraced homes and the number 47, but Carrigan had dutifully wound his way down every road, side street, and passage while she'd looked outside, waiting for recognition to strike. When at last she'd turned up Yarrow Street, the terraced homes matched the vision perfectly, and she'd instructed her driver to find number 47.

Audrey had hoped to gain an item of Miss Lovejoy's that might point her onward to another piece of information, and it had worked. But really, these were breadcrumbs, of which only Audrey could see. She needed to find something that Mr. Marsden, or the magistrate himself, could acknowledge.

How the devil did you pick that lock?

Mr. Marsden had watched her use a pair of hair pins to enter the home in broad daylight. If Carrigan noticed anything amiss, he had not said a word. Carrigan knew not to, of course. More than once, he had needed to be discreet for both her sake and Philip's.

Audrey eyed the locket, face down on the cushion. The small well for opium dust worried her. It had been over a year now since Philip had given it up, but her heart still gave an involuntary stutter.

What had started as infrequent evenings out, only to return home in a state of worrisome disarray, had become a usual occurrence. He'd often disappear for days on end. He'd insisted it was nothing, just a diversion, a means for which to escape for a short while. However, within a few months, it had consumed him. He was no longer the Philip she'd agreed to marry.

That last time, Carrigan had waited two full days outside a pleasure den while Philip was inside. She figured it was a place not unlike the Seven Sins, considering Carrigan had seen upper crust men entering and exiting, and yet he, a servant, had not been allowed entry.

Finally, he managed to sneak his way inside through a rear door, posing as staff help, and had been able to locate and carry the barely breathing, utterly delusional duke back to the carriage. Audrey had been furious and sick with worry; their argument had left her with a sore throat for days. Once sobered, he'd relented and promised her never again. He'd followed through, too. Things had gotten better.

But had he been a member of this Seven Sins club? Was that his connection to Miss Lovejoy? At least Philip hadn't been in the vision the opal locket had given her.

The idea to go directly to Lord Wimbly's home, under the pretext of calling on Lady Wimbly, crossed her mind. However, that dreadful Bow Street officer's voice whispered in the back of her mind, again and again: *I can't bloody begin to count how many mistakes you made back there.*

Perhaps she shouldn't be so heavy handed with this interview. She had no believable reason to call on Lady Wimbly, and quite honestly, with the scandal surrounding Philip, the marchioness would likely not receive her.

She needed to come around to it with a better angle. If she could corner the woman somehow... Perhaps catch her out in a place where she could not so easily scurry away... But then, Lady Wimbly would never admit her husband was having an affair with a murdered opera singer. Neither would the man himself.

Audrey felt a slip of hopelessness before stomping it down with an imaginary heel. She knocked on the wall between her and Carrigan.

"To Lord Herrick's," she said.

"Yes, Your Grace," came his muffled reply. The carriage slowed, then turned direction.

Philip's younger brother lived on Grosvenor Square. He'd

married Lady Geneva Knowlton, a baronet's daughter, less than six months ago, and considering Geneva—or Genie, as she preferred—was several years older than Michael, the love match had been the talk of the town for quite some time. At five and twenty, Genie had been settling in well as a spinster when Michael returned as a young lieutenant after the war in France concluded and began to attend the Season's offerings.

He'd been smitten with Genie immediately, though she'd been a wallflower and by no means on the hunt for a husband. She'd turned down a few proposals her first few Seasons, and when her father's finances dwindled due to a few misguided ventures, there were no more offers to either reject or accept. However, as the younger brother of a duke, Lord Herrick had no need of a plump dowry in any marriage match. Audrey and Philip had watched from afar the last few years as Michael wooed and eventually convinced the lady that he loved her, despite the difference in their ages. Now, as the new Lady Herrick, Genie had been spending the bulk of her time redecorating the house on the east side of Grosvenor Square—with a particular focus on the nursery room.

She was a few months gone, with the baby due in early fall, and ever since she'd announced the news, blushing with fierce happiness over tea, Audrey had found her visits at their residence to be something she rather dreaded. Jealousy was an awful beast. She and Philip would not produce an heir—it had been among the few agreements they'd settled on, privately, when he'd proposed the idea of marriage.

Audrey had been more than willing to forgo motherhood if it meant she would not be required to share the marriage bed with her childhood friend, who was in no way physically attracted to her. The awkwardness of that situation would have been unbearable. However, no one ever need know he never even attempted to get her with an heir, or that the marriage had never been consummated for that matter.

After two years, rumors had begun to settle in that she was

barren, just as she and Philip had anticipated. Philip's title and estate would eventually pass to Michael, and then Michael's first-born son, and life would gallop onward. Both she and Philip had agreed that a marriage of friendship was far better than anything else either of them would encounter—they each knew one another's secrets, accepted them, and were willing to guard them. Philip would not find another bride so amenable, and if she married another man, Audrey would forever wonder if her "affliction" as her mother had once called it, would ever be exposed. A marriage of friendship was the safest option for them both—and as luck would have it, they enjoyed one another's company.

However, Genie's glow of happiness over the forthcoming baby rubbed at Audrey in a way it shouldn't. Why the devil should she care? It was a baby. They were born every day.

Carrigan pulled to a stop, and in another few moments, Audrey found herself in the foyer of number 38 Grosvenor Square. New paper adorned the walls, an understated, silver-and-gray ivy pattern. The previous paper had been a pretty yellow floral, and that had been new as well. Audrey raised one brow and wondered how many more patterns before Genie was satisfied. She couldn't imagine caring enough about the foyer paper at Violet House to have it changed once, let alone twice.

Andrews, the butler, showed Audrey into the front sitting room and left. She took a turn around the room, too restless to sit and wait patiently. How long would Philip remain in that upstairs tavern room before he could come home? There would be a grand jury hearing and then perhaps a trial in the House of the Lords... but his privilege of peerage, even at the highest ranking of duke, didn't seem to be springing him from Bow Street. And from her visit earlier, she wasn't certain he even wished to come home. He was wallowing. There was not a doubt in her mind that he felt guilty about *something*.

But it couldn't be the murder.

"Audrey?" Genie's soft voice came from the sitting room

entrance. Her sister-in-law hesitated in the doorway. Her golden-brown hair was swept up into a loose bun, with two curls fringing each temple. She wore a day dress, the blue linen billowing around her to obscure any hint of a swelling belly.

"My apologies, Genie, I should have sent word first that I planned to call."

"Nonsense." A smile wobbled over her lips. She came forward, her steps equally unsure. "Michael advised me to leave you be, otherwise I would have called on you myself."

Of course, he'd advised as much. Audrey was a social pariah now that her husband sat in prison for murder. She felt a surprising burst of appreciation for Millie, who had taken the risk. Belatedly, she registered that no one else, not even Genie, had attempted to call on her. Even if Barton had turned them away, he would have passed on their cards to Greer, who would have then given them to Audrey. So caught up in thoughts of Philip and Mr. Marsden and her investigation, she hadn't stopped to give it a thought until now. It felt like all the air had fled her lungs as Genie surged forward and clasped Audrey in an embrace.

"Oh, my darling, I cannot believe this horror is happening."

Audrey tried to pull back, but Genie hung on another awkward moment. Nothing, no image or vision, formed, and another rush of unexpected jealousy arose inside her for the woman. Genie had no demons to haunt her. She was far too happy and coddled to possess them.

Unlike Mr. Marsden. The brown-haired woman that had erupted in Audrey's vision when he'd grasped her by the elbow was still in the shallow recesses of her own memory. Her delicate nose and creamy skin and full mouth. Whoever she was to him, she was important.

Audrey didn't wish to think about the officer, however.

Genie finally released her hold. She stepped away and the two of them took seats around a small cherry wood table.

"I've rung for tea," Genie said. "You will stay and visit as long as you like. Please don't feel you must leave."

Audrey hadn't—at least, not until Genie mentioned it. Just days before, Audrey would have been an illustrious guest in any household. Now, however, Genie's nervous demeanor showcased how brittle her standing in society truly was.

"I cannot stay long," she told her sister-in-law. "I only needed to be out of Violet House for a little while."

"It must be dreadful without Philip there. I can't imagine if it were Michael...if he were taken from me..." Tears glistened in Genie's eyes, and Audrey felt a stroke of guilt. Genie was indeed madly in love with Michael, and he with her, and Audrey knew the pair of them believed the same regard existed between her and Philip. Childhood friends who grew to be lovers. And while Audrey did love Philip, it had been a chore to put on the façade of deeper, truer love. She simply couldn't match the way Genie looked at Michael with such blatant admiration and longing. It tended to leave her feeling like a fraud.

"I'm worried for him," Audrey admitted, again feeling too cool and bland in the face of Genie's emotional reaction.

"Of course, you are," she replied. "Michael told me Philip isn't speaking. That he's in some horrible stupor."

Audrey nodded, saying nothing of her visit to the Brown Bear earlier, or the fact that he had broken his silence—at least with her. She didn't want Michael to know of her visit. He would not approve, and his censure was not something she needed.

"If he cannot defend himself—" Genie started to say.

"Please, stop." Audrey closed her eyes. She had already gone over every possibility during her sleepless night. If Philip was not deemed fit to stand trial in the House of Lords, he might be proclaimed insensible. Insane. He would be sent away to an asylum most likely. It had been one of his most intense fears, ever since he'd lost someone once before to such an institution.

"Forgive me," Genie said after moment. "This must be torture for you."

Audrey gathered herself, trying not to think of the things that had kept her awake last night. Like the fact that Philip could be stripped of his title, his fortune, his estates, and holdings...that he could be sent away by force the same way the first man he'd ever cared for had been.

Frederick Walker and Philip had been close at Cambridge, finding a common preference to books than to shooting, and conversation and music to billiards. In Freddie, Philip found a friend. Then, he'd become something more. Unfortunately, over a summer holiday from term, Freddie was discovered by his father in a tryst with another young man. Had it been a woman, a wedding would have ensued. Instead, Freddie's father had sent him to the north, to a place much like the one Audrey had suffered for two wretched years when she'd been seventeen years of age. She had never known Freddie Walker, but she could sympathize with him.

Philip had learned of his circumstances through gossip at Cambridge when term resumed, and he had not seen him again. It was as if Freddie had been erased from existence. Ever since, the fear that *he* would be erased had lived in the back of his mind.

"It is Philip going through the torture, not I," Audrey now told Genie.

"Don't discount your own adversity," she replied, and while Audrey knew the advice was well-meant, she bristled. The only thing that hung in the balance for Audrey was her reputation and social standing. Philip stood to lose so much more...unless Audrey could find the one who had truly harmed Miss Lovejoy.

She cast her whole attention onto her sister-in-law. Genie was a kind soul, sweet and earnest. Sometimes, Audrey wondered if Genie didn't feel gloriously lucky to have won the affection of a younger man from such solid circumstances. Though perhaps that wasn't charitable. Audrey herself had felt lucky, too, when Philip had proposed a marriage of friendship. It had saved her, much as Genie had been saved from spinsterhood.

Audrey believed Genie sincerely cared for her and Philip. She was bargaining on it, in fact.

"I've been closed up at Violet House, afraid to so much as take a breath. I thought I might convince you to take a turn with me in the park?"

It was just past two; a fashionable time for ladies and gentlemen of good society to be parading through Hyde Park. A quiver of uncertainty, and a little bit of tension, coiled in her stomach at the thought of seeing her peers, but if she could lay eyes upon Lady Wimbly and find an excuse to speak to her...well, perhaps she could find *something* useful for her investigation.

She saw her misgivings reflected in Genie's expression. "Oh. Well, of course fresh air would be good for your restless state," she began, though clearly flummoxed on what more to say.

To be seen with the Duchess of Fournier in so visible a place would be a social gamble, and Audrey was almost certain Michael had advised his wife to do no such thing.

Genie continued to waver. Audrey made her next move by feigning a gasp and averting her eyes. "Of course, I understand. How thoughtless of me. You can't possibly be seen with someone like me now. Please excuse me, Genie, I meant no harm."

Audrey stood, surprised to feel the sting of real tears behind her lashes. Perhaps it wasn't all an act, she considered as she started toward the sitting room door. It took only a few more moments before her sister-in-law crumbled.

"Oh no, please, don't leave!" She rushed in front of Audrey to block her retreat. "You are family, and I shan't give a whit what anyone says. It's absurd for you to hide away as though you've done something wrong. Now, put it out of your mind, and let's take our stroll." She gave a tight nod as if making a firm decision and left the sitting room to call for her butler.

Within minutes they were seated within Lady Herrick's town

coach and moving toward the expanse of green park a few blocks away. Audrey felt a modicum of guilt at tricking Genie into taking the stroll, but once they had been let out and were walking along the gravel path toward the Serpentine, she chose to commend herself instead.

Scores of ladies were taking their strolls, with many more men and women riding past slowly in curricles or on horseback. A fair amount of sun seekers lounged at picnics, enjoying the warm, early spring afternoon. Ladies had set up their easels and watercolors here and there, attracting lookers on and, most importantly, men.

"You see, all is well," Genie said in a sprightly voice as they walked, perhaps just a little too swiftly. Audrey had caught a few curious glances but from no acquaintances just yet.

She kept her eyes sharp for Lady Wimbly's shapely figure. The marchioness was in her mid-forties and had a penchant for hats with so much plumage one might suspect a whole pheasant roosted upon her head. She also favored the colors of autumn—shocking orange and yellow, and all too often, bronze and gold. If she were here, there would be no missing her.

"It's kind of you to walk with me," Audrey said, feeling as though she ought to acknowledge it.

She and Genie had little in common. In truth, she had little in common with most women she met. As much as she despised admitting it, her conversation generally leaned toward the realm of dull. She couldn't count the number of times she'd either been taking tea at a lady's home, or moving through Almack's, or standing in a circle of peers at a soiree and found that her tongue felt like it weighed ten stone. She'd question what difference it would make if she spoke at all. Listening in to the conversation around her, it seemed to always be as substantial as morning mist. Expected and easily forgotten.

Philip often accused her of being melancholy. Perhaps she was. Or perhaps it was just the circles she moved in that made her feel dull and heavy...and extraordinarily different.

"Another creature resides within you, my dear. I can see it whenever you blink." Lady Beatrice Gladdington had startled Audrey with this observation. They were the first words the older lady had spoken to Audrey during her stay at Shadewell Sanatorium in Northumberland. All up and down the long table inside the dining room at Shadewell, eyes had lifted, and spoons had lowered—the patients were never given forks. Prongs were a possible hazard to self and others.

"My lady?" Audrey had asked.

"It sees what others cannot," the woman went on in her singsong voice. *"It is extraordinary, wouldn't you agree?"*

The attendant had approached then, settling a hand onto Lady Gladdington's shoulder and asking if all was well. The older woman had growled, nipping at the attendant's fingers. Then, she'd laughed uproariously at the attendant's shocked expression.

It sees what others cannot. It is extraordinary, wouldn't you agree?

Yes. Audrey would agree that her sight fell into the appropriate definition of extraordinary. While Lady Gladdington had said the word with marked awe and admiration, Audrey felt only contempt for the 'creature' living inside her.

She often wished the doctors and nurses at Shadewell had been able to do as they claimed they would—to eradicate it from her mind. To make her well and normal. Unfortunately, two years inside the spartan and austere walls of Northumberland's convalescent hospital had only taught Audrey the incalculable value of pretending. Of saying as little as possible.

Looking back, it was no wonder that once she'd returned from Shadewell, she'd been afraid to speak. The anger she harbored toward her mother and uncle, the two people who had committed her to the sanatorium and then failed to visit or write for the next two interminable years, had lived on the very tip of her tongue. Whenever she parted her lips, she feared vitriol would spew out in place of tolerable words. She could hear them in her mind—unintelligible phrases and maniacal screeches that reminded her of the other patients at Shadewell. The ones that would scream out their lungs and drag their fingernails along the walls until they tore and bled.

Audrey had never been like them, and thankfully, she had been able to find a few others who were in similar positions—shoved off to a stark place where they could be forgotten by their families. Audrey spent most of her time in the library with a small group of others, though she couldn't truly count them as friends, not when she'd tried to forget them as fervently as she had. She'd returned home desperate and furious and on the edge of a dark precipice.

So, rather than risk her mother and uncle concluding that she had not been cured of her affliction and needed to return to Shadewell for another, indefinite stay, Audrey had stayed quite silent. She had nodded and smiled and made airy conversation with words that her mind could easily reach for, phrases and replies she heard ladies frequently saying. They might have sounded cold and hollow, but at least they wouldn't accidentally set the world aflame.

Genie moved off the gravel path and toward the placid edge of Hyde Park's pond, a long, curving body of water that tended to put off a stagnant odor in the height of summer. At the moment, Audrey could only trace a mineral-like whiff of it in the air.

"I wasn't being *kind* to walk with you," Genie said, finally replying after a few moments of silence as they walked. "I was attempting to be brave. Good heavens, Michael would spit fire if he knew," she said with a mischievous giggle.

He most definitely would. Audrey's brother-in-law's temper was well known and stood in stark contrast to his older and much more collected brother.

"He only wishes to spare you humiliation," she told Genie as they reached the water's edge. Their reflections rippled into view—Audrey's shorter, more voluptuous figure, and Genie's taller, lither one.

in Devon had all been given a healthy beginning or a much-needed boost through Lady Wimbly's fundraising. She and Philip had attended a few of her soirees for such benefits too.

Though Lord Wimbly attended these parties, he tended to stay silent, letting his wife take the leading strings.

"Not to mention," Genie went on after they had both walked some distance in silence, "Lord Wimbly would live as a monk the rest of his life before admitting Miss Lovejoy had ever been his mistress now."

Audrey's legs turned leaden with such sobering observations. Genie was utterly correct. There was nothing to be had in questioning Lady Wimbly after all. But then, how could she prove Miss Lovejoy's connection to the marquess beyond the opium locket? There had to be something she could obtain and show to the magistrate, or if worse came to worse, to the grand jury. The previous morning, when Michael had returned from Bow Street, he'd explained there were many steps to be taken before a trial at the House of Lords. Audrey couldn't recall them now...she'd been half listening and adamant that it would not go so far as that.

"I didn't mean to discourage you," Genie said before turning to signal the driver of her town coach, which had been following at a distance. "Perhaps we should return for tea and call for Mr. Potridge. He might be able to lend assistance with Philip's case."

As the coach drew closer, Audrey's breathing turned shallow. Yes. As the family solicitor, Mr. Potridge should be the one preparing for Philip's inquiry. He would be in touch with a barrister by now. And Audrey, as a duchess, should simply let them move along with their work while she stepped out of the way.

However, neither Mr. Potridge nor the barrister knew to consider Wimbly. They only had the same damning evidence Mr. Marsden had presented: Philip, blood-covered and in the presence of the body. With sinking spirits, she ruminated if Mr. Potridge and his barrister believed the duke to be guilty.

"You've been relentlessly realistic so far, Genie. Don't stop now. You know Mr. Potridge would merely placate us and listen with respect, but that he would not be moved by anything I had to say or suggest."

The faintest of fine lines surrounding Genie's eyes appeared as she smiled. "You sound far too bitter for your age."

"I wasn't before yesterday morning," she sighed, and Genie's grin faded. "Thank you, but I think I'll return to Violet House."

It would also be better to take her leave before Michael returned from wherever he was—likely with Mr. Potridge and a barrister somewhere, doing whatever they could to release Philip. How smug Mr. Marsden would be to see her scampering home with her tail between her legs.

"You truly believe she was not Philip's mistress?" Genie asked after they had been closed inside the coach.

Audrey nodded. "Truly."

"And yet the Bow Street officer does not believe you."

"He wishes to dismiss me and any possibility at all that Philip is innocent. He's an arrogant, intractable, offensive man."

Genie propped one thin brow. "My, he's made an impression."

When Audrey thought of the hot-tempered Bow Street officer, she fairly simmered. The cad had dared to *block* Miss Lovejoy's bedroom door as Audrey tried to leave. The outrage of it was still so fresh. As was his clean scent of oakmoss and vanilla. She'd stood close enough to trace it on the warm air between them. It had left her with a strange dizziness and racing pulse.

"What is this horrible officer's name?" Genie asked.

Audrey gritted her teeth. "Mr. Marsden."

Her sister-in-law sat taller. "Marsden?"

The note of surprise piqued Audrey's attention. "Is the name familiar?"

She had no idea how it could be. Genie might come from reduced circumstances, but she was as blue-blooded as any other aristocrat, and they most certainly did not rub elbows with Bow Street Runners—unless absolutely necessary.

"It's been some time since I last heard it, but yes. I don't know why Michael didn't mention he was the arresting officer. I'd completely forgotten about him..." Genie looked stunned as she tapped her fingers upon her lap, in thought.

Audrey leaned forward, suddenly furious with herself. Of course! The other night at the Brown Bear, Michael had said something to Mr. Marsden, that he'd known who he was. "How do you know of him?" she asked Genie now.

Disbelief filled her sister-in-law's eyes. "Don't tell me you've forgotten the scandal? I know you're no gossip, but there was no avoiding the talk when it all took place. It must have been, oh...let me see...five or six years ago? Yes, I was just about your age now, I recall."

Six years ago, Audrey had been in Northumberland, confined to a small, dark room during the night and subjected to rigorous, endless fresh air activities during the day. Ice cold baths twice a week, and a regular application of leeches to her temples once a month—to draw out the demonic possession from which Audrey's uncle and mother insisted plagued her.

"I was traveling the Continent with my aunt," she whispered. The old lie had been unused for so long that it felt flimsy and fake on her tongue. Genie only nodded.

"Still, I'm surprised you didn't hear about it when you returned. Lord Neatham, the Viscount Neatham? You must know what happened to him."

A rumble of dread scaled her spine and shivered out, under her skin. It flashed from cold to searing, then back again.

"He was shot. In a duel," Audrey said, knowing, but not really *remembering*. For as long as she could recall, the Viscount Neatham had had one functioning arm, while the other hung immobile and useless at his side. "It had something to do with his sister."

A young woman Audrey had never met, and never would. The lady had fled London in a cloud of disgrace. She'd gone to America, some said. Others said France. By the time Audrey had returned to London herself, the scandal had been old news. More scandals occurred and the story was left behind, in the past.

"*Ruined*," Genie whispered. "By the late viscount's own ward. A young man living in his home."

An icy finger stroked the nape of Audrey's neck. "You don't mean...?"

Genie nodded once. "Mr. Hugh Marsden."

CHAPTER EIGHT

The leaden sky hung low and threatening the following day as Hugh approached St. Giles-in-the-Fields. It had been a little over forty-eight hours since Miss Lovejoy had been found inside Jewell House, a few blocks over at the Seven Dials, and though her death was unquestionably murder, proper legal proceedings had to be maintained. The coroner's inquest to be held that morning at the church would be nothing short of ritual and being the officer to find the body and make the arrest, Hugh had been called to attend. He and a dozen other men would be present for the formal inquest, where the coroner, Dr. Oppler, would inspect the body, listen to witnesses, and make his pronouncement regarding the manner of death.

It would be a waste of an hour. As Hugh hurried past the west end of the church, built of blocky Portland stone, and toward the smaller brick vestry house, he thought of the numerous other matters to see to, including what to do about the Marquess of Wimbly—the owner of the home in which Miss Lovejoy had been residing.

Bloody hell.

Audrey Sinclair had been right. Belladora Lovejoy's patron had not been the duke. That didn't rule out the possibility that she had been sleeping with him, but Fournier had not been funding her—at least not by any official agreement.

Men—especially aristocrats—tended to keep their mistresses in lavish homes or apartments. No mistress living on Yarrow Street in comfortable and fashionable accommodations would ever lower herself to entertaining a lover in a place such as Jewell House. So that left a troubling question: What in hell had she been doing there?

There were a number of possibilities Hugh had been mulling over and dissecting since the records clerk at the Tower had answered a note Hugh had sent off the previous afternoon, after leaving the Yarrow Street residence. An old mate, Billy Grott, worked the records room, and while the information wasn't exactly public, Billy could be persuaded to check into things now and again so long as Hugh covered a tavern tab or two. As for the house at 47 Yarrow, it appeared to be one of Lord Wimbly's holdings, acquired some ten years ago. What he now needed to determine was how long Miss Lovejoy had been living under the marquess's protection, and where the devil her house staff had run off to so quickly after her death. Hugh wanted to question them, which meant he needed names. Until then, he could only speculate.

Had Miss Lovejoy entered into an agreement with Wimbly, only to take on another secret lover? Had Wimbly become aware of it and followed her to Jewell House? Had he been boiling with jealous rage? Or perhaps alternately, Fournier had been begging Miss Lovejoy to cut ties with Wimbly, and when she refused, he lost his temper.

Hugh ground his molars as he opened the door to the vestry house, the first drops of rain striking his shoulders and neck. Thanks to the duchess's meddling, he no longer had a nicely sewn-up case, and it pricked like nettles under his skin.

"There you are, Marsden," a voice said as Hugh stepped inside and yanked off his hat. Lord Thornton stood just outside the closed doors to the vestry's ante room, where Miss Lovejoy's body would be currently laid out, awaiting the inquest.

Thornton grimaced as he held out his arms in a show of incredulity. "What in Prinny's ballocks am I doing here?"

His oldest friend had a colorful way of speaking, though by some measure of magic it never landed as crass as it did whenever Hugh spoke in such a manner. Born and bred a gentleman, Grant Thornton had known Hugh since boyhood. It wasn't until after Hugh was no longer held in the good graces of the ton, however, that they had grown closer. Born the fourth son of a marquess, and with little chance of inheriting his father's title, Thornton had been free to do as he pleased with his life. Much to his father's displeasure, he'd chosen medicine.

However, seeing as Thornton's aim was to be a family physician and not a lowly surgeon or apothecary, Lord Lindstrom had assented to his schooling. Several years later, Thornton had emerged as a respected physician, attending to a number of families within London society.

"Language, Thornton. This is a house of the Lord, after all," Hugh said, unable to mask his amusement. His friend answered it with a scowl.

"It's an inquest, Marsden, one in which I have no role to play. Why send for me?"

"If you have more pressing matters to attend to, you are free to leave, and I'll call on you later," Hugh said. "However, if you can spare the time, I'd like you to see the victim of this case."

Thornton did as Hugh expected: He sighed heavily and assented, opening the door to the antechamber. "They're nearly gathered," he muttered.

It wasn't uncommon for his friend to sink into such surly moods. It had only been a few years since he'd lost his beloved wife in childbirth, as well as the infant daughter who'd not lived to draw a single breath, and Thornton still mourned them. He threw himself into his work to keep the memories and feelings at arm's length, but it wasn't always successful.

"Ah, Officer Marsden and Lord Thornton," Dr. Oppler, the coroner, said brightly. "My lord, I believe you are the final juror to arrive. Do have a seat. Shall we begin?"

Oppler was a rotund man with spectacles and two tufts of dark black hair just above and behind each ear on his otherwise smooth scalp. Hugh had been to many inquests conducted by Oppler, and the two of them had always gotten on. So, when he'd sent the doctor a request that Thornton be included as a juror, he had not anticipated a refusal.

Most inquests Hugh attended called together a jury of several men, as well as witnesses and others able to give testimony regarding the death at hand. Thornton was not involved in any way, but he was a respected man, educated, and notoriously even-tempered and rational. His opinion would not go unappreciated by the others gathered, not to mention that Hugh needed to speak to him on another matter after the inquest concluded.

Thornton sent him another skeptical glance before taking his seat among the other jurors, already seated in hard wooden chairs along a wall of windows. As Dr. Oppler read out the particulars about the victim, including her legal name (Mary Hoffman), her age (twenty-six), and her profession (operatic actress), Hugh took note of the witnesses gathered. The first to catch his eye was none other than Sir Gabriel Poston, the chief magistrate at Bow Street.

Sir Gabriel, who held the rank of knight, had been determined to attend the inquest, if only because of the status of the man currently within his official custody for the crime. Had it been any other crime or any other suspect, Sir Gabriel would have never dreamed of attending. However, as he was upholding the arrest of a duke of the realm, it behooved him to keep track of every detail of the case, especially as there were residents of the parish in attendance. Sir Gabriel nodded at Hugh in greeting, his firmly set square jaw as ominous as the thunderclouds outside.

Next, Hugh spotted the night watchman who'd been standing guard inside Fournier's rented rooms when Hugh had first arrived. Hugh had summoned him as well as a rag tag man who claimed to have been the first to find the body. And lastly, in the corner of the antechamber stood Mr. Bernadetto, the manager at Theatre Royal, Drury Lane. A sheen of sweat coated his pale skin. His eyes repeatedly drifted toward Miss Lovejoy's covered corpse before blinking and looking away again.

The air in the room held a note of sourness that Hugh concluded was emanating from the deceased. He'd traced the odor many times before; it never became easier to stomach. A few men among the jurors held handkerchiefs to their noses and one had pinned dried lavender to his lapel to help mask the odor.

Dr. Oppler proceeded without any more preamble. "The victim was stabbed thirteen times, the deepest wounds being directed to the victim's throat and chest, with superficial slices along the arms and hands."

He stepped forward to peel back the covering. Out of respect, the sheet remained in place over her breasts, exposing only her upper chest, neck, and face. Bluish, near purple bruising mottled her ashen skin. Her wounds, though now sewn, were still garish. Hugh's mind went back to that night, to the sheer amount of blood and gore on the bedstead.

"As you can plainly see, the neck received the largest of lacerations." Dr. Oppler indicated the long gash Hugh remembered observing with revulsion; the one that had been jaggedly done.

Mr. Bernadetto hunched over in his seat, gagged, and then vomited into the bowl of his hat. There was a moment of silence as the other men in the room shifted awkwardly, waiting for the man to stop heaving.

"Sir," Dr. Oppler said, not unkindly, "if you would prefer to wait in the adjoining room, we can fetch you when it comes time for questions."

The theatre manager did not delay in exiting the antechamber.

"There's no saving that hat," Thornton whispered as the door closed behind him.

"Pity. It was a fine hat," Hugh replied.

Sir Gabriel sent Hugh a direct glare as if to reprimand him, and then redirected his focus to the coroner.

"Well, then, to get on with things...in addition to the victim's severed carotid artery, a deep puncture wound in the pulmonary artery, and another, shallower puncture to the anterior artery were the main factors in her untimely death."

Dr. Oppler had a list of names of those in attendance, and though he announced Mr. Bernadetto to be at the fore of the list, he shuffled to the next man to give the manager a few more minutes to compose himself.

"Mr. Newton," he called, and one of the rag tag men Hugh had seen loitering around the hallways of Jewell House that evening stood up. He clasped his worn hat between chapped hands.

"I am told you were the first to come upon the scene. Can you expound on that for us?"

Newton bobbed his head, his scruffy neck and chin highlighted in a brief break of sunlight that streamed through the windows.

"Yes, doctor," he said, his pronounced Adam's apple bobbing. "I was on my way to the top floor of the Jewell to visit my brother, Reggie, who lets a room there, when I walked past number twelve. The door was open a crack. Never seen it open, so I slowed, curious like. It didn't seem anyone were home. So, I knocked and called hullo—I didn't want to barge in—but then I heard someone weeping and decided to peek inside."

Mr. Newton had taken time to practice his statement. Hugh noted the man's earnest expression as he recounted his reasons for entering the apartments.

"And what did you see?" Dr. Oppler requested.

Mr. Newton took a breath, but it faltered and caught, turning into a broken gasp. He shook his head and sealed his lips, his eyes drifting toward the corpse.

"The worst thing I'm ever likely to set eyes upon," he replied, with a nod toward Miss Lovejoy. "She was in the bed...the blood... the stuff was everywhere."

"And the weeping?" Dr. Oppler pressed.

"A man, on the floor near the bed. He was covered in it. Her blood, I mean. Rocking back and forth, muttering things. I can't say what, it wasn't all that clear. And then I ran, you see, to fetch the night watchman."

He looked relieved to be at the end of his statement, and he sat down heavily as he was thanked and dismissed. However, Hugh had a few questions that the doctor hadn't considered.

"Dr. Oppler, if I might ask Mr. Newton a question or two?"

Heads turned toward Hugh, and Thornton crossed his arms with a smirk, as if settling in for some entertainment.

"Of course, Officer Marsden." Dr. Oppler glanced at the magistrate for confirmation. Sir Gabriel tucked his chin in a nod.

"How often do you visit your brother at Jewell House?" Hugh began.

The man stood again, the anxious expression back now that more answers he hadn't prepared for were being sought.

"Every week or so, I would think. I was there twice last week, though, on account of my brother feeling poorly."

"Have you ever crossed paths with the person who resides in room twelve? Or seen anyone coming or going?"

Hugh suspected Fournier only visited his rooms in the evenings when he could use the cover of night as an added cloaking. Mr. Newton frowned and shook his head.

"None I've seen." But then his brows pinched together. "I did hear voices one time. Some hollering."

"Hollering. As in an argument?" The witness nodded, and Hugh added, "Between a man and woman?"

"I can't say as I heard a woman. These were men's voices shouting."

"Recently?"

"A fortnight or so ago, I think."

"Thank you," Hugh said, and again, the man sat back down.

Next to give a statement was the night watchman. He recounted being summoned to the rooms by Newton, finding a crowd of people surrounding the dead body, and having to push them all out into the corridor while sending a lad to fetch the parish constable.

Hugh perked up in his seat. He'd been so occupied once he'd arrived at Jewell House that he hadn't taken into account that the constable had never shown. Hugh had dealt with the arrest and the removal of the body, which was sent straight to the bone house where the coroner would claim it.

"Do you know the lad you sent?" Hugh asked, wondering why the parish constable had not come.

The night watchman gave a wave of his hand. "The one what showed up with you, Runner."

Thornton rubbed his chin, attempting to hide his smirk. Hugh only shook his head. Sir had decided to fetch Hugh instead. The question was, how close had Sir been to Jewell House to hear of the murder so quickly? If the boy regularly prowled the area, he might have seen something himself.

Hugh stood next to give his statement, his rendition of events basic and brief. There was no doubt among those present that the woman had been murdered, or that the prime suspect was the Duke of Fournier. However, Lord Thornton signaled Dr. Oppler and stood just as Hugh was finishing up.

"Yes, my lord?"

"A question for the witness," Thornton replied. Hugh braced himself; Thornton still looked moderately peeved to be sitting in on the inquest. Who knew what he was about to ask?

"You say you found the victim dressed and positioned as

though the crime was committed while...*in flagrante delicto*," Thornton said.

"That's correct," Hugh replied.

"Dr. Oppler, during your inspection of the corpse, did you confirm such activity took place?"

The doctor parted his lips, and as though mildly stunned by the question, took a moment to reply. "I did not think it necessary to conduct such an examination, my lord, considering the circumstances surrounding her discovery and...clear goings-on. Nor did I believe that her private relations before her death played any influence on her ultimate demise."

She had been found in a duke's bed, barely dressed. A woman of her ilk—an opera singer and member of the demimonde—was expected to carry out such assignations. Hugh found he agreed with the doctor in that whether she had been taking part in any sexual intercourse before her death did not matter.

However, if Thornton had bothered to ask the question rather than simply sit sulking, there was a good reason.

"Officer Marsden, was the duke found in the same telling manner?" Thornton asked.

Hugh frowned. Fournier had been fully dressed, and while rumpled and blood-soaked, he had not looked as though he'd been doing any sort of bedding. Then again, a man could very well remain clothed while being entertained by an unclothed woman. "No. He was found dressed and covered in her blood, which I thought more pressing at the time."

"It isn't your methods I question, Officer Marsden, but the decision of the coroner to not fully examine the body. With all due respect, Dr. Oppler, if she were a willing participant in some tryst, or if she were coerced, the signs would show not only upon her body, but the suspect's as well."

Damn it. Hugh wanted to cuff his friend across the jaw, and then clap him on his back. Several shallow slices to her forearms and hands had been catalogued, which indicated that she had tried to fight off her murderer. He'd noted her broken fingernails himself that night at Jewell House. His chest constricted, and he closed his eyes against the sensation of the seat falling out from underneath him.

Fournier's body had been blood-covered, but there hadn't been any visible gouges to his face, neck, or arms.

As Dr. Oppler defended his decision, Hugh had the intense desire to pummel something. Self-loathing ran like hellfire down his spine, and the roar of blood in his ears dimmed the tart back-and-forth between Thornton and the coroner. He'd been so blinded by the fact that Fournier, a peer of the realm, had been found, incomprehensible, with the body and the murder weapon that he'd failed to make the connection regarding the self-defense wounds.

How the bloody hell had he botched so fundamental an observation?

He could practically see the duchess's smug grin already. Her involvement, her risky behavior and stubborn undertaking, had claimed the bulk of his time and attention. He'd been so wrapped up in defending his arrest of the duke, and to proving that her efforts were a silly waste of time, that he'd foundered in his own inquiry.

"Dr. Oppler, may I approach the corpse?" Hugh asked.

With a pointed sigh, the doctor nodded. Though Hugh had dealt with bodies over the last several years, he never quite grew used to handling them. He flipped up a side of the sheet, careful to keep Miss Lovejoy's naked form underneath covered, and reached for her hand. The skin was unyielding and cold, the muscles and joints stiff.

The bruised cast to her nail beds matched her lips and eyelids. Hugh ran his thumb over the short, bluntly trimmed pointer finger.

"You groomed her nails," Hugh stated. Dr. Oppler cleared his throat.

"I did. Her family is arriving on the morrow to claim the body for burial."

Her body had been washed, her wounds sewn, her nails trimmed. A quick look at her long dark hair revealed someone had washed the gore from the locks and combed the tangles out. There was still a crescent of black grime under her nails, though it could have been dried blood.

"They were longer when I found her; torn and ragged from defending herself against her attacker," Hugh admitted. Humiliation seared like a hot iron against his back where he felt Sir Gabriel's eyes boring into him.

"Does the duke have wounds to match?" Thornton asked.

Hugh pulled the sheet back down. "None that I have seen."

He would not have overlooked such scratches during the duke's questioning in the hours after the arrest.

"Perhaps we should move on to Mr. Bernadetto," Dr. Oppler said after Hugh had taken his seat again. He crossed a glance with Thornton, his friend's expression one of apologetic self-satisfaction.

Lack of scratch wounds wasn't nearly enough to exonerate the duke, but it settled a heavy weight of doubt in Hugh's mind. If he'd overlooked this, what else had he disregarded?

It wasn't like him to be so careless. Then again, he'd never taken a peer into custody before. Fournier was in no way tied to Viscount Neatham or to the debacle that had left Hugh loathed by the ton. But if he were being honest, taking a peer into custody had felt inexplicably vengeful. And yes, it had felt damn good too.

Mr. Newton volunteered to fetch the stage manager, but a few moments later, stepped back inside with an apology. "He's gone, sirs. Though, he's left his hat behind in the grate."

Perhaps it had only been humiliation that had convinced Mr. Bernadetto that he could not reenter the antechamber for the rest of the inquest, but Hugh still thought it odd. He'd bothered to come in first place. Why leave?

Though vexed, the coroner moved on, asking if there were any further questions or statements the jury or witnesses wished to make. When no one spoke, Dr. Oppler pronounced the death as a murder, much to everyone's expectation, and that he would send the inquest documents to the grand jury. From there, Hugh had every reason to expect the case to be sent to the House of Lords for a trial by peers. There was no telling how long it could take, but since Parliament was currently occupied with the new king's attempt to divorce Queen Caroline, there very well could be a delay in proceedings.

"Dr. Oppler is a fine physician," Thornton murmured as they left the antechamber a few minutes later, "but he has the tendency to presume and conclude more than scrutinize. I take it that is why you asked me to juror?"

Hugh cast a look toward the grate as they walked through the vestry, and indeed saw the stage manager's felt green hat atop the ashes and charred logs.

"Not exactly," he replied. "Though your question ended up proving that I am guilty of the same shortcoming."

They stepped outside, into a chilling rainfall.

"One failure does not equal a shortcoming, Marsden. You arrested the man most likely to have killed that opera singer."

"Most likely is not the qualifier I had in my mind when I placed him in custody." Hugh searched the street for a hack.

"I have my carriage, come on," Thornton said above a cracking bash of thunder. His landau waited around the corner, the driver huddled in his oilskins. A tiger leaped from the back rail and opened the door for them. Once inside, Hugh welcomed the heat of a brazier near his shins. He took off his hat and threw it onto the bench beside him.

"I was positive he'd done the murder," he went on.

"And now?"

The driver peeled from the curb, and Hugh leaned back

against the cushioned wall. "I'm less certain. There are some questions and inconsistencies I've uncovered."

Thanks to Audrey Sinclair. He was reluctant, however, to mention the duchess's name to his friend.

"What sort of inconsistencies?"

"The duke wasn't her patron. Miss Lovejoy had an arrangement with Wimbly, and it was official enough for him to have ensconced her in a staffed townhouse on Yarrow Street."

Thornton's eyes narrowed with the new information. "Wimbly? It doesn't shock me; the man probably has several mistresses ensconced in such townhouses. Perhaps she was stepping out on him then, with Fournier?"

"I don't know Wimbly well. Is he the jealous sort?"

"We move in different circles, but his reputation is cemented. Loose morals, gambling, women, vice."

Rain knocked on the cloth roof of the landau as they turned down another avenue. Hugh suspected they were heading back to Thornton's home in St. James's Square, though he also kept an office in Wapping, near Whitechapel. Only Hugh and a handful of his trusted servants knew of it. Thornton visited a few times a week to see patients in that destitute area and offer free services. Hardly any of them left without giving Thornton something in payment though, whether it be a chicken for slaughter, a few ha'pennies, or a half-bottle of cheap whisky.

"Would you like Merryton to drop you off at Wimbly Manor?" he asked Hugh with a knowing grin.

Hugh needed to determine the marquess's role—if he held one at all. It wasn't something he looked forward to, though. In fact, the palms of his hands were fairly sweating with the idea. Hugh groaned, and his friend laughed.

"Come now, maybe the man won't remember you."

"Piss off, Thornton."

Wimbly had been friends with the late Viscount Neatham and was likely well acquainted with the current title holder.

Bartholomew. Hugh's fingers curled into his hat at the thought of his half-brother.

Thornton chuckled and sat back. "You're a principal officer at Bow Street investigating the death of his mistress. Wimbly must expect someone to come knocking on his door soon. Just be sure to use the rear door, would you?"

"Wouldn't want to blacken the man's doorstep," Hugh replied, playing along with his friend's goading.

It was easier than admitting that his low social status would prevent him from being admitted through the front door to all high society homes. Not that he'd gone knocking on any lord or lady's home in the last many years.

Thornton rapped on the roof and called to his driver with new directions. Hugh felt the carriage slow and begin to turn.

"What of the Duchess of Fournier?" Thornton said. "Have you questioned her?"

The mention of her churned up a strange toss of annoyance and reticence within him. He wasn't certain why, but he was reluctant to admit he'd dealt with the lady in question. Hugh pulled at his starched collar and the knotted cravat his valet had insisted upon that morning for the inquest. Hugh often went without the cravat, opting instead for a stock, but Basil had all but blocked Hugh's bedroom door until he'd relented.

"I have," he answered. Thornton waited, one brow raised, for more of a reply. Hugh sighed. "Her Grace is adamant that her husband was not having an affair with Miss Lovejoy."

He could tell what Thornton thought of that statement with one glance—that the duchess was either idealistic to a fault or lying to protect the duke. Just as Hugh had believed. However now, an inkling of doubt colored his certainty.

"I cannot name one lord of the realm who has not entertained a mistress," Thornton said, then shrugged. "Unless theirs is a love match, like Herrick's. Or mine with Sarah," he added softly with a glance out the window.

Hugh spared his friend a concerned glance at the mention of his late wife but knew better than to say anything more on the topic.

The duke's younger brother was well rumored to be besotted with his wife. Perhaps the brothers had that in common. The duchess was driven to prove her husband's innocence, that much was clear. Why go to such bother, shoving aside what most women would do in her situation—decamp to the countryside in shame—unless she loved him?

He considered Fournier. Tall and trim, athletic but not muscular, not unattractive. Some might even say handsome. The duchess herself stood at a shorter height, though she wasn't petite. She had a healthy flush, a generous figure, and a neck that reminded Hugh of a swan. She was far more attractive than her husband, but Hugh had known many mismatched marriages.

"What is it you're thinking?" Thornton asked.

He realized he had been staring at the floor, lost in his contemplations of the duchess's features.

"What can you tell me about her? Their marriage?"

"You know I don't socialize as much as I used to," Thornton replied.

Hugh could barely get the man out for a drink once a month. His work tied him up at all hours of the day, every day of the week.

"You will still know a hell of a lot more than I do," Hugh replied. He had shed that part of his life completely. Or at least, he had tried to. Still, rumors and memories, names and faces, hung about like ghosts.

Thornton contemplated him for a moment before briefly raising both brows—the facial tic Hugh knew preceded his friend's acquiescence. "They were wed about three years ago now. The only reason I remember it is because of the minor scandal attached to their nuptials."

Hugh's attention had already been focused, though now it was sharp as the edge of a sword. "What scandal?"

At first glance, Audrey Sinclair had not seemed the sort of woman who would endure even one bout of scandal in her lifetime. However, now that he had witnessed her picking locks and investigating brashly, Hugh wasn't surprised to hear of yet more gossip surrounding her.

"The duchess was first betrothed to another. Contracts were in the process of being drawn and banns had already been posted when Fournier swooped in and stole her away."

"Who did she jilt?" Hugh asked.

"Bainbury."

A gust of wind accompanied Thornton's answer, whistling against the side of the carriage and masking Hugh's soft huff of astonishment.

"Lord Bainbury, really?" He tamed his voice when he next spoke. "He's got to be at least two decades older than the duchess."

"Indeed," Thornton said. "Her Grace's father, Lord Edgerton, passed long ago, and it was the late baron's younger brother, the new Lord Edgerton, who aligned her with Bainbury. Thought it would be a beneficial match all around—Bainbury was well off and in need of a wife, and though it is only rumor and speculation, Edgerton did not leave his family with much by way of security."

Hugh hadn't given Bainbury a thought in years. The last time had been when news of his second wife's death had rippled out over London, even to Bow Street. Had the lady died in childbirth or after some illness, he likely never would have heard of her passing. However, that she had died by her own choice, and that the truth of it had been made public, rather than covered up with lies, Hugh had spared her more than a moment's consideration.

She'd been young, he recalled, and suffered from bouts of melancholy. Perhaps it was the melancholy that had tugged at him, making him sympathetic. His own mother had suffered as well in the final years of her life. With well-oiled efficiency, Hugh turned his thoughts away from his mother. Thinking of her would only lead him into his own surly mood.

"She got a better offer, then, and took it," Hugh surmised.

Thornton shook his head as the carriage slowed and came around a corner. "Surely a better offer, coming from a duke, but if you take into account that Fournier had known her since childhood, one could reason he decided at the last moment that he couldn't stand to have her marry another."

That might explain the duke's feelings, but the duchess very well may have seen a better future with someone closer to her own age, wealthier, and without the baggage of two previous wives. Hugh couldn't fault her for spurning Bainbury, but he also couldn't quite eradicate the twist of his gut. Instinct told him something about Thornton's story was off. His friend was only relating what had been presented to society as fact. Hugh was well aware, however, that it would only be a version of the truth.

The carriage came to a halt in front of Lord Wimbly's residence. The cramp in his stomach gave another twist.

"I'd offer to wait and drive you home, but I've a patient to visit," Thornton said.

"I always knew you were a selfish prig," Hugh replied without bothering to wink. Thornton laughed at his jest and murmured, "Good luck," as Hugh exited the conveyance.

Rain lashed at him, though the wind was calmer here on Berkley Square. He went around the back toward the servant entrance, despising the jump of his muscles and shallow breaths. He'd happily avoided any kind of interaction with the ton for nigh on six years, and now here he was, about to interview a lord all too familiar with Hugh's past life.

Come now, maybe the man won't remember you. He growled at Thornton's sarcastic comment. There wasn't a peer in the realm that wouldn't remember the scandal he dragged behind him, attached like anchors to his very feet. Something struck him then: the duchess had made no mention of it. Was it because she did not know? Or was she simply too polite to mention it?

He didn't have time to consider it further. The back door

opened after his initial knock, and he found a rosy-cheeked woman looking out at him.

"What can I do for you?" she asked.

"My name is Marsden. I'm an officer for Bow Street and need a moment of his lordship's time."

CHAPTER NINE

Greer entered the breakfast room at Violet House at half ten the following morning. She bobbed her head of ash blond curls toward Audrey, and with a poised glance at the footman hovering nearby, sent him on his way.

Once they were alone, Audrey folded her napkin on the table. "He has already answered?"

"Yes, Your Grace." Greer stepped forward and set a wax-sealed letter on the table beside Audrey's plate of kippers and toast. She had hardly been able to eat a bite, and now her appetite diminished completely.

Audrey had been awake since dawn, her mind in snarls as she paced the Aubusson rug in her room. Greer hadn't appeared at all surprised to see her lady out of bed and restless when she entered at eight. As any highly trained lady's maid would, she maintained a placid expression. Audrey could have been standing there in the nude and Greer would have calmly gone to the wardrobe, withdrawn a wrapper, and gently slipped it over her mistress's shoulders.

Not once had she parted with an unnecessary or silly word in Audrey's presence, and she did not gossip about the other servants either. Growing up, Audrey had known many a maid who gossiped and complained and shirked her duties. She felt lucky to have Greer now, and yesterday, after returning from her visit with Genie, Audrey had made the decision to ask her maid a favor.

"Thank you, Greer." With a quick curtsey, the maid retraced her steps and left the breakfast room.

The paper was not of good quality, but that was of no matter. Audrey picked it up and a breath of a vision began to take form—a dark room, candlelight, a man's hand scratching ink upon the paper—but she shoved the image away. The person who'd sent the letter was not important; the information inside was.

The previous afternoon, Audrey had skimmed the newssheets before asking Greer to engage a private investigator on her behalf—under a *nom de guerre* of course. She needed to know who owned the home on Yarrow Street, and asking Michael or Mr. Potridge, or going in search of the records herself, was completely out of the question. Someone like Mr. Marsden could get to the information much faster and without inspiring curiosity. Audrey had circled a name in an advert and Greer, asking no questions, carried out the task.

Audrey slit the wax wafer with a table knife and held her breath. During the night, she had started to fear that perhaps *Philip* owned the Yarrow Street residence. He'd let rooms in the Seven Dials, so why not elsewhere? But she released a breath when she saw the name of the property owner scrawled across the brief correspondence: the Marquess of Wimbly. Just as expected.

Her relief turned mixed as she continued reading:

The clerk I spoke to related that another individual had been looking for information on the same address earlier in the day.

Audrey sighed. Mr. Marsden. It had to be. In addition to having a man watching her home—she had spied the stranger the night before, standing across the street, underneath a lamppost for far too long a time, his attention hinged on Violet House—it seemed Mr. Marsden had taken the time to investigate into the property.

He no doubt now knew Miss Lovejoy had been kept by Lord Wimbly. A spate of unease threatened to overtake the flutter of victory. What Genie revealed the afternoon before, about the past accusations against Mr. Marsden, churned her stomach.

Miss Neatham, the late Viscount Neatham's daughter, had been ruined by the young man living under the viscount's own roof. His *ward*. Genie had not needed to explain the meaning behind that term. Neatham had felt some responsibility toward Hugh Marsden—or at least, the boy he had once been. The nanny's son. Goodness, it was unheard of, really, for a nanny to be allowed to keep her child on premises, to be raised amongst her employer's own children. Unless, of course, that child was the employer's burden by blood. And if that were the case, and if Mr. Marsden had, in fact, ruined the viscount's legitimate daughter...

She shivered. In no way did she feel she knew the Bow Street officer well, but hearing that he had done something so reprehensible, so lewd...her mind simply did not want to accept it. Or believe it.

Then again, what Mr. Marsden had or had not done in his past was not the issue at hand. He'd discovered Wimbly was Miss Lovejoy's benefactor, which had likely proved to him that Philip had not been. So, what would he do next?

Audrey's eyes skipped to the last portion of the letter. She memorized the address she had requested the private agent to discover on her behalf. There was no note of caution or a plea for her to remain a far step from said address, and a small, appreciative grin touched her lips.

She folded the letter just as the door to the breakfast room opened yet again. Barton bowed a few degrees at the hip.

"Your Grace, Lord Herrick to see you. In the morning room."

Audrey let out a breath. She figured her brother-in-law would call on her at some point in the day. He was likely upset about the stroll around Hyde Park that she and Genie had taken. Well, it had to be dealt with.

"Thank you, Barton. Please send for tea."

The butler bowed and left, and before she could follow him, she dropped the letter from the private agent into the hearth. Flames ignited the thin paper, and Audrey carried on, toward the morning room.

Michael was standing before the hearth fire there, the small flames just enough to take the damp chill off the air. He greeted her with a grimace. Michael had thick, black hair and full brows that stood out in sharp contrast to the light hair, fair skin, and finer brows his older brother possessed. The two brothers didn't look related in the least. Where Michael was of a shorter stature and broad shouldered, Philip was tall and lean—more agile looking than athletic. Michael exuded power, while Philip exuded understated intelligence.

She closed the door behind her. "I do hope you haven't come to chastise me."

"I've come to inform you on what is happening, in hopes that you will not feel the need to leave Violet House again—at least for today."

It took every ounce of her composure to maintain a tranquil, unaffected expression. "Thank you for thinking of me and of how restless I must be."

If she gave him even the slightest reason to believe she might misbehave again, he would find some way to pen her in. There was much to do, and if placating her brother-in-law with a show of meek acquiescence meant he would turn his attention elsewhere, so be it.

He let out a sigh and came away from the fire. "Philip is still at the Brown Bear, guarded by Bow Street," he said as he sat on the edge of a chair that was far too small and dainty for him.

It made Michael look big and bumbling when she knew he was anything but. She also knew he was not the enemy; he was simply restricted himself by the rules that society had set for them. This was an extraordinary situation, and for a moment Audrey tried to imagine what Michael might be going through. His beloved older brother, the holder of the family title, which had been so respected and unblemished, stood accused of a heinous crime. He was attempting to minimize the damage the only way he knew how.

What Audrey did not know, however, was whether Michael's priority was proving his brother's innocence or protecting the Fournier title for future generations. For his own unborn child, perhaps. Guilt instantly swarmed her for forming such doubt, yet it would not go away.

"He has broken his silence," Michael went on, "though only to insist that you decamp to Fournier Downs as soon as possible."

"Nothing regarding the charges?" she asked.

He shook his head, his mouth a grim, flat line. "The grand jury will discuss his indictment in two days. I want you gone from London before then."

Audrey pinned the flesh inside her cheek between her teeth. The order was not unexpected.

"I've already informed Philip that I will be staying at Violet House."

"Audrey, this is a serious matter—"

"Do not insult me further, Michael."

His eyes sharpened on her as if suddenly aware he had been patronizing her and now felt guilty for it. Just as quickly, however, he hardened them again.

"What possible good can remaining here do for you or Philip?"

She surely wasn't about to tell him her plans for that evening. They'd barely come together in her mind since reading the private agent's letter in the breakfast room.

"Perhaps none. However, even if I am not able to see or speak to Philip, I will have him know that I refuse to run away." A stinging prickle behind her eyes caught her by surprise. "I will stand with him even if I am only standing within these walls."

Michael released another sigh, this one longer and more resigned. He settled back into the dainty chair, his arms overlapping the spindly wooden armrests. "You are entirely too intractable."

She noted that he at least said it with modicum of respect.

Tea arrived then and it was another minute before they each held a cup, neither of them sipping.

"What have you and Mr. Potridge discovered?" She hoped he would part with something new and useful.

"The details are unseemly." Before she could again tell him to quit patronizing her, he went on. "And Philip refuses to say anything other than he cannot remember the crime in question."

"Not remember?" Audrey blinked. Philip had not said as much to her when she'd visited the day before. She'd begged him to form a story, any story that might get him freed. Perhaps he had done just that. "Intoxication?"

Michael shook his head. "He would not say."

Opium, perhaps. She thought of the locket from the Seven Sins still in her reticule and tried to quell the curl of worry low in her stomach.

An idea flashed up in front of her like one of her visions. "Might you send someone to the place where he was found…that time?"

Michael knew about the last time Philip had gone missing for days, when Carrigan had pulled him from that horrid house of vice. "He may have been there before going to his leased rooms," she added. "It's possible someone would remember him."

Michael set his cup of tea down with rattling force. "And if we discover he was there, succumbing to opium, what then? He was found with the body, Audrey. Covered in the woman's blood. And to his fathomless detriment—and to yours, and mine, and Genie's, and even the baby's—he has not denied doing the murder!"

His voice became louder with every sentence, his eyes wider with intensity. Audrey saw his utter frustration then. Philip's predicament did touch Michael and Genie, and yes, even the baby, yet unborn. They were all tainted now, and it was not something that could be easily washed off. Perhaps ever.

"Michael, please tell me you don't believe he did this." She had to know if she was the only one with any hope left at all.

He stood, as if unable to sit another moment, and paced away toward the hearth again. "I know my brother. Philip is no murderer." He paused, the breath he dragged in shaky. "I want to believe he has been caught up in something. That he is somehow, someway, innocent. But Audrey..." He turned to face her. "We must prepare ourselves."

She put down her tea, careful not to crack the china. "For what?"

He wouldn't say it. She didn't truly want to hear it, anyhow. They hanged murderers. They hanged men and women for far less than murder.

Michael moved toward her. "The grand jury is certain to move the case onward. However, it's possible we can avoid a trial if the House can be convinced of another...plan...for Philip."

Again, he had trouble holding her stare. He was not one to fidget. However right then, Lord Herrick looked severely discomfited. She narrowed her eyes on him. "What other plan?"

"If he were to go away...someplace where there would be no question of his harming another soul...if we could convince Philip's peers that he would be looked after..."

A cold hand tripped up her spine as Michael stumbled over his words.

"An asylum," she whispered. Like the one Freddie Walker had been shunted off to. Hidden. Forgotten. Her throat constricted.

"It is a better alternative than the noose," Michael replied.

"But Philip is innocent," she said. "You know he is, and so do I."

Not to mention that Philip would far prefer the noose to being imprisoned in an asylum for the rest of his life. It was his greatest fear. Though, of course, Michael wouldn't know as much. Philip had only trusted *her* with his truths.

Impotent frustration and rage returned to Michael's expression, causing the veins along his temples to stand out. "*Do* we know that? Do we truly?"

She gaped. Michael's retort scoured her mind of any possible response. He didn't believe in Philip's innocence? He'd given up? She curled her fingers into her palms, her nails biting into her skin. She wished she could shout, *Yes! Yes, I do know, truly.*

She wished she could tell him why and how she knew. But Michael had no idea what it was to have a secret that could strip him of his freedom at the drop of a hat. If Audrey were to tell him about Philip's true feelings, that he'd leased those rooms to meet with a man, not a woman, what would he do? She feared it would not change Michael's proposal to suggest a "retreat" in the least. She feared it would only encourage the plan.

Audrey sealed her lips. "I'm afraid I'm suddenly not feeling well enough for visitors. If you would excuse me, I will bid you a good day."

It was inexcusably rude to dismiss him in such a manner, but at the same time she could not remain in his presence without screaming at the top of her lungs. Michael was startled into immobility for only a moment, but then he nodded. "Of course. I will call on you again soon, but perhaps it would be best if you did simply rest."

He stopped just before the door. "And please, Audrey, consider Fournier Downs."

He left the morning room, keeping the door open in his wake. Audrey let out the suppressed sob in her throat. First, Millie had pleaded with her to decamp, then Philip, and now Michael. She was quite certain Mr. Marsden would also wish for her to beckon her lady's maid and begin preparations for a trip to Hertfordshire. How much simpler it would be to sweep her and her persistent objections under a rug somewhere.

However, as the letter from the private agent had related, Mr. Marsden must have an inkling of doubt now. There was nothing for her to do other than to exploit it. Wimbly had a role in Miss Lovejoy's life, and she had every intention to find out what he knew of his mistress's final hours.

Now that Michael had left, Audrey had a resurgence of energy. She stood and went directly to her study. It was a small room on the first floor, near the rear of the house. The windows overlooked a rose garden that had been maturing ever since Philip's late mother had first come to Violet House to live. In the height of summer, Audrey would leave the windows open for the scent to carry inside. Audrey would often sit at her desk, staring into the garden, wondering what it was she was supposed to do in her study, other than see to correspondence. Being a duchess was at times dreadfully dull. But it was that very dullness that shielded Audrey so well. No one paid much attention to staid, boring duchesses.

All that would be over now. A frisson of tension cracked through her chest at the thought of so many people thinking and gossiping about her. Right that very moment, most likely, in their homes and drawing rooms, in their carriages and on their strolls about town, she would be on their minds. The tension stiffened to something closer to panic.

She'd been so careful since returning from Shadewell to go unnoticed, stay unseen. So much so that she'd nearly gone through with marrying Bainbury just to avoid the scandal of severing the betrothal in order to marry Philip. In the end, however, all anyone could say was that they had not blamed her for marrying a young duke rather than an old earl.

And now, a handful of years on, Audrey had faded into the pitiful role of a sad duchess, unable to bear children. The ton would much rather discuss roguish men and bold debutantes. And now, murder.

Genie and Michael were correct in that going out in public

would invite scrutiny. Too many eyes had a way of unsettling Audrey to the point of panic. She would never make the same mistakes she had when she'd been younger, before being sent away to Shadewell. That had been all her fault, all her reckless doing, when she'd thought her ability was something that made her special.

No, she wouldn't make the same mistakes again, but she worried people might start to dig into the past. Turn up old stories about her supposed trip to the Continent and her prolonged stay with her aunt in Scotland. They might perhaps tunnel even further, to when she'd been silly and naïve enough to show a handful of village children in Hertfordshire how she could read objects.

Audrey closed her eyes against the memory. She hated to remember herself being so foolish. So desperate for praise. Well, there was no time for memories today, not when there was a Bow Street officer to sway.

CHAPTER TEN

The weak light from a glass chimney on the mantel barely touched the corners of Hugh's bedroom, let alone the lines of the woman seated on the edge of his bed. Gloria reached for his dressing gown on the post of his bedstead and wrapped herself in it. It was too large for her, and though Hugh had gone to the trouble to purchase one for her, and even kept it hanging in his closet, she ignored the silken wrapper in favor of his. He reclined on the bed, the sheets at his hips, and indulged in the languid sensation a meeting with Gloria usually provided.

Only tonight, that sensation wasn't as keen as usual. He reached for the glass of scotch he'd set on the bedside table, prior to removing Gloria's gown and then his own clothes, and tossed the liquid back. It burned his throat, but after a moment, the tension in his shoulders remained.

"You are distracted tonight," she said as she crawled back onto the pillows beside him and curled her legs beneath her.

He supposed after a year of keeping a standing weekly appointment with Gloria, she would begin to take note of his moods. She wasn't a prostitute, nor was she his official mistress. Gloria was a seamstress with Madame Gascoigne, one of the most popular modistes in town. They had met the previous year during an inquiry. A robbery at the shop, which had been resolved easily enough once Hugh questioned another of Madame Gascoigne's seamstresses. The girl dissolved into tears and confessed to helping arrange the burglary. Dire circumstances at home and her father's many unpaid debts had been her motivation.

Gloria had taken Hugh aside and advised him to take a deeper look into the father's debts. When he had, he'd discovered an underground betting racket. He'd sought Gloria out to thank her. Their mutual interest had been clear from the beginning, as had the terms. Nothing permanent, nothing with ties. A bank note arrived at her residence once a month via messenger, so there need not be a physical exchange of money between them. She visited him, and him alone, or their arrangement was at an end. And vice versa, she let it be known. Hugh had assented, unbothered by the constriction. He barely had time to entertain Gloria once a week; he couldn't imagine dealing with more than one woman at a time.

He took another sip of his scotch, wishing it would relax the tight clench of his shoulders and back. Neither spirits, nor the interlude with Gloria, had managed to erase the thoughts that plagued him since that afternoon at Wimbly Manor. It didn't matter that Hugh had been given a living—a generous one—in the late Viscount Neatham's will, and that with it, he could afford the residence on Bedford Street and a gentleman's lifestyle. To the rest of society, Hugh was nothing but a blue-collar by-blow—and a reprobate too.

He'd been turned away from Wimbly Manor that afternoon, the housekeeper and butler insisting that the marquess was out. Hugh didn't believe the excuse and had kept pressing, until the butler had lost his temper and reminded him that the marquess was under no obligation to speak with a Bow Street officer unless he was placed under arrest. He was above the law, until such a time passed. Lord Wimbly would not see him, and that was that.

"I'm sorry," he sighed to Gloria. "I don't mean to be inattentive."

She curled one of her fingers around a lock of his hair and settled in next to him, companionably. "You were hardly inattentive." She laughed huskily. "But I felt something...missing from you tonight."

Hugh frowned and turned his head to the side to peer at her. "There is no need for insults," he said, a slow grin working its way across his lips. Gloria nipped at his earlobe playfully.

"You know what I mean," she said, laughing again.

She was always so companionable; Hugh wouldn't have admitted it to her, but he enjoyed their meetings for more than just the sharing of pleasure. As a Romany from Wales, Gloria had come to London with a few of her brothers. They had wanted to put down roots, unlike their nomadic family, and she had found a place to showcase her talent with Madame Gascoigne. One of the qualities Hugh admired most about her was her direct and honest tongue. Another was her purely rational way of thinking.

"My apologies," he said again. "The case I'm investigating has seemed to demand all my energy and attention lately."

Gloria hummed understanding. "The opera singer's murder."

He shouldn't have been surprised she knew of it. There had been a number of articles in the news sheets the last two days, along with vulgar caricatures and illustrations depicting the scene. But he still furrowed his brow. "What have you heard?"

"That the duke has always been a bit uncanny," she said.

"How so?"

Gloria shrugged as she rose onto her elbow, one of her delectable legs inching over to rest atop his thigh. She swirled her fingertip in the golden hair sprinkling his chest.

"Just that he's secretive. Bland, really. No one knows much about him or his duchess. They don't stand out."

As a duke and duchess, they most certainly should have stood out among the rest of their fellow aristocrats. Hugh looked to the ceiling again, in thought.

After the inquest, Hugh had returned to the Brown Bear and questioned Fournier for a few minutes, repeating questions that the duke had already ignored before, while taking a furtive inspection of the duke's hands and arms; his neck and face. His memory stood correct: there were no defense wounds.

Hugh left Bow Street in a foul mood and had arrived at his home ill prepared for a meeting with Gloria.

"He isn't speaking," he said now. "The duke. He says he doesn't remember that night."

He didn't usually discuss his cases with Gloria, but whenever he did, he found her to be blunt and level-headed.

"Was he foxed?"

"It certainly seemed as if he was," Hugh answered, though the absence of any liquor fumes on his breath had been noted. "But I think he was just severely stunned."

"You found nothing in the room that indicated another vice? Opium? Hashish?"

"No."

"What does the wife know?"

Audrey, Audrey, Audrey. Fournier's incessant moaning of his wife's name crawled under Hugh's skin for a reason he could not quite understand.

"She is insistent that he did not have a mistress."

Gloria chuffed laughter, her lips touching down on his shoulder. "Insistent?"

"Utterly resolute," he replied, his jaw clenching again.

"What is she like? Madam Gascoigne has made a few gowns for her, but I've never spoken to her myself."

Hugh went still. "I've only just met her."

Gloria again scoffed. "You can size a person up within seconds, Hugh Marsden."

He relented. "She is stubborn and single-minded. She detests me. The woman looks at me as though she'd like to light me on fire with her glare alone."

Gloria laughed and shifted her leg up his thigh.

"She is impulsive and petulant, and there is something..." He hesitated over his words. "Secretive. She is keeping a secret. Information that might apply to the investigation. My investigation, not hers."

Gloria pushed up higher onto her elbow. "She has her own investigation?"

A frisson of tension warmed the muscles in his legs, and he could no longer lie still. Hugh sat up, dislodging Gloria from his side, and swung his legs out from the bed. Sweat crawled along his back and temples as he raked his fingers through his hair.

"She insists she will prove her husband's innocence."

Gloria was quiet. After a few seconds spent waiting for her reply, Hugh looked over his shoulder at her. He propped a brow, as if to say "*Well?*"

She smoothed down the panels of the dressing gown and cinched the waist rope as she stood from the bed. "You are doubting yourself."

"I'm not."

"I know you," she rejoined with a sympathetic smile. It only served to stab at him. "What is it that gives you pause?"

He launched himself from the bed and grabbed up his linen smalls, then his trousers. "Nothing gives me pause. I made my arrest."

Why didn't the duke have any *goddamned* scratches or defense injuries? Hugh pulled on his clothes with jerky movements. And then there was Wimbly and the house on Yarrow.

"You are lying to yourself," Gloria said, shedding his robe. Hugh paused as she let him take in the whole of her naked body before picking up her dress. The memory of the duchess and the musk of her skin when he'd blocked her from leaving Miss Lovejoy's bedroom assailed him. A hard knot formed in the pit of Hugh's stomach, and he looked away from Gloria.

Hugh left his shirt untucked, his collar undone. His feet were bare as he reached for another glass of scotch.

A pert knock on his bedroom door caught him by surprise. Basil didn't usually interrupt him during Gloria's visits. When Hugh peered into the hall, his valet held his hands behind his back and gave a short bow.

"Forgive me, sir, but a message has arrived for you." Basil's tone was clipped and brimming with annoyance.

"From Sir?" Hugh knew well the expression his valet wore whenever the lad showed his dirty face and shoes around Bedford Street.

Hugh had given Sir a job to do that morning: watch Violet House and report back with the lady's movements. With no message from him so far, he'd started to hope Her Grace was settling down.

Basil's grimace drew longer. "Quite. Delivered by a young man who calls himself *Petey*. An accomplice of your odiferous informant."

Hugh had given up reprimanding Basil for his intolerance of Sir long ago.

"What is the message?"

Sir couldn't write and so he must have sent this Petey fellow to deliver the message verbally.

Basil cleared his throat before reciting, "*You were right, guv, the lady's bloody cracked. She's at Montagu Place.*"

A twin storm of irritation and concern spiraled through Hugh as he gripped the edge of his door. He swore under his breath.

Of all the stupid, impulsive, idiotic things to do...he wanted to throttle the duchess and then lock her up in her own attic, if only for her own protection.

"Hail two cabs—fast, Basil. One for me, and one to take Miss Hanson home." He moved to shut the door.

"You need a cravat, sir, if you are going out."

Hugh scowled. "I could wear nothing at all and still be admitted to where I am going."

"But, sir, if I might just—"

"Two cabs. *Now*, Basil." Hugh groaned. "The insufferable woman and her bloody investigation!"

He slammed the door and hurried to finish dressing.

CHAPTER ELEVEN

From the street, the Seven Sins appeared to be a quiet, unassuming residence. There were no people outside the front entrance, waiting to be let in, nor were there carriages, queueing up to drop off club members. Just a brightly lit door with potted shrubs on either side.

As Carrigan drew the carriage to a stop, Audrey's resolve faltered. This was the address the private investigator had delivered, and if correct, through those doors she would find a club of sin and vice.

And hopefully, Lord Wimbly.

Carrigan shook the carriage as he descended and came around to open the door. The expression he wore did not help her courage to reassert itself.

"Your Grace, I know it isn't my place to say it, but I would much rather turn this conveyance around and return you to Violet House."

Poor Carrigan. Audrey did hate to worry him, but if the ball of apprehension swirling low in her stomach was not going to sway her, neither was his fussing.

"Where will you take the carriage?" she asked him instead of making any acknowledgement of his protestation. He grimaced.

"Around the block. There's a mews where I'm to wait."

She peered at him as she was bringing the ribbons of the mask into place around her ears. The black contraption of lace and silk, dotted with small rubies and diamonds, had been part of her costume two winters before, for a masquerade Lady Dutton hosted. The mask had been too beautiful to discard. She'd wondered if there would be an occasion in which she might wear it again, and when she'd seen a number of women in her vision of the Seven Sins wearing dominos for anonymity, she'd dug it out of her cedar chest.

"How do you know about the mews?" she asked her driver.

Carrigan had the decency to hesitate before answering. "This is not my first time here, Your Grace."

Philip. He'd been a member after all.

"I see." Audrey finished tying the mask into place, her indignation firing up her resolve once again. "When were you here last?"

Carrigan helped her to the pavement. For a large and muscular man, he looked awfully sheepish as he contemplated his answer.

"You are loyal to His Grace and for that I am thankful. But this is important, Carrigan. Anything could be leveraged either for or against him."

The driver sighed and nodded. "It was about four months ago, I'd wager. Right after Christmas."

That recently? Audrey tried not to let her driver see the prick of disappointment burrowing into her.

"Thank you, Carrigan. I won't take too long." With a hitch of her chin, she made her way up the front steps. She presented herself at the door with all the same regality that she'd exude had she been entering a fine soiree, her husband on her arm. Meeting the man at the door, his combed hair slick with macassar oil, his appraising eyes just as oily, she recognized how alone she was.

"My lady," he intoned, taking a short bow. "Your entrance piece?"

She reached into her reticule, a cornflower blue silk damask to match her gown, and withdrew the locket she had taken from Miss Lovejoy's drawer. She prayed this was the piece he referred to.

The doorman leaned forward to inspect it with a small monocle. Audrey wondered how many phony lockets were presented. It depended, she supposed, on the club dues and how exorbitant they were.

The doorman stood and lowered the monocle. "Very good, my lady. Welcome."

He stepped aside, and Audrey's limbs moved swiftly into the entrance foyer, though they trembled. She'd passed inspection. Now, for the hard part—finding Lord Wimbly.

Audrey let the doorman take her wrap, who then passed it to another attendant who swiftly disappeared into a cloakroom. Taking a quick glance around, there seemed to be only one place to go: up a twisting staircase. A slight thrumming of noise came from the first story. Audrey placed a gloved hand on the railing and started to ascend. Though the barrier of her silk gloves would likely protect her from any vision, she retracted her hand, just in case. She didn't want or need any visions tonight. When she found Wimbly, she would need her wits about her—presuming he was present at all.

It was entirely possible he wasn't, but Greer had made a discreet visit to the Wimbly House kitchen, where her second cousin was employed as a maid. Apparently, the marquess was out nearly every evening, and the driver related that most evenings he went to Montagu Place. Audrey hoped he would be in the Seven Sins loosening his cravat.

She parted through a solid wall of cigar smoke and perfume and entered a large room. The entire first level was one expansive gaming hall. Card tables were scattered around the room—faro, vingt et un, baccarat, dice—and crowds congregated at each one.

Audrey's mask covered her face from hairline to bottom lip, and her breath came hot and fast as she stared at the flesh on display. Bare shoulders, tight bodices, plumped décolletage, and many of the ladies lounged in men's laps. Some ladies wore masks, like her, but most did not.

It was exactly as her vision had been, though it was unlike anything she had seen before in person. She pictured Philip entering this room, confidently walking toward one of the gaming tables, perhaps smiling at an acquaintance, greeting them warmly, easily.

She could not do the same as she picked her way along the floor; her lips were rigid, like porcelain. Curve them into a grin, and they would crack. Her fingers clutched her reticule in a stranglehold, her palms sweating as she searched the room for the man she'd hoped to see. Now, she half dreaded it. Being alone in a place where everyone else seemed to be conversing and enjoying time together made her feel as if she sorely stuck out.

The nape of her neck erupted in a cold sweat as she waited for those she passed to stare at her with recognition. Attention did turn her way, but she'd been sure to wear a gown that would hopefully detract attention from her face and hold it around her bosom. The plunging neckline was more revealing than what she normally wore out; the gown had come from Milan, but she had not dared wear it for the shocking cut of the bodice. It did captivate attention now, mostly from male eyes as she drifted by tables, pretending at confidence.

Where was Wimbly? Perhaps it was too early yet. She'd give it an hour. Watch some of the gaming. Try to avoid saying too much.

But as she moved to the rear of the floor, near a collection of divans and smaller card tables, she spotted him.

Lord Wimbly sat in a cushioned chair at a card table, but he wasn't playing seriously. He'd angled his chair so that it faced outward, providing him a view of both the room and of the active baize green table. Men and women crowded around it, a haze of smoke above their heads. The marquess puffed on a cigar as he sought out something or someone on the main floor. Whatever was unfolding at the card table, it held no interest for him.

With a ball of dread in her stomach, Audrey hiked her chin and moved toward him, deliberately swaying her hips in a more pronounced—and she hoped provocative—manner. She felt ridiculous, mostly, but Wimbly's rumored appetite for female companions didn't disappoint. His eyes latched onto her almost immediately.

They were lined around the edges, with the skin underneath a little puffy from too much drink and late, wild nights. His jowls were just beginning to sag, not quite detracting from his otherwise handsome looks. Audrey girded herself and forced a thin smile.

Wimbly took a prolonged moment to stand in greeting. He must have hoped she would slide right into his lap. When she didn't, he got to his feet.

"Good evening, my lady," he said, and Audrey went a bit woozy from relief. He didn't recognize her. Had he, he would have called her the proper "Your Grace."

"Lord Wimbly," she replied.

He waggled his brows. "The beautiful lady has the advantage. I don't suppose you'd fill me in on your identity?"

"If I wanted to do that, I wouldn't have bothered with the mask," she replied as haughtily as she could muster.

He chuckled. "Care to join our table?"

He didn't seem to be playing at the moment, and what she had to ask him was better done in private. Or at least, semi-private. She didn't want to find herself in any alcoves with the marquess.

"I don't care for dice," she replied with an air of indifference. "But there is something I wish to discuss with you, my lord."

A flicker of excitement lit Wimbly's brown irises. Audrey masked a shudder.

"This way," he said, taking his whisky from the table and extending a hand toward one of the nearby divans. They wouldn't be alone, but they wouldn't be shoulder to shoulder with their neighbors either.

He waited for Audrey to sit before taking the section of cushion directly next to her; their thighs brushed, and she couldn't keep up the façade. She angled herself to the side, away from him. Wimbly only gargled another insinuating laugh, as if she was playing at innocence.

Audrey tried to tame her roiling stomach. Wimbly reminded her too much of Lord Bainbury. It wasn't looks that made the marquess resemble her former betrothed. Their similarities ran deeper than that. It was in the inspecting probe of his gaze, the certainty that whatever thoughts ran through his mind weren't nearly as gentlemanly as his outward manner. There was an oily quality to both men; they would keep whomever they brought close just out of reach, on the surface.

Bainbury, however, had never attempted to slide his hand along her person, as Wimbly now did. His fingers scuffed teasingly at her knee.

"Now, then, my lady," he said, still amused. "What was it you needed to discuss with me?"

Audrey suppressed the urge to bat away his wandering hand. If she were to gain any useful knowledge, she had to at least play at seduction for a brief time. "It's a scandalous topic," she began.

"I don't mind a bit of scandal." He swirled his fingers a little higher, just above her knee. They left a few blots of moisture on the pale blue silk.

"Mistresses," she whispered, attempting an alluring, husky tone.

Wimbly's swirling fingers paused. Mr. Marsden's criticism of her questioning skills rang through her head: *You are too heavy-handed.* Perhaps she was a bull in a china shop after all.

"Mistresses," he repeated, his pointer finger tapping her leg, almost absentmindedly.

"From what I gather," Audrey pressed on, "there has been a bit of a do about one of yours."

Most definitely heavy-handed. But it caused Wimbly to remove *his* hand, so Audrey couldn't feel much regret.

"Who are you? Who have you been speaking to?" His playful tone was gone.

"I have connections to Miss Lovejoy," she replied lightly, hoping beyond hope that Wimbly wouldn't guess her identity. They were not so well acquainted that he would recognize the curve of her chin or her bottom lip.

The marquess searched her face, her eyes, looking for any telling characteristic. "What of her?"

"Have you not heard?"

"Of course, I have. The whole bloody town has heard."

He didn't appear at all to be mourning the loss of his mistress. She'd been dead a few days and he was already out mixing, seeking new company. Then again, keeping a mistress did not always equate with harboring feelings.

"Miss Lovejoy was ensconced in your property on Yarrow Street," Audrey said, no longer caring to be discreet about her questioning. The marquess had clearly gone cold toward her. He shifted away from her now.

"Are you one of her theatre friends? Why are you here, speaking to me of her? I've nothing to do with what happened."

"I simply want to know about the last time you saw her. She was your mistress. Why would she be at a place like the Seven Dials when you put her up in a much finer part of town?"

His lips formed a hard line. Spots of red speckled his cheeks. "Are you a reporter? Some low brow gossip that thought she'd get a bit of a story if she sauntered in here and sat in my lap?"

His voice had been steadily rising, and though the hum of conversation was high in the club, Audrey saw glances being cast their way, especially by those on the surrounding divans.

"I am not in your lap, my lord."

"No, you are gnawing at my boot heels," he seethed. "Miss Lovejoy was murdered by a madman duke befuddled by opium, and I've nothing—nothing at all—to do with that."

"He isn't a madman!" Audrey snapped.

Wimbly's nostrils flared. He went rigid as he again squinted a good look at her eyes. He jumped to his feet and with barely controlled fury, hissed, "Take a stroll around the floor with me, won't you?"

He knows... and he was also aware of eavesdroppers nearby.

Audrey stood slowly, and when he offered his arm, she stared at it, hoping her gloves would be barrier enough. Reluctantly, she took his arm and started walking.

"Is that you, Your Grace?"

"No," she answered drolly, "I am just a low brow reporter."

He hissed through his teeth. "My god. What in the devil are you doing? How dare you seek me out here, in public!"

"I want answers," she replied. "*You* were her lover, not my husband."

He pinned her arm closer to his side as they wove between two tables. "These things are not always exclusive," he said. "She was an *actress*, for pity's sake. Nothing but a light skirted songbird. She had a number of benefactors, I'd wager."

He didn't sound jealous at all at the prospect. Audrey didn't think Wimbly was skilled enough an actor to be pretending, either.

"Do you have any idea who they were?" she asked.

"Other than His Grace? No," he scoffed.

She pursed her lips as they walked through a cloud of smoke, toward the entrance to the gaming room. He was seeing her toward the door.

"Did Miss Lovejoy tell you, specifically, that she was meeting with my husband?"

"My god. *No*, she did not, but clearly, she was, considering the way they were found," he implored, the vehemence in his voice rattling her. "You are prying into things you know nothing about,

Your Grace, and I advise you to return home at once before anyone realizes you are here, and you make an utter spectacle of yourself."

Audrey was suddenly exhausted; it felt like running up against a wall. Men had been telling her what to do during this whole ordeal. Her husband, Michael, that blasted Officer Marsden. She hadn't obeyed them, and she most certainly wasn't going to obey Wimbly.

"The spectacle has already been made, my lord," she told him through gritted teeth. "My husband is accused of murder. Arrested. I know he did not do such a crime!"

He pulled up short, his hand still latched onto her elbow. "And you thought what? That *I* must be the one to have done the murder?"

Audrey froze. Of course, the possibility had gone through her head, but now that Wimbly was saying it so plainly, she realized the absurdity of it. She had seen the dark outline, the blurry visage of Miss Lovejoy's killer, and it had not been the Marquess of Wimbly.

"No," she shook her head.

Wimbly exhaled, seemingly appeased. But far from content. "Then why approach me?"

"I need to know who else Miss Lovejoy was...friendly with."

Wimbly narrowed his eyes. "You've been nothing but brash so far, why play the part of innocent now?" He leaned closer. "You want to know who she was fucking."

The tips of her ears burned. *The cad.*

"May I have a moment with Her Grace?" a low and steady voice asked from behind her. Audrey stiffened. Recognition struck a millisecond before her eyes landed on him.

Hugh Marsden slid into view at her side, his jaw shifting with barely concealed fury. He wore a black town coat and a sooty gray, double-breasted vest. The tall collar of his white turnback shirt was sans cravat. He was not dressed for an evening out at all. Which meant he had hastened here without stopping to have a neckcloth properly tied.

Someone had told him she was here. He was still having her followed.

"Marsden?" Wimbly said, his displeasure evident. "How did you get in here? I know for a fact the proprietor wouldn't allow a miscreant like you a membership—if you could even afford one."

Mr. Marsden's narrowed eyes slowly shifted from Audrey to the marquess. She noted he didn't react, visibly at least, to the man's insult.

"We are not at a fine gentlemen's club, Wimbly. There are plenty of miscreants here. If you'd release the duchess so I might have a word with her."

Wimbly's grip was still an iron vise around her elbow. Audrey wanted to be free of it, but she wasn't finished with the marquess just yet. Nor was she eager to get a verbal tongue lashing from Hugh Marsden.

"One moment if you please, Mr. Marsden," she replied.

"*Now*," he practically growled.

Wimbly scoffed. "Working with a scum sucker like Marsden, are you? Are you truly that desperate, Your Grace?" He didn't relinquish her arm.

"We are not working together, I assure you." She speared Hugh Marsden a glare. "I have one more question before I leave the *both* of you."

The marquess finally released her and shoved her aside for good measure. "You have taken up enough of my time, Your Grace."

He kept the proper form of address, but nothing about his sneer or his tone was proper. It was clear what he thought of her and her prying. And yet, it made her want to push further, not retreat.

"When was the last time you saw Miss Lovejoy?"

Wimbly turned on his heel to leave her on the floor, but before he could take a stride, Mr. Marsden blocked his path. "This is fortuitous. I called on you yesterday. It seems you were out. Now that I have your attention, perhaps I may ask a few questions about your property on Yarrow Street."

Wimbly's black glare jumped between Audrey and the officer. "You will step out of my way, Marsden."

"I could call tomorrow if you prefer. Lady Wimbly still hosts her tea luncheon on Fridays, isn't that correct?"

The marquess's nostrils flared. His coloring reddened. "What do want?"

"Answer the duchess's question," he replied, surprising Audrey. She peered at him. "When did you last see Miss Lovejoy?"

The crowds around them were noting their intense conversation; Mr. Marsden's arrival had been noticed as well.

"Must we do this here?" Wimbly whispered.

"I find I like the atmosphere," Marsden replied. Audrey could see why. Wimbly's temples glistened with sweat. He was nervous about attracting too much attention.

"Fine. I saw her Sunday evening. At the theatre."

She'd been found in Philip's rooms Tuesday night. Audrey searched back to Sunday evening. Philip had been out, she recalled. She hadn't seen him before turning in for the night.

"And what of His Grace?" Audrey pressed.

"What of him? He wasn't there if that's what you mean."

"Tell me about Miss Lovejoy that night," Mr. Marsden cut in, as if this was *his* opportunity to question the marquess. Well, she supposed it was both of theirs now.

"She was in the production, of course. She was brilliant, as always."

"And did you go backstage after?" Audrey asked before Mr. Marsden could speak again.

"How is that relevant?"

"Did you speak to her?" she asked.

"Yes," he answered with a roll of his eyes. "She was in a wretched mood. Asked me to take her away from all of it. She mentioned the Continent."

"That she wanted to go?" Marsden asked.

"That's right, and when I put her off, she became practically hysterical. I didn't stay. Said I had another appointment."

"Was she usually that way? Distressed like that?" Audrey asked.

Wimbly grimaced. "If she had been, I would have detached from her long ago. No, she was never upset easily."

"You didn't wonder what might have caused such a mood?" Marsden asked.

"I only cared to be away from such an outburst," he answered coldly.

"The house on Yarrow," Mr. Marsden began.

"Yes, I own it. Yes, Miss Lovejoy lived there," he answered preemptively.

"Where is the staff?" the detective continued.

"I let them all go the moment I heard the news. I saw no reason to dillydally."

Audrey frowned. The man had no feelings. He didn't mourn the loss of his mistress in the least. Likely, he saw her as an object. One he could easily replace.

"Who were her friends? Acquaintances?" Audrey asked.

"How should I know? I did not entertain *them*," he bit off. "Now, you have your answers, so I will take my leave. Good evening, Your Grace." He peeled back his upper lip in a sneer and left them as quickly as he could.

Around them, the other patrons stared with curious faces and narrowed eyes.

"We have worn out our welcome, my dear duchess," Mr. Marsden murmured.

She wanted to bite off his head. Audrey turned on her heel and left the main floor immediately. She breathed easier as she took the stairs to the ground floor. The sticky residue of smoke and sweat clung to her even as her skin shivered over.

The porter brought her wrap as another footman sent for her coach.

"How dare you have me followed?" she asked as she pulled her wrap close. Her evening slippers puttered down the front stone steps. The crisp air nearly made her dizzy.

"I knew you would do something rash with that locket," he replied.

So, he'd seen her take it from Miss Lovejoy's drawer after all. Why hadn't he said anything at the time?

To see what you did with it, you ninny.

"You wanted to get me to do your investigating for you, I take it?" she asked.

He stepped up beside her, his hands in his pockets. "Hardly."

"And yet, you couldn't gain admittance to question Wimbly at his home." She faced him, defiance making her hot and loose-lipped. "How lucky for you to have cornered him in the Seven Sins just now. Thanks to *me*."

"The risk you took was idiotic."

"It was paltry. Only my reputation was in danger, and with my husband arrested for murder, that hardly matters anymore."

"Maybe I should remind you, my lady, that if you truly believe the murderer is still loose, he might not want you digging around."

Audrey's scalp tingled, and she held her tongue. That thought had not quite yet entered her mind, and she felt stupid for it. Worse, she'd allowed Mr. Marsden to see her reaction plain on her face. He now gloated.

Carrigan came around the corner with her coach.

"Yes, well, I gained some valuable information," she said, pretending at nonchalance.

"I doubt it," he muttered.

"I know the marquess wasn't jealous of her other lovers. She was not exclusive," Audrey said, using the word Wimbly had. "There are potentially other suspects."

"Who?"

"He didn't give names."

"Of course he didn't."

The carriage came to a stop beside them on the curb. Carrigan hopped down quicker than usual, likely alarmed to see Audrey standing so close to a strange man.

"Your Grace," Carrigan said, his eyes hinged on Marsden. His burly chest faced him like a shield.

"Carrigan, this is Officer Marsden."

The driver stepped closer to Marsden the moment he was aware this was no aristocrat and didn't deserve unconditional respect. To his credit, Marsden's brows lifted, appropriately alarmed.

She sighed. "Everything is fine, Carrigan. I'm ready to go home."

Audrey took the driver's hand to be let up into the coach.

"I attended the coroner's inquest," Marsden said. Audrey's feet stilled and her spine went rigid. He'd clearly intended for the blurted statement to capture her attention.

She pursed her lips, irritated his strategy had worked, and peered over her shoulder.

"You may ride with me to Violet House, but you are not invited in."

A small grin shuffled the corner of his lips. Carrigan stood aside and gestured for Mr. Marsden to climb up.

Audrey prayed she did not regret it.

CHAPTER TWELVE

The duchess did not pretend at civility for long once the carriage got moving. The hulking driver, Carrigan, had given Hugh the appropriate once over before shutting the door, a silent but clear warning on his expression. Hugh found himself pleased that the duchess had the brute on staff. The man would double well as a guard if necessary. And what Hugh had suggested while they'd stood on the curb—that perhaps the real murderer would rather her stop digging around for the truth—had cut through him with a sharp chill.

Thanks to the coroner's inquest, and the lack of defense wounds on Fournier's person, Hugh was genuinely considering the fact that he had not done the murder after all. Perhaps he'd witnessed it. Perhaps he wasn't totally innocent. But Hugh could no longer, without doubt, know it.

"You weaseled your way into my carriage with the promise of information," she said. "Either share it or I will call for Carrigan to drop you off at the next corner."

Hugh bristled. To look at her, he wouldn't have thought her so bold. Still, he couldn't help but wonder if she was only playing at it. If instead, inside, she was exhausting herself with this show of confidence.

"Miss Lovejoy's nails had been trimmed and cleaned by the coroner, but I recalled them from the night of the murder. From when I came upon the scene," he said, his body beginning to warm again with the enormity of his blunder. "They were torn and ragged from the fight she put up against her attacker."

The duchess straightened in her seat. The wrapper she wore parted, displaying the pale blue silk gown she'd chosen for the Seven Sins. The other dresses he had seen her in so far hadn't showcased the lines of her body as this one did. He forced his eyes to hold hers.

"Philip has no wounds on him," she said, breathlessly. She grinned. "You know this. You've seen him."

He canted his head in agreement. "Yes."

She slid forward on the seat, purely giddy now. "So, you must believe me now. He didn't hurt Miss Lovejoy."

He held up a hand to stay her excitement. "I'm not prepared to say he isn't involved in some way, but..." Hugh cringed inside. He absolutely detested being wrong. "I no longer believe he alone acted out against her."

She sat back, disappointed. "He didn't act out against her at all."

"That remains to be seen."

"You're just being stubborn," she replied. "You're humiliated that you missed such an obvious clue."

The woman was impossible. Infuriating. And yet, she spoke the truth. He was humiliated, and that only served to make him angry.

"The way he was found, in proximity to the deceased, means he cannot absolutely be absolved," Hugh said. "Use your common sense, Your Grace. In the very least, he saw the murder and he is keeping quiet. That makes him an accessory."

"He cannot hang for that," she replied.

"I don't think you understand. At this moment, he is the only suspect. He will be charged."

"Unless we find the real murderer."

Hugh sat back and rubbed the scruff on his cheek. He'd done this himself. He'd given her a glimmer of hope. If she hadn't been willing to stop her investigation before, she most certainly wouldn't now.

"You cannot go tromping around London asking after Miss Lovejoy's other benefactors. You will make yourself a target."

"Perhaps it will draw the villain out," she replied, then gestured toward the front of the carriage and her driver. "I have protection."

Hugh closed his eyes and fought the pulsing ache in his temple. "You'll need more than a rather large driver if you continue to be so careless."

The duchess said nothing, but when Hugh opened his eyes, she was looking out the carriage window, her jaw tight. Her chest rose and fell with agitated breaths, the parted panels of her wrap again revealing her generous curves. Irritation had mixed with concern when he'd seen Wimbly dragging her through the gaming floor at the Seven Sins. Now, another surge of frustration slammed into him. It coiled low in his abdomen.

Hugh dragged his eyes from her. This physical pull was something he had to gain control over. It bothered him. She was everything he couldn't abide—privileged, aloof, heedless of reality. To put herself in danger, to even suggest luring out a murderer, displayed a serious lack of judgment.

Audrey Sinclair was desperate, and Hugh knew all too well what desperate people could be driven to do. Especially those who lived cooped up in their townhomes with every advantage at their fingertips.

She sneaked a sideways glance at him. "Then what do you propose we do?"

"We?"

"Forgive me if I don't believe you have my husband's best

interests at heart," she replied, turning fully toward him. "You now know that he isn't the murderer, but it would be much more convenient for you if you simply chose to ignore that fact."

Hugh gnashed his teeth and sat forward. "You question my honor?"

Her expression cooled, and though his retort seemed to chasten her, she turned up her nose at him. "I've been informed of your rather *dis*honorable past, Mr. Marsden."

He pulled back slowly, searching her eyes. There it was—the barest amount of revulsion. He'd wondered how long it would be before she used the scandal as a weapon against him.

"I'm sure you've heard a lurid tale worthy of the gossip rags and believed every bit of it," he said.

"Is it not true then that you shot Lord Neatham in a duel?"

He exhaled. "I shot him, yes."

And ever since, Barty's arm had been a useless limb, tucked up into a sling. By some stroke of luck, Barty's shot had only grazed Hugh's ear.

"He called you out for ruining his sister," she pressed.

Hugh clenched his jaw. He wasn't inclined to discuss what had occurred between himself and Barty, or worse still, Eloisa.

"It's funny. You seem to know much about me and yet, I know barely anything at all about you, Your Grace."

The duchess reached for the wrapper and closed it around her tightly. Hugh had learned to pay attention to a person's body language; it often said more than they wished to express. The lady wanted to keep him at a distance.

"Why should you?" she asked. "Before this business, you couldn't have had any reason to know me."

"Why did you break with Bainbury?"

She flinched, unprepared for the question. Just as Hugh had planned.

"That is none of your business. It doesn't have anything to do with the matter at hand."

"You'd be surprised at how informative these seemingly unrelated pieces of information can be."

Before she married Fournier, she had been but an impoverished and deceased lord's daughter. Since his earlier conversation with Thornton, he'd learned Charles Haverhill, Lord Edgerton, a baron, had died alongside the duchess's elder brother. The title passed to the baron's younger brother. The new Edgerton had arranged for Audrey's marriage to Bainbury, which would have vastly bettered not just her circumstances, but those of her family. And yet the Duke of Fournier had swept in and all but stolen her from the earl. If he'd had to have her so desperately, why wait until the eleventh hour? As a duke he could have had any woman of his choosing. Why Miss Audrey Haverhill? She was attractive, intelligent, and clearly, a spitfire. Perhaps it was a love match after all. Perhaps Fournier simply hadn't known he loved her until it was nearly too late.

"Bainbury is in the past. I'm concerning myself with the present, and I suggest you do the same," she bit off. "Now, did you happen to hear Wimbly mention the Continent?"

Hugh groaned inwardly. He'd hoped she would leave that bit of bait dangling on the hook. "I did," he answered.

"It sounds like Miss Lovejoy was eager to leave the country," she said as the carriage slowed upon its arrival at Violet House. The duchess leaned forward, her eyes bright with fervor. "Do you think she might have known she was in danger?"

"Or she might have known she was in some trouble and wished to elude arrest. Once on the Continent, it's easy to disappear."

She considered his alternative motivation with a cock of her head. "Might she have gone to Philip for help when Wimbly denied her? Perhaps they had formed a friendship—"

Hugh let out an exasperated sigh and hooked his ankle on his knee. "You really are determined to believe he didn't have her as a mistress."

She snapped her eyes to his. The firm set of her jaw was at odds with how swiftly she averted her hard glare.

"You're keeping a secret from me," he stated, unwilling to play games any longer.

"Why do you say that?"

"Because I know when I am being lied to."

"I haven't told you a single lie."

"You said you went back to Bernadetto and he told you Miss Lovejoy was living on Yarrow Street."

Guilt rode swiftly across her expression. She sniffed. "Very well. I told you *one* lie."

"And you're obscuring the truth now as well. You're not naïve or unintelligent; you've proven to be quite the contrary. I'm willing to consider that your husband did not murder Miss Lovejoy, but the fact remains she was in his secret rooms, which could only have been used for one purpose: to meet a mistress."

The duchess turned her cheek, refusing to look at him or acknowledge his statement. The woman was a veritable monolith. She would not be persuaded toward reason, when even she could not deny the purpose for a secret apartment. The duke had not even had his solicitor handle the arrangements for the rooms, as most lords did when securing confidential residences.

At the coroner's inquest, Mr. Newton, who visited his brother at Jewell House often, had claimed to have heard hollering, an argument. No women's voices, he'd said, but men's voices. An argument between men.

Men.

The interior of the carriage brightened as it pulled into Violet House's drive, lamplight shedding over the duchess's figure. She held her chin high, her throat working at some knot that had no doubt formed. Hugh gritted his molars. What a fool he'd been. A damn fool! Blind as a mole. The carriage shook as her gargantuan driver hopped down.

"At the inquest, Mr. Bernadetto fled before he could be questioned," Hugh said. Her hard shell cracked, and she turned to him with parted lips.

"Fled?"

"He seemed to take ill after seeing Miss Lovejoy's corpse." He shrugged as Carrigan opened the door. "Or perhaps there was another reason he didn't wish to stay."

The sconces flanking the front doors to Violet House flickered, casting shifting light over her glossy blonde hair and the delicate curve of her neck.

"Could he have known about her wish to go to the Continent?" she mused.

"I'm sure you intend to ask him," Hugh said. She lifted a brow. "Can you wait until tomorrow? I can meet you at the theatre at noon."

He had no doubt that he would regret this. However, it was a better alternative to her rushing off to the theatre right now to badger the man. Hugh had his own questions for Bernadetto, and perhaps the pair of them could achieve more together rather than individually.

The duchess took Carrigan's proffered hand, and he helped her to the ground. She then turned back to Hugh. "I'll be at the theatre at nine o'clock tomorrow morning, if you wish to join me."

"Nine?" Hugh hopped out of the carriage and straightened his jacket.

"Mr. Bernadetto's office looked as if it doubled as his sleeping quarters, if you'll recall."

"I do," Hugh said, reluctantly impressed she had observed the same. "He will likely still be asleep."

"The early bird gets the worm," she replied.

"You are used to getting your way, aren't you?" He tipped his hat. "Good evening, Your Grace."

He started for the gated entrance.

"Carrigan can drive you," she called after him.

"No need," he replied. He'd rather hail a cab. He'd also rather

Carrigan stay close to her. The man didn't seem particularly sharp, but he was clearly protective of the duchess.

If the murderer was still loose—and Hugh was beginning to accept the fact that he was—her snooping about had likely already drawn his attention. Hugh kept a keen eye as he turned out of the drive and down Curzon Street. There didn't seem to be anyone about, watching Violet House. Except for one particular imp.

"Good work tonight," Hugh said as the scrawny lad peeled off a stone hitching post to fall into step next to him.

Sir stuck out his hand and whistled appreciatively when Hugh slapped the earned shilling into his waiting palm. It disappeared into his pocket.

"Want me to keep my blinkers on the lady's place the rest of the night?"

"No, go home. Get some rest." Hugh didn't like the boy being out on the streets alone so late at night. Sir was a scrappy thing and smart as a whip, but there were men much larger and smarter than him.

"Ain't no resting there," he mumbled. Hugh didn't know where Sir resided, or if any of his stories about his large family, all of whom he'd claimed at one point or another were sick and in dire need of money for medical attention, were even half true.

He'd have offered a cot in his own kitchen if he didn't know for certain that Sir would reject it out of pride—and that Basil would complain like a bitter old woman.

"I've got a job for you tomorrow," Hugh said. The boy practically hopped onto his toes. "Got any friends that lurk about the Jewell House?"

"You mean before or after the murder was done?"

"Before."

"A few. What d'you want to know?"

Hugh considered his words carefully. The theory he'd been struck with in the duchess's carriage was just that—a theory. But a strong and promising one.

"See if there are any rumors of men meeting other men at Jewell House."

They passed under the light of a lamppost, and Sir's expression pinched. "You mean like a molly house?"

Hugh slowed Sir's step with a hand on his bony shoulder. "I don't know if that's what Jewell House is known for but be discreet. Not a word about the murder or the lord who was arrested."

Understanding lit Sir's eyes. He touched the side of his nose and bounded away, swiftly becoming another shadow in the night.

CHAPTER THIRTEEN

The Theatre Royal, Drury Lane appeared a bit shabbier by the light of day. The façade needed a good scrubbing, especially near the sconces where soot blackened the limestone, and trash—crumbled playbills, broken glass bottles, a lady's black glove—littered the street. The red silk tapestries that hung from the side of the building gave off a rich, lustrous quality at night, gleaming in the light cast from lampposts, but the weak early morning sunshine showed they were in fact thin and bleached to a salmon color.

Audrey waited for Carrigan to stop the carriage and open the door for her, her stomach in twists. Hugh Marsden had said he would meet her there, and with mounting concern, she realized she did not dread his presence. In fact, if she were being honest, she would have preferred it. The last time she'd been in the backrooms and corridors of the theatre she'd been completely out of her element; having him at her side had given her a sense of steadiness...even if he'd been an arrogant cad. Now, after his sobering reminder that the real murderer was still loose, a chill tracked up and down her spine when she considered entering the theatre alone.

Whether or not Mr. Marsden could be trusted remained to be seen. His reputation as a Bow Street officer was on the line with this case; he couldn't possibly wish to be known as the man who'd arrested an innocent duke. However, his evident insult the evening before, when she'd accused him of only wanting what was best for himself, lingered in her mind. His honor did seem to mean something to him.

It was likely why he'd accepted the challenge for a duel from the newly titled Lord Neatham after Mr. Marsden was accused of ruining his sister—Mr. Marsden's own half-sister, if the rumor of his status as a by-blow was correct. It sickened her to think of it. It would be the height of dishonor and depravity. Had he been guilty? Why else would the young woman have fled England, draped in shame?

Carrigan swung open the door and helped her to the curb. "The Runner's here," he said in his gruff tenor, cutting his eyes toward the opposite side of the street. Audrey released a breath, which was immediately followed by another twist of her stomach, this one quite different. It intensified as Hugh Marsden came around the rear of her carriage, his hands in his pockets. He wore a gray morning coat, black trousers and waistcoat, and a curiously well-tied cravat.

He and Carrigan exchanged a terse glance, and then the driver turned to Audrey. She read his expression easily; he was wary about this visit, and about her entering the theatre with Mr. Marsden. Society gossip wasn't just for the lords and ladies; if anything, the servant class ran wild with more gossip than their employers. Carrigan glowered at Mr. Marsden as though he knew the scandal that the officer dragged behind him.

Audrey touched Carrigan's meaty forearm to relay confidence. "I'll return shortly."

He only grunted, and she started toward the theatre's front doors. Marsden fell into step beside her.

"He's not fond of me," he murmured.

"It is my endeavor he isn't fond of," she replied, then added, "Though I'm sure he also doesn't like you."

"Not many people do," he conceded. "This way."

He broke from the direction of the front doors and veered toward the side of the building.

"Where are you going?"

"The theatre is locked, but an alley door is open."

Audrey increased her pace to keep up with his long strides. "You arrived early."

"I like to be prepared."

"Is that why you've been having me followed?" Audrey had seen the tall, slim man again the night before, cloaked well in the shadows of Curzon Street. She'd put out her light and peeled back the window drape, curious to see if Mr. Marsden had stayed to be sure she didn't leave for the theatre right then. Admittedly, she'd considered it.

She wouldn't have seen the man had a passing cab's lantern not shaken light over him. He'd tried to slip behind a tree but too late.

"That has more to do with staying informed," he replied lightly. "Don't worry about the boy. Sir knows to keep his distance. Besides, he's useful."

They entered the alley and the stench of refuse and rotting food tickled her nostrils. "Boy? This was a man."

Mr. Marsden drew to a halt. His pressing stare ground her heels to a stop as well. "When was this?"

"Last night." Unease lifted the small hairs on her arms. "Shortly after you left."

"This person was standing outside Violet House?"

Her breathing slowed. "Yes. And the night before too."

Mr. Marsden peered over her shoulder and then further up the alley. He removed his hat and raked his fingers through his hair.

With her pulse tripping a beat, her breath turning shallow, she said, "You didn't send him."

He met her eyes, his jaw tight. "No."

Someone else was watching her, a man Hugh Marsden knew nothing about. He'd accused her of being too bold, of making herself a target. Until right then, she hadn't quite believed him.

"Come along," he said, his eyes searching the alleyway again before continuing toward the theatre's side entrance.

Audrey fought to remember more about the man she'd seen twice now. Both times, she hadn't gleaned more than a general outline of his figure. With an uneven pulse, she compared it to the blurred vision she'd had of the murderer while holding Miss Lovejoy's earbob. Whether or not it was the same man eluded her.

Inside the theatre, the stale odor of cigars, perfume, and lamp oil wafted under her nose, a welcome change from the alley's smell. It was dark, and she became disoriented as they turned down a corridor. The spongy carpet beneath her feet was familiar though —they had come this way the last time they'd visited.

It was in this very corridor that she'd accidentally touched Mr. Marsden and been hammered with a vision. Not his latest experience, but a persistent, clutching memory. A woman, her dark hair flowing around her shoulders. With a shudder, Audrey wondered if this memory was of Miss Neatham. With a lurch of her stomach, she realized Mr. Marsden might have involuntarily, unknowingly, shown Audrey the memory that haunted him.

"What is wrong?"

With a start, she realized she had fallen behind. Audrey shook her head and hurried to catch up.

"Nothing," she lied. Keeping company with someone like Mr. Marsden should have repulsed her. And yet, as they came to the end of the corridor and entered the familiar halls backstage, Audrey felt only curiosity.

She didn't know whether she could trust him; his true motives for arranging this meeting might still be hidden. *Trust Mr. Marsden?* It was absurd. Whyever should she? Even Philip was keeping important information from her, and the two of them had been each other's closest confidants.

The theatre manager's office door was just ahead, and thankfully this time, there wasn't another actor or actress in sight. The last time, the actor named Porter had unsettled her. He'd been furious about Belladora Lovejoy's death and had been adamant that she hadn't been a kept mistress. Of course, he'd been proven wrong—she'd been ensconced in Wimbly's property on Yarrow Street. Though, she had not been exclusive to him, he'd claimed. Had she and Porter been involved? Had he been jealous?

Hugh stopped at the manager's closed door and rapped on the painted wood. When no answer came, he knocked again.

"Mr. Bernadetto? Are you in?"

He glanced at Audrey with a silent *"I told you so"* written on his expression. Still sleeping, as he'd warned. She stepped forward and knocked a third time. She didn't have time to stand around waiting. Philip's case was being presented to the grand jury the following day, and she needed information to give Potridge; information that might help sway the jury to throw out her husband's case.

A shuffling noise came from within the office, then the sound of something heavy falling onto the floor.

"Mr. Bernadetto, we apologize for the early hour," Audrey said, her voice raised. "We have some new questions about Miss Lovejoy, and it's imperative we speak to you."

The pair of them stood staring at the door another few moments, Audrey's impatience mounting. Her restless limbs felt the intense need to move. With an agitated sigh, she threw up her hand.

"This is ridiculous. He is in there, we heard him."

Mr. Marsden's irritation wasn't much more controlled. He drummed his knuckles harder against the wood. "Bernadetto, you left the inquest without answering any of the coroner's questions. I insist you allow us in."

Utter silence followed. No more shuffling noises. Fed up, Audrey reached for the doorknob. It was locked. Mr. Marsden grumbled, then shouted, "I'm giving you until the count of three, Bernadetto, then I'm kicking down this door."

Audrey stared at him. "Is that truly necessary? I do have my hat pins—I can pick the lock."

"Yes, but kicking down the door is more assertive and much more threatening," he replied. She rolled her eyes.

"One!" he bellowed. "Two!" He stood back and motioned for Audrey to move aside. Thinking it unnecessary, but a little thrilling, she scuttled out of his way. "Three!"

Mr. Marsden raised his foot and stomped it hard against the door. In the second before his boot connected with the wood, Audrey wondered if she would be able to suppress her laughter should he fail to force the door open. A ready smile was still leaping to her lips when the door did bash open—and a grisly scene met them.

The theatre manager's office was in a state of total disarray. His desk had been swiped clear, the contents strewn all over the floor, the chairs overturned; the cabinets stood open, drawers pulled free and emptied upon the floor, leaving a mess of papers and trinkets; and lying on the floor next to the bedstead, was Mr. Bernadetto himself. Blood splattered his face and neck, soaking into his collar and onto the carpet beneath him. Audrey clapped a hand to her mouth, stifling her scream.

"The window," Mr. Marsden said, and then rushed toward it. The sash had been thrown open. With a sickening roll of her stomach, Audrey realized the muffled sound they'd heard from the behind the door must have been the intruder. Which meant he hadn't gotten far.

"Stay here!" Mr. Marsden shouted to her before leaping up onto the open sill and maneuvering himself out through the window.

"No! Mr. Marsden, stop!" she cried as he dropped from view. Audrey dashed on clumsy legs to the window, reaching for the sill

—and drawing back when she saw red stains smeared there. Mr. Bernadetto's blood.

Gritting her teeth, she forced herself forward and peered out into a side alleyway—perhaps even the same one Mr. Marsden had led her down earlier. She could see neither the officer nor any other man running away but heard shouting and the shrill blows of a pea whistle. Stymied, and increasingly horrified at being left alone in a room where a crime had just been committed, Audrey stumbled back, her eyes darting toward Mr. Bernadetto. He was utterly still. But perhaps... She edged closer, watching for any sign that he might still be alive. That he could be saved. *There*. Movement. A rise of his chest.

Audrey went to his side, staring at the gore of his slashed neck and the blood dribbling from it. His eyes were wide open, his mouth slack. Audrey crouched lower, watching his chest. No. She had to have been mistaken. He couldn't possibly still be alive, not with so much blood pooled around him and his throat so mangled.

A noise gurgled from Mr. Bernadetto's throat. She screamed and shot to her feet, staggering back.

"Audrey!"

She whipped around at her name, shouted from the corridor. Heaving for air, Mr. Marsden barreled into the office, a pistol in his hand.

"I heard you scream," he panted, his cheeks flushed from giving chase, his eyes roving over her, as if assessing her for any injury.

"I'm...I'm fine, it's Mr. Bernadetto. He made a noise. I think he's alive!" She pointed toward the man, needlessly. Mr. Marsden came forward and crouched next to the manager. He took his wrist and held still, measuring a pulse. But then shook his head.

"Damn it." He stood again, moving back out of the wet fibers of the carpet.

A strange numbness stole over her. "But I...I heard a sound," she whispered.

"Death is not always fast, even when it is certain." Mr. Marsden touched her arm, tugging her lightly. She stumbled away from Mr. Bernadetto, and she realized she'd been standing in his expanding pool of blood.

"Did you see him?" she asked, her vision unsteady. "The man who..."

"He had too much of a lead. I've signaled another street patrol. There is someone coming." He maintained a hold on her arm. Audrey felt like it was tightening. "You should sit."

She shook her head, but instantly regretted it when she felt the room tip. "I'm fine."

It wasn't true. Her breaths were too shallow, and she'd become entirely too dependent on the strength of Mr. Marsden's arm. The gurgling of air and blood escaping the slashed neck, the squelch of the carpet beneath her slippers... Her vision wiped clean. The officer's voice faded.

When her sight returned what felt like moments later, she was staring at the ceiling.

"Just lie still," a soft, deep voice said. Mr. Marsden moved into her vision, hovering above her. Audrey blinked.

"What...?"

"You swooned."

Audrey's senses were suddenly alert enough to send a flood of humiliation through her. She swatted his hand away as he tried to keep her from rising.

"I do not swoon," she insisted, even as she sat up to find that she'd been lain out on top of Mr. Bernadetto's desk. Two other men were in the room now too, standing near the theatre manager's splayed body. And in the doorway, Carrigan stood with his cap crushed in his big hands.

"No need to be ashamed," Mr. Marsden said gently. "Men

have lost the contents of their stomach at lesser crime scenes." He slid to block her view as she looked toward the bedstead again.

Her limbs were shaky as she swung her legs off the side of the desk. She must have been unconscious for longer than a few moments if the street patrolmen and her driver had made their way into the theatre.

"Goodness, I didn't cast up my accounts too, did I?"

Mr. Marsden huffed a laugh. "No." He swung a glance over his shoulder, his expression darkening. "If you're ready to stand, I'll take you back to Violet House."

She slid down from the desk, and Mr. Marsden's hands came up to bracket her shoulders. Heat flushed her cheeks and she flinched, panicking that he might pass a vision to her, like last time he'd taken her elbow.

"I'm fine," she said again, moving away from him. She felt like such a fool.

Partially to avoid his eyes, Audrey peered at the destroyed office. The papers strewn about, cabinets opened and overturned.

"He was looking for something," she murmured.

"It appears that way. Though there's no telling if he was successful in finding it."

Her first steps toward Carrigan at the door were tremulous. "What could Mr. Bernadetto have had in here?" she mused aloud.

Mr. Marsden walked with her into the corridor. "I don't know, but I doubt this was a simple burglary gone wrong. The method of the attack on Mr. Bernadetto..." He sighed. "It matches the type of wounds Miss Lovejoy sustained."

Gooseflesh spread along her arms, and she tripped to a stop as her spirits gave an expected jump. "Then that proves Philip is innocent. He's locked up right now, it couldn't have been him."

Mr. Marsden turned to face her. "It proves nothing."

"But surely if both attacks are the same—"

"The inquest for Bernadetto won't be for a few days, and until then there is no evidence to link the two murders other than a heavily mutilated throat."

Carrigan took a step closer to Audrey in the corridor, as if to protect her from some invisible foe. No, not invisible. The murderer had been just on the other side of that office door.

Mr. Marsden, too, stepped closer. He lowered his voice, his expression one of smoldering wrath. "He knew we were coming here this morning, and he got to Bernadetto before we could."

She shook her head. "That's impossible, I told no one but you and my maid and Carrigan. Who did you tell?"

He grimaced and searched the corridor behind her. "Just Basil."

Audrey frowned, curious. "Who is Basil?"

"My valet. He can be trusted."

He employed a valet? Audrey puzzled over a Bow Street officer being able to afford a staff. Then again, his personal life was none of her business.

"Our voices might have carried last night in the drive at Violet House," she suggested. "There was a man watching, after all."

"Not at that point. Sir would have seen him."

Audrey frowned again. He certainly placed a lot of stock into this Sir.

Mr. Marsden turned to her driver. "Carrigan, correct? There is an unknown man following Her Grace. She's spotted him twice now outside Violet House. Do you have any footmen who could check the perimeter of the property on an hourly basis throughout the night?"

Audrey simmered as Carrigan seemed to grow taller, his shoulders broader, and his expression flattened to something deadly serious.

"I'll speak to the butler. We'll be sure no one steps foot on the property and that Her Grace has someone with her at all times."

Audrey glared at them both. "*Her Grace* is right here, and I will decide if I require a guard."

Mr. Marsden growled with impatience. "There is a dead body in the room behind us, *Your Grace*. What more do you need to convince you?"

The mention of a dead body should have captured her attention, but it was his emphasis on *Your Grace* that did instead. For whatever reason, hearing it made her recall the way he'd instead shouted her given name when he'd heard her scream earlier. She didn't know why it flustered her so much.

Audrey forced herself to forget it.

"Mr. Bernadetto was likely killed because the murderer made a mistake," she said. "He left something behind. Some clue."

She had made a mistake too. Back in the theatre manager's office, she should have kept her wits about her and hunted down an object, some possession of Mr. Bernadetto's to help her see something informative. Instead, she'd *swooned*.

"I agree," Mr. Marsden said, surprising her. "And I have an idea who to question about it."

She straightened her shoulders. "I'll come with you."

"You're not invited. But before I leave, I'll escort you home."

Audrey clenched her hands into fists and resisted the urge to stomp her foot. "There is no need. I have Carrigan." She set her shoulders. "Besides, I'm not afraid, Mr. Marsden."

"Then someone ought to be afraid for you."

He tipped the brim of his hat and disappeared back into the theatre manager's office.

CHAPTER FOURTEEN

Porter's boarding house was one of the more respectable looking buildings in Spitalfields. Hugh wasn't unfamiliar with the East End—most of the riff raff he brought in to Bow Street dwelled in its narrow warrens and alleyways. This was the part of London that the ton chose to ignore. Hell, maybe he should have brought the duchess along with him after all. Letting her have a good look at the lower denizens might have broken her illusion of safety.

But as maddening as the lady was, Hugh couldn't have subjected her to possible danger. Not after what she'd witnessed that morning. For the umpteenth time, he questioned his foolhardy leap from the open theatre office window. As he'd given chase down the alley, seeing nothing but a blur of a man turning the corner far ahead, the thought that there might have been more than one intruder slammed into him; that he might have just left the duchess alone and vulnerable. He barely remembered racing back inside the theatre, drawing breath even, but the sound of her sharp scream coming from within the office was still staggering. The relief at seeing her unharmed, if white-faced and shaking near Bernadetto's body, had almost made him lightheaded.

Just as quickly, however, his blood boiled again.

There was more—far more—to Belladora Lovejoy's murder than what had initially met the eye. If he were to be honest with himself, the duchess's relentless pursuit for the real killer was both a knife in his pride and a challenge to correct a mistake. Now that the theatre manager had become a second victim, he was, unsurprisingly, in a foul mood.

He brought his fist down on the door to the room Sir had directed him to. After their unsettling encounter at the theatre, Hugh had paid the lad a few shillings to follow the actor named Porter and to report where the man kept rooms.

The door swung open. Porter stood alert. He filled the doorframe, his menacing glower just as Hugh remembered it.

"What're you doing here, Runner?"

"I've just come from a visit with Bernadetto." He purposefully neglected to mention that the manager was now on his way to the bone house.

"What's that got to do with me?"

He didn't show a flicker of surprise or doubt, which led him to believe that Porter didn't know of his employer's death just yet. He was inclined to believe this was not the man he'd seen whipping out of sight at the end of the alleyway next to the theatre. However, that didn't mean he was ignorant to information that might prove useful.

"Your obsession with Miss Lovejoy was a topic of conversation," Hugh lied.

He could tell which people to step lightly around, questioning them slowly and methodically. He could also tell which people that tactic would be lost on. Porter was one of the latter.

"My obsession?" he sneered. "We were friends. Nothing more."

"Not for your lack of desire."

Porter peered down his angular nose at Hugh. He used his height to its full effect, and then stepped aside, allowing Hugh to enter. He did so with caution, his hand prickling with the anticipated need to draw his flintlock pistol. The room was small and cold, with a single window and a coal stove, where a greasy pan sat with a few fish scales stuck to the bottom. The odor of last night's dinner hung in the air.

Porter shut the door and went to a chair at a small table, where colorful fabric and beads were sprawled about.

"I cared for Belladora," he said, picking up a cloud of lime green silk. A needle and thread hung from a line of stitched red beads. "And yes, I would have cared for her as more than a friend, if she'd have allowed it."

"Why didn't she?"

Porter snorted and continued stitching. A piece for the stage, Hugh presumed. "She had standards. Expensive ones, even though I told her she was being a fool."

"You argued with her?" Hugh relaxed his hand, no longer expecting the stage actor to come at him. In fact, he appeared at ease as he worked on the costume piece.

"I didn't shut my mouth and look the other way, if that's what you mean."

"You're wise to the world in which you live, Porter—wasn't her arrangement with Lord Wimbly commonplace? Why criticize her for bettering her situation?"

He glanced around him, taking in the shabby room. It reminded Hugh of the one he'd lived in after his mother's death, when he'd taken his leave from Neatham's household as a young man. The former viscount had offered Hugh funds so that he could live a gentleman's life, but he'd refused it. Out of pride or resentment, he didn't know, but he'd been angry and heartsick, and he'd wanted nothing more than to sever all ties from his father and the half-siblings that had always done well pretending Hugh was just a servant's child. Bartholomew, Thomas, and Eloisa had all known the truth. The similar features the four of them all shared could leave little doubt.

It had been Eloisa who'd sought Hugh out some months after he'd left, and after their father had passed. She'd convinced him of her sisterly feelings. God, he'd been a fool. He'd known his place within the viscount's household, but like Icarus flying too close to the sun, Hugh, blinded by what he assumed were familial ties, had tread over an invisible line.

"Bettering her situation would be one thing, but what Belladora was doing..." Porter shook his head, reclaiming Hugh's attention. "It didn't sit right. It was too incestuous if you ask me."

He flinched. "Incestuous?"

That word. Hugh didn't like how often his past had been nipping at his heels lately. Time and distance, and a hell of a lot of hard work, had finally separated his current life from his past one, so that they sat apart from each other, like oil on water.

"I told her she was playing with fire, stringing along both father and son the way she was," Porter replied.

Hugh stepped closer to the table. "Do you refer to Lord Wimbly *and* his heir?"

Porter looked up from his sewing. The glittering beads caught the light of the table lantern and sent it over his dark, pitted skin. Old scarring from adolescent spots, perhaps a case of the pox. He had no scratch marks on his face or neck, or on his hands, which continued to deftly stitch even as he held Hugh's stare.

"I told her that when they found out, she'd catch hell."

The marquess and his heir were unaware they shared her, then? The Wimbly heir, Lord St. John, could not be very old, perhaps still at university.

"And did she?" Hugh asked. "Catch hell?"

"Never happened, far as I know."

Hugh recalled Wimbly's comment from the Seven Sins. "Did she ever mention anything about wanting to go to the Continent?"

Porter scowled. "The Continent? Never. What would she want to go there for?"

If she worried about angering Wimbly or his son with her duplicity, it might have been an attractive option. Though, Hugh couldn't picture the marquess angering over her deception, even if it was with his heir. How St. John would react, however, was uncertain, as Hugh didn't know much about the boy.

"Where does the Duke of Fournier come into play?" He was asking Porter as much as he was musing aloud.

Hopefully Sir was nosing around Jewell House right then, asking what others might have known or suspected about the toff in apartment twelve. The theory that the duke had been meeting other men, rather than women, felt right.

"Belladora never mentioned him," Porter answered. "But she ended up in his room, dead, didn't she?"

"Tell me about the night of the murder," Hugh said, coming back around to why he'd made the trip to Spitalfields. "How did Miss Lovejoy seem?"

"Her normal self."

"Nothing out of the ordinary happened that night, before or after the performance?"

Porter ripped the end of the thread with his teeth and looked at his work with an assessing eye. He then set the green silk down. "I wouldn't call it strange, as Belladora received flowers and notes most nights, but there was something different about a letter she got before the performance."

Hugh silenced his many thoughts and paid close attention. Whatever Porter was about to reveal, he sensed it was important. "Different how?"

"A tiger delivered the letter instead of messenger boy."

Messenger boys had their territories staked out and would usually be readily available for any servant who opened a back door and hollered for them. Sir ran messages from time to time, but he complained it was dull work. A tiger, on the other hand, rode along with a lord who was at the reins himself, or whose driver could not spring down from the box so easily—like Thornton's driver for instance. Tigers often wore livery, just as a driver or footman, would. There was no need to question Porter's intelligence—he would know the difference between the two.

"That didn't happen often, I presume," Hugh said. Porter gave a shake of his head. "Do you know what the letter said?"

Again, Porter shook his head. But then, after a moment of hesitation, said, "Belladora was thoughtful after, though. Like whatever the letter said confused her."

There wasn't much room to pace while thinking, but Hugh took a few steps forward and back as his mind spun in different directions. "Did she share the letter with Bernadetto?"

Porter got up from his chair and started gathering his sewing supplies. "I don't see why she would've."

"Did she have a dressing room? A place she might have kept her things? This letter, perhaps?" Hugh chastised himself for not thinking to look around for her dressing room earlier.

"She had a room, sure. Hettie asked Bernadetto to clean it out, though, now that she's taking the lead role." Porter frowned. "You think the letter is important?"

"Possibly."

The actor grabbed the green silk, rolled it between his fingers, then set it down again. "Ask Bernadetto about it, why don't you?"

There was no reason to keep the truth from him any longer. He would learn of it soon enough anyhow. "I can't. He's been murdered."

Porter went utterly rigid. He stared at Hugh, nostrils flaring. "You said you were just with him."

"I lied." Porter shoved aside a chair and came toward Hugh. Quickly, he continued, "I needed to be sure it wasn't you who killed him—or Miss Lovejoy, for that matter."

Porter drew up short of Hugh. "I would never have harmed her. I got nothing against Bernadetto either."

"I believe you."

The actor seemed to lose his fury and stumbled back. "Why would someone do him in?"

It might not have anything to do with the letter Miss Lovejoy had received the night of her murder, but Hugh couldn't rule it out.

"I don't know. But if you think of anything, send word to me at Bow Street. I'll see myself out," Hugh said.

Porter sniffed and kept his head down. "The lady was right, then. The murderer can't be the toff you arrested now, can it?"

Hugh held still, the brass knob of the door cold in his palm. Admitting the duchess was right, even to someone as inconsequential as a stage actor, churned his gut.

"Thank you for your time," was all he said before closing the door behind him.

A stone tossed about in the pit of his stomach as he hailed a cab.

There was a push and pull happening within him, an undercurrent of unease. Following the duchess as she blazed ahead in her investigation was not only revealing his own mistakes with the arrest of Fournier, but also peeling back the scabs that had for so long formed a thick layer over an open wound. Every layer was a month, a season, a year he'd spent with his back turned on his past life. Now, the crust he'd built over that open wound was thinning. Self-preservation screamed at him to stop, to forget the duke and the duchess, to take the next assignment and move ever onward.

But at the same time, he couldn't possibly leave Audrey Sinclair to do as she pleased on her mission. Even after seeing Bernadetto's mutilated body, and then swooning at the horror of it, she had refused to back down. She was either absurdly brave, or asinine. Perhaps a bit of both. Either way, the danger was evident and seemed to be deepening with every passing day. A hot swell of agitation roiled inside him when he imagined what might have happened if she had gone to the theatre alone that morning...

The urge to go to Curzon Street and see if the duchess was there was both keen and grating. No, she would not stop. And because he would not have the death of the duchess on his conscience, Hugh would not either. Not even if it ended in his own self-destruction.

CHAPTER
FIFTEEN

There were many things Audrey envied about her sister-in-law, Lady Geneva Herrick: her beauty, elegance, kindness, and more recently, the fact that her husband was not being held for a gruesome murder. However, when Genie arrived minutes before Audrey was about to leave for a visit to the Brown Bear, she started to envy the woman's cunning as well.

"Come with me," Genie said the moment she entered the morning room at Violet House.

Audrey had been waiting for her carriage to be brought around and for a basket of food collected by their cook for Philip when Barton had allowed Genie inside.

"Go with you where?" Audrey asked, momentarily confused. "I'm on my way to Bow Street—"

She came forward and gripped Audrey's forearms lightly. "This is more important."

After an initial moment of astonishment, Audrey sighed and pulled free of Genie's hands. "I haven't seen him in two days."

Though missing her husband wasn't the only reason she was eager to visit the guarded upstairs tavern room. The theatre manager's murder had been widely reported in the evening papers the day before, but Philip might not yet have learned of it. If he knew that another person had been killed, if he had any idea *why*, perhaps he would finally speak.

All day yesterday, Audrey had paced the many rooms at Violet House. She had insisted to Mr. Marsden that she wasn't afraid, but even after a hot bath and a dram of whisky, images of Mr. Bernadetto's body had stayed in the forefront of her mind. He was right there whenever she closed her eyes, and the wretched gurgling of his last breaths all too clear in her memory. How long would it take to forget?

"Michael was there yesterday. He says he's refusing to see anyone," Genie said gently.

Audrey grimaced and perched on a silk damask sofa. "He'll see me."

Genie followed her to the sofa and rested her lace-gloved hand on Audrey's knee. "I can't even imagine how horrible and terrifying this all is for you, but you'll be of no use at Bow Street. However, if you come with me, you just might accomplish something to help Philip."

Audrey turned to Genie, her interest sharpened. "Where are you going?"

She grinned. "A benefit luncheon—hosted by none other than Lady Wimbly."

A few days ago, Audrey would have leaped at the chance. But now, her interest dulled, and her shoulders rounded. "I've already spoken to Lord Wimbly."

"What?" Dismay flooded Genie's smug expression. "When?"

Admitting she went to a gaming hell and known opium den was completely out of the question. Neither did her brother- and sister-in-law need to know that she had been with Officer Marsden the morning before when he came upon the grisly scene at the theatre. There had been no mention of her name in the *Times* or any other publication, so Audrey was inclined to believe that Mr. Marsden had been determined to conceal her involvement—and perhaps even paid off the two street patrols that had certainly seen her.

"It doesn't matter," Audrey said now. "I've learned all there is to know about Wimbly's relationship with Miss Lovejoy."

Any hope that he would know more about the singer's murder had fizzled out completely. There was no reason for her to speak to Lady Wimbly now.

"Are you certain about that?" Genie said. "Lady Wimbly is no fool. Surely, she's wise to her husband's...*indelicacies*. Who is to know—she might possess knowledge that Wimbly does not."

Audrey doubted much more could be gained by going, and to a benefit luncheon, no less. "I can't just drop in," she sighed. "Genie, I'm a social pariah."

She probably would be for a very long time, even if Philip was released and cleared of all charges.

Genie pushed on an encouraging smile. "I sent word to Lady Wimbly that I was bringing a friend. You're a duchess, Audrey. She won't dare turn you away at the door."

"Michael would have a fit," she said, shaking her head. "He didn't even want you to take a turn with me in the park. He certainly won't support bringing me to Wimbly Manor."

Genie shrugged innocently. "Let me handle my husband's displeasure." She stood up. "Now, you are dressed to go out, I see. If we leave now, we'll arrive fashionably late."

Audrey had selected a midnight blue day dress topped with a dark brown spencer for her trip to Bow Street. With limited lace frills and decorative stitching, the conservative gown would have looked suitable for a visit to Philip's guarded room. However, it was a bit plain for a luncheon. She considered a change of dress, but then dismissed it. Showing up uninvited was going to be scandal enough; better to at least appear solemn.

She could always visit Bow Street after. Grudgingly, she acknowledged that the potential for running into Mr. Marsden outside the magistrate's offices was also a lure. He hadn't sent word about who he'd gone to question, and Audrey couldn't quell her curiosity of what he'd learned, and whether he'd use it to help Philip or hinder him.

A prickle of guilt followed that thought. Mr. Marsden might have been belligerent, arrogant, and infuriating, but she didn't believe he would manipulate the truth or evidence, not really.

Audrey donned her bonnet and kid gloves, and left Violet House. They took Genie's town coach the short distance to Wimbly Manor, Audrey's agitation steadily rising. This was a bold move. Foolhardy, perhaps. Truly, what was there to be learned? She'd wrung all she could out of Lord Wimbly and had walked away with little more than a vague mention of the Continent—and a thoroughly vexed Bow Street officer berating her for her risky behavior.

At least Mr. Marsden couldn't complain about the risk of attending a luncheon.

The marquess's London seat was a neoclassical limestone beauty. Audrey had been invited to a number of Lady Wimbly's benefits in the past—each one devoted to the marchioness's philanthropic passion *du jour*. Children's hospices, foundling homes, and support for the Poor Law were a few she could recall. Along the way, Genie explained that this luncheon was to benefit a reskilling program at one of the largest workhouses in London, which housed poor men, women, and families.

"St. Emmanuel's has implemented a program to give new skills to the prisoners," she said.

"Prisoners?" Audrey echoed. "That makes it sound as if they're criminals. Being poor and unable to pay their debts is a burden, not a sin."

That she had not received an invitation to the luncheon smarted a little. The invitations would have gone out the previous week, well before Philip's arrest, so the marchioness had not cut her from the guest list for that reason. Audrey wondered what had prevented Lady Wimbly from including her.

"Be that as it may, they are still imprisoned in the workhouse and have little opportunity to better themselves," Genie replied.

"A reskilling program. I'm surprised at Lady Wimbly's choice," Audrey said as the manor came into view. Her stomach cinched. "Sick children and orphans tug at heartstrings. Poverty-stricken men and women don't necessarily have the same effect."

"You sound as if those heartstrings of yours have been snipped," Genie said with a surprised glance.

"Just stretched thin." Her palms grew cool and damp in her gloves. "I'm sure my apprehension isn't helping."

The carriage stopped, and Genie reached for Audrey's hand. Again, Genie's touch passed along no vision, and Audrey was reminded of another reason to envy her sister-in-law: her peaceful mind, empty of any haunting thoughts.

"Hold your head high. Don't give them anything to gloat about."

Genie's advice was unexpectedly poignant. Audrey allowed the driver to help her down, and within moments, they were being led into Wimbly Manor. As expected, the receiving room was teeming with a collection of the ton's finest ladies. The Countess of Shoreham and the Dowager Viscountess Dutton were two of the first faces Audrey recognized. Their pedigree was far too refined to cause them to lose their poise, but the excitement at seeing her lit in their eyes, and Audrey imagined they were salivating to gather information with which to gossip later.

A few others could not prevent their jaws from going slack, their eyes from bulging. Lady Wimbly herself appeared a few seconds after Audrey and Genie were left standing, ungreeted, in the entranceway. Like the countess and dowager viscountess, the marchioness's unflappable demeanor did her credit.

"Your Grace, Lady Herrick," she intoned, addressing Audrey first, as was due her rank. As Genie had said, she was not going to be turned away. It didn't ease Audrey's trepidation, though.

"I hope you received my note this morning, saying that I

would be bringing my dearest friend," Genie said brightly. She hooked Audrey's arm in a show of affection. "And there is no one dearer to me and like a sister than the duchess."

Audrey pinned the inside of her cheek with her teeth. She would *not* laugh at Genie's obvious cut.

Lady Wimbly smiled widely, easily pretending as though all was well. "I am so honored you could be here, Your Grace. It is a credit to you for showing a keen interest in St. Emmanuel's program especially with the trying events unfolding with His Grace."

Of course, she knew the luncheon would never have concluded without a single utterance of the scandal, but the mention of it so soon after her arrival knocked her off center.

Behind Lady Wimbly, every lady had quit from their conversations to look on and listen in. Audrey caught two ladies exchanging a wide-eyed glance and quickly sipping from their teacups to hide their amusement.

"Thank you, it sounds like a very important endeavor," was all Audrey replied. Bland. Uninspiring. Exactly how she should be if she did not want to draw too much attention to herself. *Good luck with that*, she thought with a stab of regret. She should not have come. Being here was not going to help Philip's case in the least.

Genie remained at Audrey's side as they were brought into the sitting room, Lady Wimbly making brief introductions to a few of the guests whom Audrey did not know—including a young, unmarried heiress, Miss Arabella Grindlay, who had spent much of her youth in Devonshire and was new to town with her elderly aunt, present as the girl's chaperone. The aunt's flat stare remained unaffected as Lady Wimbly introduced them, but the young woman's eyes brightened with recognition.

"Goodness," she breathed, "I am speechless, Your Grace. I can't quite imagine how you could be moving about in society right now, what with all you must be going through."

Silence deadened the room. There was undoubtedly a dozen

more questions all of the women would have liked to ask, but none of them dared a breach of decorum like the artless Miss Grindlay. It wasn't her fault. She was simply innocent and untried. Audrey held herself stiffly and forced a nod of acknowledgment, if not a smile.

The bell for luncheon rang, releasing them all from the awkward moment. Audrey thought she even heard Genie sigh. They followed Lady Wimbly from the sitting room.

"This is a disaster," Audrey whispered, trying not to move her lips in any definitive way. Lip-reading was a beneficial skill when it came to busy ballrooms and dinner parties.

Genie turned her head toward Audrey, a serene smile still in place. "We will determine that later."

Audrey felt ill. She'd been a fool to let Genie talk her into coming. Mr. Marsden had been accusing her of making missteps as she scoured for information on the murder, but it was only now that she felt she had made a wrong move. Here, in a place she had once so firmly believed she belonged.

None of these women were her friends. The only person to call on her had been her sister; even her mother had not yet written. The wretched news had long since reached Haverfield. With another lurch of her stomach, she realized even Genie might not have come to see her, or invited her to visit, had Audrey not been the first to reach out. Philip might be the one arrested, but Audrey was already tainted by proxy. They may not show it to her face, but the only thing anyone would feel for her now was pity.

Flashes of heat and chills attacked Audrey as the courses were served, and to make matters worse, Genie had been seated across the large oblong table and several seats down. Miss Grindlay had been placed to Audrey's left and the sour-faced Lady Timston, a baroness Audrey had never been able to prize more than a few words from in their many previous meetings, to her right. Her right arm remained cold, but Audrey's left warmed from Miss Grindlay's close leaning.

"I have heard that you went to Bow Street, Your Grace," she said, unable to keep her voice as low as Audrey would have liked. The mention of Bow Street severed a few polite yet dull conversations happening around the table.

"Was it very awful? I can't even imagine setting foot in a place where dangerous criminals are kept." The very second Miss Grindlay finished speaking, she pinned her lips together. Her eyes popped wide with remorse and her cheeks flushed with hot embarrassment. Down the table, a spoon dropped against the rim of a bowl.

"Not, of course, His Grace," she quickly stammered, "because that is certainly the grossest error any Bow Street Runner has ever made. It is...it's outrageous, it's absurd, it's—"

Audrey stopped the poor girl before she needed to find another adjective meant to exonerate Philip. "Quite right, Miss Grindlay. It is an error, and to answer your question, yes, I was at Bow Street."

Lady Wimbly cleared her throat from the head seat. "I certainly hope you did not have to bear the company of the arresting Runner, Mr. Hugh Marsden."

A murmur of recognition circled the table. Audrey met Genie's eyes and breathed deeply.

"Not for very long," Audrey lied evenly.

Across the table, Lady Dutton leaned forward, over her bowl of leek soup. "How did you find Mr. Marsden, Your Grace?"

Audrey lowered her spoon and reached for her glass of claret. Was this a trick question? Saying the wrong thing might only further scandalize her.

"Obstinate," she replied with caution.

Lady Dutton lifted her chin and sat back, giving no indication what she thought of that description.

"The man is a brute," Lady Wimbly said. "He is an absolute disgrace and blackguard. How Bow Street can depend upon someone with such low morals is beyond me. It would not surprise me in the least to learn Marsden has lied about everything and falsified evidence to implicate our dear duke. *He* might even be the one to have done this wretched business."

Audrey sipped her claret faster than intended and coughed, her hand shaking as she set the glass back down. Falsified evidence? Hugh Marsden, a murderer? Quickly, she peered at Genie, whose pale brows were raised high on her forehead.

Lady Wimbly's support of Philip was as unexpected as it was outrageous—to borrow one of Miss Grindlay's adjectives. Mr. Marsden hadn't falsified any evidence, and he certainly hadn't stabbed that poor actress to death. She parted her lips to say so but stopped as reason barreled into her head. Defending Hugh Marsden would only cast doubt on her support of her own husband. She couldn't lead them to believe she thought Philip guilty.

"He's certainly had it out for our set since that whole unseemly business," Lady Dutton agreed.

"Has he?" Genie cut in. "I haven't heard of any attempts he has made at retaliation."

It was as good a defense as he was likely to get at this table. Audrey was grateful her sister-in-law had at least challenged the ridiculous accusation. She didn't wish for her husband to be tried by the House of Lords, but she also could not abide making a scapegoat out of Hugh Marsden.

"Let's not discuss such gloomy things." Lady Wimbly dabbed at the corner of her lips daintily. "I'd like to speak on the tremendous good that St. Emmanuel's has been doing, and how, with your generous support, ladies, they will continue to reshape the lives of those most unfortunate in their circumstances." She gestured to the liveried footmen standing against the walls of the dining room, straight backed and aloof with their eyes not quite meeting the gazes of the seated ladies.

"Take these fine examples," Lady Wimbly said. "Each of these young men are recently finished from their retraining at St.

Emmanuel's and have all the skills required to be in service for the most illustrious households in town, and in the country."

Audrey took a quick glance of the footmen in her line of sight. To be in service to a fine family was a highly coveted and respected position among the working classes. It was no small thing to be a lady's maid or footman, a valet or a butler. In fact, Greer's entire family had been in service for generations, and hers was a common story. Even scullery maids and chambermaids, the lowest among the service ranks, worked with pride. These men had been given a second chance at making a living wage, and while Audrey was happy for it, it also left her feeling slightly discomfited. Perhaps it was the smugness of Lady Wimbly's tone, or the simpering looks being passed between some of the other ladies, as if these men should be indebted to them for their great opportunity.

"Even my Auggie has taken on a new valet of extreme poise and competence," Lady Wimbly said, then tittered laughter. "I must admit, I've never seen him in such a well-tied cravat before!"

Polite laughter echoed down the table, though Audrey couldn't bring herself to join in. Auggie. Did she refer to Wimbly?

"How is Lord St. John?" a woman down a few chairs asked. "He must have just finished at Oxford?"

"With top marks," Lady Wimbly replied.

Auggie, her son. But of course. He and the marquess shared a given name. The conversation turned to doting on Lord St. John, and Audrey could only be grateful. The less they spoke of Philip or Mr. Marsden, the better.

The luncheon concluded after a desert of spiced rum pudding. Restless to leave and put this whole farce behind her, Audrey caught Genie's eye when the ladies retired to the glassed-in conservatory at the rear of the manor. Despite the gray sky outside, the air within the conservatory was humid and heavy with perfume. Genie, locked into a conversation with Lady Shoreham, pleaded with Audrey with a widening of her eyes. *Patience*, it seemed to say.

She accepted a glass of champagne from a footman, one of a handful circling the pink marble floor, weaving between white-painted iron garden chairs and tables and sharp fronds of potted palms. No one approached her; in fact, there seemed to be an invisible barrier at least a few feet thick surrounding her. How ironic. Before, when she and Philip would attend parties, the crush around her would be so tight she'd often need to find an open door or balcony to escape for a breath of air. She'd hated it, but this, she thought she might hate more.

Audrey sipped her champagne and pretended to observe some of the tropical flowers Lady Wimbly's gardener had cultivated and cared for while she took surreptitious steps toward Genie, whom she fully intended to interrupt. As she walked along, the toe of her slipper bumped into something on the floor. The sound of metal raking along the Italian marble tiles echoed through the conservatory. It startled Audrey and drew eyes, but after a moment, she went on being disregarded.

Looking closer, she saw her toe had shoved something silver between two terracotta pots. Audrey bent at the hip and saw a *fleur-de-lis* crest stamped into the handle of what appeared to be a silver utensil. The same design as the ones lain out on the dining room table at luncheon. Odd. She reached for it—and the conservatory vanished down a dark and narrow tunnel.

The vision was sharp and swift. Pink marble flooring; the bottom half of a woman's vibrant blue gown with intricate floral embroidery; the flash of a footman's gloved hand holding a silver carving knife; and a woman's hissing voice: *"Fellow! Put that knife down. Who do you think you are, threatening me? I told you to burn that letter! Don't you know what it could do to me, should it be found?"*

A man's mumbled reply: *"It's tucked away safe."*

The angry woman again: *"You fool! You're trying to blackmail me?"*

"Your Grace?"

The narrow tunnel disappeared as Audrey released not only the silver utensil but her glass of champagne too. Both clattered to the marble floor. The glass flute cracked, champagne frothing over the tiles.

She craned her neck to look up and winced at the break of sunlight coming through the glass walls. Her eyes teared quickly. Lady Wimbly stared down at her with a look of distaste and embarrassment. Through her hazy eyes, Audrey noted the peacock blue dress the marchioness was currently wearing, the pattern of violets embroidered along the hem. It was the gown from Audrey's vision.

"You needn't pick that up, you know," she said as Audrey straightened her legs and stood, her head going a little light. "It appears one of my staff has misplaced a piece of silver, and they shall clean it up. Good heavens, Your Grace, you look rather pale."

Audrey cleared her head with a little shake. "No. No, I'm perfectly fine. I wasn't sure what I bumped into, that's all..."

Lady Wimbly shot a severe glare at the nearest footman.

"'Pologies, Your Grace," the man said but his voice wasn't the one from the vision. It wasn't at all cultured or refined, as all of Audrey's own footmen sounded, but it also wasn't husky.

Audrey cast a last look at the knife. Someone—one of the footmen—had been threatening the marchioness with it. What was in the letter Lady Wimbly wished for him to burn, and how exactly could it harm her should anyone find it?

"Are you certain you didn't cut yourself on broken glass? You look peaky, Your Grace." Lady Wimbly reached for Audrey's arm, but she staggered back. No more visions. She didn't think her mind could handle it.

"No, I'm fine. But I believe I should take my leave," she said, a bit breathless.

Genie came through the curious crowd of ladies, having peeled away from her conversation with Lady Shoreham at last. Her eyes were wide and alarmed, but she warmly thanked the marchioness for her hospitality as Audrey, much too abruptly, left the conservatory. She didn't suck in another breath until she reached the foyer.

"Audrey?" Genie said as she hurried toward her. "What happened?"

"I'm just a little dizzy," she answered. "The conservatory was too humid, don't you think?"

"I suppose, yes," she murmured as their cloaks were brought.

They waited outdoors while Genie's carriage was fetched.

"You're acting very strangely, Audrey," Genie said once they were settled within the carriage. "Did someone say something to you? I thought everyone was rather understanding. Cool, yes, but not cruel."

The only harsh comments made had been those about Mr. Marsden, which Audrey had needed to restrain herself from speaking out against. "No, I...I shouldn't have come."

Genie sighed and fiddled with her lace gloves. "It's my fault. I thought it would do you some good to be among our set again, and perhaps learn something useful for Philip, but...perhaps I was wrong. I'm sorry."

She smiled weakly at her sister-in-law. "And I'm sorry I forced you to leave earlier than the others."

Genie rolled her eyes. "Oh, don't be. It was insufferable, wasn't it? I'll arrange for a donation and that will be good enough."

Audrey murmured an agreement, but her mind had already turned back to the footman. There had been at least a half dozen in the dining room to serve them. Which of them had been the one to threaten Lady Wimbly with a table knife? She hadn't bothered to truly look at their faces. That both Miss Lovejoy and Mr. Bernadetto had been killed by a knife concerned her, too.

The air seemed to steal out of her lungs as a revelation struck her. *The knife.* Had the weapon Mr. Bernadetto been killed with been recovered? And had it matched the one used against Miss Lovejoy? The energy either weapon possessed would be like a confession, one the murderer had no idea Audrey could hear or see.

As far as she knew, items from Miss Lovejoy's crime scene were locked up at Bow Street, as evidence. If she could make her way into the closet that she'd seen Hugh Marsden closing and locking that first night when she'd been about to leave Bow Street, she could have a look through. Getting into the magistrate's offices should be easy. Getting into that room unseen, however, would be precarious.

It was a good thing she knew how to pick a lock.

CHAPTER SIXTEEN

It was just after two o'clock in the afternoon when Audrey set out for Bow Street. Genie had offered to have her over to Grosvenor Square for tea, but she'd declined with an excuse of indigestion—something she must have consumed at the luncheon. It wasn't entirely a lie. She did feel a bit ill, especially when she thought about the unexpected vision the silver knife had given her.

Plans formulated and dissolved as Carrigan drove her to Bow Street, and with growing unease, she realized there was little chance she would succeed. The magistrate's offices were a busy hub. A woman sneaking about would not go unnoticed.

As soon as she stepped inside, the crowd of men in the foyer confirmed it. She was immediately spotted.

"May I assist you, my lady?" a man with a copper beard and a crisp, black wool suit asked as he broke from the throng and approached her.

Audrey said the first thing that leaped to her tongue. "I'm here to see my husband, the Duke of Fournier."

The change in the man was subtle, but noticeable. He stiffened, and the warm, almost concerned expression he'd worn before, chilled.

"His Grace is not taking any visitors, Your Grace."

Audrey blinked, stymied. She couldn't simply turn around and leave—she had to get into that closet and search for Philip's things, and hopefully, the weapon. The earbob had not been enough; she should have come here days ago to read the energy of the other items within the box.

"I really must insist the duke be informed of my presence. It is urgent. Could someone go over to the tavern and alert him?"

The man's stony reaction wasn't a surprise, but it still bothered her. Using her rank to her benefit wasn't something Audrey had enjoyed the last few years. As duchess, she was, as her mother had once gloated, "a shark in an ocean of minnows."

Lady Edgerton had only been momentarily furious when Audrey broke the contract with Bainbury in order to accept Philip's proposal. Seeing her daughter wed to a duke quickly placated her. Not that Lady Edgerton had stayed in touch or accessed any of the social benefits that being the mother of a duchess gave her. Once freed of her commitment of raising her youngest offspring, her mother had been all too happy to retreat from motherly life altogether.

At last, the patrolman shifted his jaw, bowed tersely, and asked her to remain there while he *did her bidding*. The note of sarcasm wasn't lost on her. The group of men he'd been a part of before her arrival were discussing something in low voices, and one of the men was holding something for the others to see. None of them even glanced in her direction. Her heart swelled with anticipation and a touch of fear. She waited until the patrolman helping her had disappeared through the front door before slowly slipping into the corridor, just ahead.

For the moment, the narrow stretch of hall was empty. Audrey hardly took a breath as she hurried toward the white painted door Hugh Marsden had locked that first night. Reaching into her hair, she drew out the pins she'd speared into her tresses before coming to Bow Street.

A man entered the hall ahead of her. Audrey pressed herself against the wall and held her breath. Only by providence did he turn in the opposite direction, keeping his back to her. He continued on, disappearing into another room. Air shuddered from her lungs. She closed the last few yards to the door with a burst of quick steps, and, forcing her hand to steady, inserted the pins into the lock.

The locks at Shadewell had been ancient things, the tumblers inside easy to roll and release. This lock was a bit trickier. The risk of discovery pressed her to hurry. Audrey exhaled and closed her eyes. She focused on the pins in the lock instead of everything else swirling around her. The lock gave, and just in time. Footsteps sounded as did a deep, male voice.

With a gasp, Audrey darted into the closet and pulled the door shut behind her. Darkness cloaked her. It only seemed to accentuate the rapid beating of her heart. She pocketed the hairpins and removed the next items she'd anticipated needing: the same short candle and palm-sized tinderbox she'd brought with her to Jewell House the other night. This time, however, she had nothing but a small strip of wan light coming from the seam under the door to guide her hand.

After a few awkward tries, the jute in the small steel box lit, and she held the candlewick over it. The flame brightened the closet, which was large enough for two bookcases set against each wall. There was hardly any open space on the shelves; boxes packed them, along with loose files and toggled folios. Audrey held the candle to the closest shelf, where Mr. Marsden had placed the large box containing the things taken from Philip's rooms. She spotted it quickly and slid it free.

Crouching, she placed the box and the candle on the floor and wiggled off the lid. She didn't touch it for any longer than necessary. Instantly, she knew it was the correct box. A blood-stained shirt had been folded into a messy square. A pair of gold cufflinks Audrey had gifted to Philip their first Christmas together, rolled freely in the box; there was his top hat, a cravat splashed in blood, a handkerchief embroidered with Philip's initials. The items were not his alone, though. A horrible mess of ripped black lace, stocking garters, a short black, bone-and-steel corset, and a pair of black and red beaded slippers, were also inside. Miss Lovejoy's belongings.

But there was no knife. It might have been removed, perhaps to be shown as evidence to the grand jury? It didn't matter. There were other things here to hold. She looked to the cuff links again. Small, gold playing dice. Metal often held more energy than fabrics, and anyhow, what she needed was to see the apartment that night from *Philip's* point of view.

She quickly palmed them, knowing her time here, undetected, would be short. Closing her eyes, she breathed out, and let in the phantom like images.

The first few were sharp and clear: the boxing up of evidence, bloodied clothing being stuffed in, muffled voices of men. Pushing back further in time, Audrey saw Hugh Marsden crouching before her; he reached toward her face and snapped his fingers, his muffled voice asking, "*What's the woman's name?*"

Further, Audrey commanded, digging into the energy left clinging to the tiny playing dice.

The images churned up, weak and watery, like drowned silk. The glow of a fireplace, the polished mahogany of a chair leg. The angle of the vision was disorienting. Almost as if Philip was on the floor, on his side. Blurred figures darted into his line of sight—a man in dark trousers and a woman in a black silk dress. She was running from the man. She tripped. He reached for her arm and yanked her to him. Philip remained on the floor, unmoving. Unresponsive to the attack.

Audrey gripped the cuff links harder and forced herself to focus on the man in the trousers. His black jacket was bulky and ill-fitting. His face was still obscured, but he was tall and broad. The images were fading like mist. She needed more!

Light, bright and startling, flooded her vision, wiping it away completely.

Audrey opened her eyes and sucked in a breath. Standing within the wide-open closet door was none other than Hugh Marsden. He glared down at her, and Audrey's lips gaped like a landed fish.

"It appears Bow Street has been infiltrated by a peculiar breed of mice," he said, crossing his arms over his chest.

Audrey stood so quickly the blood rushed from her head. She swayed and her hand shot out to catch herself against the closest shelf. The cuff links she'd been holding clattered to the floor and rolled. Mr. Marsden crouched to retrieve them.

"I..." She had no ready excuse. He wouldn't have believed anything innocent anyhow.

"What are you doing in here?" he demanded as he stood tall again, the cuff links in his palm. He held them for her to see. "Are you taking these? This is evidence. You are not permitted to be in here." He stopped and drew back. "My god, did you pick the lock?"

He turned to view the handle as if it would tell him.

"I'm not taking anything, I merely wished to see Philip's belongings."

"You broke into the evidence closet. Do you have any idea—" He lowered his voice and looked over his shoulder. "Do you have any idea the trouble you are in?"

Sweat beaded along her back and neck. She had known the risk of being discovered, but she hadn't thought it would be Mr. Marsden himself to find her. Any other Bow Street official might have believed a silly lie and a bat of her lashes, or perhaps even an outburst of crocodile tears. But not this man. Curse it!

"I know it's impossible for you to understand, but I needed to see his things." Her mind tumbled over and over, searching for a plausible excuse for why. She found nothing but more dizzying panic.

"For what reason?" He stepped into the closet. "What is it you are stealing?"

She glared at him. "I already told you, I am not stealing!"

"Forgive me if I don't believe you. I find you pilfering through your husband's evidence box, his cuff links in hand, and you expect me to think you are doing nothing illegal?"

"Yes!"

Men's voices sounded down the hallway. Swearing an oath under his breath, Mr. Marsden came into the closet fully and shut the door. Audrey's candle still burned, thankfully. The small sphere of light danced shadows over his face.

She frowned. "What are you doing?"

"Providing you another moment to make your confession. Refuse and I'll have no choice but to place you under arrest." He angled his head, the shadows of his brows pointing devilishly. "How would that appear to the ton, I wonder. Both duke and duchess arrested within the same week."

Audrey could not believe this man! The utter gall. "You cannot arrest me for wanting to see my husband's belongings!"

"I can arrest you for breaking and entering, and for disturbing evidence from a murder."

She held his stare, searching for any indication that he was exaggerating. He didn't so much as flinch. He couldn't possibly... wouldn't possibly...would he? Mr. Marsden had more than convinced her that he didn't give a pig's knuckle about propriety or the importance of rank. He was more than happy to shock and awe. With a sickening sweep of dread, she realized that he would indeed arrest her. He'd probably have a fine chuckle and a celebratory finger of whisky afterward, too.

"I can't tell you," she whispered, her heart dropping.

"Then you leave me no choice." He turned and reached for the door. Audrey leaped forward, and without an ounce of grace, grabbed his arm. She yanked him toward her. The suddenness of it caused them both to lose their footing. Audrey slammed against the shelves, Mr. Marsden colliding into her.

"Jesus, woman!" He grabbed hold of her waist, but then, with another muttered oath, flung his arms back, as if burned.

"Please, just listen!" she said. He stared at her, still close enough for Audrey to trace his scent. Oakmoss and vanilla. She inhaled and closed her eyes, struck by the warm intoxication of it.

"I am listening," he said, his voice a low rasp. "Do not hedge or attempt to lie."

She fluttered her lashes, trying to expel the warmed vanilla scent of him. Over the last few days, she had become accustomed to his presence, to his severe mood and his exasperated tone; however, she'd also seen a lighter side to him, a dry, sarcastic wit. Concern when he thought her to be in danger. Now, he was nothing if not deadly serious. If she wasted his time, he would snap.

"You know my husband is innocent of the murder," she said softly.

Mr. Marsden's lips thinned. With visible reluctance, he nodded tightly. Audrey let out a shaky breath.

"What if I told you...there was something I could do to...to find the killer?"

His stare sharpened. "I have already commanded you to cease your investigation. After what happened with Bernadetto, are you so outright foolish that you would invite the killer's attention?"

"No, not that. It's something far less...obvious."

He frowned. "How do you mean?"

She went a bit unsteady. The closet was hot and stuffy. She couldn't possibly be thinking about admitting her secret, and to Hugh Marsden of all people! It had gotten her locked away at an asylum for two years. The last person she'd willingly discussed it with had been Philip. It had been one of the driving forces behind their marriage after all—he'd promised to keep her secret and in turn, she would keep his.

Mr. Marsden would think she was mad. He'd pull away from her. Look at her the way her mother had when Audrey had been seventeen and demonstrated her "special gift" with one of her mother's rings. The images Audrey had seen, however, had left her speechless. Her mother and her uncle, her late father's brother, had been standing much too closely in the study. When Audrey had narrowed her eyes and asked what was happening between her and Uncle Peter, her mother's porcelain expression had cracked.

Voices from the corridor filtered into the evidence closet. Both of them stiffened. Mr. Marsden must have known that if he were found here, in a closet, with Audrey, he, too, would be in severe trouble. One accusation from the duchess and his complaints about her trespassing in the closet would be moot. He already had a blemish—a dire one—on his past. It wouldn't take much to plunge him into another scandal.

However, the mere thought of lying about something so wicked, and hurting Mr. Marsden in such a way, made her feel ill.

As if he could read her mind and the terrible plot surging through it, he took a long step away. He tucked his chin.

"Perhaps I can loosen your tongue, Your Grace."

Audrey sucked in a breath at the kindling of mischief in his eyes. Hugh Marsden would not roll over and show his belly. He was ready to go to battle.

"I would need a very good reason to tell you my secret, Mr. Marsden, and I don't believe the peril of arrest holds weight any longer." She swallowed her doubt and eked out the rest. "The fact remains that I am a duchess, cornered in a closet by a man with a tarnished reputation."

Her throat closed around the greasy, repellent threat. It wasn't who she was. Mr. Marsden's nostrils flared. He stepped closer, apparently throwing caution to the wind.

"I'll give you a very good reason, viperous woman." Audrey

parted her lips, aghast at his hostility. "Right from the beginning, you've been so certain your husband had not taken a mistress, and now, I understand why."

A hollow space opened in her chest. Mr. Marsden's wicked grin stretched wider. "He has a lover. A man. They were seen."

A coldness spread throughout Audrey's body, and yet her palms began to sweat fiercely. Her heart skipped. Breaths came slowly, sporadically. How had he discovered the truth?

"No one will believe you," Audrey whispered.

Mr. Marsden cocked his head. "Do you want to gamble on that?"

He looked so smug. Audrey longed to crack her palm across his cheek.

"What do you want?" she said through gritted teeth.

"The truth. You've been keeping something from me. I want to know what it is."

"And if it's just as damning as what you think you've discovered about His Grace?"

The short candle trembled in her hand. Hot wax spilled onto her skin, and she hissed. Mr. Marsden pried the candle from her fingers and held it while Audrey rubbed the cooling wax from her burned skin.

"I give you my word, whatever you tell me will go no further than my ears."

"Your word," she said, shaking her head. "You arrested my husband, you've fought me every step of my investigation, and now you threaten to expose him. Why should I trust *your word*?"

He raised the candle, and the flame brightened his face. "I don't want to see you hurt." His eyes held hers, steady and resolute. "So long as you follow the law, I won't allow harm to come to you, and I certainly won't be the one to bring it."

There was no cunning there. Audrey found she wanted to believe him. She *did* believe him. As irritating and arrogant and combative as Officer Marsden had been throughout the whole of this ordeal, he had never once lied. He had never once given her any reason not to trust him.

Audrey stared at the flame, her lips quivering. She was out of options. She needed help, and Mr. Marsden was the only one offering.

"I'll tell you."

He let out a breath, causing the flame to jump. "Thank you. But first, we need to leave this closet."

Mr. Marsden then put his lips together and blew out the candle. The closet plunged into darkness. Audrey drew up her shoulders, and the temperature in the closet grew to stifling.

When Mr. Marsden spoke, his voice seemed to vibrate the air. The small hairs along her arms and neck stood on end. "I will leave first. If the hallway is clear, I'll cough loudly. Come out. Meet me across the street at the Brown Bear."

There was nothing left to do but agree.

CHAPTER SEVENTEEN

On second thought, the Brown Bear might not have been the best place for a clandestine meeting with a duchess.

Hugh nodded toward two men seated at the bar, their red vests marking them as horse patrolmen with Bow Street. A few more street patrolmen said hello as he made his way to a corner table. The establishment watered and fed the employees at Bow Street on a regular basis, as well as held criminals unfit for Newgate, like the duke. Had he stopped to think, he wouldn't have suggested it. However, closed into the small closet with the duchess as he'd been, he'd hardly been able to breathe let alone think clearly.

How in hell had he tangled himself up in this mess?

He half wished Sir had never fetched him to the Jewell House. If only some other poor sod had found the Duke of Fournier bloodied and incoherent, he would not be saddled with the unruly, unrelenting duchess.

He slid into a chair facing the entrance—Hugh never sat with his back to a door—and watched for the lady in question. As soon as he'd stepped inside Bow Street offices, Hardwicke had flagged him down and grumbled about the uppity duchess's visit just moments before. Hardwicke had come to the tavern to see if the duke wished for a visitor, and when he returned, the lady had been gone. *Capricious chit*, Hardwicke had called her, but Hugh had known better. The woman wasn't flighty. Instinct drove him to the evidence closet, and sure enough, there she'd been.

A curl of unease worked its way through his gut at the thought of what might have happened had any other patrolman or clerk found her kneeling there on the closet floor.

A dark green silk hat bobbed into view outside the window, and a moment later, the duchess stepped inside the tavern. She hesitated, blinking at the smoky, rough interior and the workaday patrons congregating inside. Her lips parted as she searched the room, and Hugh's discomfort increased as every eye landed on her. Her blue gaze, slightly panicked, latched onto him, and she took a deep breath before coming toward his table.

"So much for secrecy," he muttered as she settled into the chair across from him. She sat primly, her back straight and shoulders squared, her chin lifted.

"You chose the location, not I," she reminded him.

"Let's not draw this out any longer than necessary." Hugh waved off the approaching serving maid. She raised her brow, as if affronted, and turned around. "Tell me."

He didn't want to threaten arrest again should she evade his question of what in hell she was keeping from him. The truth was, Hugh wouldn't have placed her into custody. He'd already arrested a duke—arresting the man's wife for hindering an investigation would have brought Audrey nothing but more ruin, and him, more scrutiny.

She gathered a breath, her lips thinning as she removed her kid gloves; her fingers trembled slightly. What was she so damn nervous about?

She propped her elbow onto the table and extended her forearm toward him, palm open. "Give me your fob."

Hugh frowned. "Why?"

She narrowed her eyes on him and sighed. "Just give it to me."

He pulled the fob watch from his vest pocket and unlatched the gold chain. "I suppose there's no risk in you stealing it. Though I did just catch you trying to nick a pair of cuff links."

He dangled the watch over her palm, a grin tugging at his lips as the duchess glowered at him yet again. She yanked the watch from his hand, closed her fingers around it—and shut her eyes.

Until then, Hugh had never noticed the color of her lashes. Pale blonde with a coppery sheen. They rested against her creamy skin as she continued to keep her eyes shut.

"Your Grace?" He darted a look around the tavern. A few curious stares were directed their way, though probably not because the duchess had decided to take a nap.

"Shhh," she replied. Then, "You went to see that man. Porter."

Hugh leaned forward, an elbow on the table. "You had your driver follow me?"

Her eyes moved behind her lids, as though she were watching something.

"It's a single room. Small. A greasy window," she said quickly. Her pale brows snapped together. "Bright green silk. He was stitching on beads. A costume?"

Hugh thought back to Porter's sad, fishy-smelling room. He had been sewing a bundle of lime green silk, yes. He stared at her, incensed. "Did you visit Porter after I left?"

She opened her eyes, which were equally heated. "Follow you? Carrigan took me back to Violet House, and well you know it. You probably even had me watched again." She slapped the watch onto the pitted table.

He peered at it, then her. "How do you know of the costume then?"

"I saw it." She pushed the watch toward him with her pointer finger. "When I held this."

Hugh picked up the watch and ran the gold chain between his

fingers. His mind raced, searching for meaning to what she said. "You saw his room because of this?"

She nibbled on her lower lip a moment, then released it. "Objects allow me to see things." She wouldn't meet his gaze. The apples of her cheeks flushed, and her breaths came short. "Things the object itself has seen. Think of your watch, for instance—it absorbs everything that happens to you. Every place you go, every person you see. I had to wade through the memories, of you finding me in the evidence closet, of you placing the watch in your pocket this morning. I had to find something that I couldn't possibly know, or guess at, to convince you I was telling the truth."

Hugh grappled for understanding. It was outlandish. Like a Romany tale coming from Gloria's lips as she lay beside him in bed, lulling him to sleep.

He sat still a moment, stunned and confused and quiet, before slipping the watch back into his pocket.

"You don't believe me," she whispered.

"I don't think you are lying," he said quickly. Then rubbed at his eyes. "I just don't understand what you're telling me, not exactly. That you can touch an object and see into its past?"

He lowered his voice when a man's ear at a nearby table turned toward them. The duchess straightened her spine, and Hugh could see her moving into a defensive position. She'd been reluctant to give up this confession. This *secret*...she'd held on to it closely.

"Yes. But it's not just objects. I could take your hand, for instance, and..." she trailed off, another blush rising along her throat this time.

"And what?" he urged. What was it that made her uncomfortable? The mere mention of holding his hand?

"Touching skin is more difficult, but sometimes, it will allow me to see an important memory, or what is foremost on a person's mind," she finished. Then added hastily, "I prefer objects. The memories are less emotional."

He leaned forward. "The cuff links. You wanted to hold them."

At last, her eyes lifted and met his. She nodded. "Philip was on the floor of his apartments when Miss Lovejoy was attacked. There was another man present, chasing her, but I couldn't see much more than a shadow."

His mouth went dry, his head started to pound. The duchess was not jesting. She believed what she was saying, and with mounting concern, Hugh realized *he* believed *her*. He sat back, arms crossing over his chest.

"There is no earthly way you should have known Porter was working on bright green silk," he said.

"If you wish me to prove it further, let me hold another object."

"Such as my hand?" he suggested, surprising himself at the quip. The duchess did not smile as he did. She hitched her chin.

"As I said, I prefer objects. They are better conductors."

Hugh recalled touching her arm in the evidence closet. He'd held her at the waist too, but the touch had been so brief. The thought of her ungloved hand slipping into his palm, or his fingers touching her skin elsewhere, momentarily tied his tongue.

"You said this could help find the real murderer," he said once he'd batted away the inappropriate image. "How so?"

Her back rounded a bit, as if in relief. "Well, something happened earlier today. I was at Lady Wimbly's benefit luncheon—"

"Wimbly?" With a flash of ire, the other night at the Seven Sins, and the hold the marquess had on Audrey's arm, came to mind.

"Yes, *Lady* Wimbly," she repeated. "It was a workhouse benefit. The footmen were from the workhouse, and one must have dropped a knife in the conservatory, and when I bent to retrieve it, I saw a most peculiar image." She stopped for a breath. "Lady Wimbly and a footman had an argument right before luncheon.

She accused him of trying to blackmail her by keeping something he was supposed to have burned, something that could destroy her."

Hugh shook his head. "What was it?"

She folded her hands, which were still gloveless, atop the table. "A letter." She leaned forward. "And he was threatening Lady Wimbly with the knife."

Hugh considered these fragments of information. None of this was evidence. It was only what the duchess's...*vision* had shown her. Nothing he could present to Sir Gabriel or the grand jury or any sane person in London.

"Do you see this footman? In your...in your mind?" he asked, uncertain what words to use.

She shook her head. "No, the memory was his, but if I could hold something of Lady Wimbly's—"

A hot coal inside him flared to life. "No. I don't want you going back to Wimbly Manor, not if she's employing a dangerous man."

"But if I could just see the footman's face, I might be able to tell if he is..." She let the rest of her sentence fade away.

"If he is what?" Hugh asked. When she hesitated, he added, "You promised the truth."

Her temper showed in the jut of her chin. She paused to collect what she was going to say, but Hugh already knew he wasn't going to like it.

"Miss Lovejoy's earbob. I found it the night you followed me into Jewell House."

The reckless visit had infuriated him. It was there he'd learned the Duchess of Fournier would prove to be a thorn lodged just under his skin.

"What did the earbob show you?" he asked. Then again, if an object revealed memories of the one who possessed it...

The duchess's flushed cheeks paled. "The murderer," she said tremulously.

Hugh tightened his jaw. "You saw his face?"

"It was shadowed, and the image was blurred, panicked. But...yes."

Had it been anyone other than a duchess of the realm seated across from him, telling him that they could see an object's memories, he'd have stood up and walked out. However, he'd spent too much time in her presence not to know she was firm minded and anything but fanciful.

"So, if I could access something belonging to Lady Wimbly—"

"No," Hugh barked. He checked his voice—eyes and heads turned in their direction.

"If you think this footman is involved, you're not to go near him," he finished in a near hiss. "I don't like where this is going. There are too many connections to Wimbly."

She frowned. "The marquess or the marchioness?"

"The heir as well," he replied. Then, because it no longer felt as enormous a secret as the one the duchess had parted with, the one he was still struggling to understand, he explained. "Miss Lovejoy was also mistress to young Augustus."

"Auggie?"

"Do you know him?"

She peered out the window, nibbling her lower lip again, as if thinking. "No, but the ladies were speaking of him today. He's just out of university."

"Porter said he attended many of Miss Lovejoy's performances. Father and son shared a lover." His gut twisted at the thought. "Though, I don't believe either of them was aware of it."

"I'm curious where Auggie was the night of the murder," she said, her eyes still hinged on the window. She seemed to be musing to herself, her fingertips tapping rhythmically on the table. They drummed to a stop. Audrey looked to him. "You could question him."

It couldn't be done, no matter how much he did wish to question St. John. "On what grounds? The inquiry isn't warranted—

I've already arrested someone for the crime, and the grand jury is sending it to the House of Lords."

If word spread that the arresting officer was now chasing down other leads, he'd be a laughingstock. It was damaging enough that there would be talk of his meeting with the duchess at the Brown Bear. He could say she was disgruntled; that she followed him inside, begging to see her husband. He could pretend to be vexed by her persistence—it wouldn't entirely be false. But Hugh knew his honor wouldn't allow it.

"Then I will speak to him," she said. "I'm certain I could find out where he is—"

"Absolutely not."

"Please stop interrupting me."

"Please stop suggesting ludicrous situations."

She slanted a brow at him. "What is so ludicrous about a duchess speaking to the heir of a marquessate?"

"Your very situation does—His Grace stands accused of murdering the man's lover," Hugh replied.

She hinged her jaw shut and took in a breath, rather than make another comment. Hopefully, she could see the wisdom in what he'd pointed out.

"Young Augustus has a penchant for the theatre?" she finally asked after a momentary silence.

"Apparently so." He could sense another plan forming in that crafty, belligerent mind of hers.

"I could finagle a chance encounter with him at the opera. If I happen to bump into him there, he could hardly snub me so publicly."

Hugh's immediate reaction was to say no again, but reluctantly, he recognized the possibility of such an encounter working in their favor. St. John's whereabouts the night of the murder would be illuminating. Even more important, though, was the letter St. John's mother had wanted burned.

"How do we know which performance he will be attending next?" Hugh asked.

The fact that he did not immediately trample her idea seemed to surprise her. The duchess was speechless for a few seconds.

"I can have my lady's maid make some inquiries. She has a cousin in Wimbly's employ."

"Servants chatter like magpies; if he is informed of your interest, he'll do what he must to avoid you."

"Greer is careful. I trust she'll know how to proceed."

He shook his head. "It's a bold move, attending the opera while the duke sits in custody."

A fine blush rose and fell from her cheeks, quick as clouds racing across an autumn sky. "I suppose society might regard it as callous."

"And you don't mind the gossip?"

She suddenly appeared weary, her confident glow fading. "Mr. Marsden, I am already ruined in the eyes of society, no matter what the outcome is. My only desire is to save my husband from the noose." She stood from her chair. "A little more gossip can't hurt me now."

She was right; scandal would stay attached to the Fournier title for at least another generation, perhaps longer. However, by all appearances, the duchess didn't seem distressed by that in the least. Her sole concern was for her husband.

"Admirable, Your Grace," he commented, ignoring an odd and quick pang in the center of his chest.

"Some would call it reckless and shortsighted," she replied with a sad grin.

Many would. He kept the thought to himself. "You'll let me know what your lady's maid discovers? Send word to my home, 19 Bedford Street, *not* Bow Street." He frowned. This meeting was not going to go overlooked and neither would a missive from the duchess.

She gave a tight nod. "I'll send word. Good afternoon, Mr.

Marsden," she said primly. The back of her green spencer jacket and the skirt of her day dress were his to admire as she turned. But then she paused and spun to meet his eyes again. She hesitated before taking a step closer to his side of the table.

"I thank you," she said softly. The words were so unexpected, he held his breath as she continued. "For not treating me terribly when I told you my secret."

Hugh sat back in his chair, uncertain how to reply. Uncertain about all of what she'd told him and demonstrated. He knew one thing, however: someone, at some time, *had* treated her terribly for it. He flexed his hands into fists and rapped the wood of the table.

"I can't say that I understand it. But you certainly have my attention, duchess."

A spark of surprise lit her eyes and she nodded daintily before turning to finish her exit. Through the window, Hugh watched a girlish grin stretch her lips as she walked away. He rubbed his chin, suppressing his own smile, before taking his leave.

If he was going to be attending the opera, he had some arrangements to see to.

CHAPTER EIGHTEEN

Like most of the upper echelons of the ton, the Duke and Duchess of Fournier rented a box at the Theatre Royal, at both Drury Lane and Covent Garden. They had mostly remained unused since Audrey and Philip had wed. It wasn't that Audrey didn't enjoy the theatre—she was captivated by the actors' abilities to assume a character's role and portray it with such convincing emotion. They made it appear so natural, so easy, all while more than half of the audience was busy chatting and looking around the room at who was present and who was not. That was what Audrey disliked about the theatre—the stage performance was never the reason any of them were in attendance.

Ironic how Wednesday evening, she was not in attendance at Covent Garden to watch the performance of *Artaxerxes* either. She had become what she disapproved of. She supposed, however, that if she could get a private moment with Lord St. John, it would be worth the hypocrisy.

Greer had made her inquiries at Wimbly Manor, where her cousin Bethany was a kitchen maid. Bethany's beau was a footman at the manor, and he'd reported that the younger Augustus had turned down an invitation to a dinner at Lord and Lady Granger's on Wednesday evening as he would be attending the performance at Covent Garden. Whether or not it was an excuse, or the truth, remained to be seen.

True to her word, Audrey had written the pertinent details on a slip of parchment, but before she could send a footman off with it to 19 Bedford Street, she glanced through the morning room window and spied another avenue of communication. She marched outside and across the street, to where an odorous young man of about eleven or twelve was attempting to hide behind a lamppost.

"Your employer is expecting this. Please deliver it," she told the boy, whose soot- and grime-creased hand accepted the note as if it were a dead mouse.

He'd gaped at her, speechless.

"Why does Mr. Marsden call you Sir?" she asked.

The boy straightened his back then and stuffed the note into his pocket. "He called me 'boy' at first, but when I told him I weren't no boy, he started calling me 'sir.' I says I prefer that, and it stuck."

She'd bit back a smile at Mr. Marsden's humor.

A response arrived that same evening, delivered by Sir to her back door and brought to Audrey by Greer. *I'll see you there*, was all it said. She'd set the slip of paper on her lap, running her fingertips along the inked words. She'd opened her mind, allowing the paper to show her the image of her kitchen maid, scowling at Sir as he presented her with the message, then further back, to the image of Mr. Marsden at a desk, folding the note and handing it to the boy.

She couldn't picture Mr. Marsden attending the opera. It was unlikely he even possessed the proper attire. Then again, he did employ a valet. With that thought, she'd asked Greer to bring her the most conservative gown she owned.

Her lady's maid had only blinked when Audrey explained it would be for the opera but had asked no questions. Instead, Greer made her opinion clear in the choice of dress: a deep maroon silk with black pearl trimming and not a ruffle or frothy bow in sight. As Mr. Marsden had said, with the duke about to go to trial for murder, attending the opera would be scandalous. A benefit luncheon was one thing. An evening at the opera was quite another. A somber gown would not dissuade the gossips from lighting London's upper crust on fire with the news of her outing, but at least she might appear solemn, attempting to keep a firm chin through it all, rather than celebratory.

She began to sweat on the ride to the theatre, despite the late April chill. Even during normal circumstances, she deplored having so many eyes assessing her, and tonight it would be an onslaught. If St. John was not seated in the Wimbly box across the theatre from her own for the first act, she and Greer, who had come as her companion, would certainly not stay past intermission. But that still left her with an hour or more to endure the endless stares and whispers.

Carrigan pulled into the queue of carriages and as soon as she was helped to the curb, eyes found her. Heads bent together and lips moved swiftly. She took a breath and cut her gaze straight ahead as she walked into the theatre, trailed closely by Greer.

"Would you like me to await you in the withdrawing room, Your Grace?" she asked. It was where the rest of the maids would be.

"Thank you, Greer," she replied. "Don't be alarmed if I don't meet you during intermission."

She nodded knowingly and departed. Audrey took the carpeted steps to the third level, where her box was located, and as soon as she entered, she closed the door and stood with her back against it. That had been a lot tougher than she'd suspected it would be. Not one person she'd passed had so much as nodded in greeting, let alone addressed her.

Attending Lady Wimbly's benefit luncheon had done nothing to repair her tattered status among the ton. Audrey was now a social outcast through and through. A part of her—a very large one—wished to flee. Just turn around, find Greer, and meet Carrigan in the queue outside. It would be easier. However, there would never be a time again when eyes did not stare, and mouths didn't whisper. Best to stay and see through the task she'd set out to accomplish.

Several frenzied heartbeats later, Audrey released a long breath and stepped from the shadowy recess of her private box, into the light. Faces turned in her direction, the most obvious ones from the long benches of the house seats below. After a thorough sweep of each row, where the lower gentry classes were seated hip to hip, her chest tightened. Unless he was running late, Hugh Marsden wasn't in attendance. Perhaps he hadn't been able to secure a ticket after all.

No matter. Audrey could accomplish her goal with or without him. She peered across the house floor to the partitioned private boxes, stacked five high, a dozen to a row. Most were filled with their occupants, including the Wimbly box.

A young man sat with an insouciant slouch, as though already bored, surrounded by two ladies and two men. A chime of recognition echoed in the back of her mind. She had seen this young man before, though not at any of Lady Wimbly's parties. He had dark hair, the style a bit long to accentuate the soft curl of it. He was handsome in a refined and haughty sort of way. Beside him, Audrey recognized Lord Ashbrook, the heir to an earldom, and his sister Lady Mary, but the other two guests were unfamiliar. They all seemed merry, except for St. John.

His attention drifted toward her box. She quickly cut her eyes away, not wanting to be caught staring. But then, she startled as her eyes met with a person who had already been looking at her. He sat in a box on the second level, in a fine black suit and a snow-white cravat. Hugh Marsden held her stunned gaze, the corner of his lips resisting an amused grin.

Audrey snapped her parted lips back together, the momentary

lapse of decorum embarrassing. What on earth was he doing in Lord Lindstrom's private box? The man seated next to him wore a suit just as stylish and bespoke as Mr. Marsden's, though he was unfamiliar. Lindstrom, a marquess, had a handful of sons. This might have been one of his spares, since it certainly wasn't his heir, Lord Chandler. Audrey quizzed the Bow Street officer with a frown and a widening of her eyes as she shifted them toward his companion, but of course, he had no way of explaining just now. It didn't matter anyhow, she supposed. He was here as he'd said he would be, and at intermission, she would make it her mission to bump into St. John.

Looking up at his box, she was again put off her guard to find the young man staring at her. She drew in a sharp breath and forced a gracious nod of her head in acknowledgement. St. John's expression was flat, unaffected, and yet the way he shifted his gaze toward the stage without recognizing her greeting, hinted at tension. As if he was unsettled by her presence.

Perhaps Greer's cousin hadn't been as circumspect as Audrey had hoped. St. John might know that she was here for him, not the performance.

The orchestra in the pit below had started to warm their brass and strings, and finally, were ready to begin. As the stage filled and the music and voices rose toward the muraled plaster ceiling, Audrey stole quick glimpses toward the Lindstrom box, then the Wimbly one. St. John seemed to be totally devoted to the performance, while his companions whispered and laughed together. It was as if he was doggedly trying not to meet Audrey's eyes again. Although, it was just a suspicion. She had no earthly idea what was going through his mind, or if her presence even registered.

On the other hand, she and Mr. Marsden clashed eyes time and again. Whenever she caught him watching the performance, his expression was as bored as St. John's.

Feeling ill with agitation, the minutes slowly ticked forward. Finally, the first act concluded. Intermission was upon them.

Audrey stood, palms damp within her maroon gloves. With what felt like a stone in the pit of her stomach, she left the private box and made her way to a refreshments room on the second level. A bell would signal them back to their seats for the second act in thirty minutes, and until then everyone would bombard the large room for punch and sweets.

As expected, the throngs of operagoers were thick, the air humid and close. Perfume and cologne filled Audrey's nose as she entered the long room, alone. And good lord, she'd never felt more alone than she did right then. Once again, eyes settled on her and bodies shifted away, as if just by being in her presence they, too, would be tainted.

She maintained what she hoped was a regal, unaffected expression as she whisked a glass of champagne from a table. Her eyes darted from person to person as she sipped, skating over the looks of censure, awe, and pity. After a few minutes of mounting unease, she saw St. John within a small grouping of people near the refreshments table. He stood tall, his chin lifted, hands clasped behind his back as he observed the conversation around him without participating.

Audrey sipped her champagne and made her way toward him. She wasn't stealthy enough. He caught a glimpse of her approach, and his eyes widened with poorly masked alarm. A memory slammed into her then. While walking through Hyde Park, near the Serpentine with Genie just a few days before, he had been picnicking with friends. He'd been wearing a linen suit and boater hat and had quickly turned away when he and Audrey had met eyes.

Just as Mr. Marsden had said he would, St. John now made to avoid her. With a nod to those around him, he slipped to the right, behind another throng of operagoers. She narrowed her eyes at his attempt—as if it wouldn't only increase her determination.

She followed him, threading through the room while keeping her eyes on his back and the dark curls trailing below the silk brim of his top hat. At last, a woman stepped into St. John's path. At her sides were two younger versions of herself, and all three wore coquettish grins. Audrey hastened forward. This was her chance.

"Lord St. John," Audrey said as she appeared at his side. "I'm so happy to bump into you. I wondered if I might implore you to pass along my gratitude to your mother—" With artificial surprise, she belatedly gaped at the woman and her two daughters, as if she had not seen them standing there before now. "Oh, do forgive me. Were you speaking?"

The woman's false smile had been replaced with flared nostrils and a tight stretch of the lips that now only slightly resembled a grin. "Not at all, Your Grace. My daughters and I were...just moving on, weren't we girls? Come along. Good evening, Your Grace. Your lordship," she said and with a quick curtsey, whisked her daughters away.

Whoever the woman had been, she'd known the duchess on sight, and as Audrey had hoped, hadn't wanted to be in her company a moment longer than necessary. Gracious, the woman had not even taken the opportunity to introduce herself. She truly was a leper among the ton now, it seemed. And as St. John, the future Marquess of Wimbly stiffened at her side, she realized he, too, wished to escape.

"I will pass along your good words to my mother, Your Grace." He bowed and started to move away.

"I hoped to speak to you on another matter as well," she said quickly, stepping alongside him again. His agitation was palpable, though not like his father's had been at the Seven Sins. While Wimbly had been incensed, St. John seemed cagey. Eager to be away. She glanced up at him, and from this angle, noticed a small mole on the side of his left cheek. For a moment, she forgot what she was about to say.

"I believe I can speculate on what matter you refer to," he said, keeping his voice low.

She blinked, distracted. "I believe you can," she agreed.

"I have nothing to say," he said, his eyes skipping around, landing anywhere but on her.

"I only wish to know more about Miss Lovejoy and how she might have come to be at His Grace's apartments that night." She expected him to snort and say something along the lines of *Isn't it obvious?* Instead, he kept his jaw firm, his expression glacial.

"She was not his mistress, but yours," Audrey added.

St. John huffed and shook his head, eyes rolling toward the ceiling briefly, as though he'd liked to have denied it.

"Was she not?" Audrey pressed.

He faced her fully. He appeared much like his father then: irritated, pushed to the edge of anger. Still, there was a note of panic in his voice when he all but hissed, "You are dallying with a situation you don't know the first thing about, Your Grace. I believe Fournier would wish you to step back and let things alone."

She peered at him. The way he called Philip 'Fournier' rather than 'His Grace' gave her pause. Had he and St. John been acquainted?

"What would you know of my husband's wishes?"

The younger man straightened his back, composing himself. "Any respectable man of quality would not wish for his wife to be conducting herself in this fashion. You are not with Bow Street, Your Grace. You are a duchess."

He sounded like Hugh Marsden now—at least, it was how the officer had sounded when she first started searching for the truth. Thinking of him now, she cut her eyes from St. John's and searched the crowd.

"I have information that Bow Street has been dismissing," she said, if only to tempt St. John out of stalking away from her. When she failed to spot Mr. Marsden and turned back to the young man's eyes again, she startled at his pointed glare.

"What information?" he demanded. Intensity rolled off him, practically slapping Audrey in the face. She blinked, and when she didn't respond, he stepped closer. His height pressed down over her, and his cheeks flushed.

"What are you aware of?"

"Tell me where you were on the night of the murder, and I'll impart some of the knowledge I possess." It was a gamble, one made before she could think. What information *did* she have to give him, other than what she had gleaned from the few objects she'd held? The earbob, the cuff links, doorknobs, and newel posts.

"You want me to tell you that I was there? That it was I, not His Grace, who killed Belladora?" He snorted in derision and continued to speak, though Audrey's ears grew muffled as at last, the memory came together. She knew where she had seen St. John and his noteworthy mole before.

"I'm sorry to disappoint you, Your Grace, but I was with friends that evening. We went to a boring soiree and then to Vauxhall for a bit of real fun. Hunt them down and badger them with your questions if you're so inclined."

St. John turned on his heel—and collided with Hugh Marsden. The two men staggered, feet tangling, arms reaching out for purchase. It caused a burst of commotion, which was readily observed by those around them.

"Good God, man!" St. John finally freed himself of Hugh's clumsy grip and tugged the lapel of his jacket. Audrey narrowed her eyes on the officer, who was just about the least clumsy person she'd ever met.

The man Mr. Marsden had been sitting with in Lord Lindstrom's box clapped St. John on the shoulder and gave a hearty chuckle, flashing straight white teeth. "Forgive my friend, St. John. He isn't accustomed to these sorts of crushes."

St. John straightened his cravat, his already peeved expression souring more. He ignored Mr. Marsden entirely. "Thornton," he said. "I don't usually see you at these productions."

Mr. Marsden met Audrey's dubious gaze briefly as his friend,

Thornton, rumbled laughter. "You could say I'm expanding my cultural horizons."

Thornton's grey eyes landed on Audrey. He made a short bow before turning his attention to St. John, clearly waiting for an introduction. To speak to her before one was made would be considered rude, and this Thornton fellow clearly knew as much.

Reluctantly, St. John cleared his throat. "May I introduce Her Grace, the Duchess of Fournier. Your Grace, this is Lord Thornton, son of the Marquess of Lindstrom."

Lord Thornton bowed again, this time more deeply. "A pleasure, Your Grace."

Audrey canted her head, keeping her eyes hinged on Mr. Marsden, who had seemingly recovered from his awkward drunken sprawl.

"Still keeping questionable company, Thornton?" St. John muttered, taking a cold glance at Mr. Marsden.

"I pride myself on it," Lord Thornton replied lightly, grinning. He turned to Audrey. "You and my friend have met, Your Grace, I'm aware."

"He arrested the duke," St. John nearly growled. "You're beyond the pale bringing him among us, Thornton."

"I was simply doing my job," Mr. Marsden put in.

"Your job," he snorted, dismissively. "You are a reprobate. Good evening, Your Grace. Thornton." With that, St. John slipped away.

Audrey watched him go, brimming with excitement. St. John's anger over the arrest of the duke had been the lynchpin in her theory.

Lord Thornton whispered something in Mr. Marsden's ear, then with an assenting nod, he withdrew as well.

"I assume you don't wish to stay for the second act?" Mr. Marsden asked her.

Numerous eyes bored into her back, and heat swamped her chest. Here she stood, conversing with the man who arrested her husband. Audrey could only imagine the tsunami of gossip about to flood London.

"I am fetching my maid and leaving." She turned on her heel and stormed away from him.

It had to be done, for appearances sake—something she hated, especially considering she would have much rather told Mr. Marsden what she had just discovered: St. John *had* been at Jewell House that night. He'd been the very last image the doorknob to the building had shown her, the murky and smoky energy dissolving into nothingness as St. John barreled down the stairs. She'd noted the mole on the unknown man's cheek then but had promptly forgotten it and him—until tonight.

Greer was waiting for her in the receiving room. The maid only had to see Audrey's expression to know that they were quitting the opera.

The brief ride home was utterly quiet. Greer's discomfort and curiosity and Audrey's muddled thoughts mingled to create a black storm within the carriage.

St. John had fled Jewell House before the body had been discovered. Before the murder, or after? She tried to recall whether he'd had blood on him in her vision, but the energy had been evaporating; she had barely been able to make out his face. The only thing she was certain of was that he knew more than he was claiming. Also, whatever Lady Wimbly had wanted the footman to burn was evidence that might implicate her son—and exonerate Philip.

When she and Greer finally stepped through the front door to Violet House, Audrey only wanted a finger of whisky and a hot bath before slipping into bed and sleeping for a dozen hours. Like a turtle, drawing its head into its shell, Audrey wished for solitude. She wished for the whole world around her to stop and hold still for as long as it took her to know how to breathe again. To know how to piece together what to do next.

Unfortunately, Barton announced a visitor just as he was removing her cloak. She whipped her head toward him.

"A visitor?"

"The officer from Bow Street. He insisted on seeing you, Your Grace, though I threatened to throw him out into the mews if he so much as set one boot—"

Audrey held up her hand. "Where is he?"

"In the kitchen, Your Grace. Shall I get rid of him?"

She closed her eyes, exhausted. But if he had come here at this late hour, after that fiasco at the opera, it was for a reason. "No. Show him to my study."

"That room is unprepared," Barton replied, sounding sorry for it.

"I will light a few lamps," she said, brushing off her butler's concern.

"Will you want tea, Your Grace?" Greer asked.

"No, thank you. He won't be staying long."

Audrey started for the small room on the first floor. Philip's study was far larger, and much more masculine, in comparison. Audrey's study had been done in soft blues and greens and creams, the furniture a honey oak rather than dark mahogany. It suited her, and it was the one room in all of Violet House where she didn't entertain visitors.

Why she'd told Barton to send Mr. Marsden there perplexed her. If she saw him in her study, it might not feel like a true meeting. Or perhaps it was only that the room would feel isolated from the rest of the city, set as it was at the back of the house, the drapes drawn. No one would need know Mr. Marsden had visited at all.

She arrived at the darkened room at the same time as a footman. Two lamps were glowing, a third wick being brushed with a flaming taper when Barton's knock rapped the closed door. He opened it, and with great displeasure, announced her visitor.

"Officer Marsden, Your Grace."

The footman placed the glass chimney onto the lamp and turned up the wick. Mr. Marsden stepped inside, still wearing his opera attire, though the cravat had loosened a bit.

"Thank you, Barton. Stephens. You may leave us," she said, though she knew the butler and footman would not go more than a door or two down the hallway.

Mr. Marsden waited until the door snicked shut, then whistled. "He doesn't like me."

She crossed her arms. "Calling so late at night is unseemly."

The officer rubbed a hand along his jaw as he glanced around the room. "Especially after we ran into one another at the opera."

"Yes. Especially," she bit out. "Mr. Marsden, why would you cause such a scene, bumping into St. John the way you did?"

He unbuttoned his jacket, and she noticed the gloves he'd been wearing at the opera had come off. He reached one unadorned hand into his waistcoat pocket. "To obtain this."

A gleaming gold pocket watch appeared in his palm. He let it drop, catching it by the chain. As Audrey stared at the object, understanding reaching her slowly.

The ungainly stumble. The tussle of arms and hands. Hugh Marsden had *stolen* Lord St. John's pocket watch.

CHAPTER NINETEEN

"You picked his pocket?" Audrey asked, her jaw loose.

"I'll return it somehow, but I recalled you saying that objects are easier to...see into." He looked and sounded uncomfortable, but as she realized what he'd done and why, a vise closed around her throat. When she spoke, her voice was raspy.

"How do you know I didn't convince him to tell me what he knew?"

He propped a brow. "The pair of you looked ready to do battle."

"Well, it just so happens I learned a great deal from my discussion with him," she said, and then proceeded to tell Mr. Marsden what she had remembered from her earlier vision. Proof that St. John was at Jewell House, that Lady Wimbly might be trying to protect his involvement somehow, and that the letter she mentioned could have grave consequences.

"Not proof," he said after a moment of consideration. "This information isn't tangible. It's not proof unless I can hold it in my hand." He held the pocket watch out a little farther. "Tell me what it shows you."

The round watch ticked back and forth like a pendulum. Her eyes followed it. Apparently, Mr. Marsden intended to view her as she read the object.

The beating of her heart was unsteady, her arms quivery as she stepped forward to accept the offering. The warm gold met her fingertips and she inhaled, opening the door to the first memory the object had to show her: her butler's incensed visage, sneering at Mr. Marsden. Audrey pushed back, peeling her way through clear images of his ride to Violet House, to the busy refreshments room at the opera, to the lush hallway at the theatre. This image was a bit foggier, having been layered over with newer ones since. But all was still visible. St. John, following the tall, proud Lord Ashbrook, his sister Mary on his arm. Ashbrook, glancing over his shoulder. His dark brown eyes meeting Audrey's—or rather, St. John's. A slight curve of his lips; an assessing sweep of the lord's figure, from crown to foot before facing forward.

The grainy memories fell apart completely. There was nothing now but black fog. She sighed and her study filled her vision once again.

Mr. Marsden stood with his arms crossed. "Anything?"

She ran her finger over the watch case cover, the etching simple. It appeared to be a clover.

"I'm not sure," she whispered, uncertain if she should voice her suspicion about Lord Ashbrook. The look he'd given St. John had not been one of friendship, but of lust.

Philip had always said that there were many men like him in London, and the world over. More than anyone liked to let on. Being attracted to the same sex was like an invisible flag that he carried and only others like him could see. Philip swore up and down that his great aunt Marta had carried on a love affair with her best friend Lavinia for decades under the guise of two old maids living in the country together. Theirs was not an unusual story either.

Mr. Marsden stepped closer. "What was it?"

She snapped to attention and held the watch back out to him. "I saw things from tonight, at the theatre."

He accepted it by its chain, then dropped it back into his pocket. "Nothing more?"

"The further back I push in time, the dimmer the images become, I'm afraid."

He was disappointed; Audrey could see it in the deep breath he gathered before attempting to straighten his cravat. She considered staying silent about Lord Ashbrook. Hugh knew about Philip's secret now, but it didn't make speaking about intimacy of any kind more comfortable.

She started out with, "What do you know about Lord Ashbrook?"

Mr. Marsden paced away from her, toward the fireless hearth. "He is the second son of a viscount, but when his elder brother died a few years back in a carriage racing accident, he became heir. Why?"

Audrey nodded. She recalled the carriage accident now. The tragedy had garnered much attention that summer.

"He was with Lord St. John tonight." She hesitated before adding, haltingly, "Something makes me wonder if perhaps Lords Ashbrook and St. John were...or are...carrying on a liaison?"

He had ambled toward the window, completely obscured by a heavy tapestry drape. He turned, his interest piqued. "What gave you that impression?"

She shrugged, the gown she'd worn that evening growing hot and heavy. "A look in Lord Ashbrook's eyes. A certain smile he gave St. John."

Mr. Marsden rubbed his jaw. "If you're right, another question arises."

She nodded, knowing where he was heading. "If St. John prefers men to women, then was Miss Lovejoy truly his mistress?"

"He could enjoy both men and women equally, could he not?"

he replied, giving her a pointed look. Flustered heat rose to the tips of her ears.

She moved toward a shelf of books to keep from looking at him. "Yes, I suppose."

A moment of silence ensued. A question was building in his mind; she could sense it through the thick, tense quiet.

"I take it that isn't the case with the duke?"

She ran her finger along a few of the books' spines. "It's how I knew for certain he couldn't be meeting with Miss Lovejoy."

Audrey was curious as to what she would see on Mr. Marsden's expression. Revulsion? Apprehension? Philip had once, he'd admitted to her, dreamed of acceptance from those he loved, like his brothers Michael and Tobias; but some of their disparaging comments about molly houses and buggery and unnatural acts had made it clear where they would stand on the issue.

However, society had rigid rules that required following. Walking outside the lines of those rules caused people to question your mental ability, your very soul.

Mr. Marsden walked the perimeter of the small study, hands in his pockets, brow furrowed. "He was meeting with another man at Jewell House. Might it have been St. John?"

Audrey had been slowly coming around to that speculation too. Philip had been meeting a man in those rooms, but not knowing who it was had been a kind of protection from the truth. Putting a face to the man was a different feeling altogether.

"I'm sorry if this is difficult for you," Mr. Marsden said softly.

She turned from the books in time to see his earnest expression. "Thank you." It was difficult, though perhaps not for the reasons he assumed. The infidelity alone did not injure her as much as Philip's keeping it a secret from her.

"I could ask Philip," she offered before anything more could be said.

He shook his head. "I'd rather you not come to Bow Street again."

Audrey parted her lips to argue that she would go wherever she pleased, but he continued, "We were seen at the Brown Bear together by some other patrolmen, and I've been fielding questions about your involvement." He cleared his throat and rocked back onto his heels a bit. "About *our* involvement."

"Oh." They *had* been spending more time than was proper together. More questions would surely arise after tonight at the opera, too. She eyed the drapes, thankfully pulled.

"I will speak to His Grace," Mr. Marsden offered.

"He won't tell you anything."

"I might find a way to convince him." He came toward her, his hands still in his pockets.

A bubbling of apprehension drove her forward, and she met him at the arm of the sofa. "With threats? I won't allow it."

He held up his hand. "No threats. You have my word."

Audrey drew back, uncertain. She trusted him, but how he planned to convince Philip to speak about his deepest, darkest secret, however, mystified her.

"Very well," she said. "I won't go to Bow Street. But Mr. Marsden, please, make it clear to him that you discovered it on your own, that I...that I wasn't the one who revealed..."

Philip wouldn't believe she would say anything. Would he?

He nodded. "I'll be clear."

A few seconds ticked by. It was time for him to leave. There was nothing more to be said, and yet Hugh breathed deeply and asked, "Indulge my curiosity for a moment?"

She shifted back on her heels a little, curious herself at what he might be about to ask. She could say no; bid him goodnight. He would turn to leave, surely. Instead, she nodded.

"Did you know from the outset? His feelings, I mean...before you wed?"

Strange. Audrey had never discussed this with anyone, except Philip, of course. But at this personal question, she felt like opening the door wider rather than slamming it shut.

Her heart beat faster. "Yes."

Surprise leaked over his expression in the barest twitch of his brow. "The duke saved you from a marriage to Bainbury, and you accepted him as he was."

Audrey pressed her lips thin, her defenses rising. "It wasn't as transactional as that. We were already friends."

At the time, she'd been accused of being a fortune hunter, of breaking a marriage contract to elevate herself in society and wealth. There were some who believed it had been a love match, and Audrey and Philip had certainly tried to exude that in the first year of marriage. Standing close, smiling at each other, Philip lavishing her with presents and adoration.

"Yet you knew he would never be able to give you his heart," Mr. Marsden said. It was a question posed as a comment; something she imagined he did regularly with those he arrested and interrogated at Bow Street.

She stepped past him suddenly regretful she'd been so accommodating. "You know nothing of his heart. Philip loves me, and I love him."

"Though differently than other married couples."

"What does that matter? There is nothing stronger than a marriage based on friendship and trust. That requires heart as well, Mr. Marsden."

Her voice had been steadily rising, and the sudden hush in the study now was startling. She took a breath, trying to calm herself as the officer mulled over her declaration.

He walked toward the door, where she'd thoughtlessly stepped. It seemed her mind had decided she was done with this conversation.

"I can't argue with that." He paused at the door and met her surprised gaze. "I only hope he is as devoted to you as you are to him. I'll take my leave. Good evening, Your Grace."

He slipped from the room. Audrey's lips gaped, her shoulders sagged. Devoted? Of course Philip was devoted to her. He'd made mistakes, had caused some pain, but had, for the most part, stayed committed to their marriage agreement—he would keep her secrets, and she would keep his; he would never require her to share his bed. They'd also agreed that should either of them take a lover, they would be honest and upfront about it. That had not happened, she knew now. He'd gone behind her back. But that didn't mean he wasn't devoted. Did it?

Audrey went to her room, but as she stripped out of her gown and sank into the hot bath Greer had prepared, Hugh Marsden's parting comment clung. It settled into her pores and refused to be scrubbed out.

IF IT HAD BEEN any crime other than murder, especially one so horrific as Miss Lovejoy's, the Duke of Fournier would have been released from Bow Street almost immediately. He would have been allowed back into the comfort of his home, free to leisure about with his daily routine while he awaited progress on the status of his legal case.

However, the magistrate had deemed His Grace too much of a risk, to himself and to others. There was also the high probability that the duke would abscond to the Continent to avoid trial. He had the means and the contacts to make it happen. So, he'd been locked up for the past several days. Still, the room above the Brown Bear tavern was a sight better than anything a commoner would have seen at Newgate.

Hugh climbed to the second level of the tavern, to where the duke was being held in his makeshift cell. A maid was being sent over from Violet House each day with a basket of food, though most of it was left untouched. The basket sat outside the locked door now, on the floor. The constable guarding the room had a will of pure steel to not have dug in himself already. Hugh lifted the parcel, heavy with biscuits, a small jar of honey, cured meat, and a hand pie. He knocked on the door, unlocked it, and shoved it open.

The duke was sitting upright on his cot, reading a book. His own clothing had also been delivered to him from Violet House and so he at least appeared clean and put together, though he'd left his collar undone, his sleeves rolled to the elbow. He glared at Hugh.

"What is it?" he demanded, as if Hugh had trespassed onto his ducal property. He bit his tongue against an inflaming reply.

"We need to speak." Without waiting for Fournier to agree, Hugh placed the basket on the otherwise bare table and pulled out a chair. He lowered himself into it.

"I have nothing to say to you," Fournier announced.

"It concerns the duchess."

As he'd hoped, the statement lured the duke to the table. His face tightened with concern. "What about her? Has something happened?"

Good. At least the man appeared to care for her wellbeing. Hugh gestured to the chair opposite his, and with a resigned sigh, the duke sat.

"What is this about?"

The man had no patience for preamble, and neither did Hugh.

"You should know that I've discovered what you were really using that apartment at Jewell House for." Fournier sat rigid, expressionless. "Her Grace said nothing. In fact, she went to great lengths to conceal the truth. About her own secret as well."

Now, the duke's steely-eyed glare changed. His nostrils flared and he sat forward, as if about to speak. But then, he sat back again, holding his tongue.

"She displayed her ability and explained how she's been using it to investigate Miss Lovejoy's murder," Hugh went on.

Fournier seethed. "She would never. Unless you forced her hand."

Hugh shrugged. "I may have persuaded her to come forward with it."

He slammed his fist on the table. "Leave her alone, Marsden. She has nothing to do with this."

It was the most the duke had said to him to date. Hugh wasn't about to relent now.

"Unfortunately, she has much to do with it now that she's cast herself as your liberator. Her Grace is determined to see you redeemed." He tossed aside the corner of the napkin covering the basket. "Biscuit?"

The duke ignored the blithe offer. "I don't know what you did to force her hand, but Audrey has suffered enough for what she can do. If you dare use this against her—"

"I have no intention of revealing her secret. Or yours, for that matter." Hugh removed a biscuit. "May I?"

The duke rolled his eyes to the ceiling and waved a hand. Hugh took a bite. Rosemary and salt exploded on his tongue.

"You really shouldn't let these go to waste," he said, mouth still full.

"I'm not sitting here to discuss biscuits with you, Marsden. Tell me what you want."

He thumbed the corner of his mouth and a crumb there. "Are you involved with St. John?"

The duke's fury vanished; his expression slackened, and he sat back in his chair, as if someone had shoved him square in the chest. He said nothing.

"St. John was there that night. I know because the duchess saw it in her unique way," he went on.

"What does it matter now? You have your man."

"The real murderer is still loose and has already killed again." Hugh rolled his shoulders, trying to release some tension. It didn't work. "Her Grace won't relent until he is caught. She could find herself in a great deal of danger."

He didn't reveal that she had been with him the day

Bernadetto was murdered, or that someone had been spotted following her. Diverting the duke's attention and focus wouldn't be wise.

"Don't pretend to care for my wife's welfare."

Hugh locked eyes with the duke, his pulse picking up tempo. "I aim to keep her safe—something you, at this moment, are unable to do." The duke seared him with a glare, but Hugh continued, "To do that, I need to know more about St. John's visit to your rooms that night."

The request hung in the air between them, as did the pointed insinuation that Hugh was better poised to protect the duchess. After a moment, Fournier's provoked expression changed: a softening of the lines around his eyes.

"What does it matter?" he shifted in his chair and quickly added, "He had already left."

Finally. The wall the duke had built around the events of that night had been breached. Hugh proceeded cautiously, aware of Fournier's extreme discomfort.

"Had St. John arranged for Miss Lovejoy to meet you at your rooms?"

"Of course not." The duke clenched his jaw. He lowered his voice. "We always met alone."

Audrey had made it clear women didn't tempt the duke, so a rendezvous between the threesome would not appeal.

"When did she arrive?"

Fournier rubbed his temple. "I don't know. St. John had left already, and I'd...I'd taken a dram of laudanum. We'd fought, you see, and I was on edge."

"What was the argument about?" Hugh leaned forward. "Miss Lovejoy?"

Fournier grimaced. "No, no. She had nothing to do with it. I knew, of course, that he was seeing her, but...it didn't matter. The issue was about his mother."

"The marchioness," Hugh murmured, recalling the duchess's report of an argument between Lady Wimbly and the footman.

"She'd grown suspicious of Auggie's outings and had him followed. We were discovered, and Lady Wimbly demanded that he end things with me."

"Did he?"

Fournier shook his head, eyes still hinged on the open door to his room. "No. But he didn't tell me about her demands; he kept me in the dark, and all the while Lady Wimbly was threatening to reveal what she knew. Finally, that night, he did say something and...I became angry. If I had known what she was threatening..."

"You would have ended things yourself. To protect the truth," Hugh guessed.

The duke gave a slight nod.

"Do you recall when Miss Lovejoy arrived?"

He sat back, less rigid than before. "I remember a knock on the door, and her asking what I wanted."

Hugh frowned. "How do you mean?"

"She seemed to want to know what *I* wanted her there for, but...I hadn't invited her."

"Are you certain St. John didn't?"

He glared. "I've already told you—he wouldn't have."

Hugh got up, restless to move. Now that he had the duke talking, he was less worried about another lapse of stubborn silence.

"Someone sent her to Jewell House. Or invited her," Hugh said. "Do you remember anyone else arriving? Anything of the attack?"

Audrey's vision of the attacker had lacked any defining details. Male. Tall. Broad. But her mention of Lady Wimbly's new footman, straight from a workhouse, strummed a connective thread inside Hugh.

Exhaustion paled the duke's face, the puffy skin under his eyes dark. "No. Nothing. I've been trying to remember, I truly have, but...

but the *laudanum*. I don't understand why it affected me as it did that night. I couldn't see, couldn't stand. It felt like my head was on a whirligig, spinning, spinning." He closed his eyes and buried his face into his palms. After a few moments, when he lifted his face again, his eyes shone as he held Hugh's stare. "I was right there, in the same room with her, when she was attacked. I did nothing. I didn't stop it. I couldn't. I might not have killed her, but I may as well have."

Fournier stood and pushed back the chair roughly, then paced away from the table. Hugh let him go. He wasn't worried about the duke making a run for it—it was more than evident that he was intent on blaming himself, even though he was innocent.

"Where did you get the laudanum?" he asked when the duke looked to be calming.

He crossed his arms and started back for the table. "Why?"

"It sounds as if it was tampered with. Something could have been added to it."

He shook his head fervently. "The bottle was in my coat pocket all evening. No one could have touched it."

"Not even St. John?"

The duke lashed him with another glare. Hugh took note of his blue eyes, his handsome looks. He attempted to envision the duchess on this man's arm and could not deny the odd satisfaction he felt in knowing that their marriage was not traditional.

"Are you suggesting he drugged me?"

"I think someone did," Hugh answered. "As for the timing of its effects, you must have consumed it while you and St. John were together, or immediately after."

The duke pulled out his chair again and sat, his gaze distant. His brow creased. "We each had a scotch."

"Poured from your own decanter?"

Hollowing disbelief spread over the duke's face. He rasped, "Auggie brought the bottle. It was from his uncle's distillery, up north."

"You are sure he drank from it as well?"

When the duke nodded, Hugh stood, restless to move.

"If he knew the scotch was laced, he wouldn't have consumed it," Fournier insisted.

"Or he might have and made sure to leave before the effects could strike him down."

The duke shook his head, resisting. He didn't want to consider the possibility that his lover had betrayed him.

"Someone sent Miss Lovejoy to your rooms, and I'm willing to bet it's the same person who wanted to be sure you were inebriated." Hugh took no comfort in what he was now realizing. "Your Grace, you were framed for this murder, and it looks like the Wimbly marquessate had a hand in it."

CHAPTER TWENTY

A visit from her brother-in-law the next morning was inevitable, Audrey knew, and sure enough, as soon as the hands of the clock reached the noon hour, Lord Herrick showed up on the doorstep to Violet House.

The chatter about her attendance at the opera the night before, and then the commotion in the refreshments room during intermission had fired through the households of London's ton, among servants, and even into the morning's scandal sheets. Her own home, however, felt like a tomb. Greer was more reserved than usual; her eyes avoided Audrey's. Barton, too, kept a solemn expression, though it might have just been residual annoyance for her unsuitable visitor late last night. While poring over everything that had been said between them, on reflection, Audrey had to admit Hugh Marsden had pushed boundaries. Inquiring about her relationship with Philip had been overstepping, but even more disturbing was how willingly she'd replied. Had welcomed the chance to speak about it, even.

Audrey was in her study, standing at the window with her arms crossed, gazing out onto the side lawn when Barton announced her visitor.

"Lord Herrick to see you, Your Grace. I've placed him in the front sitting room."

Better there than in the study. She'd made a mistake bringing the officer in last night; it was her sanctuary, and his presence within it had likely been the reason she'd let down her guard. Had she greeted him in the sitting room or morning room, like the rest of her callers, she would have kept the conversation direct and aloof.

As she entered the front sitting room now, Michael stood like a marble statue behind the sofa, his hat placed on a cushion. He clasped his hands behind his back, his chin held high. Audrey read his irritation instantly, and almost chose not to dismiss Barton; Michael wouldn't explode in anger with the butler watching. But knowing it was cowardly, she nodded to Barton, and he took his leave.

As soon as the door closed, Audrey spoke. So did Michael, and their voices overlapped.

"It's not as bad as you think."

"What in Hades were you doing at the opera last night?"

Audrey sighed. Even though she'd been expecting this, it was still frustrating that she had to form a lie. At least with Mr. Marsden, she didn't need to pretend.

"I needed to get out," she said lamely. Michael gave her a withering look.

"You've been out, Audrey. Numerous times, I'm told." He came around the sofa, his hands resting on his hips. She hated the flutter of unease in her chest. "You've been seen in the presence of that Bow Street officer too many times for my liking. Tell me what is going on."

Admitting that she had been conducting her own investigation into the murder would only lead to more of Michael's condemnation; she'd kept quiet about it for this very reason. However, now, instead of fearing Michael's reaction, she was aggravated by it. Didn't he believe in his brother's innocence? What had he been doing these last many days to help Philip? Other than looking into placement at an asylum.

Audrey squared her shoulders, no longer content to back down. "I won't apologize for refusing to hide away here while Philip faces a trial."

"How is your reckless behavior going to change anything?" Michael ran a hand through his thick black hair. Philip had received his mother's fair complexion, and Michael their father's darker one. He'd also inherited the former Duke of Fournier's angry pulsing vein down the center of his forehead.

She wished to blurt out everything: that she and Mr. Marsden were working together to find the real murderer. However, Michael would surely expire right there on the carpet if she admitted the unvarnished truth.

"Audrey, the gossip is rampant. Officer Marsden was at the opera last night and the two of you were seen in conversation. I've also had word from a friend that you joined him at a tavern on Bow Street; the two of you, alone."

Mr. Marsden had mentioned he'd been fielding questions since they met at the Brown Bear. She wished to know how he'd responded, if only so she could have some idea what to say to Michael now. Her mind turned up nothing but blank space. It did look terrible from an outsider's point of view. To be meeting with the man who'd arrested her husband was certainly suspicious. She should have been more cautious. Then again, if she'd been cautious, she never would have learned the things she now knew about the murder. *Still not enough,* she admitted.

"I have my reasons, Michael. I ask that you trust me. Everything is for Philip."

He looked ready to throttle her. "I have already ordered you to leave the legal proceedings to myself and Potridge, or do you imagine you have a better grip on the law than the barrister we have engaged?"

Fire leaped to her tongue. "And what has come of that? Philip is still being held and his case is going to trial."

The flare of insult and then anger in her brother-in-law's eyes stoked a bit of guilt. Lashing out at him wouldn't help her. He was doing what he thought best for his brother, and so was she...and yet, neither of them had managed to free Philip yet.

Michael paced away from her. "If you believe I am not hunting for something, anything, that can help my brother, then I wonder if you truly know me, Audrey."

More guilt dragged her stomach low. "I didn't mean to disparage you, or make it sound as though you don't care for him."

Michael nodded, as if accepting her apology.

"How do you plan to prove him innocent?" she asked, truly curious. She'd been so focused on her own methods that she hadn't stopped to consider what Michael, Mr. Potridge, and their engaged barrister had been doing up until now.

His hesitation, the way he only glanced back at her briefly, did not give her a good feeling.

"You must see, Audrey, that the evidence against him is substantial. If he were to plead to a bout of an unsound mind, a momentary lapse of sanity, he might be spared the noose."

The air in the sitting room went dry and thin; Audrey could barely take in a breath as she stared at Michael. Her temples pounded, her vision careened.

"You...want him to plead guilty?" she whispered. "You want him to say he lost his mind?"

"It is the best way forward," he said. "I've a lunch today with Lord Westborough, the House leader, to discuss Philip's immediate release into the custody of Gibbets Sanatorium. A stay there would certainly restore his mind and give the public some sense of peace—"

"Why would you do this?"

He peered at her with narrowed eyes. "Do what?"

"Give up on him! He isn't the murderer!"

Michael shook his head and reached for her arm. "I understand this is difficult, but the evidence is damning."

She jerked away. It was clear now. "You think he did it."

He hardened his jaw and thinned his lips. Her eyes stung and filled with tears. Philip's own brother believed he'd lost his mind and mutilated his lover.

She spun around, unable to look at him another moment.

"I know you've resisted going to Fournier Downs, but I must insist. If Westborough agrees to my terms, you should decamp before Philip is removed."

She said nothing but felt her heart toll in her chest. His immediate release, Michael had said. They would send him to the sanatorium right away? Today, even?

Michael took his leave when she refused to look at or speak to him again. Her mind spun, her breaths came quickly.

The night before, she'd promised Mr. Marsden she wouldn't go to Bow Street to ask Philip about St. John. She'd assented to him questioning Philip instead, and she was in twists wondering what he had learned. If only he would send a message or perhaps show up at the servant's entrance again. But how could she stand by and wait? Especially now that Michael was so close to having Philip released into the custody of a sanatorium. It was just a nicer word for insane asylum. Just as Shadewell had been.

She couldn't let it happen. Promise or no promise to Mr. Marsden, she had to find evidence against St. John or Lady Wimbly *now*. Before they took Philip.

The footman. He told Lady Wimbly the letter was tucked away safe, but surely not amongst his things at Wimbly Manor. The marchioness would have turned his room over to find it. Was he even living at the manor? Or perhaps he was back at St. Emmanuel's. If she could get a list of the men's names that the workhouse provided for the luncheon, perhaps she could share it with Mr. Marsden, and together, they could look for the one who had scratches to his face and neck. The odds were long, but it was all she could think of at the moment.

Audrey checked through the front window; Michael's carriage had already left.

"Barton," she called, and a moment later, the butler entered the room.

"Your Grace?"

"I'm going to my room. I don't want to be disturbed, not even by Greer," she said, then whisked from the sitting room.

No doubt the staff would believe she was sorely vexed by Lord Herrick's visit; surely Barton heard their raised voices and would pass along the order for privacy. Going to her room and wallowing there seemed a natural thing for a lady to do after such a distressing conversation.

No one, not even Greer, would know Audrey had left Violet House. It was best they all thought she was abed. Sneaking out to visit a workhouse would even alarm her devoted lady's maid. There was no other option, though. She had to find that letter, whatever it may contain.

She dressed quickly, choosing her plainest day dress, an olive linen with a puce spencer. The dress was still too fine for her to be mistaken as working class, but perhaps she would not draw too much attention to herself.

The adjoining door to Philip's room was unlocked, and once inside, Audrey went to the door, listening closely for any footsteps. Hearing none, she slipped into the corridor and to the servant's stairs at the back of the house. When no noise came from the stairs, Audrey took them quickly, pausing at the bottom, where they emptied into a hall off the kitchen. Voices drifted from the kitchen, but the washroom to the left was silent. She dipped into it, and the washroom door led to a minuscule courtyard. It was totally obscured by trellis and boxwood hedges, and Audrey walked toward the street without being detected. If Hugh had his young spy watching Violet House, he might not have even spotted her.

A hansom cab stopped for her along Curzon Street, and considering it was still daylight, she didn't worry as she had when she'd gone to Jewell House past midnight.

It took about a half hour to reach St. Emmanuel's, and still Audrey didn't quite know what she was going to say once she arrived. Only when she was stepping down from the hansom and paying her fee did some half-formed idea come to mind. Philip's imminent remittance to the sanatorium continued to drive her, and oddly enough, she didn't worry about her own actions as she approached the stone edifice of the workhouse. It looked every inch the penitentiary it was for the poor men, woman, and children inside.

Audrey brought the solid iron knocker down onto the wood door, one of a pair, and larger than the barn doors to her carriage house. A small square of metal slid aside, revealing a window and a man's face. The porter wore a hat and had a scraggly red beard, his skin underneath chapped and flaking.

"Wotcha want?" He peered at her as if she were no more than a fly on a horse's backside. As shocking as it was, it was also welcome.

"I am looking for the master here," she responded, attempting to sound firm. "It has to do with money due from the Marchioness of Wimbly's benefit luncheon."

She hoped the mention of money would open the door for her. The scraggly-bearded porter slammed the small window and then a moment later, the deep thunks of locks being thrown sounded. The door opened on massive iron hinges.

"This way, missus," the man said, and immediately started away.

Audrey hurried to keep up with him. The courtyard-like interior was packed with men dressed in striped shirts and caps. They were sitting on benches and stools, or directly upon the dirty, wet flagstones. A few were hammering stones to break them; some were working mortar with pestle, grinding some whitish dust. With a shudder, she noticed a collection of animal bones piled nearby. The men glanced up at her with sharp, assessing eyes. Some mean and desperate, others hopeless. Audrey quickly looked away, wondering how anyone at a place such as this freed themselves of these walls.

The man led her to an office, dim and smoky and smelling of a peat fire. Another man, equally scraggly, with a soiled shirtfront and stained underarms, sat in a chair, his heels upon his desk.

"What's this, Grover?" he asked, bringing down his heels as his eyes set upon Audrey.

"Lady says it's about money due to us," Grover, the porter, replied, unable to mask his excitement.

Audrey's stomach dipped; perhaps she should have thought of another excuse.

"I'm here on behalf of the Marchioness of Wimbly. It seems one of the footmen from the benefit luncheon she recently hosted is due a wage and left before receiving it. I am to locate him."

The pair of men quizzed each other with a glance, then shifted it to Audrey.

"What's his name, this footman?" the master asked.

Heat flashed up her back and out along her shoulder blades at this unexpected question—though she should have expected it. To be caught so unaware worried her. What more had she not taken into consideration? *Fool*. She'd acted rashly, out of desperation and panic.

Her mind scrambled to produce some answer. "That is, well... something of a challenge. You see, the butler cannot recall the man's name."

"Then how're we supposed to find him, eh?" the master retorted.

She licked her lips, more heat rising to her cheeks. "Perhaps if I could take a list of names back to the butler, he would recognize it."

The master spread his arms out. "I don't got no list of names, do I? Grover. Who do you recall went to this *soiree*?" He dragged out the last word as if it was an amusing joke.

The porter pinched his brow, as though thinking. "Billy Parker, Jim Gent, Charlie Harris I know went because he nicked a bottle of gin from the—" Grover caught himself and cleared his throat. "Well, never mind that. Let's see...Hobarth went and he said Fellows was there too..."

He kept listing names, but Audrey's attention snagged on that last one. Fellows. In her vision, Lady Wimbly had whispered, "*Fellow! Put that knife down.*" Audrey had thought the address odd at the time, but now realized she might have been calling him by his name. *Fellows*, not fellow.

"Fellows," she said, cutting off the porter. "Yes, I think that is him."

The warden frowned. "Thought you said you couldn't remember the name."

"It just came to me now, hearing Mr. Grover say it," she said lightly, adding in a giggle to appear even more vapid—and hopefully, easy to dismiss.

"*Mister* Grover. Ye hear that?" the porter said, rocking back onto his heels and pulling at his stained collar. The warden scoffed. "Fellows paid his debt and sprung from here a few days ago, miss."

"Do you know where I might find him?"

The workhouse master leaned forward, forearms flat on the desk, chapped hands clasped together. "The board of guardians hasn't seen no coin from the marchioness and yet Fellows is to get his first?"

"Oh, well, ah...Mr. Fellows was so competent that I am also to pass along an invitation to interview for a permanent position."

She could imagine Mr. Marsden, rolling his eyes at the weak

fib. The master sneered. "Fellows, eh? Must've turned over a new leaf, him."

The porter at her side snorted. "Fellows, in service to a fine house?"

The footmen on display at Lady Wimbly's luncheon had appeared rough, without the polish most men in service have, but something told Audrey that these men were doubtful for more reasons than just Fellows's appearance.

She cleared her throat. "If you wouldn't mind sharing where I can find him?"

"He's got a shanty now. Bragging about it, he was. The Jackdaw," Grover said.

A shanty? "And where does he moor it?" she asked.

The master sat back, no longer interested in her visit now that he knew she had no money for him. "The Thames of course, near St. Katherine's wharves. Ain't a place for a lady goin' alone, mind you."

Audrey exhaled, her chest expanding. "Thank you, I'll be sure to bring someone with me." She backed out of the office, eager to be on her way and find the person she did, indeed, plan to bring with her.

Within a minute of walking away from the workhouse, she flagged down a hansom.

"To 19 Bedford Street," she told the driver.

CHAPTER
TWENTY-ONE

The magistrate slammed his fist onto the desk and the boom echoed around the office.

"For Christ's sake, Marsden, you've already brought in a duke—now you want to take a marquess's son into custody?" Sir Gabriel Poston, chief magistrate at Bow Street, kept his fingers clenched into the fist.

"Not custody. I want to bring him in and ask a few questions about Belladora Lovejoy. He was her lover, after all." Hugh had spent a good hour after his discussion with the Duke of Fournier trying to figure how to untangle the connection with St. John in a clear way for Sir Gabriel, without exposing the duke's secret.

There was no doubt that should Fournier's affair be discovered, he would be tried and convicted for buggery and sent to an asylum or sanatorium—even if he was cleared of murder. Same sex affairs were illegal, and many considered those who carried them out to be not in their right mind. Just last year, Bow Street had raided a rumored molly house and arrested half a dozen men; under accordance of the law, they'd been sent to prison, a few of them clapped into the stocks and left to endure pain and humiliation as the crowds jeered and lobbed at them everything from rotten vegetables to dead cats.

Sir Gabriel leaned back in his chair, his stomach straining over the waist of his trousers. The magistrate was a lover of fine food, good wine, and comfortable chairs, and it showed. He'd taken over operations at Bow Street from his predecessor some dozen years before and could spot a lie like a hawk spots a mouse.

"There are no more questions needing to be asked, Marsden. Fournier's case is closed."

Hugh frowned from where he sat across the desk from the magistrate. "You mean it is moving ahead to trial."

Sir Gabriel exhaled. "I mean closed. He's a bloody duke. Lord Westborough has agreed to shunt him off north, to some asylum in the Highlands or some such. It's over. He's being escorted there tomorrow."

Hugh gripped the arms of the chair. "When was this decided?"

Sir Gabriel incised him with one of his legendary cold glares. He didn't need to respond for Hugh to know what he was thinking. That it didn't matter when it was decided or how, just that it had been and to let it go. Sir Gabriel never enjoyed dwelling on one case for too long; there were too many criminals and arrests to be made to spend much time on any one of them. Usually, Hugh was of the same mind. The more arrests he made, the better his living.

This was different though.

There was little he disliked more than admitting he was wrong, except, perhaps, having to voice it to his supervisor, his mentor. Sir Gabriel had trained him, shaped him into the officer he was. He could turn and leave the office right now. He could save himself the trouble and humiliation.

His conscience, however, stood firm.

"I believe the duke is innocent." The words rolled from his tongue and took with them a weight from his shoulders.

Sir Gabriel held still, his stare changing from exacting to stunned. "You what?"

"I brought him in for the murder, and at the time, it felt right. But I cannot deny the details of the case I've learned since then—"

"Details you've learned alongside the Duchess of Fournier."

The magistrate had his finger on the pulse of Bow Street; he knew what, who, when, and where, always.

"She has a vested interest in her husband's case," Hugh allowed.

The chief magistrate stood, his impressive height and bulk dwarfing Hugh and making him once again feel like a young, fresh-faced street patrolman full of doubt. "She is running in circles, Marsden. I've had a man on her for these last many days, and she has caught you up in her aimless foolishness."

Hugh snapped his eyes to Sir Gabriel's. "You've had someone following her?"

Unexpected ire bubbled in his chest. Audrey had seen a man outside Violet House and on her tail on more than one occasion. Perhaps not the murderer after all. Momentary relief snubbed out when he remembered he'd been shut out of an official part of the case. *His* case. "Why didn't you tell me?"

"I wanted to be sure the duke's wife wasn't somehow involved in his lover's murder, and your distaste for the upper echelons of society is well known," Sir Gabriel replied, guttering a laugh as if Hugh should've known the answer. "I didn't think you could be unbiased. Apparently, I was right, only it's gone in a much different direction than I anticipated."

Just as everyone in the duchess's set knew of Hugh's past, so did the men at Bow Street. It wasn't often they had reason to visit the homes of London's elite, but whenever they did, Hugh was not the man to go.

Sir Gabriel came out from behind his desk. Hugh met him at the corner. "What do you mean by a different direction?"

"You must cease this dalliance with the duchess before it ruins you."

"*Dalliance*," he scoffed. "It's nothing of the sort."

The magistrate held up a thick finger. "A cloud has hung over you since the duel with Neatham. Becoming mixed up with a duchess is throwing oil onto the fire, and well you know it. Bow Street doesn't need it. *I* don't need it."

Hugh wasn't naive—he knew how things would look. It was why he'd asked her to stay away from Bow Street. He'd be content to remain invisible to the ton for the rest of his life...just not at the duchess's expense. He couldn't walk away from this case when he knew she would not let it go until her last breath. Now that the duke was about to be released into the custody of some institution in the north, where he could be forgotten, swept under the rug... Once the duchess learned of it, she would panic. Do something reckless. *Again.*

"St. John is off limits," Sir Gabriel announced, his voice booming. Hugh could only nod. Arguing would earn him nothing but a desk assignment. Anyone who got on the chief magistrate's wrong side found themselves with a stack of files and paperwork no one else wanted to be saddled with.

Hugh quit the office and stormed down to the ground level, where his own cramped closet of an office was located near the back of the building. He hadn't gotten four steps from the base of the stairs when he heard a raspy, pre-pubescent voice hurtling profanities at the front desk clerk.

"I'm tellin' ya, ya nugget brain, I've got to see him now, an' it be important—more important than what you're doin'!"

Hugh's heels dragged to a stop. He backed up and entered the front room. Sure enough, Sir stood before the clerk, who was busy scowling at the boy, his cheeks red.

"Now listen here, you scum sucker, this is the last time I'll tell you to get out—"

"Sir," Hugh bellowed. The boy twisted his rail-thin upper body toward him.

"Finally. Been tryin' to get this fish-faced clod to tell me where you was for a quarter hour."

Hugh raised a hand to the clerk, a signal to let it be. "Why are you here?"

He hadn't asked the boy to report to him. For a heartbeat, he hoped Sir brought news of another crime, something to drive Hugh's mind from the Lovejoy murder. From the duchess. It was what Sir Gabriel wanted. No doubt it would be easier, better, to move on and leave everything having to do with the duke and duchess in the past.

"Your fancy lady," Sir said. "I been keeping my peepers on her, just in case, and I thought you might want to know where she's been."

He braced himself. "Nowhere good, I imagine."

"The workhouse called St. Emmanuel's. Got there by a hansom and then left again. Heard her tell the jarvey Bedford Street."

"*My* address? Did you follow her there?"

"Nah, I knew you was here," he answered.

Absently, Hugh took a few ha'pennies from his pock and tossed them to Sir. "Nicely done. Good initiative, lad."

The copper coins disappeared into one of the boy's many pockets, and Sir tugged the brim of his cap. Hugh stared over the boy's head, awareness ripping into him. She'd gone to the workhouse to find the footman, to hunt down the letter Lady Wimbly had wanted burned. It was dangerous. Desperate.

She knew. The duchess had learned of her husband's imminent removal to the institution. She was acting rashly and was going to confront the footman alone.

"Come with me," Hugh growled, and then bolted toward the station's front door. Sir followed, a shadow on Hugh's heels.

There was no need for a cab; Hugh's home on the corner of Bedford Street and Maiden Lane could be reached in only a few minutes if he ran—which he did. He kept stride with Sir, the young boy holding onto his hat and pumping his arms.

The duchess hadn't taken her driver, Carrigan. Which meant

she'd most likely absconded from Violet House without any of the staff knowing.

Hugh barreled up the front steps to his home and swung the door wide. "Basil!"

The valet entered the hall, dressed to go out with his coat and hat. "I was just about to come to Bow Street, sir. You had a visitor, the Duchess of—"

"Where is she?" Hugh peered into the front room, but it was vacant.

"Gone, sir. She left a message for you. Said it was quite urgent." Basil took a folded piece of paper from his pocket. "I hope you're not angry, but I had a look and indeed, I thought it was prudent to come to you right away."

Breathless from the run and from his bottled apprehension, he took the note.

The footman's name is Fellows. The letter is on a boat at St. K. wharves. The Jackdaw. Meet me there. I'll be careful.

Hugh crumpled the paper in his fist. "Like hell she will be," he grumbled. "Damn woman!"

If St. John and the marchioness were involved, as Hugh suspected, who better to assign the killing than a man they'd rescued from a workhouse? The letter. It had to be something incriminating. Something the killer held onto for insurance.

"Did she say anything else to you?" he asked Basil. Alarm crinkled his valet's brow as he shook his head.

"No, sir. Her Grace seemed to be in a hurry. I offered her a carriage, but she left on foot."

"She can't walk to the wharves from here. When did she leave? How long ago?"

"Fifteen minutes at the most," Basil replied, removing his hat.

If she'd caught a hansom quickly, she might be arriving at the wharves right at that moment. He swore under his breath.

"Basil, keep your coat on and go to Bow Street," he said. "Ask for the chief magistrate. Tell him I need a few patrolmen at the St.

Katherine wharves right away. Let him know the duchess might be in danger there."

That should light a fire under Sir Gabriel's heels.

"What about me?" Sir asked.

Hugh peered down at him. "How well do you know the docks?"

He shrugged a knobby shoulder. "Like the back of me hand."

"Then you can help me find the duchess," Hugh said, and with that, the two of them raced into the falling dusk.

CHAPTER TWENTY-TWO

The Tower of London stood as a black monolith against the umber glow of sunset. The damp weather was bringing in a mist off the Thames. Within the hour, Audrey figured the St. Katherine district would be swimming in the thick brume. The natural cover would have been appreciated now, however. She paid the jarvey and he cracked the whip, the carriage trundling off and leaving her alone on a narrow street.

To her left was a busy warehouse, its doors open with cargo boxes, spools of rope, and open-slatted crates stacked into precarious towers. The workday was not yet over, and the commotion of the busy warehouses, taverns, and shops filled the air.

No one paid her arrival any mind; the laborers continued with their hauling, their shouting, and the people passing her didn't so much as tip a hat or make a nod. *Perfect.* Here, now, she was nobody. Not worth being seen. If she were going to make her way onto Fellows's shanty and find the letter from the marchioness, she needed that obscurity. With any hope, the shanty would be empty, Fellows himself still out working. Maybe even at Wimbly Manor.

If not, well, at least she could discover where Fellows lived, and she could wait for Hugh Marsden to arrive. His valet had taken the note and was sure to deliver it, but Audrey hadn't been able to wait. Patience was not her virtue, and Philip's removal to Gibbets Sanatorium could even be happening tonight. Doing so under the cover of darkness would be beneficial for Westborough, Michael, and the other lords who had agreed to the alternative.

Hugh Marsden had commanded her to stay away from Bow Street, and a quick look around the wharves and riverside in St. Katherine wouldn't necessarily be dangerous.

To her right, the Thames was a cluster of activity, with ships and boats of all kinds either sailing or moored. From dinghies to clippers to tugboats, there was hardly any part of the riverfront wharves that wasn't clogged. Doubt took over. These were all working vessels, nothing like a shanty. She imagined Fellows's houseboat would be small, rustic.

Walking farther upriver, the wharves thinned out and smaller boats bobbed in the black, brackish water. The fog rolled in a little more, a bell clanging somewhere in the distance. Gulls screeched overhead. The smell of the river and the undeniable stench of refuse and fish turned her stomach. One got used to the odors, she imagined, though she didn't think she'd be able to cleanse it from her nostrils for some time.

A few children—two boys and a girl, their faces dirty and their shoes worn—ran toward her, looking as if they were racing. Audrey held up her hand.

"Wait, children, excuse me." All three children slammed their heels into the stone street with matching looks of alarm. "I wonder if you could give me directions to a particular shanty that moors in this area?"

The children continued to stare at her. The little girl's eyes stuck on Audrey's shoes, the polished boots practically gleaming like fairy dust in comparison to everything else in the vicinity. There was the possibility they would pickpocket her, but she hadn't brought much with her anyhow.

"Which shanty?" one of the boys asked.

"It's called the *Jackdaw*," she said

The boy started to speak, but the other one slammed a forearm into his chest, holding him back. "What's it worth to ya, lady?"

Audrey bit back a surprised grin. She couldn't fault them for making it work in their favor. She reached into her skirt pocket, where she'd kept her coin purse, and without removing the pouch, extracted a few coins. The children's eyes brightened when they saw the copper pieces.

"Betcha got more'n that in yer pocket," the same boy said.

"Perhaps, but this is what I am offering you. Unless..." she shrugged, pretending to consider, "I need to ask elsewhere."

She made to put the coins back into her pocket.

"No, no," the boy said, holding out a hand to stop her. "We know all the shanties 'round here. We'll take ye to *Jackdaw*."

The children took to the task with excitement, turning in the opposite direction and weaving between carts and drays and crates. Audrey followed, hoping they weren't just leading her into an empty alley to steal her purse. As they ran toward the quay, in the direction of several shanties and dinghies tied up to weirs, she breathed a little easier.

Some of the boats had their insignia carved into the bows, some had them painted on plaques, and others still had no insignias at all. Many had roofed compartments and windows, and others were tented with only canvas sheets. A few were moored so closely they rubbed up against each other, buffered only by blocks or buoys attached to the outside of the vessels.

"There." The enterprising boy pointed.

Audrey's heart swelled and her stomach clenched as she laid eyes on a long shanty covered with two pitched canvas roofs. *Jackdaw* was painted in white on the bow of the withered vessel. She worried her lower lip. Now what? It didn't look like anyone was aboard, but the two canvas tarps obscured her view of the shanty's living quarters. She couldn't search it if Fellows was inside.

She felt a tug on her skirt. The little girl dropped her hand quick and whispered, "The man who lives on this one looks mean."

Audrey's attention piqued at the fright in her eyes. She found she understood the girl well. "I don't wish to run into him. Before I board, I'd like to be sure it's empty."

The younger boy picked up a glass bottle near a pile of trash. "Easy." He lobbed the bottle straight at the *Jackdaw* just as Audrey let out a strangled, "No!"

The bottle landed on the deck and smashed. All four of them froze, the little boy seeming to realize right away what he'd done. Fellows could burst from the covered area and chase them down for a thrashing. And if he saw Audrey...

A few seconds passed like whole hours with her breath lodged in her throat. Then, after another handful of seconds of stillness from the *Jackdaw*, the little boy tugged his hat, victoriously.

"Well?" he said, holding out his hand.

She dropped the coins into his palm with a relieved grin. "Nicely done. Though perhaps not the method I would have taken."

The children whooped and divided up the coins before scurrying back the way they'd come. She watched them go before turning back toward the shanty. The light of sunset had grown even more dusky; orange and brown streaked the fog hanging just above the water. The shanty was small. It wouldn't take much time to search. She could be done within a few minutes.

The dock ran right up against the boat, and holding onto the low rail, she swung one leg over. Thankfully, the cut of her dress gave her enough room to not go toppling onto the boat's deck. She felt the easy undulations of the Thames beneath her feet. She had never cared for boats, or open water, and as she made her way around the smashed remains of the liquor bottle, her legs felt unsteady.

Just to be sure, before she peeled back the canvas flap to the tented area, Audrey called out, "Hello?"

Her voice warbled, her pulse knocking hard in her neck. No answer. Letting out a breath, she pushed aside the flap. The space was cramped and dark, though a few worn spots in the canvas let in the dim light from outside. There was a single table and chair, some crates with liquor bottles set atop them, a cot and blankets, a small stove, and a pail of coal next to it.

Beyond the living space, there was a messy collection of fishing traps and poles, nets, some buoys, barrels, and a grappling hook, and then another opening in the canvas tent cover, leading to the stern. She took a few steps toward the cot and found a balled-up set of blue and gold livery. The same as the Wimbly staff.

This was indeed Fellows's boat.

Audrey riffled through the crates; they were filled mostly with bottles of liquor. Where would he have put the marchioness's letter? Would he think to hide it? Or perhaps he'd done as she'd asked and finally burned it. A single long stride took her to the stove. It wasn't warm, indicating it hadn't been lit for hours. She opened the grate to a smoking pile of coal ash. In the coal bin, there were nothing but lumps of black. In another metal bin was what looked and smelled like human excrement. She crinkled her nose.

Faster. She had to find it and flee. She had trouble breathing as she turned to view the shanty again. *It's tucked away safe*, he'd said. *Safe*. No, he wouldn't have burned it. The marchioness had been angry with him for defying her orders, accused him of blackmail. He had kept the letter as some type of protection. More than ever, Audrey needed to know what it said. Needed to see how it could help Philip.

She peered at the livery again; the state of it, wrinkled, cast aside without care, said much about the man's appreciation of Lady Wimbly's charity. If he wasn't wearing it, that meant he was elsewhere today. A thread of worry twisted in the back of her mind.

She picked up the footman's coat, then pulled back the untucked blanket. When she had been at Shadewell, she'd kept special things hidden from the attendants inside a slit in her mattress, under her pillow. An extra biscuit wrapped in a napkin, a beautiful piece of quartz she found on a walk one day; too sharp to be allowed safe for her, the attendant had made her drop it. On the next walk, she'd scooped it up unseen and hidden it in her mattress.

Audrey tugged the flat pillow aside, and then lifted the bedroll from the cot's frame. Victory swelled in her throat, and she snatched the folded piece of paper that Fellows had tucked between the cot's crossed wooden legs. The paper wasn't cheap; Audrey felt the smooth linen weave between her fingers. With trembling hands, she unfolded the note. Her mouth went dry.

Belladora,

Meet me tonight at my new rooms after your performance. I have something important to discuss with you. I think you will be quite pleased, my songbird. Jewell House, 3rd flr., #12.

-W

It was dated the day of Miss Lovejoy's murder.

Audrey sucked in a breath. *Lord Wimbly* had invited her to Philip's rooms, claiming they were his own? But then, how did the marchioness know of the letter? Perhaps she had instructed him to write this note? But then why had St. John been there?

She didn't know all the answers, but the intention was plain: Miss Lovejoy had been lured to Jewell House on false pretenses.

A creaking floorboard was all the warning Audrey had that she wasn't alone.

Then, a low, rough voice said, "She told me to burn that."

Audrey spun around, fumbling to shove the note into her pocket. A man stepped through the split in the canvas panels. Fellows stood a full head taller than her and wore the common clothes of a laborer, trousers and shirt, a patched jacket. His collar was open enough to display several scabbing lines across his neck and at his chin. Defense wounds from Miss Lovejoy's nails.

"Told me to get it back and destroy it," he said.

Audrey's blood pumped, hot and cold at once, and she put together how Fellows must have gotten the letter. "Miss Lovejoy left it at the theatre. You went back for it, but...Mr. Bernadetto saw you."

He'd been the one to slash the theatre manager's throat, and to leap through the open window and run. The destruction of the office had been in effort to find the letter, and he had.

"The old man shouldn't have read it."

"Why didn't you burn it?" she asked, if only to keep him talking. She needed time to think her way out of this.

"I know what I am to her. Hired hand. Expendable. She might've got me out of the workhouse, but she could just as easily point a finger at me to save her own skin, if something went afoul."

Audrey took a step back—her skirts brushed the cot. He shook his head.

"You should've stayed out of it," he said.

"You murdered an innocent woman."

He scoffed. "She was a whore."

Audrey breathed in through her nose, disgusted. Terrified. He had no remorse for what he'd done, and he'd think nothing of killing her, too.

He took a step toward her. Audrey jumped back. He laughed. "Where do you think you can go? You're a far step from your fancy manor now, aren't you?"

"Someone knows I'm here. A Bow Street officer. He's meeting me," she said rapidly, hardly breathing. Lies. She'd left a note, but she had no idea if Mr. Marsden would come, or how he'd find the *Jackdaw*. Still, she hoped it would give the killer pause. Make him reconsider.

Fellows chuckled again. "He's nowhere near here."

He launched forward, shoving aside a chair between them. She grabbed the pail of his refuse and without hesitation, flung it into his path. The contents splattered over him as Fellows batted away the pail. Audrey ran past the stove and toward the back of the shanty. The opening on the other end was her only chance.

Without breathing, without thinking, she jumped over a spool of rope on the floor, sweeping an arm at a stack of empty fish traps as she passed. The netted cages tumbled behind her, though she didn't know if they delayed her pursuer—she didn't dare look. Fishing line and poles brushed her shoulders as she made for the back of the shanty; her toes caught on something hidden in shadows and she pitched forward. Her hands caught on a metal pole and she landed hard on her side, the wind driven out of her—along with any sense of promise that she'd make it off the shanty safely.

Giving up, however, was not an option.

Still holding onto the metal pole, Audrey slashed it out in an arc, behind her before even looking to see where Fellows was. Her senses had known he was close, and indeed, he'd been reaching for her ankle when the end of the pole connected with his face. Blood spurted, he bellowed and pulled back, and Audrey scrambled for footing.

She stumbled through the flaps, her shaky legs threatening to fold beneath her. The stern was packed with debris, covered with more tarpaulin—there wasn't a place to step. And no dock to jump out onto—it must have ended midway along the length of the boat. Now, there was just open water. Audrey started for the railing, heedless of the fact that she couldn't swim, when Fellows burst from the flaps. Blood streaked his face, but it was the small pistol in his hand that her eyes stuck to. The nose of it was aimed right at her.

A deafening crack. A blast of searing pain. And Audrey went sprawling back, toward the water.

CHAPTER TWENTY-THREE

The report of a pistol echoed across the wharves just as the little girl pointed Hugh toward the dilapidated *Jackdaw*. Through the thickening mist, the figure of a woman stumbled back, over the stern, and splashed into the water. *No.*

"Audrey!" Hugh broke away from the young urchin and bolted down the connecting wharves, dodging debris and slipping on the wet, corky wood. He kept one eye on Audrey's billowing skirts in the water and the other on the man who'd shot at her.

"Fellows! Stop!" Hugh shouted. The man jerked toward him, then flashed into the covered portion of the shanty.

His instinct was to give chase and apprehend him. The man was a criminal, a murderer. He needed to be stopped before he could harm anyone else. But Hugh's attention shifted to Audrey in the water, and he knew there was only one choice.

"Sir! Get the carriage!" he shouted over his shoulder. Hugh reached the end of the dock and without hesitation, plunged into the water.

Audrey wasn't far from his reach, but as he broke the surface of the briny, refuse-filled Thames, she seemed leagues away. The cobwebbed spray of her golden hair showed the pins and combs at the back of her head. She was face down, and she wasn't attempting to thrash or swim. Her heavy skirts would drag her under any second.

Hugh pinned his lips together against the foul water and finally reached her, flipping her over so that her nose and mouth were in sight. Blood streaked her chin and tinged some strands of her hair pink. The bullet had struck her. Hugh hooked her with one arm and pulled at the water with his other, toward the dock as the shrill blare of a pea whistle split the air.

A commotion on the wharves stole his attention, though only for a moment. He kicked his water-logged feet and cut his arm through the water, toward the dock.

"Audrey," he gasped. "Audrey, can you hear me?"

A glorious sound punched through the racing pulse in his ears and the splash of water: the choking gargle of a cough.

He grabbed onto a piling, where several small hands latched onto his wrist and clutched at his coat sleeve.

"It's the lady!" the young girl exclaimed. She, and the two boys she'd been playing with, heaved, and though their combined strength did little to assist him out of the water, he was grateful they hadn't scampered away. The two boys grabbed at the duchess's arms, keeping her afloat as Hugh hauled himself onto the dock. He then dragged her up next to him. She moaned as he laid her down onto the wood.

"Blood," the girl whispered.

A dark stain bloomed against the drenched, deep green fabric of her upper right shoulder.

Hugh tore off his sopping wet jacket and then yanked at his sleeve, ripping the threads. He balled up the wet linen and pressed it to her shoulder. She screamed at the sudden pressure, and her lashes fluttered open. Terrified, deep blue eyes met his.

"It's him," she gasped, her lips purple, bits of debris and dirt clinging to her brows and cheeks. The Thames was polluted and writhing with pestilence. He pushed the thought of anything contaminating her wound from his mind and focused on what to do next.

"Mister Hugh!" The wharf rattled uproariously. Hugh tore his eyes from her; Sir pointed toward the black roof of their waiting carriage, closer now than it had been before. At the head of the wharf, two uniformed patrolmen had tackled whom Hugh hoped was Fellows, and several more men were rushing toward the melee. Basil had reached Bow Street, and Sir Gabriel had taken Hugh's request seriously. *Thank God.*

He scooped the duchess into his arms. Her drenched gown and limp form were a burden, but his legs held as he rushed, as swift-footed as he could, toward the carriage. There was only one place he could think to bring her; one person he trusted.

"Number eighteen St. James's Square," he told the jarvey as the man assisted Hugh into the carriage, Sir leaping in on the opposite side. "As fast as you can, goddamn it!"

The jarvey slammed the door and the chassis rocked madly.

"Where are we going, Mister Hugh?" Sir asked.

"My friend. He's a doctor."

"The tall nob, with the chops?"

"That's the one," he said, knowing full well that Sir had taken to following him around London, waiting to make himself useful in any capacity. Today, it might have saved the duchess's life.

Might.

The wound bled profusely, and worry knocked against his thoughts. There was no room in his mind to consider it further. He cradled her as the driver took his orders to heart and careened from the wharves. She shivered and groaned, wincing with every movement. He hated that the rattling motion of the carriage caused her pain, but the faster they arrived at Thornton's, the faster he could treat her shoulder.

"Stay awake, Audrey," he told her, dispensing with her title and proper form of address. He needed her to hear him; perhaps even shock her a little.

"It was him," she murmured, her eyes opened to slits. "He killed her."

"I know." Hugh gathered her closer, their soaked figures both shivering now. "St. John was with the duke that night, and his mother had given him orders to end their relationship."

Audrey's eyes flared open. "The marchioness. Letter. My pocket."

If the Thames hadn't fished the letter out of her pocket, the water would have destroyed it by now. Hugh cringed at the lost evidence.

"She wrote it," he guessed. Lady Wimbly had led the singer to Jewell House and had hired Fellows to kill her there. How had the marchioness known her son would be gone by the time Miss Lovejoy, and then Fellows, arrived?

"P-pretended to be Wimbly," Audrey confirmed, jerking her head as she tried to nod. She grimaced. "My shoulder...the bullet."

"I'm taking you to my friend Thornton. He's going to help you. Audrey, you have to stay awake."

"I should have..." she started, but then her next word tremored.

"Waited for me? Not gone to the wharves alone?" he interjected. He clenched his teeth against more of a reprimand. He couldn't scold her, not when she was like this.

"Brought a pistol," she finished. Hugh barked a laugh.

"Yes, I think you should have too," he agreed.

The carriage tottered around a sharp corner, and outside, he spotted the familiar wrought iron fence and elms outside Thornton's home. At last.

The driver whistled to the horses. The next collection of minutes was a blur of shuffling Audrey out of the carriage without causing her too much agony, sending Sir ahead to alert the butler and Thornton himself, and then Hugh pushing his way into the foyer.

"Goodwin, tell me he's in."

The butler snapped his fingers to a footman and maid, who'd rushed into the front hall to view the commotion. "Yes, of course, sir. Take her straight to the back wing," he said, but Hugh was already on his way.

Thornton kept an office in his home at the back of the house, where patients could enter and leave without being seen from the square out front. Hugh kicked open the door and was two steps inside the office when Thornton entered through a side door, Sir on his heels.

"A bullet to the upper right shoulder?" Thornton asked, already serious and focused. Ready. Hugh's thighs trembled, knowing Audrey would be cared for now. He laid her onto the examination table.

"Yes. And a dunk into the Pool of London."

Thornton scowled at the poor luck as a young maid rushed through the door Sir was still holding open, her hands swiftly tying on a pinafore. His assistant, Hugh presumed.

"And yourself?" Thornton inquired as his assistant produced a pair of steel shears and handed them to him. He made an incision in the sopping green fabric of Audrey's bodice and began cutting upward, toward her collar.

"I am fine. Uninjured," Hugh answered, impatient. The duchess's cheeks were ashen, her lips dusky purple, but her eyes were partially open.

"So c-c-cold," she stammered.

"You'll be warm soon, Your Grace," Thornton assured her.

The gown's fabric fell away, and Thornton gently rolled Audrey to her side.

"W-what are you—" Her stammering objection fell silent as she continued to shiver.

The assistant sliced the ribbons from her boned corset.

"Your Grace, forgive the impropriety but I need access to your wound," Thornton informed her.

At the first glimpse of her bare back, Hugh stepped away, averting his eyes.

Lying her down flat again, Audrey made small mewling noises. Each one daggered Hugh in his gut. Thornton pulled off her sopping corset just as his assistant draped her with a swath of white cotton.

"The bullet entered the outer deltoid and has lodged there," Thornton announced. "Miss Matthews, hot water, alcohol, and forceps."

Audrey moaned as the assistant flushed debris and blood from the wound, and then held her still as Thornton inserted the narrow forceps. Hugh's stomach turned and he fought the irrational desire to clock his friend in the jaw. He was helping Audrey, saving her life, and yet anger roiled inside him. Not for Thornton, no. For that Fellows blackguard. The man who'd murdered Miss Lovejoy, had most likely killed Bernadetto too, and who'd held no qualms about shooting the duchess.

"Mister Hugh," Sir whispered, appearing at his elbow, as usual. The normalness of it relieved him. "Want me to keep my blinkers on this Wimbly lady?"

He'd been listening in the carriage. The marchioness hired Fellows to frame the duke. What he couldn't be sure of was if St. John had been in on it or not.

"Got it," Thornton announced, followed by a clink of metal as the extracted bullet fell from the tips of his forceps and onto a tray.

Audrey had lost consciousness, her waxy complexion giving Hugh another curl of fury mixed with nausea.

"A clean entry," Thornton said, stepping away as his assistant staunched the bleeding.

"She'll live?" Hugh asked.

"I'll clean the wound again, suture it, and get her warm and dry. Infection is a possibility," Thornton answered as he wiped his hands on a length of linen. "But the damage is minimal. There is nothing more you can do right now, Hugh. If there is somewhere you need to be regarding whatever happened here, this is the time."

His friend knew him well. Hugh looked at Audrey and nodded tightly.

"Take care of her," he said, needlessly. Thornton would not leave the duchess's side. He motioned for Sir to follow him from the room. "I'm going to Wimbly Manor. Head to Bow Street and find out what's come of Fellows's arrest."

Sir nodded and dashed away, disappearing before Hugh even emerged onto the front steps.

Goodwin followed him. "I will have a carriage brought around for you, sir."

"Thank you, but I think I'll go on foot." Hugh needed time to comb through his approach at Wimbly Manor—and time to let off enough steam so that he wouldn't geyser as soon as he laid eyes on either St. John or the marchioness.

It was a ten-minute walk through the now darkened streets, which were thick with a soupy fog, the kind London knew so well. With any hope, Wimbly Manor had not yet heard of the fracas down at the wharves; then again, Fellows might have given up Lady Wimbly the moment he was in custody. Whether or not Sir Gabriel would believe him was another story altogether.

Knocking on the front door was a risk, but Hugh had to get in legitimately. He wanted Lady Wimbly on edge and angry. As his hand slammed down upon the manor's door, he had but two avenues of potential success.

The butler appeared and instantly took in Hugh's wet visage. His hat was gone, lost to the Thames, and his clothing was still soaked. The butler sneered at him.

"You again." He recalled him from his previous attempt to speak to Wimbly a few days ago. "What is it you want, Runner?"

"A moment of Lady Wimbly's time."

"The lady is out."

It was entirely possible she was, though it was still too early for any social function.

"It's imperative I speak to her. Please, tell her it's about St. John. Tell her, *I know.*"

At the mention of the heir's title, the butler's brow arched with annoyed interest. Servants knew everything, and something about his new scowl said he knew what Hugh spoke of.

He stood aside. "Wait here."

Hugh stepped into the grand foyer, his boots squelching. His untidy appearance might just do him a favor and unsettle the lady of the house even more. The butler had turned into a room beyond the twisting front stairwell a moment ago, and now, he emerged.

"Her ladyship is indisposed and asks that you return tomorrow afternoon."

Hugh sighed. So, it would be Avenue Number Two, would it? "Tell her that Fellows has been arrested and that I will most certainly be back."

The butler frowned. "Fellows?"

"Fellows," Hugh repeated, loudly. A glass clinked and fabric rustled within the sitting room. The butler turned his head, having heard it too.

The marchioness would not be prepared to run out the back door of the manor and flee. She would require a few things first.

"Stay here. I will inform her ladyship," the butler intoned, and then entered the sitting room again. Hugh slipped out through the front door, onto the front steps. He then went around the manor to the mews, toward the carriage house, where within a minute, as he'd expected, a groom began to ready a pair of horses and a small brougham.

Hugh waited, unnoticed, behind an ivy trellis. Within ten more minutes, two shadows quickened through the fog: Lady Wimbly and her maid, a valise in each of the servant's hands.

"Did you put the laudanum into your son's bottle of scotch, or did St. John do it himself?"

Hugh stepped out, and Lady Wimbly came to a halt. Her maid knocked into her elbow and gasped. It took the marchioness a few seconds to recover. She turned to the maid. "Go fetch Beckett. I want this riffraff turned out."

"Yes, miss, and while you are at it, signal for a street patrol. Kindly inform him that Chief Magistrate Poston will be arriving within the quarter hour."

Lady Wimbly spun toward him. "You lie."

"You know Fellows has been arrested. It's why you are running —because he will talk. He won't go down for the murder of Belladora Lovejoy alone. That's why he kept the letter and stashed it on his boat."

The maid hesitated, looking between her mistress and Hugh, eyes glassy and wide. At the mention of the letter, the marchioness hitched her chin. Her face, lightly lined, regal by any standard, froze into a mask of panic. She didn't need to know the paper had been destroyed.

"What letter?" she demanded. "I've nothing to do with that villain or murder."

"Well delivered, your ladyship, except for the slight tremor in your voice."

She flicked her hand at her maid, encouraging her to continue to the carriage house.

"Stay where you are, if you please, miss," Hugh said. She'd alert the grooms to his presence, and in his current state—cold, soaked, and fatigued—he wouldn't be able to fend off more than one or two.

The maid froze in place.

"I could scream for help," the marchioness said.

"But you won't. You know it's only a matter of minutes before Bow Street arrives. I'm here to make a bargain."

She canted her head. "A bargain?"

"You don't want your son's private life put on display and dragged through the mud, and I am here to see the same is done for Fournier."

He needed to appeal to her to get her to speak; justice was required for Miss Lovejoy's death but that didn't mean two other men needed ruination.

"State your business," she finally commanded.

"Was it laudanum in the scotch? I didn't find a bottle at Fournier's rooms at Jewell House. I presume you had your hired man take that with him after he finished with his bloody task."

"I've told you—I have no idea what you are talking about," she insisted, and this time, the annoyance on her tone rang true. But there was something else there as well. Something harsh, bitter.

"You arranged for the duke to be incapacitated enough for Fellows to make it appear *he* had stabbed Miss Lovejoy to death," Hugh pressed on, thinking of the blood found on the duke's hands, his face, his clothes. The boning knife next to him on the floor.

How easy it must have been for the real murderer to drag Fournier across the room, into the slain singer's pooling blood, and then position him back on the floor.

"But the risk," Hugh said, the accusation unfurling as he put it together in his mind. "The risk was great. Dear Auggie was there; he'd had some of the tainted scotch. How did you know he would leave in time? Before Belladora arrived. Before Fellows did."

There was no chance the marchioness would have allowed her son, the heir to the marquessate, to be implicated in a murder so gruesome. Her entire world, her family name and legacy, would be ruined.

A sixth sense warned him, but too late. Cold metal pressed against the back of Hugh's skull. He knew the shape.

"Unlike you, Marsden, I am thorough in my actions. I find peace in order, in precision. Lift your hands."

Hugh exhaled through his nostrils. "Wimbly."

The marquess stood behind him, in the shadowy corner of the carriage house exterior. The nose of a pistol nudged Hugh a little more insistently.

He raised his hands. "I underestimated you."

"You lost your focus," the marquess said. The steady weight of his flintlock in his hip sheath disappeared as Wimbly claimed it, though after the jump in the Thames, the powder would be useless anyhow.

Much like Hugh right then.

After that evening at the Seven Sins, he had written off Lord Wimbly as a clueless ingrate. He didn't care about the death of his own mistress, but he also didn't care enough to be jealous of her supposed connection with Fournier. He would have had no motive to kill her when he could find another woman to replace her so easily.

Porter had been wrong. Wimbly *had* known about his son and Miss Lovejoy. And he had known something more.

"Belladora told you about Auggie and the duke, didn't she?" Hugh asked.

"Augustus!" the marchioness hissed to her husband. "What are you going to do?"

Within a minute, the carriage that the grooms were preparing would be ready and emerge into the courtyard.

"Was she blackmailing you?" Hugh mused aloud. "Did she ask for more money, hinting that she might otherwise let the knowledge slip? You needed to be rid of her, and you also wanted to be rid of your son's lover."

Two birds, one stone, as it were.

"I'm thankful for Belladora, actually." Wimbly sounded far too calm for a man who was holding a gun to another person's head. "Learning of my son's transgressions from the likes of her was far better than learning of it from one of my own set. No, she didn't blackmail me. She knew her place."

"Then why kill her?"

Lady Wimbly's maid clapped a hand over her mouth and made a soft yelp. She and the marchioness huddled, uncertainly, together in the courtyard. Lady Wimbly, however, didn't act as surprised as her maid. She knew of her husband's actions, though how involved she'd been remained unclear.

"It was as much a lesson to my son as it was a guarantee that Belladora would remain silent on the matter," he replied.

"And Fournier?"

"You must know he would rather hang for the murder than speak of what he was truly doing in those rooms."

It seemed the marquess had the duke pegged correctly.

The carriage house doors opened on their hinges, and the jangling of tack and hooves on paving stones followed.

"*Augustus*," the marchioness again pleaded.

"You will be riding with us, Marsden," Wimbly announced.

He couldn't possibly put a bullet in his brain here, at Wimbly Manor. He'd wait until they were in the countryside. Lead him into the woods. Leave him there to rot into the forest's undergrowth.

As the horses pranced to a stop in the courtyard, and before the driver could throw the brake, Hugh took a gamble and dodged to the side—the blast of the pistol walloped his eardrum, but he wasn't hit. Spinning around, he blocked Wimbly's right arm and pummeled him in his soft gut. With a hard twist of the marquess's right hand, the pistol—a double-barrel flintlock—clattered onto the ground.

The marchioness screamed as the grooms and driver shouted, trying to bring the spooked horses under control.

In his wet clothing, Hugh's movements were slower and more constricted, and the marquess landed a ridge of knuckles into his jaw. It only stunned him momentarily. His ear still ringing, and his vision unsteady, Hugh rammed into him, tackling the man to the ground.

Strong hands latched onto Hugh's arms and shoulders, trying to pull him off the marquess.

"Neatham should've shot you when he had the chance in that duel!" Wimbly seethed as another pair of hands grabbed Hugh and successfully tore him away.

The grooms, Hugh figured, believing they were protecting their master. They held him back, locking his arms out and to the side.

"And I should have had better aim," Hugh replied, all caution tattered and tossed to the breeze.

"You don't understand the first thing about good breeding." Wimbly lurched for his flintlock and leveled it at him again, prepared to set off the second and last shot. "I am within my rights to shoot, and no one will miss you, you bloody bastard."

The men holding him scattered. Hugh stayed rooted to the paving stone.

"I might."

A hammer clicked back on a second pistol a mere second after Audrey's voice entered the courtyard. Hugh lowered his hands as Thornton appeared at Wimbly's side, another double-barrel flintlock trained on the marquess with unwavering conviction.

"Give it here," Thornton ordered. Wimbly's scowl grew apoplectic as he turned the gun over. Thornton pocketed it.

Hugh spun, searching for Audrey, and found her approaching from behind the marchioness and her maid. She had a thick shawl wrapped around her, her wet hair hanging loose around her shoulders.

"What are you doing here? Your shoulder—"

"I'm fine," she replied. "I remembered something after you left. The letter Fellows kept; the endearment used. *My songbird*. It's what you called her too, Lord Wimbly. At the Seven Sins, do you remember? A light skirted *songbird*."

Audrey took a step closer. Hugh saw her tremble.

"The marchioness didn't write that letter pretending to be you. You wrote it yourself."

"I hear you went into the Thames, Your Grace," Wimbly said, dismissing her revelation. "I'll wager that's where the letter still is."

Audrey reached into her gown's skirt pocket and withdrew a piece of wilted and rumpled paper. "The ink has run in spots, but unfortunately for you, it's still legible."

Hugh didn't care if she was bluffing—she was brilliant.

From the corner of his eye, he saw Wimbly hand dart under his jacket.

"Thornton!" Hugh barked. The gun the marquess had confiscated from Hugh shone in the light of the carriage oil lamp.

With a growl, Wimbly aimed at Audrey and pulled the trigger. Hugh dove toward the duchess, but the pistol only gave off a muted *pluff* of a discharge and a small spark. Wimbly stared impotently at the useless weapon—until Thornton slammed his fist into the marquess's jaw. He disarmed him, then tossed the flintlock back to Hugh.

He caught it, his heartbeat slowing as he looked Audrey over. Her eyes were wide with alarm at being shot at yet again but was otherwise unharmed.

Hugh turned to Wimbly's driver. "The marquess needs a ride to number four Bow Street. And on second thought, Wimbly, I think I will ride along with you."

Thornton nudged the marquess toward the conveyance.

"Susan, fetch our solicitor," Wimbly snapped at the marchioness.

She gathered her skirts. "Fetch him yourself," she spit, and then turned on her heel and stormed back toward the manor.

Hugh watched her go, unconcerned. She was as low as her husband for knowing the truth and trying to conceal it, but she hadn't been involved in the planning of Miss Lovejoy's murder.

"She'll be on her way to their country estate before morning," Audrey said as she joined Hugh at the carriage.

"Once news of all this gets out, she won't ever return to London. Nor will St. John, I imagine," he replied.

Audrey touched his sleeve. "Mr. Marsden, if the marquess tells the magistrate about Philip and St. John and why he hired Fellows—"

Hugh took her uninjured shoulder in his hand and stepped closer, lowering his voice. "I will talk to Wimbly on the way to Bow Street. He knows he's finished, but he won't want to muddy his son's name any more than he already has. It won't take much to convince him to claim mere jealousy of his son's involvement with Miss Lovejoy drove him to plan the murder and attempt to pin it on the duke."

For the marquess, protecting the family name had been his ultimate logic, and to him, murder had seemed an equally logical action. It seemed so pointless, all of it. The aristocracy always had seemed that way, at least to Hugh. All of them working so hard to perfect their façade and cover up their truths, their secrets. Everything that made them *real*.

He let out a breath, still holding Audrey's good shoulder. She trembled. "You need warm, dry clothes."

"I'll have Lord Thornton's driver bring me home," she said.

He peered at her. "Your being so readily agreeable makes me suspicious."

"Still suspicious? Even after I just saved your hide?"

He huffed a laugh and held up his hands in surrender, reluctantly letting her go.

"Merryton," Thornton said, greeting his driver as he appeared in the courtyard, likely drawn from his post at the earlier commotion. "See Her Grace to Violet House and then meet me at Bow Street."

What Hugh wanted was to see her to Violet House himself. The lady, however, was more than capable.

"A hide for a hide." Hugh hopped up into the carriage. "I think this means we're square, Your Grace."

She took a playful curtsey, made all the more difficult with her wet gown and injured shoulder, as the driver snapped the reins. As the carriage circled the courtyard and headed toward the street, Hugh sat back, grinning.

"This could be a problem," Thornton mumbled from the opposite bench, his pistol still trained on Wimbly, who was already sporting a large bruise on his eye.

Hugh frowned, his smile slipping. "What might?"

His friend tipped up the brim of his hat and crinkled his forehead. "She is a duchess."

The meaning of his statement landed like a stone. Hugh scowled. "Don't be an arse."

Thornton chuckled, but Hugh didn't appreciate his humor. His friend's assumption rankled. He knew full well what Audrey was. Whatever Thornton thought he'd seen, he was wrong. She might have turned out to have more depth, more substance and courage than anyone he'd known within the ton—other than Thornton himself, of course. But she was still a duchess. A married one, at that.

After the duke was released and cleared of all charges, they would have no reason to enter one another's social spheres again. Audrey and her duke could carry on and start to repair the damage done to their reputations. It wouldn't be easy. But Hugh didn't want to see it be any more difficult than it already promised to be. He shifted his dark glare toward the marquess.

"Wimbly, we need to discuss your confession before we reach Bow Street."

CHAPTER TWENTY-FOUR

The home was nondescript and narrow, but well kept, and from where she stood on the front steps, Audrey considered just how suited it was to a man like Mr. Hugh Marsden. The limestone exterior of number 19 Bedford Street was clean, but not pristine; the windows tidy, but not gleaming. There were no adornments or potted shrubbery outside his plain black front door. It was as straightforward as the officer was.

She let go of a breath and brought the knocker down thrice.

It had been over a week since the night of Wimbly's arrest. Philip had been released at once, and Audrey had met him in the front hall at Violet House, where they had clung to one another, their cheeks wet from tears. After a long, hot bath and an overlarge meal, Audrey and Philip had stayed awake into the early hours of the morning reviewing everything that had happened.

When he'd seen her bandaged shoulder, Philip insisted on calling for their doctor first thing the next morning, to be sure her wound wasn't festering. Dr. Ryburg had allayed the duke's worries —Lord Thornton had done an admirable job. Philip, though relieved, had still been furious with her decision to face Fellows alone.

However, he was too happy to be home and absolved from all charges to remain angry with her for very long.

The door swung open, and Mr. Marsden's valet, Basil, peered down at her. His expression gave away no hint of a reaction at seeing her, though she knew her appearance here at Mr. Marsden's home was irregular.

"Your Grace do come in," Basil said, politely stepping aside.

Audrey entered, as invited, and behind her, Greer, too, alighted into the modest home. It would make tongues wag if anyone were to see her at the Bow Street officer's home, but if she were to be seen arriving alone, it would be a disgrace for both her and Mr. Marsden. They were only just emerging from one scandal; there was no need to willingly plunge them into another.

"Thank you, Basil. Is Officer Marsden at home?" she asked as the valet snicked the door shut.

As it was a Sunday afternoon, she hoped he would not be at Bow Street.

"He is," Basil replied, his eyes lifting toward the stairs behind her.

Mr. Marsden was taking the stairs, shrugging on a jacket over his shirtsleeves. "Aud—Your Grace." The near slip of her given name flustered her, and for a moment, she forgot why she had come.

"Officer Marsden." Her tone sounded unnecessarily rigid. She hadn't meant it as a reprimand, but his chagrinned expression hinted he'd taken it as such. He came off the last step and gestured toward a room to the right.

Audrey sent Greer a glance. Her maid nodded before stepping aside, Basil politely guiding her into the room to the left, to wait. Mr. Marsden followed Audrey into what appeared to be a sitting room that doubled as a library. The furniture was unpretentious, though clearly of good quality and most certainly masculine. Leather, mahogany, wood panels, and dark tones reminded her of Philip's study.

Mr. Marsden lived in comfort and was of apparent means much more suited to a gentleman than to a working-class Bow Street Runner.

"How is your shoulder?" he asked as he came to stand before the fireless hearth. Audrey realized she was staring at the room and snapped to attention.

"Healing well," she replied, rolling it a little as if to demonstrate. "Lord Thornton called on me earlier in the week to check in. He's quite an exemplary physician."

Mr. Marsden crossed his arms. "He's a good man. I'm glad to hear you're well. And the duke?"

Unexpected strain wove itself through Audrey. They were respectful comments and questions. Civil. But they seemed to come from a chilly distance. It had only been a week since she had seen Mr. Marsden, but already, the time she had spent with him seemed like another life. She'd been given no opportunity to see him the last several days, let alone speak to him. It was partially frustrating, suddenly feeling penned in. Limited. As Philip recuperated at Violet House and she allowed her shoulder to heal, she'd been restless and despondent. Which made no sense, considering her husband was home and safe. It was what she had wanted most.

Her smile felt forced. "He is well, thank you."

Silence stretched another moment, with Mr. Marsden standing solid as a statue. She cleared her throat. "I've come to say thank you and goodbye."

He winced but swiftly smoothed his brow. "Goodbye, is it?"

"The duke and I are leaving tomorrow for Fournier Downs. I expect we will stay through the summer."

Even though Philip had been vindicated, there had been few shows of support the last week from the people who had once called him friend. The Duke of Fournier still stank of scandal and except for Michael and Genie, he and Audrey had found themselves quite alone.

Fellows had been arrested and charged with the murders of

Miss Lovejoy and Mr. Bernadetto and had been locked away in Newgate. He would hang, there was no doubt about it.

The Marquess of Wimbly's fate was a bit more complicated than that. He'd denied hiring Fellows, but the letter Audrey had found on the *Jackdaw* had dried out and though the ink had run, the letterhead cast no doubt that the paper had come from his private stationary. The marchioness had decamped to their country estate, as expected, but her lady's maid had quit and given her statement to the magistrate, relating what she heard the marquess confess—everything except, thankfully, the mention of St. John and the duke being involved romantically. Whether Mr. Marsden had convinced her to stay mum on the topic, Audrey wasn't sure. She leaned toward that assumption, however. Paired with Lord Thornton's own statement, the magistrate had sent the case to the grand jury. From there, Audrey could only hope it would continue to trial.

Belladora Lovejoy and Mr. Bernadetto deserved that much, at least.

"I see," Mr. Marsden said, nodding slowly. "The fickle ton is showing its true colors."

Though it was a snide comment, it relieved her. At least Mr. Marsden was sounding more like himself.

"I had already seen them, thank you," she said with an arch of her brow. Though he allowed a half grin at her reply, they fell into another strained silence.

Perhaps coming here had been a mistake, but Audrey had not wanted to leave London without at least acknowledging his help in exonerating the duke. And in saving her life.

"Thank you—" she started to say, just as Mr. Marsden blurted out, "I'm sorry—"

They each sealed their lips. He gestured to her with a hand. "Duchesses first."

Though she was quite interested to hear what Mr. Marsden was sorry about, she wanted to say her piece and be done with it.

"I know that I wasn't exactly easy to work with," she said, ignoring the cant of his head and instant mocking scowl. "But without you, the duke would be locked up in an institution. And I would be dead. So, I thank you."

He seemed to absorb her words, the scowl fading rapidly. In its place settled unmistakable reticence. Mr. Marsden clasped his hands behind his back and straightened his shoulders, looking awfully uncomfortable.

"Yes well, I should apologize for my behavior when we first met. I shouldn't have been so short-tempered or brusque. I judged you too quickly."

She could understand why, now that she knew of the bitter and chaotic break between him and Lord Neatham. How could she blame him for his prejudices, really, when he had suffered total exile for an act she could not—did not—believe he committed?

"I know people like me haven't been kind to you," she whispered.

"They aren't like you at all." The rejoinder was so quick, it could only be heartfelt. Audrey warmed as she met Mr. Marsden's earnest stare, then looked toward the front hall.

"I should go," she said, refusing to name the sudden stab in her breast or the sour dip of her stomach.

Mr. Marsden let her reach the open door to the foyer before he spoke. "Thank you. For trusting me."

Audrey knew he did not just mean with Philip's case. She'd revealed a part of herself to him that had frightened her for so long. Ever since her commitment at Shadewell, and the betrayal she'd felt from her mother and uncle, and even her sister, she had feared anyone else knowing of her affliction. And yet, Mr. Marsden now knew and treated her no differently. A part of her wished he would have at least been a little cruel or condescending. It would have given her a reason to dislike him, to regret baring herself to him. Instead, she now felt a reluctance at leaving for Fournier Downs that had nothing to do with the loss of London society.

A smile trembled to her lips before she cut her eyes from the Bow Street officer and left the room. Greer came to her side at once, and together they left number 19 Bedford Street.

She thought it unlikely that she would ever have another opportunity to encounter Officer Hugh Marsden. As Carrigan helped her into the brougham, Audrey wasn't certain if it was relief or regret making her impatient to be in the country.

"To Violet House, Your Grace?" Carrigan inquired.

She took one last look at the windows of Mr. Marsden's home and gave a nod.

THANK you for reading Murder at the Seven Dials! Please consider leaving a rating and review on Amazon and reading the next book in the Bow Street Duchess Mystery series, Death at Fournier Downs. Keep reading for a sneak peek of Audrey and Hugh's next thrilling investigation!

DEATH AT FOURNIER DOWNS

A BOW STREET DUCHESS MYSTERY

Fournier Downs, Hertfordshire
August 1819

The chirping of crickets was a demented symphony, unending and shrill. If Audrey listened to their song too intently, the sound would drive her to insanity. So, she made sure to keep up a one-sided conversation with Fortuna, her dappled gray mare, as she led her through the overgrown rye grassland. The fields were thick with wild carrot, red campion, and purple harebell, and the heat brought out a sweet, peppery scent from the soil. It made her think of vibrant sunrises, thunderstorms, and puffy white clouds trimmed by slate gray skies. Audrey breathed it in and sighed.

"I wish there was some way to bottle that smell and transport it to London," she said to Fortuna as the mare nosed a clump of meadowsweet and tore the roots up. She huffed through her nostrils and shook her white mane.

"I know, I know, you don't want to talk about the end of summer, do you?" Audrey brought the horse to a stop along the matted deer path and let her munch on another few sprigs of meadowsweet. "Neither do I."

She and her husband Philip, the Duke of Fournier, had arrived at their country estate at the beginning of May and had been lazing about for the whole of the summer months. At first, their respite had seemed doomed. Only a few weeks after their arrival, Philip had taken to his bed with a nasty malaise. Headaches, fever, coughing; he had been miserable for weeks. So much so that his younger sister, Cassandra, who had been with Philip's brother Michael, and his wife Genie at a house party in Kent, had decided to travel to Fournier House and help Audrey care for him.

Cassie was supposed to have had a summer filled with more routs and house parties, and even a trip to Cumbria, all in preparation for her first season as a debutante—something Cassie had been excited about for as long as Audrey could remember.

However, she'd given it all up to stay at Fournier House with Philip. Audrey suspected it wasn't just out of fear for his health either.

They had come so close to losing him in April, when he'd been accused of murdering an opera singer. Found at the scene, covered in the dead woman's blood, the duke appeared to be guilty. Audrey, however, hadn't believed it, and for good reason. Against the wishes of the Bow Street officer who had arrested Philip, she launched her own investigation. Using her irregular—but oftentimes convenient—ability to see the memories that clung to solid objects, she had tracked down answers in the case, object by object. From the opera singer's earbob to an opium locket used to gain entry to a gambling hell to a pocket watch, and even a pair of Philip's cuff links.

Principal Officer Hugh Marsden had eventually realized the truth and helped her to close in on the real killer, but not before Philip was mere hours away from being committed to a sanatorium for the insane. Exoneration had saved his hide, but his reputation had been badly damaged—as was Audrey's. Decamping to Fournier Downs, the duke's expansive estate in Hertfordshire, had been an easy decision to make.

It had not, however, lived up to expectations.

The Duchess of Fournier dismounted into the grasses and let Fortuna amble off to munch on more flowers. She picked a few sprigs of red campion to weave into the horse's bridle. As much as she dreaded returning to London and seeing her old acquaintances, she also didn't think she could take much more of this solitude in the countryside. The boredom of it was slowly driving her mad. Cassie was showing signs of distress too. Her usual bubbly and bright demeanor had faded over the last few weeks.

She'd lived with Philip's great aunt Hestia in Scotland since their mother's death. With two of her older brothers being newly married, and a third, Tobias, finishing up at Cambridge, Edinburgh had been the best place for her. But now, she was ready to begin looking for a husband of her own. Michael and Genie were to take her in for the Little Season in the fall, even with Genie about to enter into confinement for her first child. Still, they had agreed it would be better for Cassie to be hosted by Michael, rather than Philip. All due to the murder scandal, of course.

A few months in the countryside would not be enough time to cure the taint of disgrace, even if to Audrey, it felt as though they were suspended in time here, protected and absolved.

A dash of motion across the field caught her attention as she was braiding the stems of some flowers. She squinted against the sunlight. The sky was nearly cloudless, leaving the sun unimpeded. Heat beat down upon her shoulders, and a fine sweat had built up on her skin, under her linen riding habit. Ahead, the field sloped toward a stone wall, bordered by tall alders, and an open gate that led into a stretch of woodland. A woman in a white dress popped in and out of view as she ran through the trees. She passed the mouth of the stone wall, giving Audrey a better view. Her bright red hair was unmistakable—it was her friend Charlotte, the Countess of Bainbury.

What in the world was she doing all the way out here, on Fournier Downs parkland?

"Charlotte!" Audrey shouted, but the countess gave no indication of hearing her. She kept running, past the gate and into the woodland.

Audrey lifted the hem of her voluminous skirts and called to Fortuna. The mare, of course, was all too happy to ignore her, favoring instead a patch of meadowsweet across the field. Grinding her teeth in annoyance, she stalked across the field, all the while wondering what had brought Charlotte out here. And why should she be running?

Lord Bainbury's estate, Bainbury Park, was several miles away. It did not even border the Fournier Downs parkland. Rather, it was beyond their neighboring estate, Haverfield—Audrey's own childhood summer estate.

There were multiple walking paths and riding trails that crisscrossed through all the countryside, so she supposed it would be possible to reach Fournier Downs on foot. But it was a great distance, and Charlotte had never been overly fond of exhausting herself in nature.

Audrey clicked her tongue to Fortuna and grasped her traces at last. Mounting her horse, she then led her toward the gate. Something about her friend's running did not sit well. To be all the way out here, alone, and seemingly in a panic... Audrey gave Fortuna's ribs a gentle press with her heels and increased her pace.

It felt good to have a destination for once. With nothing to do and hardly anyone to see, the days at Fournier House had passed in timeless ease. Audrey woke each morning wondering how she might be able to fill the day that lay ahead. Philip spent most of his time in his study, poring over estate ledgers and plans, while Cassie played the pianoforte or painted, and Audrey either read or took Fortuna out onto the downs for hours on end. Bringing a footman with her would have been more proper, but Audrey liked to be alone. She'd find a good spot to spread a blanket in the grass and either nap or read while Fortuna grazed nearby, her tail whipping at persistent flies. Sometimes Cassie joined her, but even though they liked each other immensely, she and Audrey didn't have much to converse about beyond the one thing they had in common: Philip. Cassie's conversation had grown thin the last few weeks, and Audrey supposed hers had as well.

She reached the gate and turned left, in the direction Charlotte had taken. The light coming through the boughs of the trees fell in dappled sweeps of gold and shadow, and the cooler air was an instant relief. There was no sign of Charlotte, though she had been moving quite quickly and several minutes had passed by the time she'd mounted Fortuna and started to follow. The countess could also be obscured by the thick stands of trees filling this part of the forest.

"Charlotte!" Audrey shouted again. Her voice carried, and a few birds in the limbs above scattered. Fortuna huffed impatiently as Audrey held the horse still and listened. Waiting. But again, there was no response from her friend.

She and Charlotte had been acquaintances when they were younger. Charlotte, the only daughter of the Viscount and Viscountess Prescott, had spent her summers here in Hertfordshire at Greely Park, the viscount's country home near Low Heath. It wasn't far from Haverfield. Shortly after Audrey broke her betrothal to Lord Bainbury in order to marry Philip, she had been astonished to hear that Charlotte had agreed to marry the older earl instead. There were at least twenty years between them, and the earl had already lost two wives. The first to a wasting disease, and the second to a tragic suicide. Her maid found her dead in bed one morning, a muff pistol in her hand.

Audrey had felt sorry for Charlotte, who had likely had little say in whether she married the earl or not. Audrey herself had been forced into the betrothal, which had been arranged by her mother and uncle, Lord Edgerton. But upon seeing Charlotte for the first time after the wedding, her friend had seemed content.

"We don't have a love match like you and Philip," she'd

admitted to Audrey once. "But I am quite satisfied with my situation."

For some reason, Audrey always felt guilty when people spoke of her "love match" with Philip. He'd whisked in at the eleventh hour, stealing Audrey from Bainbury with all the flare of a man in love. But it hadn't been love between her and Philip; it had been a safe agreement between longtime friends.

Besides, Philip was a duke. Even Audrey's mother could not complain...at least, not publicly.

Audrey pushed Fortuna onward, into the woodland, around trees, trying to spot her friend again. Soon, she pulled on the reins, discouraged.

"I think we've lost her," she told Fortuna. Her stomach twisted with worry. Charlotte had to have been running fast to have disappeared so quickly. Ladies never run.

Not unless they are in trouble.

A curl of unease worked its way through her, and she tried to ignore her instinct.

"Let's keep on," she said to Fortuna, leading her mount forward again. There was a trail ahead that would take them back to the stables at Fournier House. Perhaps that had been Charlotte's destination?

A scream rent the air, followed immediately by the shrill ruckus of ravens cawing. Audrey whipped around in her saddle. The ravens were still at it, their cries coming from deeper in the woods. Heart pounding, mind racing, Audrey tugged Fortuna's traces and started in the direction of the birds.

"Charlotte!" she shouted as Fortuna wove between trees. Something had happened. Her friend was in some kind of danger. Had she crossed paths with a wild boar protecting its piglets? Or a lynx, or some other wildcat?

The ravens beat their wings, darting overhead through the thick green foliage. Audrey aimed Fortuna in their direction. Soon, the alders, pines, and white beams began to thin. Fortuna deftly leaped over a downed pine and Audrey drew her to a hard stop. Ten yards ahead, the land dropped off into a craggy open pit. This was the old citrine quarry, one of Philip's ancestor's enterprises that had not withstood the test of time.

Audrey breathed heavily, the utter stillness of the wood unsettling. A single, sharp caw from a branch above jolted down her spine. A lone raven spread its wings and leaped into flight, soaring over the quarry's edge. With shaking legs and arms, Audrey dismounted. She held the leather traces a few moments longer than necessary.

"Charlotte?" she called, though her choppy breaths made her voice sound wheezy.

She didn't want to go to the edge. Didn't want to look down into the open pit where, if memory served, blocks of rock lay scattered as scree at the base of the abandoned quarry. Intuition loomed like the black belly of a rain cloud.

Audrey could mount her horse and ride back for Fournier House. She could gather a group of footmen and stable boys and lead them back here, and they could then search for Charlotte together. But she knew in her heart that would be cowardly. Last April, she hadn't backed down once on her quest to prove Philip's innocence. It had nearly gotten her killed.

"Stay," she told Fortuna, and then with as much false nerve as she could gather, went to the edge of the quarry. The drop was at least a hundred feet.

Audrey swallowed a scream and covered her mouth. Far below, Lady Charlotte, the Countess of Bainbury, lay broken. Her eyes were open, but she wasn't moving. Her red hair had fanned around her like a halo of radiant light in a sacred painting. Blood splashed the rocks near her head.

Behind Audrey, a stick snapped. She dropped her hands from her mouth and turned, but it was only a pair of red squirrels skittered up a tree, chirping at one another. Fortuna loped toward her mistress, perhaps sensing need. Audrey, her legs weak, took her by the traces gratefully, and mounted swiftly.

"Come, hurry," she whispered, the sensation that she was not alone in these woods crackling along her skin with rushed impatience. "We have to get help."

She dug in her heels and rode back toward the path to Fournier House, her eyes stinging with tears. It would be too little, too late. There could be no help for Charlotte now.

"Cor, is there anything out here what's not grass, sheep, and trees?"

Seated on the bench across from Hugh Marsden, the young street urchin stared out the carriage window with a sneer of disgust.

"Are you really complaining about the countryside, Sir?" Hugh asked, suppressing a grin. It wouldn't do to let the boy know that he found him more amusing than he did vexatious. Hugh had asked Sir to come along with him into Hertfordshire for practical reasons, but he couldn't deny that getting him out of London for a week or so would be good timing.

Not only were the rookeries in London little more than rank stink pits at this time of the summer, in the last few months the street gangs had been ramping up in violence. Sir had come around with a few black eyes, and though the lad wouldn't breathe a word about what happened, Hugh could easily guess. Sir had made it clear he wanted nothing to do with the gangs; unfortunately, gangs didn't generally like being refused.

Sir sat back in his seat and crossed his arms. "Strange, is all. There's too much sky if ye ask me."

"And not enough pockets to pick, I imagine," Basil, Hugh's valet, muttered.

"Aw, come off it, Baz, ye know I don't do that trick no more."

Basil gave a roll of his eyes and adjusted his spectacles. He'd insisted on joining Hugh, even though he'd been told it wasn't necessary. Multiple times.

"I will not have you presenting yourself to a viscountess without a properly tied cravat," the aggravated valet had said.

After that, Hugh didn't put up much more of an argument. Basil was serious when it came to cravats. The man ran Hugh's household and small staff, which included a cook, Mrs. Peets and a maid, Greta, who came in a few times a week to tidy and do the wash. Basil also hadn't had a holiday in ages, and Hugh suspected he wanted a bit of fresh country air now that London's own had turned humid and stale.

Not that this would be any sort of a holiday. A woman was dead. Her mother believed there had been some foul play.

Yesterday, Hugh, a principal officer at Bow Street, had been called into Chief Magistrate Sir Gabriel Poston's office. The magistrate slapped a letter onto his desk and gestured toward it in his rough, no-nonsense fashion.

"You've been hired to investigate a death." He'd gone on to explain what little the letter had provided.

Lady Bainbury, the Countess of Bainbury, had been found dead. Her husband, the earl, was claiming it was an accident. The countess's mother, Lady Prescott, refused to believe it. She had been advised to send for Officer Hugh Marsden by none other than Her Grace, the Duchess of Fournier.

Audrey.

Her name, written in black ink scrawl, had loosened something inside his chest, something tight and constricted. Like a fist clenched for too long, the muscles were reluctant to release.

Hugh had set the letter back on the desk and told the magistrate to find someone else.

"This lady what we're visiting," Sir began as the hired coach and four rumbled and shook down a post road toward Greely Park. "She's a viscountess?"

Hugh's pocket watch read half four. They should be arriving any moment now. He slipped the watch back into his waistcoat pocket and fought rising irritation. It wasn't Sir he was irritated with but himself.

"Yes, Viscountess Prescott. But *we* are not visiting. I am. You and Basil will wait with the carriage while I interview her ladyship."

Sir groaned and slumped down in the seat like a petulant child. If he wasn't the smartest, scrappiest, most resourceful urchin Hugh had ever known, he would have left him in London.

Basil swept away a clod of dirt that had floated in through the open window and landed on his cuff. "I sincerely hope there are acceptable accommodations in Low Heath."

Hugh knew next to nothing of the village closest to Greely Park, Lady Prescott's estate. Just that it was in Hertfordshire. If it was anything like the other villages along the post road, it would have a posting inn and tavern, and a stable, at the very least.

"Hopefully we don't have to stay on for long. A few days at the most to sort things out," Hugh said.

Sir Gabriel would be having himself a grand chuckle right now, he imagined. He'd refused to have another officer summoned for the job. *Your duchess is asking for you, Marsden,* he'd said. *The last thing I need is her hoity toity self, storming in here, asking why I sent the wrong man.*

Had the Duchess of Fournier been in London, there was no doubt she would have done just that. Last April, he'd had a devil of a time keeping her from getting herself killed during her unorthodox investigation into Belladora Lovejoy's murder. She'd been shot in the shoulder just before the true killer was caught, and Hugh had felt a barbed friction under his skin for days after. Frustrated, bloody angry, and blissfully relieved.

Once Audrey and the duke left for Hertfordshire, that friction faded slowly. Arresting thieves and burglars, drunkards with tempers, and run-of-the-mill murderers, had buried the memories of that remarkable case, in which Hugh had arrested the wrong man—something that still pricked like a thorn.

"No doubt you want to return by Friday evening," Basil said, arching a brow.

"Shut it, Basil," Hugh replied, more peeved than usual with his valet. He was a perpetual sarcastic snob who felt entirely too secure in his position. There wasn't another valet in all of London who would provoke his employer with a sarcastic remark about his mistress. Basil was the epitome of grace when he saw fit, and yet also managed to be as petulant as Sir at times. No wonder the two of them rubbed each other the wrong way.

Next to him on the bench seat, Sir snickered. He was probably only eleven or twelve, but that boy knew more than he should.

"Miss Friday's real pretty, she is," he said.

Hugh glared at him. "Mind your manners, Sir."

He pouted. "What? I didn't call her ugly."

"You shouldn't ever mention a man's mistress in conversation," Hugh replied.

"Why not?"

"It is considered rude."

Sir rolled his eyes. Hugh fought another grin. Sometimes he felt like his own father whenever he tried imparting wisdom and manners into the young lad. Lord Neatham, the sixth Viscount Neatham, had never shirked his responsibility to teach his sons how to behave in polite society. That Hugh was not his legitimate son, and would never be required to enter polite society, had not stopped him from instilling the knowledge just the same.

Hugh had been raised alongside his half-brothers, Bartholomew and Thomas, as well as his half-sister, Eloisa, and had absorbed every last drop of wisdom the late viscount had offered. He sat back in the carriage as it trundled toward Greely Park and sighed. A hell of a lot of good it had done him.

"Maybe ye should marry her then," Sir said after a moment. Hugh jerked his head toward him.

"Marry who? Miss Hanson?" A spate of cold sweat rushed the back of his neck. Gloria Hanson was his longtime mistress, and while they had a comfortable arrangement, there was absolutely no desire rampaging through him to make her his wife. He was quite certain Gloria felt the same way.

Sir shrugged. "Why not?"

The question hung in the carriage like a miasma. Basil met Hugh's eye, then looked away, apparently uninterested in weighing in.

"Men do not marry their mistresses," he replied, hoping it was enough.

"You lot don't make much sense," Sir muttered.

Hugh wasn't sure he did not agree with him. Thankfully, at that moment, they turned into the drive for Greely Park.

He'd left Bow Street the day before with the beginnings of a searing headache, the stabbing pains beginning the moment he'd gritted his teeth and ripped the letter from the magistrate's desk. In the last few months, he'd been all too happy to pretend London's polite society did not exist. After the close of the Duke of Fournier's case, and his and the duchess's departure from London, Hugh had found himself thinking far too often of Audrey and in turn, the *ton*. And thinking of the ton only led to reflecting on his own past, which only ever put him into a foul mood. It was in that irritable, foul mood he'd stayed for a few weeks, until he'd quit thinking so much about the duchess. Exhausting himself at work and increasing his meetings with Gloria from one night per week to two, then three, had helped.

However, with that letter and this assignment, the barbs of irritation had immediately set in again. She was here, in Hertfordshire. The duke's expansive estate of Fournier Downs was only ten miles or so from Prescott Manor. A subtle thrum of expectation had lived under his skin since he'd barked at Basil to begin packing his things.

Lady Prescott's estate was a somewhat modest neoclassical

home, ivy and roses creeping up the sides of its pale sandstone exterior. The hired coach's wheels rolled over the half-moon drive of crushed gravel, which was centered by a fountain topped by a winged angel clutching a harp. Hugh rolled his eyes at it as he pulled on his deerskin gloves. Basil had insisted he wear them while presenting himself to her ladyship, the dowager Viscountess Prescott. That it was a hot, humid afternoon with a rainstorm on the horizon and his palms would be sweating buckets did not matter. Appearances and formalities were everything, at least among the Quality.

The coach came to a stop. Sir sat forward to peer out the window, his jaw loose, showing off two crooked front teeth.

"I'll return shortly," Hugh said, then descended. The front door to the manor opened and the butler came out onto the front step.

"Officer Marsden, I presume," he said. "Her ladyship was expecting you, however she has since become indisposed. If you'll follow me, Her Grace, the Duchess of Fournier will receive you."

Without waiting for a reply, the man turned and entered the foyer. Hugh's feet weren't swift to follow. Instead, it felt like a stone of weight had been added to each one. She was here? He shouldn't have been surprised. She'd written the letter on Lady Prescott's behalf, after all. A footman stood patiently, waiting for him to enter so he could close the door. Hugh doffed his hat and kept after the butler, who moved with the elegant efficiency that all proud head servants possessed. He paused within the entrance to a room, announced the constable, and then stood aside to allow Hugh entry.

As if he'd been carried in on a dizzying wind, Hugh swept into a sitting room—and came to an abrupt halt. Audrey Sinclair, the Duchess of Fournier, slowly rose to her feet.

"Officer Marsden." Her voice was soft, her gloved hands clasped together in front of her waist. It was a nervous motion, as was the hesitant smile to touch her lips.

Warmth pooled in his stomach, and his shoulders stiffened. Momentarily, he lost his train of thought. He'd forgotten the deep cerulean blue of her eyes. The fullness of her mouth.

"Your Grace," he replied, then cleared his throat and remembered to make a short bow.

Audrey gestured him toward a chair before retaking her seat. She nodded toward a maid, who left, presumably to fetch tea.

"Lady Prescott wished to meet with you, but she isn't faring well. I hope you don't mind speaking to me on the matter?"

"No, not at all." He eyed the chair warily. He'd already been sitting for several hours in that rattling coach. Instead, he laid his hat on the cushion and clasped his hands behind his straight back. "How may I be of service?"

The duchess got to her feet again and crossed the room, toward a pair of open French doors that led to a terrace. Her upswept hair had been styled to leave artful blond ringlets to trail down the nape of her neck and over her shoulder. The bodice of her pale blue gown accentuated her voluptuous figure, and Hugh took a deep breath before averting his eyes.

"Lady Bainbury, Charlotte, was a good friend of mine," Audrey began, her fingers still twisting together as she looked out onto the terrace.

"My condolences." He didn't know what more to say. He'd always found the lengthier an expression of sympathy became, the cheaper it sounded.

Audrey turned toward him, her cheeks pink with a new flush. "The earl is saying it was an accident, and already the rumors are spreading that it was suicide, like the previous countess. But I know it was neither of those things."

Hugh hitched his chin, struck by the glittering intensity of her stare, at the set lines of her jaw. Last spring, she'd been just as adamant that her husband had not been having an affair with Miss Lovejoy and was innocent of the gruesome murder. At first, Hugh had dismissed her as naïve; it was a well-established tradition that married men of the ton took mistresses. However, he'd soon come to understand she was correct. The duke had been having an affair with a male lover, not a mistress, and he was indeed innocent of the murder.

Hugh stepped around the chair, toward her. "Tell me what you know."

Read Death at Fournier Downs now!
Available on Kindle Unlimited

ABOUT THE AUTHOR

Cara is an author, reader, and history lover. She loves to read and write across genres, but her heart is reserved for romantic historical fiction and mystery. She lives in rural New England with her family. When she's not writing, she's freelance editing, driving her kids everywhere, burning at least one side of a grilled cheese, or avoiding doing laundry.

ALSO BY CARA DEVLIN

The Bow Street Duchess Mysteries

MURDER AT THE SEVEN DIALS

DEATH AT FOURNIER DOWNS

SILENCE OF DECEIT

PENANCE FOR THE DEAD

FATAL BY DESIGN (October 2023)

The Sage Canyon Series

A HEART WORTH HEALING

A CURE IN THE WILD

A LAND OF FIERCE MERCY

THE TROUBLE WE KEEP

A Second Chance Western Romance

Printed in Great Britain
by Amazon

39364298R00171